OF SAINTS AND SINNERS

More by Brooke Shaffer

The Timekeeper Chronicles

The Chivalrous Welshman
Time to Kill
Tick Tock
Windup
Stopwatch
Free Time (Summer 2020)

The Hands of Time
In the Hands of the Enemy (Fall 2020)

Singles
Of Saints and Sinners

Of Saints and Sinners

a novel of
The Timekeeper Chronicles

Brooke Shaffer

Black Bear Publishing

Published in Michigan by Black Bear Publishing.

ISBN:
  Hardcover: 978-1-7336954-2-8
  Softcover: 978-1-7336954-3-5
  eBook: 978-1-7336954-4-2

PROLOGUE

THE PRISONER AND THE PRIEST

He shuffled into the tiny chapel, feeling very conspicuous, but also very weak. His body was starved and wounded. Worse than that, though, his soul was heavy, crushed under the weight of his sins. The distance between him and the priest seemed to stretch on forever until he sat in the front pew.

The priest was perhaps fifty-five years of age, maybe closer to sixty. He had blond hair that was quickly turning white and falling out almost in clumps. His build remained large and strong, though his back was bent and he moved with the obvious pain of arthritis. He nodded once to the gaoler who moved back a pace. Then the priest pulled up a chair and sat down in a heap.

"What is your name?" the priest inquired.

"Walter Forbes," the man answered, studying his feet.

"Is it? If I recall correctly, your given name is Owain, named for our ancient king."

"My wife called me Walter. It was a more proper, more British name, but still slightly uncommon."

"Your ex-wife, whom you beat and murdered."

Owain glared at the priest. "I don't deny that I beat her, but I did not murder her."

"Yet you murdered her father."

"And five of his associates, including the man who killed Paige and our daughter."

The priest leaned back in his seat as comfortably as he could manage. "Mr. Fforidd...Owain, the Church is in the business of mercy. Often we advocate for the prisoners here for reduced sentences or even clemency.

You are here on very serious charges, and you are a known drunkard, brawler, thief—quite frankly, you are a criminal. The Lord extends the hand of justice just as readily as the hand of mercy." He sighed. "It is unlikely that we can exonerate you of your crimes, but we may be able to keep you from swinging."

"For what purpose? So I can rot in my cell?"

"Saint Paul made good use of his time in prison."

"If I recall correctly, he was still executed."

"What I am saying, Owain, is that even if you were to spend the remainder of your days here, I am sure that, with the help of the Church and good behavior, you could make it worthwhile. Perhaps, in time, you could earn privileges. But it has to start here. Today. You have to talk to me."

"I didn't ask for this."

"Did any of us ask for salvation? The light came into the darkness, and the darkness did not understand it. I am offering you a chance to make the right choice. You are sentenced to hang in two weeks. Seeing you walk in here, I can sense your heart is heavy and your soul is suffering. Perhaps the Church cannot dissuade the courts, but perhaps you can walk up there with a clear conscience."

Owain let out a breath and studied his hands for a moment. His fingernails needed trimming, but he was not permitted any sharp tools. If he didn't kill someone else, it would be himself. Besides, did it matter whether a dead man had trim fingernails? Finally, he nodded.

"All right. I'll talk. I don't think you're going to keep me from swinging, but I think you're the only person who has ever cared to listen."

The priest dipped his head. "Why don't we start at the beginning?"

Wales

Chapter One

The Child

My given name is Owain Fforidd. That's F-F-O-R-I-D-D, but it got changed to F-O-R-B-E-S in order to make it sound more British, but that comes later. I am the eldest of my ma and pa's five living children. My ma was Gwyneth. My pa's given name was Owain, but because his pa was also named Owain, he elected to go by his middle name Teo. I have only one brother also named Teo who is four years younger than me. My sisters are Missy, Mary, and Adith. All of them are deathly afraid of me.

From a young age, I was defiant. I was a fighter. When I was three, I tried to stone one of the barn cats. I couldn't say why. Maybe I'd heard about it in a Bible story and wondered how it worked. My pa switched me a good one for that. I had no sooner recovered from those wounds than I was back getting into trouble. This time it was a chicken. I had caught it and tried to rip its head off. When I couldn't do that, I went for its wings. Again, my pa switched me for it. I couldn't say why I did either of those things, except something about it fascinated me. Maybe it was the crunching of bone. Maybe it was being confused about the butchering process. I don't know, but it thrilled me.

My first sister was two years younger than me, and an absolute angel. I hated her for it. I would beat her and rip her hair and do everything a boy is not supposed to do to a girl. She rarely wandered far from our ma and my attacks were short-lived, but I always considered them worth it to see her cry and watch the bruises blossom on her skin. Pa punished me and I learned to bide my time.

When Teo was born, my ma and pa swore that they would make sure he would never end up like me. We were to be kept as far apart as possible and have very little interaction. Of course, this was going to be difficult seeing how our house had only four area in a single large room, one door between them, and there was a lot of work to be done on the farm. It was easy at first, since Teo couldn't walk or talk or otherwise leave our ma's side, but that would change as we got older.

As soon as Teo was walking and able to get more than three feet from our ma without bawling, I went after him. Sometimes I threw things at him. Sticks, rocks, anything I could get my hands on. A few times, I managed to really hurt him. Once, I hit him in the head with a rock and knocked him out. There was blood everywhere, and my ma thought I'd killed him. She wailed until my pa saw that he was still breathing and took him inside. They labored over him for a while to fix his wounds and ended up calling for a doctor, which cost a pretty penny. My mother refused to leave my brother's side for days.

After four days, he woke up. He had no idea what had happened. It took another week or better, but he healed and was back up and running after our ma and pa, being the good son they had always hoped I would be. He didn't remember the beating, but after that time, if he even saw me across the yard, he would go running.

My pa had reserved his punishment for me, to be determined based on whether or not Teo lived. Only because Teo had lived did he not turn me over for murder.

O wain shook his head and looked out the little window.

"Can you imagine? A murderer before I could read and write. And my own brother. Do you think maybe it was the Lord trying to warn my parents what I was going to become? Do you think they ought to have saved themselves the trouble and just drowned me?"

The priest frowned. "What happened next?"

M y pa gave me more lashes in that one session than he had combined up until then. He lashed me until I was practically shitting blood. Then he took a stick to my knuckles and broke both my hands and several fingers so I would never be able to do such a terrible thing ever again. Probably the only reason he didn't kill me was because of my ma. Bless her soul, she showed me more mercy than I ever deserved.

When I first woke up from being tended, my pa sat down with me and had a talk. He made me memorize the story of Cain and Abel, constantly asked me if I wanted to be sent away and under the Lord's curse for trying to kill my brother. I always said no, but more because I knew it was what he wanted to hear, not because I had any deep reflections, or even cared.

I stayed abed until my lashings healed enough that I could move and get around, though my hands took many weeks to heal. In that time, I suppose I sobered up a bit as I became fully dependent on others to help me eat, get dressed, and do anything for myself. I devoted myself to my letters, learned to read. I even memorized whole chapters from the Bible and recited them after supper. My parents held out hope that whatever demon had beset me had gone. I guess there was a time when we were actually happy and functional. But it didn't last long.

With our family happy and functional, once my hands healed, my pa decided to show me more around the farm and introduce me to more chores. Maybe if I was put to work with real man chores, my strength and aggression could be fulfilled. But there was a fine line between using my strength and challenging it, even defeating it. As long as I won, I was generally satisfied. If something proved to be too difficult for me—mind you, I'm only five or six years old at this point—then I would go into a flying, frothing rage. I would destroy everything I could get my hands on, or I would find tools to amplify my destruction. Shovels, rakes, axes, and so on. When my pa came calling for a switching, I ran.

I went without supper many nights, more nights than I had it, yet I was not a small child. I was strong. And I was fast. Getting stronger and faster every day. There were some days when I was able to get a head start on my pa and manage to outrun him, or maybe he simply gave up the chase. I would either come home eventually, or I would get my due out in the real world. I think he may have started to give up on me around that point.

But I would run to the neighboring farms, hide in their barns, terrorize their animals, throw rocks at their children. Once, I was in the barn with a neighbor's daughter and their donkey. I antagonized the donkey until it bucked, hitting the girl in the face. It broke her nose, her jaw, and ruined her pretty looks for the rest of her life. And I got away with it because I was able to run and escape without anyone seeing me, and because she couldn't remember what had happened or who had been there.

I wasn't always so lucky, though. Sometimes I got caught. Actually, most of the time I got caught. The neighbors would switch me themselves, then drag me home so my pa could have his turn at licking me with the cord. I had more scar tissue than flesh on the back of my body, and I hadn't even gotten into any real fights, not like I would later in life.

Teo and our sisters learned to stay well away from me, and they were every bit the children our parents hoped they would be: polite, kind, caring, respectful, hard-working. Most often, they looked at me with pity and confusion. Why was I so angry? What was it about my life that I hated? Truthfully, I still don't know the answers to those questions. I had a loving ma and pa, loving family. I had good discipline—I didn't think so at the time, but looking back, I deserved everything I got and never got more than I deserved. We had food and water; the farm was doing well. On the days that I could be made to sit still and do work, I did good work. To an extent I might have even enjoyed it. We had good relations with the neighbors, and they all had children who were of an age, potential friends if I had cared to make any, even potential wives and husbands for all of us.

W as there no activity you enjoyed other than violence?" the priest cut in, seeming to remember himself half a second after he spoke. "Unusually strong men are often feared, true, but they are a great asset, especially on a farm."

Owain nodded sullenly. "Yes. I know. Unfortunately, I was only feared. As for an enjoyed activity that wasn't violence, there was one, though you may be shocked to know of it."

"Oh? And what is that?"

"Cooking."

"Cooking?"

I enjoyed cooking. I enjoyed butchering, too, don't get me wrong, but I enjoyed cooking. Perhaps it came from being sent to bed without supper most nights, and staying away from home as much as I could. I still had to eat. I could catch any of the small farm animals, and my pa had taught me about hunting and trapping game, but there's a huge difference between a field-dressed game animal and a home-cooked meal. My ma was an unbelievably good cook. All the women in the area were, of course, but my ma was just special. Well, I'm sure everyone says that about their ma, but she was. She could taste any dish blind and tell you exactly what was in it and what it needed to make it even better.

Sometimes, when I wasn't in trouble, I would watch her cook, ask questions, make suggestions of my own. My ma always obliged and encouraged my fascination with food. Later, in private, I would overhear my pa lament that cooking was to be done in the home by the women, ma and daughters. My ma agreed, but said that any activity which kept me from throwing things, getting angry, and torturing either the animals or my siblings, she would encourage it. Obviously, my pa had little choice but to agree.

To that end, he tried to get me into butchering instead. Perhaps it was a way to marry cooking and violence, give me a purpose and an outlet for my rage. I already knew how to butcher chickens and rabbits, but my pa showed me how to do goats, sheep, and cows, too. Those were a little harder, even for a strong nine year old such as myself. No matter how angry I got, the animal was always stronger still and could seriously hurt me. I had to learn how to maneuver them, subdue them. Soon, it became less about the actual butchering and more about just winning.

I know my pa was trying his best to find something that would fulfill me, satisfy the aggression, but nothing could. Pitting me against animals bigger and stronger than myself did not teach me patience or duty; it only taught me how to read my opponent and how to exploit weaknesses.

Of course, it also taught me a lot about pain. I can't tell you how many times I got headbutted by an angry goat and broke ribs. The cow trampled me once, too. Broke both arms, multiple ribs, and there was some internal damage, too. Like Teo several years before, I lay abed, struggling to hang on. My ma watched over me, prayed for me. She sought the help of the local chapel, that while I was weak, perhaps they could drive out whatever demon had possessed me.

Like the time my pa beat me to within an inch of my life, I sobered up for a time again, as I began to get better. It was hard for me to eat, to breathe. I had little use of my arms for a time. Again, I was dependent on others just to get through the day. The pastor spent many days at our house, at my bedside. He tried to get to the root of my problem. My parents were loving and supportive. We had food. The farm was doing well. Why was I so angry? What was I trying to accomplish? What was I trying to prove? Why did I feel the need to fight against all that was good?

I had no answers. But the more I thought about it, the more my mind twisted his words. I resented the pastor, for thinking that anything was wrong, for thinking my parents beat me, for thinking we were poor and unable to look after ourselves. I resented my parents, that they had sent for him in the first place to talk to me. Did they think I was a fool? Did they think me deaf and dumb? Did they regret having me, as if I was some kind of taint on the family?

Well, that I may have been, but I couldn't see it at the time. All I knew was that everyone was looking at me as though there was something wrong with me and I ought to be discarded for it. They all hated me and wanted to get rid of me.

I seethed for many weeks, as my arms healed and my abdomen no longer hurt. I wasn't even back to full strength before I took up my antics again, worse than I had ever been. This time around, instead of just sending me to bed without supper, I was made to sleep in the barn. If I wanted to act like a wild animal, I could at least sleep with the animals. I took my punishment in stride and tried to hold my head high, but the onset of winter is a powerful motivator to make amends in order to sleep in my own bed again.

Often, evening conversation was stunted and awkward. My parents wanted to include me, bring me in, try to make me a normal part of the family, but it just couldn't happen. When I was out of the room, I could hear them talking and laughing. All my siblings loved to sing. My ma did, too. My pa liked to listen, but he couldn't carry a tune to save his life.

Then I would walk in the room, and everyone would fall silent. Someone would make some off-handed comment, try to start some interesting small talk on the most mundane topics, but it never really caught on. And all my mind could think was that they hated me, wished me gone, wished me dead, wished I had never been born and then life would be absolutely perfect. I hated them for it, and I spent most of the winter sitting on my bed, brooding, seething, looking for ways to get out. Could I run away? To where? How would I survive? I knew I would have to be sharp and cunning.

The winter was long and cold that year, and I was afraid it might never end. Maybe God knew of my plans and was going to send winter continuously, until I had no choice but to concede and just stay home. A foolish thought, but children have many foolish notions.

As soon as the weather turned and spring looked like it was on its way, my pa put me to work. There was never a time in the day when I wasn't doing something, most of it hard work and heavy lifting. He was trying to exhaust me, and it worked for a time. I would no sooner finish my breakfast than my pa would putting something in my hands, telling me to do this or that.

With the welcome break from the winter and the cabin fever that had enveloped us all, I didn't argue. But once the weather warmed and the snow melted and I no longer shivered getting into bed at night, my restlessness began again. I didn't want to help out on the farm. The other kids were getting older. None of them liked me. None of them wanted me. Which was just as well because I didn't like them and I was tired of being stuck in the same house as them. I was tired of sharing a room with terrified Teo, and I hated hearing my sisters in their room, laughing, giggling, playing, and carrying on in innocent girl things. Several times, I went in their room to beat them, break their things, and tell them to shut up.

Eventually, my pa banished me to the barn once more, once I became too rowdy. But that was exactly what I had been waiting for, a chance to get out, get away without anyone noticing. I did not fight as my pa walked me out to the barn that night and sent me to the loft. I can still remember walking up the ladder and watching all the cats hiss and scatter. But I lay down in my customary spot. My pa left and locked up the barn.

I waited a short time until I knew they would all be asleep. Then I slipped down to the ground where I knew there was a loose board in the wall. I wiggled it out of place, squeezed through the opening, and replaced the board. It would be like magic. Then, when I could see that all the lights were out and the house was quiet, I ran away.

Chapter Two

The Urchin

It was two days before my parents found me. Unlike young Jesus, however, they didn't find me in the chapel. Luckily they found me before the police did, and the fact that I'd stolen a lady's purse was made into a misunderstanding based on the sheer fact that the lady I stole from did look a bit like my ma. She'd asked me to retrieve her purse, and I just grabbed the wrong one. There were more words, but in the end, I was dragged home, switched, and sent to bed without supper. Afterwards, my pa gave me a good talking to, shaming me for causing my ma to worry like she had.

I was allowed back into the house to sleep, but only while my pa went around looking for how I'd gotten out. He found the loose board and spent a good half a day securing every single board on that barn and ensuring that all the locks and latches were snug and secure. My ma chastised him, asking if they were running a farm or a prison. My pa pointed at me and said that their prison was far nicer than what I'd be sleeping in if the law got a hold of me.

Owain scoffed and shook his head. "Damn him, but he was right. A hayloft sounds like pretty swell accommodations right about now."

The priest dipped his head calmly. "Perhaps...I can ask and arrange for better accommodations."

"I'd sleep in the shit shack if it got me out of the black cells."

"I will see what I can do. What happened next?"

I learned to pick locks, what else? Locks, latches, boards and barricades, there was nothing I couldn't do given just a sliver of space to do my work, even from the inside. My pa would walk me out to the barn in the evening and lock me in with the animals. Once he was gone, I'd just slip out using my custom-made lock-picking kit. I'd run around, causing mischief here and there, then return to sleep a bit and be found in the barn in the morning. My parents thought they'd finally succeeded at containing me, at least at night. Sometimes, it was just the best they could do.

The neighbors quickly learned that my ma and pa were not poor parents. It wasn't them, it was me. Or maybe it was them, punishment for some sin they had committed. But regardless, they were doing their best to try and keep me under control. My pa loaded me down with work during the day, but exhaustion no longer worked. I was too strong for that now. And unless he was standing there watching me—and sometimes, even while he was—I would run off and do my own thing. And sometimes...he would let me.

I joined a little street urchin gang when I was ten, or maybe eleven. We were all of an age, but I was the one who stood out. I was the biggest, the strongest, the boldest. I would get into trouble and do things the other boys only talked and snickered about. They were in the little street urchin gang because they didn't understand the concept of what a gang was or what they did. The other boys thought a gang was a group of friends who went out, pulled on girls' hair, stole bread and vegetables from vendors on the street, then went home at the end of the day to a family who was most likely oblivious to their actions. Some of them weren't even poor farmers, but sons of wealthy parents who thought they were doing something absolutely dastardly by getting their stockings dirty.

My ideas were a little different. I didn't just tug on a girl's pigtails, I pushed her down, beat her up, and took anything of value, be it cheap jewelry, toys, money. If she had a brother trying to defend her, most often, I could beat him up, too, and take his valuables. I learned the art of pawning and reselling. I didn't just steal from street vendors, but from stores, walking in their doors and taking something off the shelf.

Ａnd you did this all at night? Or during the day?" The priest shifted position. "When did this happen? You lived over an hour's walk from town."

Ａt first, it was just easy stuff at night. Swipe something from the neighbor's yard, something left outside of a vendor's booth or a store, rob someone who who unlucky enough to be out at night, that sort of thing. I got good at it. And I was always back home in time to slip back into the barn, or so it was for a while.

My pa caught me one night, sneaking back in. He'd heard one of the heifers bellowing in labor pains during calving and gone out to check on her. First he made me help with the calving. Once the calf was safely delivered and nursing, he got himself cleaned up, then took a switch to me. He'd didn't stripe me a lot, maybe two or three times.

I'll never forget the look on his face or the slump in his back when he hung it up after those couple times. In the shadow of the lantern, I saw what he would look like as a frail old man, with loose wrinkles and tired muscles, aching knees and a bent back. I saw him as he felt when he looked at me. Exhausted, defeated, unsure what to do or what lay ahead. Between the calving, the switching, and this sudden insight into my pa, I did not move as he went to the door and opened it.

"If you want to leave, then leave," he told me.

I just stood there, certain it was a trick.

"Get out, Owain. Stop shaming me and your ma. Stop terrorizing this farm and our good neighbors. We've tried to be a good family for you, but if you don't want none of it, then just leave."

He didn't stop me as I walked out the door. He just closed up like normal and took the lantern back to the house. He didn't even look my way.

I won't say that I suddenly changed and ran back to him, trying to make amends. I didn't really want to make amends. But there was a certain thrill in disobeying the rules, in pulling the wool over their eyes, in besting them as they tried to cage me. But I had always envisioned a grand victory, where they wept as they conceded defeat. My pa had taken that away from me. He didn't succumb to me. He threw me out. Like trash. Or that was how I perceived it.

Trash. I wasn't wanted. I was never wanted. They wanted all the other kids, the ones who were perfect and submissive. They never wanted me. So I turned my back and ran.

I returned to town, now fully committed to my new life as a thief. I had no choice. The only one feeding me was myself. The only one clothing me was myself. The only one watching out for me was myself. Sure, I could bully the other so-called "gang members" into doing stuff for me, but at the end of the day, I was alone in the world, king of my own castle. Everything I did was about me.

It didn't take two months for me to get caught stealing from a store and apprehended by police. Problem was, they hadn't gotten the message that my family no longer wanted me, and they dragged me back home. My pa was polite and thanked them for bringing me back. But once they were gone, he was ready to turn me away again.

My ma begged him not to, citing the Prodigal Son. My pa said the Prodigal Son came home of his own free will, not dragged by police. Still, he conceded to her. She took me inside, gave me a bath, clean clothes, and a hot meal. She spoke all about the happenings around the farm. Two clutches of chicks had hatched and were doing well. The calf was growing stronger every day and would make a good breeding bull. Her garden was doing well, but it was going to be a dry summer, so water had to be hauled up from the creek some days.

I stayed home for a couple of days, even helped with a few chores as I deemed them worth my time and interest, but my rage had quelled and my interest was gone. One night, I simply wandered off again, back to town.

You were looking for the excitement of sin," the priest stated. "The thrill of the chase."

Owain nodded. "Yes. When my pa turned me away and told me to leave, he had retracted his hand of authority over me. It was a hand I could no longer defy, except if I did defy it, I would have to become a good son. So I was caught, you see? Or so my mind said. But there was always the hand of authority in town, called the law, and the law enforcers, and that chase never ended."

I was twelve years old the first time I went to jail. I had broken the window of a storefront and stolen some goods. I don't even know what the store was or what I stole. I just wanted to cause trouble and something I saw sparked my interest. The law caught up to me a day later while I was sleeping. Because I was only a boy, I only spent a few days in jail. They were trying to scare me, I think, make me see what I was facing if I kept doing what I was doing. I should have listened.

As it was, after three or four days, the police took me home to my parents. This time, they made no show of having been looking for me or waiting for me to come home. My ma still loved her son, but I could see she was perhaps becoming afraid for me, if not of me. I was just starting to become a man, and I was set to become a big one. A strong one. My pa thanked the police for doing their duty, but said to hold no illusions. I was a fighter. I was a troublemaker. If they needed to teach me a lesson, then they had his full permission and support. The police promised to do their job well in the future.

Once more, my ma gave me a bath, fixed my clothes, and got me something to eat. I don't know that I said three words to them the whole time I was there. My pa let me stay the night in the barn, but when the sun rose and the cock crowed and morning chores began, I had to be gone. So I was.

By this time, I was gaining quite a reputation among other young troublemakers. And I don't mean the mischievous little boys from before, who caused a little trouble, then went home to their mothers. I mean kids who were like me, homeless, without a family, caring only for themselves. There's a pecking order when it comes to people on the streets. The strong dominate the weak. I was strong. Not the strongest, because I was not yet a man, but I was getting there.

When I was thirteen, I challenged a boy named Bill to a fight. There was certain turf at stake, you understand? I wanted it. I wanted the turf and the kids who went with it. Bill led those kids—and by kids, I mean sixteen to twenty years old; he himself was probably eighteen—and I wanted them under me, not him.

I lost the fight, in the end, but I gave him a little something to remember me by. I'd bitten off part of his ear. He squealed like a pig when I did it, hanging onto his back with all my might, chomping down, until it just...ripped. He bled. And he almost went down. The only thing that really saved him was that one of his buddies didn't like the idea of being told what to do by a thirteen year old kid, so he clocked me in the back of the head. Knocked me out cold.

When I came back around, the other kids were gone, but those who were under me were not only impressed, they were mesmerized. I was strong. I was vicious. Even some kids who wanted no part of the gang wars came to me and asked to be part of my little gang; they wanted me to protect them. I agreed. I enjoyed having the power. Oh, I told them that I cared about them and would keep them safe from the likes of Bill and his friends, but it was, at the heart of it, a lie. I cared for no one but myself.

The police were coming to know me, too, very well. I did a three-month sentence for stealing a couple chickens. After that, I learned to delegate responsibility. I took the kids who looked up to me and we formed our own family, our own society with our own rules and how we did things. A couple of boys were responsible for finding food. A couple more went after money and small goods to pawn. A couple of homeless girls who had fallen in with us went after clothing materials. Seeing how they were blossoming into women, they had more leverage to take valuables from rich men as well, which they did. I was building a small empire, or so my mind thought. The police knew that much of the activity was coming from my mind, but they could never trace it back to me in a court of law. They might have, if anyone ever told, but they were too loyal to me.

I was fourteen when I first knew a woman, a prostitute in a brothel on the south side of town. That opened up a whole new world for me. Unbecoming as all teenagers are, I learned quickly. I didn't like it when they laughed at me, giggled behind long eyelashes. I wanted power over them, total control.

Sex is a powerful force," the priest said, nodding. "And for men, it does tap into our desire for power. But we must also learn to be as Solomon and be a gentle lover, aware of our lover."

"How would you know what it's like?" Owain asked perhaps more sharply than intended. He let out a breath. "But you are right. I didn't understand that second part, about being a gentle lover. I just enjoyed the feeling, wanted more of it, wanted more power, more control."

Having discovered sex, I began to disdain my crew, those who had served me loyally, brought food and clothing and looked to me for protection and direction. But many of them still blushed at the thought of sex, even if they were of an age. The younger ones I barely acknowledged. The only ones I began to care about were a couple of girls. They saw the power of sex and were ready to consign themselves to the brothels. As long as they were part of my little gang, I slept with them. Even after they'd gone to the brothels and taken up residence in the sex houses, I still slept with them; I just had to pay for it. But then I began to feel as if they were mocking me. Once they had stolen money for me, and now they stole money from me. I stopped seeing them. For a short time, I stopped going to the brothel completely.

Instead, feeling very foolishly like a man, I, at only fifteen years old, decided to challenge Bill again for his territory. He'd not been idle either, but he was still bigger than me, and he was ready to rip my face off after what I did to his ear.

The difference the second time around was that I had finally grown into my strength, and would continue to do so over the next several years. The second time, it wasn't just about being an annoying child relying on speed and agility, though I still had those. This time, I was able to meet Bill almost squarely in strength as well. Unfortunately, we never did find out who would have won, now that it was a fair fight. The match had drawn a crowd, a large enough one to warrant the attention of the police. They broke up the fight and dragged us both to jail. We were placed in different cells.

I didn't see it, but I heard it and found out later that Bill had gotten in a fight with another man in his cell. Except that man was a lot bigger and meaner than him. The man beat him bloody, beat him until he went unconscious. He just...never woke up.

I was released six months later.

The priest stood, ancient joints creaking like old wood. "I should very much like to continue this conversation, but the hour grows late and, alas, we must both return to our cells."

Owain felt a blanket of dread drape itself around him. He swallowed and said, "Yes. I suppose we must."

The priest patted his shoulder, ignoring the sudden advance of the guard, as if Owain had any strength or desire to hurt the old man. "Fear not, Owain. God has not forgotten you, and confession is good for the soul. Furthermore, I will speak to the warden and see if perhaps I cannot persuade him to free you from the black cells."

"That would be greatly appreciated."

"Sleep well, my son."

The guard tugged on Owain's chains and pain lanced through his wrists and ankles. He winced and cast a last, long glance at the priest before being led away.

Interlude

The Warden

Everyone was sound asleep as Father Forthill made his way out of the chapel and into the larger gaol. He didn't know which was worse, the silence or the screams. Beaumaris was a rather comfortable prison, all things considering. Some of the inmates were permitted to work, and almost all of them got to see the sunshine once a day. And a meal each day, too. There was plenty of controversy surrounding the prison, that it was too humane for its inmates, and while Forthill believed in treating all men with dignity, there were days when he, too, wondered, if allowing such niceties was a good idea. Lord knew he'd had the wool pulled over his eyes a time or two, when he was younger and more naive about the human condition. That was why he had to choose his advocates carefully. If he ever got it wrong and a criminal who had been granted clemency returned to his old ways, especially if it got someone killed, he could be deposed as the chaplain and excommunicated entirely, dismissed as senile and easy to fool.

As it was, he was a bit unsteady on his feet, and considering whether he shouldn't retire to a country chapel, to be among the more placid members of the flock. He didn't want to be accused of being senile, but if an inmate got it in his head, Forthill wouldn't have a chance in a physical confrontation. Across from the chapel, he let out a breath and began the hike up the stairs, much to the dismay of his knees and hips. How many times a day did he make this journey? It was getting harder and harder with each trek. Whose idea was it to put the office upstairs? Father Forthill would certainly like to have a word.

As expected, the warden was working late in the governor's office, a lamp burning low, a bottle of whiskey sitting next to it. A fire in the corner stove faithfully churned out waves of heat, a cooking pot set up on a rack to cool. The hour was hardly seven o'clock, but the days were short still, winter mercilessly beating the countryside.

"Father, how can I help you?" the warden, a young man by the name of Nathaniel Dillon, inquired. He was perhaps thirty-five years old, a bear in his own right, though Forthill was willing to bet that if motivated, Fforidd would be able to best him easily. "Did you get a confession from Fforidd?"

"He's never denied anything," Forthill said, puzzled.

"Telling a lie is not the same as not telling the truth. Not always. I was wondering if he'd admitted to anything more." Dillon made a gesture. "Please, sit down. Drink?"

The aging man sat down across from the warden and accepted a small glass. The warden grinned when the priest's face screwed up. Finally Forthill pushed the glass back to him. "People indulge in sin because it feels good. That..."

"Well then, this wouldn't be considered a sin for you, would it?" Dillon chuckled, pouring himself a glass and downing it without batting an eye. "So it all works out in the end. Now then, why are you here?"

Forthill was careful in choosing his words. "I was curious to inquire—"

"Please, Arthur, you don't have to approach me like a child trying to roundabout ask his mum for a sweet. Out with it." Forthill couldn't decide whether the man was amused or annoyed.

"I would ask that Owain Fforidd be moved out of the black cells."

For a long moment the warden just stared at him, studied him, as if searching for the punchline to a joke. Finally he leaned back in his chair. "You know I can't do that."

"Why not?"

"He's scheduled to hang in two weeks. He's a vile murderer. He's in the condemned cell where he belongs."

"And if you had only two weeks left on God's green earth, would you not want to spend it on the green earth and not under it, a living hell, darkness before eternal darkness, God have mercy that maybe I can save his soul beforehand?"

"If he is destined for eternal darkness and torment, what's two more weeks? If you do manage to save his soul, then the Lord will surely give him a nice plot of land with all the greenery he can stand. And until then, he can serve out the governor's justice." He went on before the priest could protest. "On top of that, he is considered a danger to the other prisoners. A man with his history alone is bad enough, but I'm not going to send a murderer to run around beside a hog thief. Even Hell itself has different levels to keep the baddies apart; you yourself teach that, don't you? I'm sorry, Arthur. I can't do it."

"You can't or you won't?"

Dillon rolled his eyes and cracked his neck. Forthill thought he heard a muttered curse. "Why are you asking for this, anyway? Fforidd isn't the only condemned man here, and you only just spoke to him."

"He is a penitent man, warden. Even if I cannot keep him from swinging, perhaps a little show of kindness at the end...Nathan, it may be the only kindness he's ever known—"

"He had a loving family. Two, in fact. His parents and the farm he grew up on, and he even had money, a wealthy wife and newborn babe."

"The only kindness," Forthill reiterated, "that he has been of a mind to appreciate."

"If he is penitent, as you say, then he can understand and appreciate the consequences of his actions before emerging into Paradise. If he is yet damned, two weeks pales in comparison to eternity, wouldn't you say?" He continued before the priest could speak. "We're not going to debate this all night, Arthur. I'm ending this here. Fforidd is not going to be moved from his cell."

The priest let out an even breath, sending up a silent prayer for patience so his anger wouldn't consume him. And then, in the stillness of his soul as emotions and reactions warred, a small thought was placed in his mind. Taking a level breath, he dipped his head and said, "I understand. I would, however, like to continue meeting with him."

The warden assented without a fuss. "Of course. Confession is good for the soul, and who knows? Perhaps we shall one day see him in Paradise." He shrugged. "Was there anything else you needed, Father?"

"No." Forthill stood. "Thank you for your time, sir."

Forthill turned but didn't make it past the door before the warden spoke again. "I know you're a Protestant and yet we still call you Father. Just a matter of familiarity, propriety in a sense, I suppose." Forthill turned. The warden went on, "I'm Catholic myself. But I know enough about men—be they men of God or men of the world—to know when they've got something more in mind than what they say aloud. I've been around criminals my whole adult life, and a lot of them are better than you at hiding their intentions."

The older man did his best not to react to the man's words, but he knew he failed. The warden nodded slowly. "I can see those gears turning, Father. Don't go over my head on this. Don't go to the governor or the other priests or even the Catholics. Honestly, I don't know what you see in the man but it is an excellent excuse to cut your career shorter than his life. You're a good chaplain, Father. Done a lot of good around here and in other prisons. Fforidd isn't worth it."

Forthill frowned and said, "Neither was the thief on the cross. And he admitted as much. Tell me, Nathan. Will the Lord remember you so well?"

The words came out unbidden and sharper than he intended. He turned and walked away before the warden could reply or else see his fluster. Rarely did he ever lose temper, and never had he spoken with such absolution, such surety, to a man who was, in a sense, placed over him. He was to respect the governing bodies as the Lord had appointed them over him. There were times to refuse and rebel, but for his part, he was to do it politely, with respect, not with such cutting words. And if he'd had any hope of keeping his position at the gaol, it was surely gone now as long as he advocated for kindness for Fforidd.

Not even mercy, just simple kindness. Was that really too much to ask? He wasn't asking for clemency, wasn't asking for a commutation, just simple kindness, a chance to see the sun, feel the grass in the exercise yard, breathe fresh air. Forthill couldn't even imagine what demons awaited Fforidd's return to the cell. If a soul was damned, the demons didn't wait for something as petty as death before beginning their torture.

Beaumaris Gaol was on an island. Forthill did not stay on the island, but lived on the mainland and made the crossing twice a week. Once for service, once for confession and, if need be, last rites. The ferryman was not pleased about the crossing in the dark and wintry cold, but it was only a narrow crossing—you could see from shore to shore—and the ice was continually broken up by laborers or others. It could not be allowed to freeze, lest a prisoner escape and attempt to cross. As long as it was water, men were confined to the island but for the ferry.

Once safely on the mainland—which, in itself was a bit of a joke considering the British Isles, were, well, islands—it was a half hour by horse and cart to the little house he called his own. He shared the parsonage with the priest who led the services in this local chapel. When Forthill walked in the door, the stove was hot, the fire warm, and the tea kettle was just starting to whistle.

"I was beginning to worry," Father Peitr Worthington said, pouring two cups. "Thought perhaps the crossing had frozen or the boat tipped over. Mighty windy out there, isn't it?"

Worthington was easily fifteen years Forthill's senior, but apparently someone had forgotten to tell him so. He walked and moved and spoke like a man half his age. Even his hair refused to turn gray while Forthill's blond hair had long ago abandoned him, in more ways than one.

"That it is," Forthill agreed, using the cup to warm his hands for a moment. "No, no. All is well, or it would be."

"Troubling confession?"

"The confession does not trouble me so much as the warden's response to it."

Worthington waved a hand. "The warden's response is always the same. They committed a crime and he is committed to seeing that they serve their sentence to its full."

"He is a stubborn man, and he is young enough to be my son."

"Why don't you tell me what happened?"

So Forthill did. As soon as he mentioned the name Fforidd, also called Forbes, Worthington's expression darkened, and he sipped at his tea thoughtfully. Forthill talked about the meeting itself, how haggard and desperate Fforidd had looked, his words, his mannerisms, his thoughts and reactions to the things he had done—and consider that he was speaking only of his childhood and teenage years! They had not even begun to broach his adult life! Then he talked about his meeting with Dillon, including his sharp parting words.

When he was finished, the two men sat in silence for a long minute. Finally Worthington asked, "Are you really so surprised at the warden's reaction?"

Forthill heaved a sigh. "No. I understand his reservations. I do. But even the thief on the cross—"

"The thief on our Lord's right hand was repentant. The thief on his left was not," Worthington reminded him. "We both know that Fforidd was prone to bouts of depression and repentance, but he always went back to his old ways. Fforidd is or was also highly manipulative. Dillon knows this as well. The warden is looking out for the guards and, to an extent, the other prisoners. He's doing his job, Arthur. If you are able to save his soul, then would it not be better for him to depart this life and join the chorus of angels, rather than live with this burdensome chain about his neck?"

"I'm not asking for clemency. I'm asking for kindness," Forthill said. "What is so difficult to believe about that? If I can save his soul, then so much the better. But how are we supposed to save souls if we show no measure of kindness to men when they are most vulnerable?"

"He will see the sun on his last day."

Forthill shook his head. "Not good enough."

Worthington rubbed his eyes and sighed. "Arthur, the only way you will convince Dillon to let Fforidd see the sun is if you can show he is not a danger. The only way to prove that he is not a danger is by delaying his sentence long enough that he will have cycled through his mood swings and shown that he is not at risk of losing control; he is still a strong man from what I understand. Considering how his cycles can last for months to years...that's a long time to spend in the dark hoping for just a chance to glimpse the sun again. If it were me, I would sooner hang myself."

A minute passed. Then two. Worthington stood and tossed a small log in the fire. Forthill stared at his tea, a black mixture with sparks of red as the fire reflected in it for just a moment. Then the stove door swung closed and the older priest returned to the small table.

"Arthur, you have to consider where this leads, how you are going to get there. You have to consider what lies in the interest of Mr. Fforidd. You probably won't get him to see the sun again until he hangs. You're not going to push back his sentence. But if you can save his soul, then he can depart this wretched life and be with our Lord. And why should we covet the days on Earth when glory is so much better that mortal man can hardly fathom it?"

After a long moment, Forthill nodded. "Maybe you're right."

Worthington's expression was gentle. "If we had our way, we would need only to open our mouths and mankind would repent. But men have free will, and we must reap what we sow. Fforidd may be able to be saved, but his mortal punishment must still be served."

Forthill wordlessly agreed, and with that, Worthington finished his tea, then headed to one of two sparse mattresses set up near the stove. Forthill remained at the table, going over the conversation, knowing that what the older man said was true, but in his heart, he knew it wasn't right. This wasn't how things were supposed to be. Fforidd's life could not end at the end of a rope. It would not. He was as certain of that as the snow that would be waiting for him in the morning. He could not see the condemned man's life path, but he knew it was one of remarkable significance, a flower that bloomed where others only withered because it had the fortitude to stand up to adverse conditions, to thrive against the tide, to use this tragic experience in unimaginable ways.

Lord, You are showing me something of great importance, Forthill half-thought, half-prayed. *But what is it? I don't understand.*

It is not on you to understand, a small voice whispered. *Your job is only to do what I tell you.*

Fforidd is scheduled to hang in two weeks. I won't be back in the gaol for another four days.

Then you will have to do it quickly.

Forthill stared at his tea which was quickly growing cold. Then he looked over at Worthington. The man could fall asleep at the drop of a hat, and he was already snoring.

What do You want me to do?

Take up a pen and paper and write this...

So it was that Forthill spent the better part of the hour composing a letter as dictated to him by nothing more than a whisper. No, not even that, for it was not audible. It was more as if someone were tugging strings on his heart, playing him like a piano, and he interpreted the music and transcribed it as letters and words onto paper. All the while, his mind wrestled with fear and doubt. Was he doing the right thing? What if it made things worse? Fforidd was already condemned to death, but he could be sacrificing his own career. Country chapel aside, he could be ostracized completely. Then where would he be?

And yet the music kept thrumming through his chest and his nib scratched along the paper, words flowing out of him as they had never done before. Well, that wasn't quite true. He'd done this sort of thing once before, years ago, when this same little heart piano player had told him to apply for the chaplain position in the gaol. He hadn't wanted to. Had never dreamed of such a thing. Perhaps now the reason why was being fulfilled. Perhaps he had been brought to Beaumaris Gaol all those years ago to simply wait for this one man.

Suddenly, it was as if a second instrument had been added to the mix, a violin. The piano and the violin played together in perfect harmony, an enchanting rhythm, and his pen scratched faster and faster. Yes. Of course, it was so clear now. How had he not seen this immediately upon meeting Owain Fforidd?

What plans do You have for this man? Forthill wondered silently.

The piano player did not reply.

Chapter Three

The Inmate

Between my fifteenth and eighteenth birthdays, I had done more time in jail than out. I stole, I got in fights, and I was no different in the cells of the jail. I earned a reputation, and I liked it. I was a big man, strong, and I didn't care about anyone or anything. Cross me if you dare. This attitude which had once won young street urchins to my cause now drove them away in fear. I was a dangerous class of criminal, far beyond mere desperation. I had crossed into sadism.

It was four days since Owain last spoke with the chaplain, though he never would have believed it. Time passed differently in the black cells. It was at once one day and a hundred days that he had been down. He never knew whether the screams came from his own mouth or someone else. Sometimes he couldn't even be certain that he hadn't already died and gone to Hell. The shadows played tricks on him, taking on a life of their own. Slithering, snarling, snapping, making him long for the comfort of something so simple as a rat.

He'd scratched his left arm until it bled. Likely he would contract an infection and die. Which would take him first, the infection or the gallows? Trick question. The Grim Reaper would take him any way he could.

Soon it became that I almost had my own reserved cell, ready and waiting the next time I got caught doing something bad. If there were others in the cell, they knew very well which corner was mine, and they scattered just as soon as they could. Men begged not to be in a cell with me. One man killed himself because he was so afraid.

Honestly, I don't even remember that I did anything to any of them. Maybe a little physical intimidation because of my size, maybe I roughed them up a bit just to make a point, but I don't know that I actually hurt them. My reputation hurt them more than anything. And I enjoyed that almost as much as I enjoyed the fighting and everything else.

Those chaplains would come by, and it was amazing how many people confessed and repented, begging to be saved from me as much as their sins. To some, I was the Devil himself. I think those chaplains must have gotten some kind of award for most souls saved just because of me.

There is no such reward within the church," the priest, Father Forthill, told him, smiling gently. "However, our reward will be great when we stand before the Lord. And who knows? Perhaps you did inspire some real change in some of those people, change they never would have experienced if a living devil hadn't shown them what lay in store for them in Purgatory. So you see, the Lord can work in mysterious ways. This all happened some ten or fifteen years ago and we are just now seeing the fruit of that unusual seed."

It was meant to be uplifting, but Owain found he could take no comfort in it. Maybe some souls had been saved because of his intimidation as a living devil. What would it take to save his soul, then?

After a time, I simply became the head prisoner. The guards realized they couldn't defeat me, so they allied with me, or they tried to. I became their weapon. Any time a prisoner didn't do as they were told, I was given free reign to beat them within an inch of their lives. The women I was free to use. In exchange, I got a little better food, a little better blanket. Problem was, I was also forced to stay longer in the jails rather than be released. And as my reputation preceded me, the prisoners learned to behave.

One jail tried to recruit me, hire me as a guard. I took the job for a time, but I knew it wouldn't work out. I wanted no one over me. I wanted to do whatever I wanted whenever I wanted, free reign to come and go and do as I pleased. Completely. No rules but my own. And yet, there was also the memory that when my pa had seen that in me and released me, it was no longer fun. I derived my pleasure from the defiance, the struggle.

We struggle not against flesh and blood," Forthill said. "We struggle against the enemy of our soul."

Owain studied his fingernails for a moment. At some point in the last few days, most of them had broken off, usually painfully, most of them bloody to one degree or another. He looked up at the window in the chapel, stained glass with steel bars over it, the Christ in a cage of His very own. But it was still sunlight glittering on the floor in front of him.

"What happens to the soul when it becomes its own worst enemy?" he asked. "Is there any soul to speak of, to save?"

"There must be," the priest told him. "Or else we would not be talking."

My role as a guard failed, and I did more jail time because of it. When I was released was the first time I felt any semblance of lucidity. I was bored, but I was not frustrated. I was calm. Maybe a bit lethargic. My reign of terror appeared to be complete, and now I didn't know what to do.

So I went home. Well, first I should say that I got a drink, and then I went home. Alcohol was still a bit new to me, and it didn't take much for me to get drunk. I stumbled up the path toward home.

I don't know who saw me first, but it was Teo who met me. He was sixteen or seventeen by now I think, a good, decent, hard-working, strong young man. Spitting image of our pa and everything our parents had hoped I would be. But he wasn't as big or as strong as I was, and I beat him easily. I beat him until he was pissing blood and could only see out half an eye. Then I got bored and ambled off to the barn where I made myself a bed out of the straw in the loft and fell asleep.

My ma...God bless her and give her every reward I could never have...my ma was the only reason my pa and brother didn't drive me off, call the police, or shoot me themselves. I was still her boy and she wouldn't let family hurt family if they could help it. She treated me right when no one else would or should have. Food, clean and mended clothes, a warm and dry place to sleep...I wish I could go back and tell myself to be appreciative, be grateful, take the chance to change my ways...

But I didn't. At some point, lying in my nest in the barn, I got the idea to spread my terror elsewhere. I would be like a one-man army, terrorizing the countryside, pillaging and plundering goods from every home, raping the women, claiming everything as mine. I got up and left without so much as a goodbye to anyone in my family.

I went south, terrorizing the countryside as I went, announcing my presence, letting everyone know that I was coming. Even the police. They were ready and waiting for me, and I was back in jail again. None of these prisoners knew me, so it was just another conquest, another place for me to establish my reign of terror.

Again I became head prisoner, the one who got first pick of the food, stole food from the others as I pleased, took their blankets, their clothes, beat them if they refused to submit. Some repented, begged to be freed. Some sought to ally themselves with me, but I had no interest. I was strong enough on my own and had no need for them to dog my heels and slow me down.

The guards quickly came to know my face, my antics, my strengths. They said my only weakness was that my bouts of ferocity were pretty short-lived. Once I knew I was the dominant, the absolute winner, I grew bored and quickly turned my attention elsewhere. Word of this spread, and it quickly came to be that the best way to beat me was simply to outlast me, to wait. Surrender was met violently, but even a small fight easily won could stave off further injury from a true brawl hard fought.

This infuriated me, that I had any weakness and that others were learning of it, but it was perhaps the only part of me that I could not overcome. I could not bring myself to sustain the fury and the rage and the strength. I almost could not bring myself to care. Oh, I was angry, but this anger soon abated as I got another drink, got in another fight, and inevitably landed back in jail.

With this weakness in mind, the police and the jailers tried to concoct plans to exploit it, to prevent my crimes or make it easier on themselves when they were ultimately forced to confront me. Other clergymen were called upon to see if a more sanctimonious solution could be found.

I was too dangerous to leave on the streets, but I was almost too dangerous to have in jail, either. Most of my time was spent in black cells, with no light, no food or drink but occasional bread and water. The guards hoped to weaken me, but even at my weakest, I was still equally as strong as they were.

There was no easy or readily available solution to my terror, my rage and my antics. Sometimes, I think the guards released me just so they could alleviate themselves of my terror for a short time before dragging me back. I think perhaps they were more merciful to the other prisoners after seeing what I could do, what real evil looked like. They were too happy whenever I moved on to the next town, the next county, became someone else's problem.

Eventually, it came to pass that I was just known everywhere in Wales. The villages did not easily forget the day the Devil came to town, though my time spent there was short, often just long enough to steal food or maybe sleep in a barn. The cities knew me very well as I established myself as a firm presence, again staking out a reserved jail cell.

Come the fall time, the harvest time, I would have a period of sobriety as I faced the oncoming winter with no home, no fire, no food. Strength alone would not keep me from freezing to death. But I was far from home, and many were afraid of me.

I sobered up for a time, moving from farm to farm, looking for work in exchange for a bowl of soup or a place in their barn to sleep. Those who did not know me agreed, though warily, as I am an intimidating man. Or I was. Those who did know me, assuming they spoke to me beyond threatening to call the police, sometimes they simply gave me food in an effort to make me go away, pass them by for my mischief, take my antics and violence elsewhere. This pleased me greatly, and I threatened many a farmer.

As the winter grew deeper and the work grew less, I stopped asking and started taking. I broke into root cellars and stole canned goods. I took chickens from coops. Being a man on the run had taught me much about survival, the art of the chase.

But, eventually, I wandered my way back home and helped myself to a place in the loft. No one knew I was there; they didn't come outside in the cold unless they absolutely had to. The hay and straw had been meager that year, and they were thin on resources, so the loft wasn't well insulated. Certainly it was colder than I remembered it being. I finally went down to sleep in the pen with the cow and her calf only a month old. Of course, the cow didn't want anyone near her calf. They slept on one side of the pen and me on the other, but it was still warmer than the loft.

My ma found me in the morning, just this side of warm. She was out to milk the cow, which she did. She gave me the shawl off her back to wrap around my own shoulders and a bowl of warm milk to drink. She talked to me as she milked the cow, as if I were merely home for a visit and not possibly running from the authorities again.

She told me about happenings in the family, about my younger sister who died of the flu just a few months before. She was only seven years old when she passed. Sorry to say, but at the time, I could conjure up no feelings for her. I did not weep for her, but neither did I scoff at her for being weak. Quite frankly, I didn't know her. I was twenty-four myself and was out of the house by the time she would have any memories of me. I felt nothing. Maybe it was better that way, at the time. I could see my ma still grieved, but there was work to do on the farm, same as always.

She also told me about my pa, how he was considering buying some land from a neighbor; it would basically double the size of the farm. The elderly neighbor couldn't take care of it and his children had run off to the city to make their fortunes. My pa was going to plow it for the old man in the upcoming year, and if it did well, he would buy it, let the man continue to live in his house until he died.

And my ma told me that Teo was in love with a girl. Had been for some time. She fancied him, too, apparently. Very much so. Everyone could see it, but they always denied it. Our pa was going to see about marriage arrangements, in secret if necessary, but it was going to happen eventually. It was as inevitable as the spring thaw, though it seemed far away at the time.

Owain shifted uncomfortably, the shackles echoing in the empty chapel. "I can't explain it well, but something about that conversation sparked a little humility in me, a little shame. My actions had been nothing but despicable for years and always brought shame to myself and my family. And yet my ma still gave me the shirt off her back and a warm meal, a place to sleep, and she could pick up a conversation, even if one-sided, as though we were simply meeting up for tea to catch up after months of being apart."

" 'If your enemy is hungry, feed him. If thirsty, give him drink. If he is cold, give him your shirt and your cloak also. And you will heap burning coals upon his head,' " the priest recited, nodding sagely.

But Owain shook his head. "No. It wasn't that. My ma did not see me as an enemy, either to hate or to do good. Most times, she just saw me as her son and she did good to me because I was her son, not to heap coals upon my head. And sometimes, I don't think she even saw me. I think she saw my soul, she saw what I needed, what my spirit craved."

"Mothers can be like that. They know us even before we are brought into the world. It may be that as the Lord knits our flesh together, He also gives our mothers special instructions about us, shows them how to look at us. Perhaps He gave your mother even more special instructions, showed her the path you would take."

"If that is the case, she ought to have drowned me when she had the chance."

Still, her kindness toward me there in the barn as she milked the cow stirred something in me. I finished the milk, returned her shawl, and stood. She thought I was leaving and asked me to stay, but I simply went about doing the remaining chores as I remembered them, feeding the horses, the chickens, the goats. I braved the cold and snow to fetch water for both the animals and the household. My mother made the excuse that the buckets were too heavy for her to take back to the house, and so I had to carry them.

My ma had my pa cowed before he could say three words. I was home, I was helping, and even so, it was the middle of winter. He wasn't going to cast out her son like a leper. I remember my pa saying that I was worse than a leper but just as unwanted. I think that was what quelled my growing shame and desire to be good for a time. My ma loved me, but my pa hated me, wanted nothing to do with me. He would deliver me to jail himself if given the chance. I took it as a challenge and promised myself that we would get even one day.

I don't even know what we would get even over, except I had reached a point where I simply desired to dominate, especially him, the man who had released me into the world, who had thrown me out of my home, who would do it all over again a thousand times if need be. But for the sake of my ma and the fact that it was still the middle of winter, I refrained for a time and behaved.

I ended up sharing a room with Teo, the same one we'd shared as boys. He was deathly afraid of me, I knew, but he did not run away or back down. He just went about his day as if I didn't exist. We rarely spoke to each other.

Once, I did try to be friendly and I asked about this woman our parents said he liked. He wouldn't tell me her name—perhaps he considered me a danger to her, which I would have been, had I been of a mind to hurt him or her—but he did admit to me that he liked her very much and did want to marry her. He just wasn't sure how to go about asking. It was the closest thing we ever had to a friendly, brotherly discussion.

As for my sisters, they were not overly interested in me, though they knew well to fear me, especially Missy, who was old enough to remember my antics as a child. They stayed in their room or flocked around our ma or pa, looking for protection, or witnesses at the very least.

It was a tense couple of months. When the spring came, I made no pretense about wanting to stay. I knew they didn't want me, and I told my ma to not try and talk me into staying. Things were civil this time around. Might as well keep it that way for as long as possible.

Unfortunately, on my way out, Teo did confront me, one on one. Words were exchanged. I didn't need a drink to be provoked into a fight. I don't know what was going through his mind that he thought he could challenge me. Perhaps he'd been reading too much about David and Goliath. I just know that I left him on the ground, bloody and barely conscious. Any kind of shame or humility, anything that might have started me on a better path, anything that kindled that spirit over the last few months all dissolved. I went to the nearest town, the closest pub, and got a drink.

I spent the spring and summer as I always had, making my way from here to there, fighting, stealing, spending time in jail. I was a national nuisance.

In the fall, I did return home. The lines were more defined than they had been when I left. My pa hated me, had basically disowned me already. Teo despised me, though I will still contend that the fight was his fault. My sisters were afraid of me and wanted nothing to do with me, as if I might violate them. My ma still loved me, though I could see the constant cycle, the uncertainty, it was wearing on her as she aged.

It hurt. I didn't like the feeling, the pain, the guilt. I helped on the harvest for a few days, but I was an extra hand to be tasked with meaningless errands, not someone to be relied upon. Eventually, I ran. I was a coward. Perhaps I still am. No, I know I still am. Once a coward, always a coward.

I spent that fall doing menial work on various farms. I was known, and my tasks were thankless, everything everyone else didn't want to do, and my pay was a pittance. A threadbare blanket with holes, some leftover stew with a piece of crusty bread. I hated such living, so I again resorted to stealing whatever I wanted. I did this through the late autumn and into the winter.

Sometime in the winter, around Christmas, I got drunk and broke into a root cellar. On my way down the stairs, I fell and ended up breaking my leg. The noise woke the farmer. I took what I could and managed to hobble out of the cellar. But the bone was sticking through the skin and I had not only my footprints in the snow but the blood trail, too. Not only that, but the homeowner spotted me and shot me from a pretty fair distance. It wasn't lethal, but with everything else going on, I went down.

I was sentenced to nine months in jail, and I was to do labor just as soon as my leg would allow it. Of course, there are plenty of chores to do in jail that don't require the use of a leg, so I was put to work almost right away. Several times I got in fights with other inmates, the guards, even myself a few times when I was truly delirious. I think the last month or so, they just kept me in my cell and didn't bother to do much more than give me my rations, every two or three days as they remembered I existed.

It was mid-September when I was released. I was given a recommendation to find honest work on a farm for the harvest. It was more of a formality, really, a commonly rehearsed script to try and get convicts back on the path to righteousness. None of the guards held out any hope that I would change.

I made my way back home. But this time, something was different. When my ma found me again in the barn in the morning, she explained just what was different. Teo had gotten married in the spring. His wife was Maisy, a girl I vaguely knew of but didn't really know. Apparently she had escaped my reign of terror as a child somehow, which only worked in Teo's favor, I suppose. Anyway, the neighbor whom our pa had bought the field from had died. Teo and Maisy now lived in the man's farmhouse and worked those fields. Once our pa got too old to work, the plan was, he'd sell the whole thing back to Teo. It would be a grand inheritance for his only son.

That comment hurt me in a way I can't describe. I always knew my pa hated me, and I'd figured he'd disowned me, but to hear it confirmed, and to hear it from my ma, it pierced me like an arrow. My pa disowned me. My brother was a grown man starting a family, had a wife and land and everything that I should have been. Even my sisters were growing up and getting married. And here was I, still doing the same fighting and drinking and terrorizing the whole countryside from Caerdydd to Abertawe, the same actions and nothing to show for my miserable life. I was very nearly thirty years old, had nothing but the clothes on my back and whatever I could steal that would fit in my arms.

I stayed with them for the harvest. The whole harvest. And I helped. Most often, my pa was out in the fields with Teo. If I was out there, I was always sent away on meaningless errands better suited for little boys. I spent more time in the house with my ma and remaining sisters doing women's work, canning and preserving and cooking. Don't get me wrong, I enjoy cooking, but it was still demeaning, all things considering. I was still unbelievably strong, still a big man, I should have been out helping all the farms, doing things that might otherwise require three normal men. Instead, I was in the kitchen with the women, like a woman, like an invalid, like an unwanted parasite.

During the harvest, I slept in the barn. As a gesture of good will, I would have the horses ready by the time my pa came out to plow. He ignored me completely, did not say so much as thank you. When my ma came out in the morning to milk the cow—which was when I would get up and get ready—she told me that my pa wasn't even grateful, not even secretly. He'd made the statement that he would sooner die trying to do it himself than accept my help.

After the harvest was taken in and the snow began to fall, I was permitted to sleep in the house, but I would not take the room I had once shared with my brother. I would sleep in the kitchen, near the stove, like a dog. My job was simply to keep the fire going, retrieve wood, chop wood when needed.

Without Teo and Missy, I had no one to even try and connect with. While the rest of the family would play games at night or read from the family Bible, try to pass the winter any way they could, I simply stayed by the stove, unwanted. Sometimes my ma would come and sit with me and talk, try to cheer me up, but I knew it caused trouble with my pa, the same way he might confront her over a secret lover. He hated me. Maybe he wanted to kill me.

Sometimes, at night, when I was adding wood to the stove, I wondered what it would be like to kill myself. It wasn't that I was seriously contemplating it at the time, but I wondered what the sensation would feel like. I'd been in plenty of fights, but I was always the victor. What would it feel like to die, or to even consider death as an option? I often wondered about God, sitting there and listening to them read from the Bible at night. Did He hate me? Would He send the fires from the stove to consume me one unsuspecting night? Did He even understand why I had always been so angry? Had He made me that way? If so, why?

In the morning, I would usually make the loaf of bread for the day. Once, I even went out to the barn in the middle of a snowstorm and milked the cow myself, did all the chores so my ma didn't have to. My ma was grateful. My pa made some comment about how at least I was better at being a woman than I ever had been being a man. Maybe that was where they'd fallen short. Maybe God had gotten a little confused on which parts to give me. The comment stung.

The weather had just turned its face back toward spring when I announced that I was leaving. My pa wished me good riddance. My ma asked where I planned to go. I'd never really announced my leaving so formally before, so this was unusual. I told her that there was nowhere in Wales I could go where I wouldn't be known as a drunken brawler. There was nowhere in Wales where I would be taken seriously if I said I wanted to change. If all I faced in Wales was rejection, then maybe it was time to leave Wales.

My ma did not like the sound of that, and she all but forbade me to go, even as my pa all but offered to help me pack my bags. Except I didn't have any bags because I had no worldly possessions. At the very least, she got me to stay until the threat of winter had truly gone and it was safe to travel again without fear of freezing to death on the side of the road.

Then my ma made me a brand new set of clothes and a bag to put them in. She got me all cleaned up and told me to make a good impression wherever I decided to go. My pa told me good riddance, but he also said that he prayed to God that this was the instance that changed me, that maybe it wasn't too late for my redemption. As long as I didn't become Catholic. Then there was no hope of redemption for me.

I stopped to see Teo before I left, maybe for good. We didn't fight, but his demeanor had changed. Maisy was pregnant with their first child, and he didn't want my taint to touch their unborn baby.

That was the last time I saw Teo, and the best thing I can say about it was that we didn't fight. I just said goodbye, turned around, and started off, to where I did not know.

Chapter Four

The Vagabond

For a short time, I did stay in Wales, meandering here and there, hoping to find honest work, trying to convince people that I wanted to change. There were a few hesitant offers, but one drink and an argument that ended in a fistfight quickly closed those doors. I made my way east and north, to England.

It was a land I'd never seen, though it looked remarkably like Wales, as you might imagine. I knew the language well enough, but my heavy accent pegged me as an outsider, and not a welcome one at that. Some folks near the border knew who I was, and they knew well to stay away from me. When I finally reached truly foreign lands where people did not know my name and reputation, my status as a foreigner was enough to stop many people from asking for my help or otherwise accepting my offers of assistance.

I traveled all over the English countryside. Sometimes I found work. Sometimes I found a drink. I really did try to stay clean, and I'd like to think I did a decent job of it. I won't say I never ended up in jail, but I never passed out drunk, didn't have any blackouts that I can recall, didn't cow other prisoners to my will, didn't frighten the jailers. I will say that it was a new experience for me, not being absolutely dominant, and the anxiety over it nearly tore me in two.

I think that was my first experience seeing myself as two entities, seeing my rage as its own beast, a thing that I not only had to control, but that I *could* control. I was the master of this creature, the master of this beast. It did not come out of its cage unless I said it could. My cage of will was not a strong one, however, and it escaped more than once.

Recognizing that you have a problem is the first step to healing," Forthill said. "You can't fix a problem that you don't acknowledge exists."

Owain nodded absently. "Maybe, but even if you acknowledge that the dam is leaking, it does no good if you don't know how to fix it."

"Very true, and demonic forces do not take kindly to their acknowledgment; they will go on the attack immediately."

"Don't I know it."

Once I made my rage and my need to hurt and conquer a semi-tangible beast to cage and control, it fought against me. Just trying to talk to people normally and make a kind offer of assistance on their farms, it was like trying to speak while a rabid dog chewed on my limbs, and it was something only I could see. Sometimes I reacted to this internal battle, and people turned me away because of it, thinking me a sick man.

I also had another dilemma. The beast was rage and hatred and the desire to conquer, to dominate. If I wanted to conquer it, did that mean I was indulging it or defeating it? I had no way to know. This, too, kept me up many nights.

But, all things considered, my life as a nomad in England wasn't half as bad as my life in Wales. Most nights I had either food in my stomach or a warm, dry place to sleep. Sometimes I had both. Sometimes I had neither. But I was drinking less, I was fighting less, and I was in jail less. Life wasn't good, but it was better than it had been, than it could have been.

Eventually I made my way to London, and the first thing I did was send a letter to my parents, just to let them know that I was alive and well, let them know I wasn't in jail and things were looking up.

Have you ever been to London?" Owain inquired.

"Yes, once," the priest replied.

"Then you know that it is a large city. One man can't hope to take it all in, in only a day."

"I would concur."

It was perhaps one of the single greatest battles against the beast that I can remember. London was huge. I could dominate this city, one block at a time. I could bring thousands of people to their knees. I could rule a whole network of jails and prisons. I could rule a criminal underground so vast and so powerful, no one would dare try to take me in.

Perhaps it was that last part that gave me an advantage to defeating the rage beast. I've never wanted to rule anything or command men. I'd abandoned the idea of a gang long ago. I was still a coward, a selfish man only interested in himself and his own well-being. That didn't stop the beast from tempting me, though. If nothing else, it tried all the harder to make me fall. And in a city crawling with pubs, the beast could have stayed quiet and let the everyday culture tempt me for him.

London was—is a vast city of contradictions. It was at once unbelievably wealthy and yet obscenely impoverished. Grandiose mansions reached for the sky not a hundred yards from hovels and slums. Sprawling docks stretched as far as the eye could see, and still more were under construction. Sailors of all varieties were in port: rich merchants, poor merchants, military, foreign traders, passenger vessels, and plenty of shady characters as well, possible pirates and smugglers. And there were a number of markets. Overshadowing these markets were the banks, massive financial institutions for all kinds of monetary needs. People moved all over in every fashion. Walking, horse and cart, and there was even an underground system under construction.

Even as my rage beast desired to dominate this city, the more human part of me was awed and terrified by the sheer magnitude of human activity. My one disadvantage was my one advantage, being a foreigner. On the one hand, I wasn't known. My anonymity meant I could have a fresh start. As long as I stayed clean, I could maybe make a life for myself, an honest existence.

The disadvantage was that I was a foreigner, and certainly not the only one. The city was flooded with foreigners, most of them poor Irish fleeing the Famine. The French, the Italians, the Dutch, the Asians, the

Arabians, foreigners, yes, but rich ones, come to do banking, trading stocks and bonds, and investing in currency. I could not even imagine pretending to be one of them. My presence, my power was gained through strength and intimidation. The power gained in the city was of a more subtle variety. Size and strength without a business mind would win me nothing but a crown of mud from the slums.

With the flood of Irish immigrants into the city at the same time, jobs were scarce, wages were low, and mistrust of foreigners was high. Even though I wasn't Irish, Wales was close enough for Londoners to disdain, and I didn't have enough money to persuade them to think otherwise. Opinion of Welsh folk wasn't very high to begin with.

It was all so much to take in, and I almost turned tail and went home. It's easy to gloat over my own power when I'm king of a hundred. Realizing that I was but an insignificant body in a city of over a million people, it quieted my inner beast for a short time.

I had only a little money, enough to get me through a couple days until I could find work. Dock construction was all the rage. It required a lot of strength and it was dangerous, which meant they needed even more expendable labor. A strangely strong Welshman? I could do the hardest, most dangerous work, and they could pay me half what they were paying the rest of the crew. But seeing how I was coming in with only the clothes on my back, I couldn't say no, and any honest wages sounded good to me.

In all reality, I enjoyed the work. Well, perhaps what I mean to say is, I enjoyed showing off how big and strong I was. I could get work done that no one else could do, and I hardly broke a sweat. It made me feel good, and it placated the beast for a while. I wasn't in charge of anyone, we were all doing the same grunt work, we were all under the thumb of a very cranky foreman, and I could prove myself the best.

I suppose it's my own fault for thinking I was somehow in the clear. I knew what power felt like, and my demon craved power won in opposition. It enjoyed the pushback. Half the time, it wasn't about the victory, but the fight.

Most of the men I worked with were English, but there was a noticeable Irish presence as well, all of them poor. They all hated me even as they couldn't get along without me, not when my size and strength made some aspects of the work that much easier. So while I was the best and always proved it, there was little pushback. I began looking for ways to make them need me, manipulate situations where I would have to be called to help. Failing that, I got smart and began thinking of ways to provoke them into a fight without being obvious that I was the instigator.

Owain paused and shook his head, his neck wretchedly stiff. "Perhaps the worst kind of evil is the kind that learns. It learns how to be better, smarter, more subtle, disguising itself as good and provoking others into being evil without their knowledge."

"Perhaps," Forthill began thoughtfully, "but every man is responsible for his own actions. They were no more compelled to react than you were to act. The provocateur may be the cause, but he is by no means the only one at fault."

"Does it matter? I probably would have hurt them anyway. There were a couple instances where I could have gotten someone killed. All to satisfy the beast inside me."

"Then it could be that the Lord permitted them to react in order to save their lives. Be grateful for it, then. The Lord works everything for good."

Looking at his manacles, Owain found that he could see no good here. Maybe Forthill was right and hundreds or thousands of souls had been saved, thousands of souls destined for Heaven because of him. If he was the Lord's tool in that way, did it excuse his actions? If he wasn't an intentional tool of the Lord and it was more of a convenience thing, would the Almighty Father still discard him? Was there any hope for his soul?

Eventually, even for my size and strength, the foreman was forced to fire me because of the complaints and the division among the men, the only real division being them against me. But I was given my wages and told to get out.

It didn't matter a whole lot because dock construction was a massive undertaking. It still is. Actually, construction of any kind in London is a huge undertaking, and it wasn't hard to find work as long as you were willing to work for next to nothing. I jumped from job to job, the beast always coming back to haunt me, telling me to dominate. Sometimes I was able to resist for a time, but I always gave in eventually.

I was renting a single room at the time. With an array of jobs, I was able to keep the money coming in, but having been homeless for many years, it was not my first priority like it was for some. My first priority was always myself and my immediate needs, and a room I considered luxury shelter.

I'm talking about food and drink. London is a crossroads in the world, and there were plenty of dining options to be had. With my background and my low wages, I was relegated to the shadier establishments in town. And I fit in very well, as you might be able to imagine. For a time, I was able to restrain myself. I developed a plan where I would put money on the counter and tell the keep to give me food and not more drinks than the money would cover.

The problem came when I started working. Every job started out the same. I was big and strong, and the foreman always liked me. The crew liked me, too. And sometimes, at night, we would go out to the pub together. I would do my honest routine, get a plate of food and a couple drinks. Then the other men would start buying rounds, or just buy me drinks. We would get drunk. Sometimes, if the mood was light, the beast remained caged and we would have a jolly drinking time. But more often than not, I would get violent. Then things would happen.

Once, I woke up in jail. I lost my job, as you might imagine.

Usually, though, once the other men realized that my strength could be turned against them as easily as it worked for them, they would start to shun me. We wouldn't go out anymore. They excluded me from conversation. One crew became openly hostile.

Suddenly rejected, I grew angry. And I would begin another cycle of provoking them to anger, of creating situations where they absolutely required my assistance.

D id you have no one?" the priest inquired. "No one at all? Friends, even of the shady type? Did you ever write to your parents and your family back home?"

"Any friends I had were short-lived, once they realized how volatile and selfish I was. I had no allies in a fight. My demon convinced me I needed none. I could usually win any fight single-handedly, and no friend or ally would do anything once the police got involved. Some would drunkenly fight the police themselves, but if I was in a scrap, no one was going to attack a cop or otherwise come to my aid. If I went down, normal men would have no chance. It was their own selfishness, I suppose, but in a way, I respect them for it. I would not have expected them to operate under rules I myself did not follow."

"And your parents?"

"I'd written them when I first arrived in London, but I did not write to them after that. There was nothing to tell. I was working. They were farming. And I was ashamed that I hadn't made much of myself. A job was good, but it only served to feed my alcoholism. I could have quit my job and just gone back to my old ways just as easily."

"Why not write, then? Even that sliver of light, the desire to be good, that could be seen as a victory, surely. Accountability is a powerful thing."

"Everything looks clearer when it's behind you," Owain sighed, still not looking at the priest. "It does me no good now."

A nd I did have a time where I felt a surge of strength, productivity, an urge to better myself. After being fired from my last job, I decided to take what unholy talents I did have and hope to turn them to an ultimate good use. Instead of constantly working on construction projects in the slums and low-income areas, I got myself cleaned up real well and presented myself to companies and projects of somewhat better means. I was big, I was strong, and being well-groomed at least got them to look at me. My accent and lack of mastery of English nuances gave me away and kept me from becoming anyone important, but I did get a decent job as a laborer on slightly better projects. Instead of digging sewers and building docks, I was building homes and businesses. It couldn't be done fast enough as people from all over the world continued to pour into the city.

Not only did it pay better, but I was afforded the opportunity to learn and educate myself some. I greatly improved my reading, my speaking. I worked on my accent so it didn't mar my speech so much. In London, a hint of an accent means you're a potential wealthy investor. A heavy accent means you're a fool. I also improved my mathematics. I learned how to multiply and divide, even got to a point where I didn't need to use paper.

I suppose that somewhere in my mind, aside from the basic knowledge I was acquiring, I was also learning how to be better at being evil. My beast evolved from a starving dog attacking everything, into a clever cat looking for a way to get what it wants. I figure that my intent was to learn a few things, make more money to be able to present myself better, get an even better job, learn more, and so on. I would enter by big picture fraud and fill in the details later.

I never really had an end goal on this line of thinking. My demon had always had a desire to dominate through brute force and intimidation. Victory was easy. The goals were simple to achieve. With this new line of thinking, I had to think further and further down the line, into the future. With my new job, I was learning names, faces, becoming loosely connected with people. Sure, these people saw me only as a laborer, but, after all, London was big. Who was going to know who I was in another part of town?

Of course, I still had a lot to learn, and I failed to take into account that wealthy people had more resources than me, which included the ability to get around town wherever they needed to go, and they liked to talk. I was caught once on the north side of town. I was still known only as a laborer and politely, if haughtily, asked what I was doing among the rich and famous. I managed to weasel my way out of that one, and I resolved to keep my head low until I had the means to make the jump.

It wasn't going to be easy because that required substantial means. Even if I wasn't out brawling like I used to, I still drank. Heavily. I was still living in a rented room and didn't consider rent my highest priority.

On top of that, anything nice that I did get, I had to be sure I kept safe. I was living among my own kind, after all. I couldn't be seen with any fine possessions in the slums or by anyone who knew who I was and where I lived. I was, really, living a double life.

In the morning, I would get up, go to work. In the evening, I would go home, grab my nice clothes, fix myself up nice so I almost couldn't be recognized, and I would just walk the streets, try to get myself seen, make myself known among the upper class. I listened more than I spoke so I could pick up on news, learn the language of the wealthy, and interject myself only when I was confident that I would not be discovered as a charlatan.

Then, at night, I would return home, hide my fine things, and go out drinking. I would return home to get hardly a few hours of sleep before returning to work.

O wain sighed and let his face drop into his hands. "God, I hate myself."

Forthill said nothing as Owain wept silently for a minute or two.

"You know," he said finally, "It might not have been so bad, except for what happened next."

"What happened next?" the priest inquired gently.

"Nothing that can't wait a few more days, I'm sure," the gaoler interrupted, walking up and grabbing the chain to haul Owain to his feet. "It's time for you to go back to your cell."

"It's hardly suppertime," Forthill protested.

"It's dark. You ought to be heading back to the parish yourself, ain't you? The weather is fine right now, but it won't take nothing for a storm to blow in."

"Please." The priest stood and smoothed his robes. "May I pray for him first, at least?"

"Pray for me," the gaoler sneered, "that I don't cut his throat myself."

Nevertheless, he stepped back two feet and Forthill prayed for Owain. The priest didn't even get past the "Blessed Father," before Owain was bawling. No one had prayed over him—specifically, intentionally prayed over him—since he was a small child. Even then, his mother had always prayed for an end to the rage and for the demons to be expelled from his soul. The priest prayed for peace, for comfort, for a clear conscience, for rest for his soul, for the love and wisdom of the Holy Spirit. Never had anyone ever associated those things with him, never mind asked God to give them to him.

"In Thy Name, Amen," Forthill finished.

"All right, off you go," the gaoler grumbled.

"And what is your name, sir, that I might pray for you as well?"

That gave the man pause, but only for half a second. He was pale-skinned, but likely that came from being in the prison as much as the prisoners. Brown hair that was almost red sat in a thick mop on his head, freckles dotting his cheeks. But he was a bear of a man, with broad shoulders, a thick chest, and meaty arms. He was almost Owain's size, and Owain was at his weakest. It might have been a fair fight, tipped in the gaoler's favor seeing how he did not appear to want for food.

Finally the big man gave the priest an almost unreadable look and replied, "Cassius."

Forthill was not fazed. He simply dipped his head and said, "Well then, Cassius, I shall be certain to pray for you in the coming days. After I have prayed for Mr. Fforidd here."

The gaoler, Cassius, grunted, shook his head, and hauled Owain along like a disobedient dog.

It wasn't a long walk back to his cell, his black cell, but for Owain, it was simultaneously a thousand miles and yet a single step. His ankles were bloody, his feet swollen, wrists and hands not much better. Beaumaris Gaol was supposed to be the height of prisoner comfort, but he felt little of it. The man who had murdered his father-in-law and several of his associates did not deserve to understand the word "comfort." He dare not even whisper it for fear of being beaten.

Even as the shackles and his mistreatment made the trip painful, it was still preferable to his cell, dark and cramped and crawling with rats, listening to the screams, unsure whether they came from other cells or his own mouth. Didn't matter, he supposed, it was all the same in the end. Death, torture. Maybe he ought to tell the priest not to bother asking for a postponed sentence or any sort of mercy. In fact, just kill him now.

Talking about the road that brought him here only made his stomach twist until he thought he would be ill.

"You make me sick," Cassius growled, forcing him up the steps. "You are a disgusting waste of human flesh. I'll be glad to see you to the noose."

"At this point, I think I shall be glad to go," Owain said in a small voice.

The gaoler snorted indignantly. "You know what I hate most about some of you prisoners? You try to act so noble toward the end. Even in your last days, you're selfish dogs, pretending to care about your crimes and your soul so as to win over the weak hearts of the priests, get them to pray for your soul so you can enter heaven ignobly." He spat. "Despicable. Utterly wretched, filthy, disgusting swine that you are."

"*Ie*, but even swine are useful."

"Shut up." Cassius paused, turned, and swung at him with a huge fist. It caught Owain sidelong against his cheek. A smaller man might have stumbled and perhaps fallen back down the stairs. Being a veteran of many fights, Owain simply took one step back to steady himself and push away the pain. He'd learned not to fight back, and he'd learned how to keep going, act normal even as he was tugged along and feeling slightly dazed.

The condemned cell was just around the corner from the top of the stairs. Here Cassius stopped just long enough to get his keys and open the door. Owain might have likened it to the gaping maw of Hell, except it was frigid cold. Cassius pushed him into the murky blackness. He stumbled, sucking in a breath but not daring to cry out as the shackles cut into his ankles and he couldn't catch himself well with his wrists bound together.

The door swung shut, but then a rectangle of dim light shone through a small port. Owain scrambled up to get his wrists through. It was rare that his wrists were unbound, and he always took the opportunity to free them. His ankles, however...his ankles had not been free since his arrival. He counted it a miracle that he could even walk.

His arms fell to his sides as the iron was undone. He felt tears streaming down his cheeks into his beard, a small moment of joy. Then the rectangle of light disappeared and he screamed in terror and frustration, his heart, if not his mouth, begging God to bring back the light. A lantern, a match, he would take anything.

But he would be given nothing because he deserved nothing. Not light, not mercy, certainly not forgiveness. In the dark, he could hear the scuttling of the rats, that small sound, the little scratch of claws on stone or straw. The cell wasn't long enough for him to stretch out and sleep, and if he sat against one wall, he could put his legs out and touch the other. There was a bench along one of the longer walls. Half of it was a seat, the other half the latrine which he had to scrub once a week, or maybe once a month. Sometimes it was hard to tell.

He sat on the seat and tried to cover as much of his body as he could with his sparse garments, lashing out at the invisible rats. Sometimes the hits connected and the rat would let out a surprised squeal and then a hiss. Most times, though, he lashed out at empty air, and he was forced to wonder whether the rats were there at all or if it was just his mind playing tricks on him.

Sometimes, during the day, there would be a very dim light that came through under the door and around the cuff hole, just enough that Owain could see his hand in front of his face. The light only last maybe an hour at the height of the day, but he soaked up every minute of it. Once or twice a month they might let him out in the exercise yard. The first time, he'd been so afraid, he almost begged to be taken back to his little crypt. But he had to take what he could get.

But he would be given nothing because he deserved nothing. He was a brawler, a drunkard, a murderer. Swine had more use in society than he did. Swine could be butchered and eaten. He would die, but that was the extent of it. They would bury him in a common grave in the cemetery, brush off their hands, and go about their day.

The only other time he saw any light was at feeding time. It was supposed to be every day, but there were times Owain was fairly certain that it had been at least two if not three days. Why waste food on a dead man, after all? They only needed to keep him alive long enough to hang him. He didn't need to be healthy to kill him properly. In fact, being sick and weak might make it a little easier, make his neck easier to snap.

Owain slept fitfully; somehow he'd become talented enough to throw off rats in his sleep, though it did little good. Aside from rats being persistent sons of bitches, he would wake up to other sounds, worse sounds. Sometimes they came from the other cells, sometimes from his own mind. Many times they sounded the same. He couldn't even decide whether he preferred the unknown sounds or the known nightmares, reliving his crimes over and over and over again, from childhood all the way to the murders that got him here.

He woke up, face wet, body freezing. Stiffly, he forced his legs to function and got all his joints moving again, if just barely. He sat up. Another day in darkness. Right where he belonged. He was scheduled to hang in a little over a week. It was said that men could survive almost a month without food. He did not expect to be fed that day, whatever promises were made, but a bowl of bad gruel was given him at some point in the day. He knew about where it was in the darkness, but he did not move to take it. He could hear the rats again, their noses telling them what was going on, telling them that food was in the vicinity. Claws scratched on straw and stone. He could hear the wooden bowl scraping on the floor as the rats assaulted it.

Let them, he figured. They could use it more than he could. He was going to be hanged in a week and then it wouldn't matter. Sighing, and taking advantage of the rats' distraction, he pulled his legs up close, lay down, and closed his eyes.

THE EXECUTIONER

"So, how is our penitent murderer this evening?" the warden asked, not looking up from his paperwork as the chaplain stood in the doorway.

"Gloomy," Forthill replied, helping himself to a seat.

They sat in silence for a long moment, unspoken tension threading through the room like violin strings. Forthill forced himself not to waver in his resolve as he stared at Dillon who intentionally ignored him, making busywork for himself.

After a good five or ten minutes, the warden set everything aside, steepled his fingers, and sighed, finally meeting the chaplain's gaze. "I know what you did, Father."

"What did I do?" Forthill questioned innocently.

"You sent a letter of appeal to the judge, asking him to push back Fforidd's execution date. Your claim is that you are hard at work extracting a religious confession from him and to hang him in the middle of his story could be harmful both psychologically and spiritually, that deeds left unconfessed could damn his immortal soul. Given the difficulty of the passage here and your infrequent visits, you estimate that you would need approximately six months to go through everything with him." Dillon's voice had gotten louder as he went on and he was standing now. "Six—months! That is utterly outrageous! Unthinkable!"

"How so?"

"He is a condemned man sentenced to hang. He condemned himself and he confessed to everything. He was found at the scene of the crime, fully and openly admitting to everything."

"Everything with which he was charged. But there is a greater heaviness on his soul. I am sorry you cannot see beyond your own narrow, legalistic views. I am not asking for his sentence to be overturned; I am asking for time to prepare him to meet the Lord."

"You're here twice a week, and that's when weather is favorable. That means he goes five days without seeing you. You think he can't make his peace by himself? He has nothing better to do. And furthermore, he is a drain on our resources. He is condemned to die. He will hang. Might as well do it sooner than later, save us all time and grief."

Forthill shifted position. "And whose grief is that, Nathan? Yours? Will you weep over this man?"

"I weep over the men he killed, the families he ruined."

"Then you ought to weep for him as well, for his wife and child were also murdered."

"He has no claim to them. And we are not having this conversation."

"You keep saying that, yet you insist on defending yourself and your decisions."

Nathan gave him a look. "Are you not doing the same?"

"Perhaps. But my goal here is to save his soul that he might enter Paradise and be with our Lord. You seek only to justify your own actions."

The warden breathed heavily for a few seconds, then sat. "You know, you're not the only one who can write letters. And you're not the only one who knows judges and magistrates and councilmen." He put up a finger. "One letter from me, and you're gone. All I have to say is that a prisoner has gotten to you. Manipulated you, threatened you, and in the interest of your safety, I would like you to be removed. Seeing how this particular prisoner is already condemned to death, I would also request that he be hanged immediately. No flair, no pomp and circumstance, maybe not even a ceremony. Maybe he won't even leave his cell, just go in and kill him. Could be a bullet in the head, strangulation, anything I please. Where will his soul be then?"

"Where will yours?" the chaplain countered. "That you should take such pleasure in hurting those in your care...that is the wretched filth here, not Fforidd."

"In my care? Am I running a school, a charity?"

"You know exactly what I mean. What do you have against this man so much that you will not permit me to continue this work?"

"I am trying to do my job. A sentence comes down and I maintain it in the strictest fashion. What would happen if other prisoners heard about this, that they could buy time just by talking to the chaplain? A hog thief may not care because he does not wish to spend more time here than he has to. A walking dead man? Extending his own pitiful life, giving him ample opportunity to plot an escape, assault the guards. We're not fooled, Forthill, Fforidd is hardly a weak man even in his current state."

There was a part of Forthill that wanted to get up in arms, defend himself, raise his voice, but he did not. He sat quietly and nodded calmly. "I respect your position, Nathan, I do, though it may not seem like it. And I understand that there are many shifty men out there who would gladly take advantage of a man's kindness, take advantage of a clergyman. But tell me something: if all men are unable to change, why do we let them out of here? If we know that a hog thief will always remain a hog thief and will continue to steal hogs, why bother to let him out? Mr. Fforidd has come to his senses, perhaps too late to do anything more with his life, but with enough time to save his soul. The thief on the cross had less time with the Lord and yet he was saved."

"Then perhaps you can speak to him at the gallows," the warden growled. He leaned back in his chair, his expression exhausted and unimpressed. "I'm going to meet with the judge next week to discuss this unauthorized letter of yours. You know what I'm going to tell him?"

"To remove me from my post and have Mr. Fforidd executed posthaste?" the chaplain ventured.

The warden shook his head. "No. Six weeks. I'll give you six weeks to finish up your soul searching with him. It's more than I'd like, but know that I also respect your position. I respect you. Think you can handle six weeks?"

"I make no promises, but I should think so. I believe the weather is about to make a turn toward spring."

"Whatever. Six weeks. If you like, I'll do my best to make his execution date on a sunny day, that he might see the light before he hangs."

"That would be very good."

The warden shook his head, muttered an oath, then grumbled an apology to the chaplain. Forthill forgave him, then excused himself from Dillon's office.

It was a peaceful return to the chapel that night, brutally cold, but the skies were clear and the stars twinkled overhead. Nevertheless, he quickly ducked into the parsonage where Worthington was just tossing another log on the fire before apparently preparing for bed. He wore only his night robe and had extinguished all but one candle at his bedside.

"So, how are things in the land of stone and sorrow?" the older priest inquired politely.

"Stony and sorrowful, I'm afraid," Forthill answered, removing his shoes and outer garments. "But not without hope."

"Still speaking to Fforidd, then?"

"Yes. And more good news." He spoke of his letter and Dillon's compromise, six months to six weeks. Less than he'd wanted, but more than he'd expected to get in the end. He'd simply been fishing for anything at all. Why had he doubted the Lord's provision?

"Sounds like quite an endeavor." Worthington's tone was carefully neutral. "Fforidd has continued to be repentant and forthcoming?"

"Most certainly. He has a fascinating tale to tell, going from brute strength and almost animalistic instincts to a cold, calculating mind. I admit, I'm eager to hear the rest of the tale, as bloody as I know it is going to be."

The older man grinned. "Now we hear the truth from your lips. Perhaps your calling is not to be clergy, but a criminal investigator. Perhaps you should look into the budding field of psychology, studying the reasons people do things, examining their minds."

"If I understand it correctly, this 'psychology' bases everything on that blasphemous, naturalistic view. People search for excuses, but every man is accountable for his own actions to God Almighty. I simply wish to know what those actions are or were."

"Yes, you keep telling yourself that."

"What is that supposed to mean?"

"Why are you so concerned over this one man? Every other prisoner you have spoken with, condemned or not, you have done your job and gone your way. What makes Fforidd so different? Why stick your neck out for him?"

Forthill sighed. "I don't know. It's just something the Lord has led me to do. Something is being accomplished here. I don't understand what it is, and I may never know, but something is happening for the Holy Kingdom. It may be that we do not know the fruits of this seed until the last day when we are joined with the saints."

"And there you go thinking a little too far ahead. Why don't you see how the next six weeks turn out?"

Forthill chuckled. "Yes, I suppose you're right. Comes with old age, I suppose, being fanciful."

"Watch yourself, young'un. I'm still older than you."

"And so you are."

The two of them retired to their respective beds. It wasn't two minutes before Worthington was snoring, but Forthill remained awake, staring at the shadows as they bounced on the ceiling. It was nothing new, seeing the shadows created by the fire in the little stove, but tonight they seemed to speak a warning. It grieved him in ways he could not explain right away.

Then he considered that Fforidd did not have even this luxury of shadows. Nor heat. He was lying alone in the cold and dark. Not even alone; he was sharing his small space with rats. Forthill had seen the scars and the chew marks.

Maybe I'm making a huge mistake, he thought, sighing to himself. *He wants to die more than the warden. To spend your life in the darkness, waiting and just hoping to catch a glimpse of the light. What demons speak to him from the shadows? Should I speak to Dillon and tell him to go ahead with his desire to remove me and kill Fforidd? Am I getting sentimental, or foolishly idealistic? In no situation would such poor conditions be the ideal. Fforidd has confessed to much. Surely the Lord will show him mercy.*

Forthill muttered half a dozen prayers for Fforidd's soul before yawning and rolling over. As comforting as his surroundings were, he found he could not enjoy them. He was here among friends, with a warm fire, and a tea kettle where the water was likely still warm.

Why have you put this man on my heart, Lord? he prayed silently. *What impact will we have on each other? Will I see him again in Paradise one day?*

He sincerely hoped so. His uncertainty delivered him into a restless sleep, but he remembered his dream vividly.

He found himself walking through a gorge that was sandy and desolate. Animals were everywhere, mostly cows, dead, stomachs pulled out of their bodies. The stench was unbearable, and Forthill gagged. He looked for the nearest rock wall and began climbing. He found good purchase, but when he was halfway up, all his purchase points under his hands and feet slid out and he fell. As he was falling, he felt something tighten around his neck. Before it could tighten and snap his neck, the rope broke, and he continued to fall.

He hit the ground. But instead of the dry gorge, he found himself in a grassy field near a beach. The air smelled of salt and he could see a shore, far in the distance. He walked, unbidden, toward the beach, the water. As he did, he discovered he was actually walking on the water and the distant shore had suddenly become very close indeed. He stepped on the far shore and found himself looking up a slope to a cave in the side of a mountain.

This is not your life, a disembodied voice said.

"Whose life is it?" Forthill asked aloud.

No one answered.

The ground began to shake. Forthill went to his knees. As soon as he hit the ground, he startled awake. It was morning again.

He did not speak of his dream to Worthington, and it plagued him for several days until he returned to Beaumaris. As he prepared to enter the complex, one of the gaolers motioned for him and mentioned that Dillon wanted to speak with him. Forthill took a breath, said a prayer, and went up to the warden's office.

"You wanted to see me?" he began politely.

Nathan motioned him in and bade him sit.

"I spoke to the judge," the warden said, casually pouring himself a drink. "We debated, at length, the appropriate course of action, given the circumstances. I tried to be reasonable, offer up my six week compromise, but he would have none of it." He downed the drink, set the glass down, and stared at it as he sighed. "You got your six months."

"I...did?"

"Most priests I know would at least give some thanks to the Lord that they got what they wanted," the warden grumbled, half to himself. "See, there's a thing going around these days, an idea. It started here, in Beaumaris, the idea that maybe we ought to treat prisoners more humanely. That's why our prisoners get one meal a day and they get to go out and see the sunshine if they've been good. Well, that idea seems to be resonating more deeply with some, and the judge believes that any and all spiritual cleansing, as long as it is genuine, ought to be conducted to its full extent. He believes that because Fforidd has nothing to gain, that he is still going to be executed no matter what, that he is most likely earnest in his desire to change, or confess, whichever the case. So, he is willing to give you the time you say you need to make sure Fforidd's soul is at peace and in good standing with the Lord."

"That's wonderful news."

"Yes, well, the judge is lenient. Mr. Fforidd seems to have other ideas."

Forthill felt his heart sink. "What do you mean?"

"He's stopped eating. He's gone on a hunger strike, going to starve himself to death."

"And you're going to let him?"

"What do you want me to do, give him one of my tits? We're not going to force him to eat. In fact, we've considered withholding the food entirely. We feed our prisoners, not the rats, though the rats get most of it anyway. But if you're up for a secondary challenge in this unique case you've taken on, might be you convince Fforidd to start eating again, or your six months will be spent mostly in one-sided conversation."

The chaplain sighed and pinched the bridge of his nose. "All right. All right, fine, I'll talk to him. After I make my normal rounds, I will speak to him in the chapel, as per usual."

"Of course. I don't mean to hold you up. You're excused."

The way he said it let Forthill know that he still wasn't happy about the arrangements. But there was nothing to be done. Forthill stood, wished the warden a good day, and left the office, momentarily disoriented as to what he was doing there and why he felt as though he'd forgotten something. Right. His talk with the warden normally came after the rounds, not before.

Rounds, those days that weren't Sunday service, typically consisted of visiting all the inmates, asking if they had family they would like him to speak with on their behalf, or if they had any prayers for him to intercede on. Most of the responses were rude, sarcastic, or otherwise unable to be taken seriously for a variety of reasons. But he endured, allowing his attention to skim over the superficial until he could pick out the one man who had something deep and meaningful to tell his family, or another man who wanted prayer for himself or someone else. There were a few women in the prison as well, and they were usually pretty sincere. They usually wanted him to communicate with or pray for their children, if they had any, tell them their mother loved them, ask God to look out for them.

Rounds could be long or short, take only a couple hours or half the day. With Fforidd, he could safely judge a minimum of two, maybe three hours.

This day, few of the prisoners were serious enough to even warrant walking in the room and asking for communique or prayer requests, but he did his job dutifully. He couldn't just brush them off completely, after all. If Owain Fforidd could be saved, so could anyone if they had a mind.

He finished his rounds and went to the chapel, letting a gaoler know that he was ready to receive Fforidd. The gaoler did not appear enthused, but he did as he was told. Five minutes later, Owain Fforidd was marched into the room.

Four days without eating hadn't had much of an effect, if Forthill wanted to be honest. Fforidd remained a big man who lived every day in a small cell in his own filth, fighting rats and shivering with cold. He sat down quietly in the pew.

"The warden told me that you've been refusing food," Forthill began.

"I'll be hanged before I starve," Fforidd said softly.

"No, you won't. I sent a request to the judge to stave off your execution. He's allowed for six more months."

"So the rats can eat me first?"

"So you and I can continue to talk. Your soul can be saved, and I want you to leave nothing unsaid."

Fforidd studied him with unusual blue eyes. "You really think there's hope for me, don't you?"

"All who call upon the name of the Lord shall be saved. That is a promise. God does not go back on His promises."

The prisoner frowned and studied his hands. "He may not, but I did."

Chapter Five

The Banker's Daughter

It happened that I did get better work with better pay, and I was able to get out of a flea-infested, sewage-smelling slum and into a flat that was merely dirty. The lock on the door actually worked, and the windows didn't have nearly the draft my old rented room did. The piss pot and the washbasin were clean, too. It was the nicest place I'd lived since leaving home, which ought to say something in its own right.

At work, I was a well-known laborer, and it came to be that my services were wanted. People asked for me. Foremen wanted to hire me for my strength. I was proficient in reading, writing, and mathematics, but that was too much for them to handle, I think, the idea that an immigrant laborer might be intelligent. So the managers never respected me, but other laborers did. Some for my mind, most for my strength. I still intimidated them, mostly so that if I ever came to blows with a foreman or a manager, I would have supporters. I'd abandoned the idea of being in a gang long ago, but lurking among the wealthy had taught me the importance of having connections and backup.

I still walked among the wealthy in the evenings and made connections. The connections came very easily for me. Most of the elite enjoyed bragging about their wealth and their wealthy exploits, but I never did. I gave up precious little information about myself and my dealings, and I think it intrigued them. On one occasion, a businessman offered to buy me dinner and talk business. He knew I was a laborer, but when I demonstrated my proficiency in math and reading, he asked if I might be interested in heading up a business venture he was seeking. I was interested...until he said the words "dock construction." Never again, I said. He tried to tell me that I would not have to actually labor, but I'd been laboring too long to buy that. The foremen always ended up working. And besides, I never really minded working. I was strong, I enjoyed the physical toil. Pretending to be wealthy made me friends and kept my head above the slums, but politics was exhausting. My inner beast was cunning, but it was still a beast; it still wanted to fight.

So I returned to my routine, though I did notice that some of my wealthy connections drifted away. I didn't know what rumors the businessman had spread about me, but my anger began to rekindle. I pushed myself harder in both areas — laboring and lurking — just to prove that I could be better than whatever he said about me. My goal was divided between splitting his skull and stealing his wealth.

I reached a point where I decided that simple working and collecting money wasn't going to be enough. I had to put some of my charlatan knowledge to the test. I went to a bank and opened an account. I deposited a quarter of my earnings into this savings account and decided to start playing a little in investing. Half of my earnings went to the investments. The other quarter was what I lived on, and most of that still went to alcohol.

Owain paused and studied his hands for a long moment. "What is it about the need to dominate that drives people? For so long I thought I was the only one. Perhaps everyone in Wales thought that, too. But when I was in London, I saw it everywhere. Rich, poor, men, women, all seeking to dominate. For the poor, this was most often physical. For the wealthy, this was done with cunning and politics and strategic placement of wealth."

Forthill frowned and shifted position in his seat. "We are all fallen creatures. As we wallow in the pit of our sins, we try to push others out of the way, climb on top of them, just to stick our heads above the crowd, above the water, and say, 'Here I am!' But what many don't realize is that it is those at the bottom, the down-trodden, whom the Lord sees and hears more than those who are shouting above the crowd."

"What punishment awaits those of us who beat the others down in order to elevate ourselves?"

"None, if your soul has been cleansed and your sins forgiven."

How he wished he could believe that.

I tracked my investments and used this new experience to further myself among the elite, get my name out there. I was investing. I had money to lose. It was how the rich gambled. Seeing how gambling and drinking often go together, I learned how to gamble well. I watched, I waited, I listened, and, most importantly, I learned how to brag subtly. I can't really describe it; it's just something rich people do, I suppose. As naturally as breathing, they brag without bragging.

At any rate, after an initial flunk where I lost a good portion of my investments, I learned how to earn it back, reinvest, and increase my wealth. I never dealt in the thousands or millions of pounds, but I did well with what I had. Once, I sent a hundred pounds back to my parents, to help them, show them that I was doing well, that I was turning my life around. I really did mean well. And they were honest gains, too. Whether or not they believed me, I don't know.

One day, I decided to up my charade and buy myself some new clothes, just one step above what I had been wearing, always trying for the next rung of the ladder, just a little more, just a little more. So I went to the bank and asked to make a particular withdrawal. Well, I'd been drinking some, and when I drank, my accent came back, thick and heavy. The clerk was clearly disgusted and tried to shortchange me. I got angry and roughly tried to explain this to him, but he denied it.

And that...was when I first met Paige. She heard the commotion and came to investigate. After hearing about the situation, she determined that the clerk was indeed in the wrong. It did not matter who I was, where I came from, or how I spoke. If I was a member in good standing at the bank, I was to be treated with the utmost respect.

I think it was that encounter which piqued my interest in her. I'd seen her, I was sure, and I saw many women, but none captured my attention like she did at that moment. Maybe because she was the first woman since my mother to ask that I be treated well. And she was the first woman making that request and got it answered. She did not look down at me, did not do any of this grudgingly, but very stoic, very matter-of-fact, very...businesslike. And the clerk listened. He had to.

Don't misunderstand. Paige was a very attractive woman. Wide hips, curvy chest, long neck, round face, and dark eyes. Her dress made her look like a porcelain doll, and yet she walked with the confidence and grace of a cat. She loved hats, and the one she wore that day was a simple floral arrangement, no veil of any kind.

All the same, while attractive, I was unsure how to act around women of this social class. Certainly I'd never entertained the idea of marriage. My experience with women was primarily carnal. On the one hand, I knew that I could never hope to advance my station and support a wife at the same time. I was still very selfish. On the other hand, I had no idea how family dynamics worked in the city. In the country, everything is pretty straightforward; the city is a whole different beast.

Anyway, I thanked her and went on my way. The following month, I was in the bank again to work some of my investments and I ran into her in the hall. She inquired as to whether my experience with the bank had been satisfactory as of late. I assured her it was.

"If you don't mind my asking," I said, "how does a woman hold so much power in the bank? Does your husband invest here?"

She laughed and answered, "No, not at all. I am as yet unwed. No, my father is Jonathon Balk. He owns this bank."

That stopped me cold, and I couldn't say why except I suddenly felt very unworthy. I felt as though she would see right through my charade, that she would call me out for my clothes and my rudimentary knowledge, expose me for the country Welshman that I was, a criminal at that. I knew that some women of wealth simply wanted to bask in it, and others used it to their advantage to give themselves power. It was an intriguing and terrifying prospect.

As for Paige, however, she was essentially a representative of her father's bank. She had to ensure that his customers were taken care of. Maybe she thought that I'd already known who she was at the time the clerk shortchanged me, and to not intervene would have projected poorly on the bank and so her father.

One thing I did not miss, though, was how she explicitly mentioned that she was unmarried. While I had inquired about a husband, she did not have to tell me anything about him, or else she could have lied. But what she said and how she said it, maybe it was my own fault I interpreted that as an invitation.

She saved the conversation.

"So, unless my ears deceive me, and they rarely do, I should think you are sporting a Welsh accent," she commented. "Is that true?"

"Your ears remain trustworthy," I told her.

"How does a Welshman come to invest in one of the wealthiest banks in London?"

"Through my own hard work."

"Truly? That is fascinating. I'm sure you've heard, but opinions of the Welsh are not fond among the English. Likely you've heard all the ghastly rumors and lies that the newspapers and the Catholics spread about your people."

Oh, I had. That we fornicated among our family, with our farm animals, that we were uncultured and barbaric, that our language was inherently pagan and resembled the tongue of devils. I knew it very well, and my stiff silence was apparently enough of an affirmation for her, for she nodded in understanding.

"Yes, it is unfortunate. It is even more unfortunate for the small-minded. You need only look about you to see slums everywhere in London. For the business-minded, poverty only breeds poverty and it brings down the rest of society. Most bankers and aristocrats would sooner see the peasants die in their own filth. And if they're foreign, no sweat at all."

"And why are you telling me this?" I asked cautiously.

"Because my father believes in motivating the lower class to work. They earn a pound, he earns ten pounds, civilization is brought to those who are true barbarians, everyone is happy. Get them out of their filth, expand his investments, diversify his portfolio."

"Don't put all your eggs in one basket lest you drop it and they all break."

She grinned. "Such a charming analogy. Anyway, my father has investments in many countries in Europe, even Asia, can you believe it? But it does him little good if his home is a hovel. He wishes to see the great city of London thrive, but there is filth everywhere. And it's not getting any better, what with the Irish and their Famine especially. My father wishes to invest in the British Isles, to make them a shining beacon to the world, with London at its center. This includes investing in Ireland, Scotland, and Wales."

I folded my arms and tried to present an appropriately curious posture. "Sounds intriguing. If your father is serious, would he care for some advice from a Welshman?"

"Of course. I will speak to him about it. How shall I contact you, Mr...?"

"Fforidd. Owain Fforidd. As for contacting me..." I couldn't tell her to meet me anywhere—it wouldn't be proper—but especially not at my dump of a flat. "I will return here in one week. If your father wishes to meet, we shall do it then."

She was a remarkable woman," Owain said. "She really was. Beautiful and smart. Is it wrong for a woman to be so?"

Forthill frowned. "God made men to be leaders, but that does not mean women are incapable. There are many good women leaders in the Bible. Deborah, for example. But I believe in order for it to work, the goals must be the same between men and women, else all spirals out of control."

It made sense. But then, the past always looked the clearest.

I had no clue what I was going to tell a wealthy, knowledgeable English investor about investing in Wales, and I had only a week to figure it out. I may have been selfish, but I wasn't ignorant. Wales had little love for England, and the thought of an English investor coming to "spread civilization" would not be well-received. The Welsh were simple, but hardly stupid. They preferred their quiet lifestyle to the hustle and bustle of London and the like. If a Welshman wanted excitement, he left his small town and went to Caerdydd for a spell. If he wanted to live like they do in London, he went to London. He didn't make London come to him.

I tried to explain this to Mr. Balk, but he was unmoved. He did not believe all the rumors of the crude, barbaric Welsh folk, but he also didn't believe in leaving people alone, either. Civilization must expand, and all who stand in its way shall perish.

The only thing I was able to keep him from doing was completely razing the Welsh countryside and so collapsing all dreams of proper civilization expansion. If he wanted to avoid nationwide riots or worse, start small. Invest in what was already there: fishing, farming, and imports. He was more interested in the importing and exporting businesses; it was the fastest way to grow his influence and secure a foothold in a fledgling market. By the time other investors took notice, he would already be established and they would be fighting him for dominance.

I simply left him to it. Honestly, I was more interested in his daughter, Paige. She was not present while we spoke, but I did overhear part of her conversation with her father afterwards, and it was very detailed, very involved. She knew what was going on, and she had her own opinions about it.

It was after that when I really considered my situation and made the decision to risk almost everything I had in an attempt to acquire a better amount of wealth and jump up several social stations, enough that if anyone figured out where I lived, that it might be in modest standing. If I did well enough, I might be able to quit laboring and focus solely on investing.

I risked everything, leaving just enough to drink my way through the weeks until I felt confident in looking at my return. I avoided Paige and the bank as much as possible, avoided the wealthy social scene completely when I could.

When I finally did return to the bank to check my investments, I not only had enough to quit my job, but I found a decent flat as well. It was easily the nicest place I had ever lived.

I s it wrong to want nicer things?" Owain wondered aloud.

Forthill shifted position. "The Lord places us where we are for a reason. It is not wrong to aspire to greater things, but we must learn to be content when the Lord says no."

The prisoner looked at him. "What about when He says yes?"

The priest dipped his head thoughtfully. "Then we must give credit where credit is due, praise the Lord for his mercy and grace, use these things wisely and for His glory."

"But if He knew how selfish I was, how selfish I was going to be, why did he let things happen the way he did?"

Forthill was silent for a long moment. Then, "I don't know. But I suspect that even now, things are in motion, and great works are being done, even if we can't see it."

"Easy for you to say when your time on Earth doesn't have a countable end date."

The priest said nothing to that.

When I spoke to Mr. Balk the following day, he proclaimed his investments slow, but a slow success nonetheless. He didn't mind it, though. A slow success is better for building trust and a foundation for future investments, rather than a quick success that dissolves just as quickly and leaves behind a carcass no one wants to go near. He thanked me for my investment advice. Frankly, I was stunned. I'd only been in the business a couple years, and most of my knowledge was parroted from what I'd heard others say. I was learning, but part of it was still bluster. I didn't know what I was doing. But he apparently thought I did. My inner beast found pleasure in this, that I was sneaking my way up the ladder without half the life and business experience they had.

It was then that I inquired after Paige and voiced some hesitant intentions. Mr. Balk liked my investment advice. He liked me far less. I was still a country Welshman, born into no money, having no station, no family, and my English was still accented. I was a self-made man, but I could just as easily lose it all and then where would I be? Investing and banking was a risky business. He said he'd suspected my intentions, so he'd had me investigated a bit—thankfully, only in the financials, not in the criminal. He said that I often risked too much and had poor money management skills. How could I hope to support a wife and family if there was no guarantee that we would even be sleeping in the same bed each night. What if I lost it all and wound up on the streets?

Furthermore, just my very name would degrade her family line. A nobody Welsh name, showing up in the middle of a proud English line? Hardly!

Perhaps the only thing that saved me further embarrassment was Paige's intervention. She particularly enjoyed eavesdropping, and she overheard this conversation as well. She intervened and said she found the proposal charming and delightful, and also delicious for the investment business. Mr. Balk could take me on as an investment and banking apprentice of sorts and send me to do all the foreign investments and investigating potential opportunities. She could clean me up to be a proper Englishman, and if she went with me, she could ensure that all deals were made with the bank's best interests in mind. The only reason she couldn't do it now was because no one would take a woman seriously, and she had no husband. Furthermore, having a Welshman on as an investment agent might make the locals in Wales—and possibly the reluctant Ireland and Scotland as well—more open to allowing English banking and investment.

It was brutal and selfish and highly politically-motivated, but logic dictated that it was a decent offer. Of course, Paige had other suitors vying for her courtship and her hand in marriage, but none of them brought anything new to the table that Mr. Balk could not already offer. I could bring him the rest of the British Isles. If I was cleaned up well enough.

He agreed. But he made it clear that he was immensely skeptical. He was seeing this as business first, romance second. I would have to change myself so completely that even he could believe that I was a born and bred Englishman, and Mr. Balk was undoubtedly a scrupulous man.

The first thing that had to change was my name. Forbes was a fine last name, Paige decided. It was close to my family name, but just sounded more...English. "Fforidd" anglicized, she said. As for my given name, she decided on Walter. It was not a true English name, but everyone knew Owain was Welsh. The Welsh were looked down upon. I forgot where she said Walter originated, but either way, it sounded foreign enough to be enticing for other investors, and yet it was still pronounceable.

I wasn't entirely against changing my name, either. It sounded like a fresh start, a chance for me to leave behind my old life and my old crimes, though I knew my inner demon was still lurking in the recesses of my mind. I'd gone celibate since moving up my station, and the beast craved lust and sex. It wanted Paige. It wanted to dominate and take its pleasure.

But I focused on being a gentleman. Paige quickly learned that I wasn't as sophisticated as I'd portrayed myself to be, but then she commended me on my ability to pass off as rich anyway. She told me that it would come in handy when dealing with other bankers and investors, being able to bluff while simultaneously calling others out. I wasn't so sure, but I went along with it. I learned better manners, etiquette, all the finer points that would really help sell the image that I was a proper gentleman.

She also helped me lose my accent, though she and her father had a bit of a dispute as to how to go about it. Her father wanted to train me to be a proper Englishman. I ought to speak like a Londoner. She got the idea to mold my English accent to be an American one, when it wasn't its natural Welsh accent, that was. A Welsh accent would win over the Welsh and maybe the other Celts. But there was an overabundance of English investors with London accents. The competition was droll. But Americans, now, Americans had money. They had money, influence, and who didn't want a piece of the New York Stock Exchange? She would be the face of London, I could rope in the rest of the British Isles and bring the other side of the pond just a little closer.

America was a risk, Mr. Balk said, with fractured tensions perhaps leading to civil war. But then, if war did break out, stock prices would hit rock bottom. If they could wait out the war, maybe invest in supplies for the winning side, they would all but secure their presence in America. With one foot in London and one foot in New York, they could rule the world of Western banking. They would be rich, influential, nothing could stop them.

It was not lost on me that most of their plans exclusively involved them, and I was little more than a pawn to expand their influence and help them get what they wanted. I confronted Mr. Balk about it once. He told me, sternly enough, that at the moment, I was simply an associate of his—not even that, an apprentice. An experiment, even. His daughter was fascinated with me, perhaps thought she was in love, but until we were married—and his tone said this was highly unlikely—he had little reason to treat me as if I were anything more. I was a Welshman who'd gotten his attention and was proving useful in his business endeavors. Nothing—more.

I didn't like that answer. My beast certainly didn't like that answer. And there may have been some heavy drinking involved that night. When I asked Paige about it, she told me not to worry. She'd have me fixed up in no time and that her father would have to believe that I had changed because to not believe was to doubt his daughter whom he adored.

And as things stood between us, we were doing very well, I thought. We laughed, we talked. She sometimes flirted, maybe a little more than what was proper. She also enjoyed my story of being a humble Welshman turning into a wealthy London banker. On the rare occasion that she was able to get out and travel with her father, she enjoyed the countryside and watching all the hard-working farm folk, be they English, Welsh, or something else entirely. She loved the countryside and the scenery, or anywhere that was away from stuffy, smelly London. Make no mistake, she was a city girl and liked city life, but she always envisioned the country as a breath of fresh air, a holiday trip as it were.

Owain paused again, studying his hands thoughtfully. "Do you think there was any way it could have worked between us? Was there any way it could have been saved before things got bad?"

Forthill frowned. "Love and marriage is about service, sacrifice, giving all that you have and all that you are to the other person. Were either of you doing that?"

"I thought I was. I tried to think about my parents, how they loved each other and worked things out. I either couldn't recall because I'd never cared, or else I couldn't figure out how to apply it to city life, wealthy life. In the moment, all we knew was love and, at least for me, lust. Maybe not even love, but...fascination. Infatuation. We were simply new things to each other. I'd never really liked a woman before, and she thought my being foreign and her pet project to turn me into a proper Englishman was exciting." He sighed and shook his head, staring at the floor. "There never was anything there, was there?"

"Perhaps, but even ill-advised marriages can work. Marriage is an oath before God, after all, and, as we are created in His image and called to love one another, I have seen dry wells bring forth life again. It is a remarkable and very satisfying thing to witness."

If God ever approved of our relationship, His voice was drowned out amid a chorus of societal outrage, especially among the upper class. As you know, the Welsh are overwhelmingly Protestant and we have our myriad of little chapels. These Londoners whom I associated with were all Catholic and preferred their grand cathedrals. I attended Mass obediently, but I never felt anything except indignation and disdain. It may have just been from the well-to-do among the congregation, but it may have been from the Almighty, too. How was I to know? One day at confession, the priest asked if I wished to confess my sin of being a foreigner, that the Lord could use even a former barbarian like me. I may have punched through the wicker screen, seized the priest, and perhaps threatened him. I never went back to confession, just followed Paige and her father and all of them to Mass on Sunday.

And anyway, I didn't care. As far as I was concerned, my parents had been obedient Christians their whole lives and still they toiled away on the farm. I'd run away, shaken my fist at God, and become a self-made man. I'd caught the eye of a beautiful woman and was apprenticed to her father and set to double or triple my fortune. Maybe God had some bit of mercy on me, maybe not. But I had no need of Him, He evidently never needed me, and I considered Mass a simple truce to confirm that we would stay out of each other's way.

How great was my arrogance that...why did I think that?" Owain interrupted himself. "Crossing Mr. Balk was foolish enough; why did I think God would simply sit back and let me...do what I did? Why did He not strike me down while I stood hypocritically among the masses?"

The priest's gaze was soft. "Because He is a patient, loving God, who woos quietly and waits for you to return. If He'd struck you down, your arrogant, selfish, godless soul would be tormented in Hell for eternity. But by being patient, here you are, returning to Him."

"And what of Paige and the men I murdered?"

"The Lord alone knows what happened to them, and they made their own decisions. You must not worry about the actions of every man. Cannot the Father use even the weakest and most reviled of us? Paul is the most...appropriate example I can think of in this situation."

Owain sighed and rubbed his face, dirt scraping on dirt, and that was being optimistic. "I know."

"The Lord forgives freely, Owain. But perhaps harder than asking for forgiveness is receiving it and believing that you are forgiven."

Harder than that, I think, was asking for Paige's hand in marriage. My first barrier was my own fear. I had no idea how to be a husband or a father. Again, I had nothing good in my past life to brag about, and my recollection of my own father was muddled with bad experiences and general apathy. I again did not know how to apply country living to city living. Everything I knew about city families came either from the slums or the wealthy, and I had little desire to emulate either. I wanted to be good, better than the poor families who hated each other, better than the rich families who played each other like chess pieces, seeking alliances and betterment of station, amassing combined fortunes. Both sides sickened me, but I knew of nothing else.

My second hurdle was her father. He'd commented on several occasions that he was impressed at how far I'd come, that he could almost believe I was at least an American, if not an Englishman. This was high praise coming from him. I'd also learned much under his tutelage on money, banking, investments, and my own fortune increased significantly.

One morning, he called me into his office and said that perhaps I was ready for a trial run. He was going to send me to Wales to see if I couldn't drum up some prospects in Caerdydd and perhaps other areas, investigate the market. I knew he was testing me, sending me to my homeland, seeing if I was going to come back. I told him I would go, but I wanted Paige with me.

"Absolutely not," Mr. Balk said. "It would be improper for her to accompany you without being your wife."

And I looked at him dead in the eye and asked, "So...is that a yes?"

Chapter Six

The Honeymoon

We were married within six weeks, and I think no one was more stunned than I that Mr. Balk had said yes. I don't believe it was because he actually liked me, but rather because it was economically and politically advantageous. But in the heat of the moment, we were both thrilled, perhaps the only two who were. Even the priest did not look enthusiastic about marrying us, but there were no legitimate reasons we couldn't be married. Social scandal was not enough, however much her entire family and half the upper class of the city wanted it to be. Mr. Balk had said yes, and so it shall be.

One thing I will mention is that, although I was now socially known as Walter Forbes, I never actually legally changed my name. If you look in the records, you will find Owain Fforidd and Paige Balk. She took my name out of propriety and so became Paige Fforidd, but in public we were known as Walter and Paige Forbes.

I think that was when the beast started to return in its more carnal nature. Like other aspects of my "barbaric" homeland, she found the lovemaking thrilling, though I was forced to wonder if proper English gentlemen were really any less...enthusiastic, I shall say. Maybe she thought that, like every other aspect of rich English life, sex would also be a rote, proper affair. I was less so, but I digress. Celibacy had annoyed the beast, but marriage and the marriage bed reignited its lustful passion. I was in charge, I was dominant, I was to maintain control at all times. Part of it was the gentlemanly desire and need to defend the household, but most of it was sheer, primal domination.

Of course, this all came about slowly. In the moment, everything was fresh and exciting as she came to live with me and share my life, not that it was much different than what it had been other than she returned to a different bed at night.

Three days after our wedding, we spent a week at her father's country villa, though even that was a mansion compared to what I was accustomed to. And when we returned, it was back to the same routine.

About three weeks after the wedding, Mr. Balk informed us that we would both be going to Caerdydd to investigate prospects. The venture had been put off too long; other investors were beginning to wonder what he was up to. He had to stay ahead of them. He informed us that there would be less time to consider offers; we had to make quick decisions, establish ourselves before others started heading that way. What could we do but agree?

That trip was where, although I still maintained a very happy exterior, I really began to battle the beast again. Paige was used to nothing but the finest. Now, of course, Caerdydd isn't exactly a great voyage from London, but the idea of stopping anywhere but the finest accommodations was nearly unheard of for her. I could be happy as long as there was a roof over my head. Barring that, I could sleep outside as long as it was dry. Paige would have none of it. And she took forever to be ready in the morning. She made me take time to be ready as well. It took several days to reach Caerdydd, and I didn't see a reason to get dressed up for each day we were simply on the road. The carriage was nice enough, but we didn't need to wave a banner announcing to all the bandits on the road that there was money for the taking.

But it all came down to appearance when we arrived at each inn along the way. Again, the nicest inns only. Sometimes we would cut days short because one town had a nice inn and the next one didn't, or we would ride long into the evening for the opposite reason. We represented Balk Banking and Investments everywhere we went, and it always demanded the utmost lavish. I was loathe to inform her that few Welshmen knew who Balk Banking and Investment was other than another snooty rich English bank who hated and looked down upon poor, dumb Welsh folk. If we wanted to win their hearts and minds—and most importantly, their money and business—simply having me speak Welsh to them wasn't going to be enough. We had to not be what we were because that was why they were having such trouble investing in Wales in the first place.

The beast took every little annoyance I experienced on the road and held onto it, slowly building up a mental wall between me and her. Quite honestly, I don't know whether the nightly love helped or hurt things, but things didn't get much better when she began her woman's blood the day we arrived in Caerdydd. We didn't even really fight that night at the inn, but there was certainly a hostile air between us. By morning, we resolved that the trip had been hard, she was having a tough week, and it was a little nerve-wracking for both of us to do these potential investment deals all on our own. If we could make it through this trip, we could make it through anything. How idealistic.

The first day was a nightmare, not quite a disaster, as we met with the Welsh banks. They had little love for England, and my changed name was the only thing that kept me out of trouble. I was sure they knew who I was, but the disparity was too great to want to put words to their suspicions. If they were wrong and accused me of being Owain Fforidd, then they'd just delivered a great insult to a very wealthy English banker. They were suspicious, but not stupid. The economy was too great in London to simply brush it off and put short-term pride over long-term gain. They just didn't want to get ripped off, and I didn't blame them.

All the same, we got nowhere the first day. Or the second. The best we got by any of the banks or investors, despite our apparent willingness to work together, was a "consideration." Of course, if anyone didn't grow suspicious of a willing and cooperative Englishman, I would be worried. Paige was beside herself and growing more frustrated. She worried that her grand plan was going to fail before it ever got started, and then she started asking me why my Welsh-ness wasn't working to win their hearts and minds—and more importantly, their money and business.

Finally I told her to take a day off. Go shopping or do whatever she wanted to do. I would talk to the bankers myself. She agreed. I waited until she was gone before getting rid of all the English finery and approaching the bankers and investors one more time, this time as myself.

Several of the bankers pinned me right away, called me out on my identity. There were accusations of fraud. It took some clever persuasion and a lot of bank notes to prove to them that I did have the money I said I did. A couple of the men not only closed the doors on investing with us, but locked and barricaded them as well. But a few were willing to listen. My money was genuine, and so were my motives, those being, I wanted to be king. In my younger days, I fought my way to the top. These days, I traded and invested. I would do nothing that didn't advance my cause and further solidify my fortune. That was generally true of any banker, humble or greedy, and they could say little about it—specks and planks and all that. The difference now, though, was that even as I worked for an English bank, I myself was Welsh and would not sell out my own people. True, I had done horrendous things, was a known drunk and brawler, but I was still Welsh. I invested in Wales and wanted to improve it.

I wasn't sure quite what that looked like, but it was enough to get them to listen. Paige and I returned the following day and continued to negotiate. It took a couple weeks, but we were in business. We invested mostly in the factories in southern Wales, blacksmithing, glass-blowing, those sorts of things.

After Caerdydd, we went to Abertawe and managed to invest in a few shipping lines. Paige wanted to go straight for the major shippers, but I talked her into the smaller lines. The large lines were already invested in, already sought after. If we invested in the smaller lines and they succeeded, we not only built loyalty with those lines, but the proportional return was greater as other investors tried to get in on the profits.

How did the beast feel about all of this?" Forthill interrupted, his expression saying he probably hadn't meant to say this out loud, but there it was. "It has been documented that young men may mature out of crimes of impulse, and I certainly believe that demons will change their temptation tactics to suit the person, but how did that dynamic fare? You are still a large man, very strong. You could have continued on in your ways."

Owain managed the smallest of smiles. "It's odd. I was thinking that would be a question to ask you, except I think I know the answer, and it makes me sound like you. It's something I contemplated a lot, and still do. I think maybe God tried to rescue me once, send an angel to speak sense into my ears, and that was how I made the decision to leave Wales and better myself. But as you said, demons change their tactics to keep their prey. All mine had to do was shift the focus from fighting for power to using my newfound cunning for power."

After a moment, the priest nodded. "So it would seem. The common element appears to be power."

"Yes, but I still don't understand why. Later in life, men crave power as we are pitted against one another. What was my obsession with it as a child? The eldest child, at that? What sparked my rage? What demon possessed me as a babe? I don't understand."

"Nor do I. And perhaps we never will except that it has led to this moment of your redemption. Perhaps it was the only way for the Lord to carry out His hand of justice, or maybe His hand of mercy. Perhaps your actions have set in motion things we cannot yet begin to comprehend. Even Rahab did but a single act of kindness and found favor with the Lord."

"Rahab didn't kill six men," Owain pointed out flatly, then sighed. "I suppose I will be able to ask the Lord myself soon enough. All I can ask for, I suppose, is that it was worth it and hundreds of thousands of people join the Kingdom of Heaven."

"Owain, the angels rejoice at the repentance of but one sinner. Maybe this time that sinner is you."

Perhaps, but at the time, I worshiped at the altar of greed and power. Paige wanted more immediate results, bigger clients, but I wouldn't allow it. We couldn't swarm in or else the market would become flooded too quickly. We had to remain discreet for as long as possible, solidify our holdings, and make out with some worthwhile returns before showing our hand. Paige could be impulsive, even reckless. It was one of the things I loved about her, that she had spirit, that she could provide a new perspective even if it was wrong. In an odd sort of way, I enjoyed arguing with her. One part of the beast sought to dominate her through every argument, even tempted me early on to physical means of dominance. The other part of the beast thought about molding her and turning her into an ally. If only she could see things my way. I suppose that is another area I went wrong.

Paige said I was overly cautious about the investing. I said I was merely being patient. Whatever the case, we'd already pushed our limits with the Welsh bankers and investors, overstayed our welcome, and they wanted us to move on. She was eager to go home, and I wanted to get out of Wales before news of my return got around and she found out just who I was really.

The morning we departed from Abertawe, Paige declared that she wanted to meet her in-laws. The thought was utterly terrifying, but I couldn't tell her no without telling her why. And besides, I'd made something of myself. Maybe I really could make things right, show my parents that I was a new man.

So we went north. Again, Paige insisted on all the finery she was accustomed to. I tried to explain to her that my parents were but humble farmers. I don't know what she expected to find, but she still seemed surprised when we arrived and there was, indeed, a farm. Maybe she thought I meant that my parents owned the land and hired hands to work it. But it was that moment when she understood just how humble my beginnings were, how meager my familial means, and she didn't even know the half of it.

Naturally, my parents were rather confused when a carriage stopped in front of their house. Indeed, they didn't even recognize me at first. They presumed us to be bankers or debt collectors or some such, and my pa wasn't having any of that. It wasn't until I spoke that they knew it was me. My pa was speechless, but my ma rejoiced, hugging and kissing me and praising God that her boy had found purpose and meaning and fortune in life.

Now, Paige did not speak Welsh. She had no desire to learn Welsh. Her interest in the Welsh went as far as bank business and being civilized, but she was hardly an ethnographer. On the other hand, my parents did know English, but tension between the Welsh and the

English meant they didn't like to use it very much.

I asked my parents in Welsh to not tell Paige of my horrendous past. My ma chastised me for keeping something from my bride, but agreed, if only to keep the peace in her home. My pa had words about that as well, but, he said, in the interest of keeping the peace and for the hope of making amends and building a new life, he would honor my request to the best of his abilities. He never said he was proud of me, but he was heartened, encouraged to see how far I'd come. Even if I was working for a bank—and an English bank at that—as long as I wasn't a drunken brawler whose postal address could be legally described in terms of jail cells, I was doing something with myself and being a good man.

I didn't tell my parents that I still drank. I didn't want to worry them. Paige knew I enjoyed drinks, but then, so did most of the upper class. The only thing she hadn't seen yet was my temper, my rage, my beast. I intended to keep it that way. At the time, I just wanted to talk to my parents and leave without any horrifying incidents.

We ended up staying with my parents for three nights. At the end of it, as we were leaving, my ma told me that while she was glad I had made something of myself and I wasn't drinking or fighting anymore, I really could have done much better with my choice of wife.

I t's not uncommon for mother-in-law and daughter-in-law to not get along," Forthill chuckled. "Or father-in-law and son-in-law for that matter."

Even Owain could not deny that the memory was amusing. "Perhaps. But there is a difference between city folk and country folk. I was a country man who never quite found his place in the city, certainly not among the upper crust. Paige was in a similar predicament when we stayed with my parents."

M y parents' home was not an inn, and my ma's kitchen was not a restaurant. Nor was my ma a maid. To say that Paige was not accustomed to housework or kitchen work is a bit of an understatement. The first night, Paige expressed her confusion but also naive delight about my humble upbringing and country life in general. The second night, she was clearly frustrated, but said she was glad that I appeared to be having a good time reconnecting with my family. The third night, she declared that we were leaving.

I found it humorous that she was as out of place in my world as I was in hers, but that amusement was also laced with irritation. She didn't get it. She didn't understand that was how I felt in London.

In all honesty, for as much as I was annoyed with her displacement and overt frustration, I wasn't faring much better. I was glad to get out of my fine clothes and back into something comfortable. But when I went out with my pa in the morning, while I left as if I knew what we were doing and I was simply falling back into a rhythm, I really didn't know a whole lot. My pa gave me chores fit for a prepubescent boy because they were easy. In the hard tasks, he used me only for my strength and did all the intricate work himself. It was humiliating. It made me mad.

S urely you must have talked about things," the priest interrupted. "Did you make amends?"

"How do you know when you've made amends?" Owain countered.

W e talked, yes. He asked about my life in London, asked how I did it. I assured him it was all through legal means. He said that there was nothing truly legal about banking, only that the laws had been written so it looked that way. But at any rate, I did honest work, invested, got wise, made money, worked my way up. I hadn't been in jail for some time, so that had to count for something. I didn't tell him about my drinking, but something about him and the way he looked at me said he knew. I was richer, but I hadn't changed a bit, not really.

All the same, he did say that he was glad for my fortune, that I had gotten it together and made something of myself. He said that they had received the letter I sent them initially, as well as the money. It had actually helped save them and the farm when they had a tough year. It made me feel good, actually, to know that I had helped them. It made me feel better to know that they had received my gift and used it rather than throw it away because of who I was and what I'd done.

I offered to give them some more money so they could buy whatever they needed, or else they could tell me what they needed and I would buy it for them. Or perhaps they could come live with us in London. My pa adamantly refused to go to London, or leave the farm at all, and he also refused any further gifts. He didn't trust bank money to begin with, and more things required more attention and more care. Him and my ma had reached a point, with all but one child gone from the house, they were going to cut back as much as possible and bring in just enough for themselves to get by, just the two of them.

It sounded odd to me that they would say such a thing. I asked about Teo and Maisy. With me gone, he ought to have been the one to step up and take care of our parents. And hadn't they promised the land to them?

Nope. Teo and Maisy were no longer in the area. Teo had refused to take any of my money, and he and our pa had a disagreement about it, a heated disagreement. Our pa took the money, and he was able to survive. Teo refused to have anything to do with it. When they fell on hard times, he had taken Maisy and their infant son south to the glass works.

My pa and Teo exchanged letters frequently. Life was hard in the glass works. The pay was dismal, food scarce. Teo was often sick, as was the baby. Maisy was exhausted and discouraged. Less than a year later, Teo declared that they were soon heading for America, the land of opportunity.

I knew the notion hurt my pa, seeing both his sons move away to distant lands. True, London wasn't all that far, but I was hardly his favorite son whom he desired to communicate with. No, the good son was leaving for new lands. Better lands, perhaps, but an ocean and a lifetime away. It was especially troubling for my ma, and my pa told me not to bring it up to her.

As for my sisters, they'd remained in Wales at least. One lived in Abertawe; had I known, I might have visited. The rest were in the area, married to good men or about to be, as in the case of my youngest sister Adith who was due to be married in the next couple months. She was courteous toward me, highly suspicious. She knew my reputation more than she knew me, and I got the distinct impression that I would not be welcome at her wedding. Still, I congratulated her and wished her well. She did not know what to make of such a kindness coming from me.

"What wretch of a man am I that kindness is cause for suspicion?" Owain asked of no one in particular. "What about you? Or the warden? Or any of the gaolers? Am I simply a lost cause? Do they doubt my sincerity?"

Forthill frowned, sighed, but nodded haltingly. "Yes. They do doubt your desire to repent. The warden harbors a particular disdain for you."

"And you listen only because it is your job to do so?"

The priest shifted position. "Do you know how many times I have asked for a stay of execution for an inmate?" He paused for a moment, then held up one finger. "Once. For you. Because I believe that there is a chance for redemption for you, for your soul, and perhaps some even greater glory will come of it."

Owain regarded him. "Has anyone told you that you are insane?"

"Frequently. Even other priests have told me that they would not go so far for you and just leave you to your judgment." Forthill continued before Owain could speak. "I tell you this not for my own vanity, that you may admire me, but that you may recognize the mercy of the Lord and the love He has for you to give you this opportunity. Men have cast you off, but the Lord knows your heart, and He knows your sincerity. This may very well be your last chance for a true confession. The Lord gives every chance He can. Take it. Be sincere. The Lord is your only Judge now."

The convict heaved a sigh as he stared at the dirty floor. It was swept daily by the other inmates, but there was always a permanent filth about this place.

He nodded. "I am sincere, or as sincere as I know how to be."

I was sincere when I told my ma I loved her before we left. I was sincere when I told my pa that I would do my best to be a good man and make him proud of me in the end—he did not look convinced to my eyes, but he did not speak aloud his misgivings in front of Paige. I was sincere when I told Paige I was glad for her patience over the few days we stayed with my parents. I think she was equally sincere when she declared that it was nice to visit during the day, but she never wanted to return and stay the night ever again. I think she was also sincere when she said she worried that the visit had been too long and perhaps I had lost some of the posh refinery she had so painstakingly instilled upon me. I would need fixing.

It wasn't all bad, of course. One we were safely out of range of country influence, her idealism and fantastical images of farm life returned. She and my ma had rubbed each other the wrong way, but Paige still saw a certain charm in country life. So long as country life stayed in the country and far away from her in our rich city life.

Her opinion of country life wavered back and forth. She seemed to be more intrigued by the idea of it in her mind, but when faced with reality, she much preferred London. But at one point, her opinion changed at just the right time that she decided that she'd been tainted by the country and the only way to fix it was by hiring a cook and a maid for our home. I had man's business to attend to, and seeing how she was also vested in the bank and the investments, she couldn't sit idly by like a common housewife—such as my ma—to cook and clean. She had affairs to tend to, you see?

I will admit, more than once, it crossed my mind to wonder whether she was truly faithful to me. She bowed to the decisions of her father and myself, but she seemed to hold more sway over the operations of the bank and other banks than was proper. Any sway at all is somewhat unusual, but she had more than that. Maybe it was just the beast being possessive and paranoid. She'd been a virgin on our wedding night; there was no doubt about that. If she'd been in the banking business with her father for any length of time and had considered selling herself, she would have done it already with no need for a husband, and certainly no need for me.

Anyway, we returned to London. She hired a cook and a maid the next day. The day after that, we went to the bank and spoke with her father of our expedition, less the visit to my parents' homestead. Most of the details were left out, such as how I'd really persuaded the bankers and businesses to partner with us. For one, Balk would most certainly have disapproved. He was a shrewd man and very intelligent when it came to investing among his own folk and those who thought like him. But he was of a mind that anyone who didn't think like him was a fool and should be looked down upon. Hence his treatment of me. To that end, it seems contradictory to say, then, that he was less interested in the means of the bargains and more concerned with the bargains themselves, the ends versus the means. At the end of the day, what did the numbers say?

He was not overly enthusiastic with our results. He thought we should have taken more risks or else bullied the Welsh bankers into more favorable deals. He blamed me for being too sympathetic. At the same time, the logic following our decisions was fairly sound. If we played our cards right, he would have the Welsh markets in shackles to his bank in the long run and no one would be able to compete. That was how he put it. Quite honestly, putting it in those terms made me sick, as if I'd just betrayed my whole country. Bad enough I'd terrorized it, now I'd sold them out to a foreign power. I could do nothing right by my homeland. I still can't, it seems.

It would be a market to watch, he declared. It was a gamble, anyway, and he'd sent us with money he could afford to lose. He would let those investments sit for a year or two before checking up on them and seeing if they might be worth pursuing further. The economy was booming, and Wales would not sit anonymously for long. With its ports and farmland, all it needed was a little civilization from its English neighbors. As for me, well, maybe I wasn't entirely useless.

He dismissed us then, as if we were simply underlings for him to command and not family. He may not have liked me or considered me family, but Paige was still his daughter, and he was dismissive of her as well. My beast did not like that. I tried to be as polite as possible when I asked if he had anything else for us, other markets to look into. Ireland, maybe, or Scotland. He just said no, not yet. He wanted us here. We ought to learn the bank some more, learn more about investing.

It was the way he said "we" that infuriated me. Maybe he really was dismissive of Paige because of her choice of husband. Maybe he knew how men like me operated and he was intentionally trying to get under my skin. But I would not allow myself to stand idly by while he ignored his own daughter and lumped her in with the likes of me. I told Paige as much and asked what more needed to be done. Maybe she was part of that plan, if there was a plan. And she told me I had to clean myself up more and become even more of an English gentleman, basically eradicate everything about me that was Welsh.

So that is exactly what I tried to do.

CHAPTER SEVEN

THE BUFFOON

To say that I was unprepared for married life would be a gross understatement. I understood more about farming than I did about marriage. Consider, then, how I had often shirked my chores and was a miserable embarrassment to my parents in that area alone, and it should tell you a little bit about how much more disappointing I was when it came to being a husband.

I think the only thing I was good at was my husbandly duty, and you know what I'm talking about. Of course, such a thing was not unique to husbands, which was why I was good at it. Sex was not a foreign concept to me. If the idea that I had not been chaste before marriage ever crossed Paige's mind, she never said anything, nor could she do anything about it. Actually, I think her greater fear was being barren, as months came and went with no baby in her belly—but that's another matter entirely, which I'll reserve for the moment.

But it was about the only thing I could do well without even trying, or that was the way I saw it. As I said, it is something not unique to married men.

Things that are unique to married men, however, were not only unusual for me, but almost foreign, and it doesn't escape me that most or all of these are what you, Father, call the fruits of the Spirit.

Love. The only thing I really knew of love came from my ma, and I do thank God I knew even that much, else my definition of love was little more than sex. In my mind, love was acts of service. In my world, this had come in the form of cooking, cleaning, all the things that we had hired a cook and a maid to do. With them taking care of those duties, what was left for me? I thought of other gentlemen and how they doted on their wives with jewelry, fashions, and other finery. I tried to do the same. Paige loved the attention, but she had a keener eye for money, and my foolish spending was not the best for our finances. Her father helped us on more than one occasion when I spent money on her and so could not pay the help. This brings me to...

Gentleness. I did my best to explain to Paige what I was trying to do, that I was trying to show her that I loved her. I did this calmly, trying to tell her how much I loved her. I even took some of the blame on myself. I was good at math, yes, but I wasn't always good with money. This was why I was always so cautious with our investments. If I didn't intentionally play it safe, things could get out of hand. I was aware of the problem. Her help in refining me was doing wonders in my money management skills, but I wasn't perfect. I tried to be a nice as possible, I really did. I didn't blame her, told her I loved her, tried to reason things out...But she just didn't listen, and then things would get heated.

She would take the compliments in stride, but often replied that jewelry was fine, but I could do better by not loving her into poverty where the slum rats would rape her just for having fine teeth. I could never decide whether this was an intentional jab at my humble origins or just her loathing for the impoverished in general, but my beast always determined that it was an insult to be taken personally, which brings us into...

Kindness. I had a few things to say about her and her family as well. Yes, I was wealthy and economically part of the upper crust, but I was still a Welshman. No one ever let me forget it. Just as they always had something to say about me, around me, to me, well, I had my own opinions. They wanted to know why the Welsh, the Irish, the Scottish, were all so wary of partnering with an English bank? Well, I would tell her. They were tired of being treated like garbage, as lesser human beings, slaves if they were anything. The Irish especially were treated poorly because of their Famine and need to find food and work anywhere they could. When it came to me, I was tired of being surrounded by thousands of tiny kings and queens who all looked down their nose at the working class and disdained anyone, such as myself, who worked hard and desired to make more of themselves. I was tired of being assigned my place in the world. I was my own human being and I would work hard and do what I could. We all returned to the mud in the end. This attitude also affected my...

Goodness. I had spent most of my younger days in jail or on the streets. Many nights I went to sleep on cold rock with an empty stomach. But I had gotten smart and worked my way up from literally nothing. No name, no family, no home, no money. And now I was a wealthy investor. I had been modestly wealthy even before I met Paige. I knew it could be done for those with the right motivation and the right mindset. Some days, I had great sympathy for the poor. Most days, though, when I was laden with self-pity and defending myself mentally against all the attacks—both real and perceived—from those who considered themselves my betters, I hated the poor. I hated them for being poor, for doing nothing to improve themselves. I hated them for wasting their lives looking for sex, drugs, alcohol, anything to pretend that they weren't where they were and how they were. I would give them nothing, no food, no money, because I knew it would not help things.

And no, I was not completely blind to my hypocrisy. Because even as I hated the poor, I knew that I was really hating myself, putting myself in their shoes. And to that end, I had no...

Peace. None. Not really. Rarely did I put my head on my pillow at night and feel good about myself. I felt like a hypocrite, a degenerate, a charlatan, a criminal on the run though I had done nothing wrong. I looked at the poor on the streets, and as much as I hated them, I only hated myself. Sometimes I wanted to give up everything and return to the streets. That was my station in life. No one in the upper class wanted me, and the slums were familiar territory. I knew how things worked there. I knew how to dominate. I knew how to get by. But even as I considered that, I also knew that it would do little good. I had lived in that world for far too long. I knew it would only be a matter of time before the beast returned and things would get ugly. There would be no peace. The beast did not leave me alone because I was rich, but at least it felt more manageable, and I spent less time in jail for it. But this lack of peace also robbed me of my...

Joy. I loved Paige, I loved my life. I admit that I loved my money and not having to worry about what I was going to eat or where I was going to sleep. The problems of the upper class felt so petty sometimes, and I was glad to have them. But I had no joy, for the reasons I've already gone through and listed. I could take no pleasure in anything I had accomplished, and it made me feel as miserly as Mr. Balk. Perhaps he had his own beast he dealt with. Even the sadistic pleasure I had once felt when physically dominating an opponent was nowhere to be found. Life simply went on. Banking, investing, numbers, counting, percentages, payments, all very dull. My bestial days had been violent, but the victories were always clear-cut, always obvious. If my opponent yielded, it was a victory, and I claimed the spoils, whatever they may be: food, shelter, sex, some combination of the three. If my opponent won, well, that was a rarity in itself, and I always went back for revenge, so it was never a solid defeat, really. If I landed in jail, well, that could go either way. I was in jail, but it was shelter, and there was at least bread and water.

Victory was not an attainable goal in wealthy society. Victory was an ongoing endeavor, almost as wearisome as Paige continually fixing me up to be an English gentleman. There was never an end in sight. My accent always needed improving, my vocabulary, my mannerisms. Fashion was always changing and I should do my best to be of the latest style, just like my father-in-law. If I couldn't manage that, then I had to be able to fudge it a little, play it off. This greatly tested my...

Patience. What little I had of it. I wanted victory, I wanted an end goal. I was tired of doing laps; I wanted to cross the finish line, at least in something. Give me one small victory, something to claim as my own. Long-term had stretched into endless as we got into more and more serious investing. Math and numbers consumed our days at the bank but the calculations never ceased. That was bad enough, but as the months wore on, Paige fretted about having a child. I had no qualms about making love to her, but her incessant worry over becoming pregnant wore on my nerves. I tried to get her to calm down and let things happen was they would. She would calm down for a little while, at least until her next blood. Then she would cry and worry again. Once she was finished, she demanded that I put a child in her. I tried, believe me, but more than once I considered going down to the slums she hated so much and asking a destitute mother if she would like to give her child a better life. But I knew better than that. Paige wanted her own child, a proper English baby, not another slob that would need cleaning and fixing. Bad enough she had to deal with me. She did say that once, and that broke my...

Faithfulness. We'd only been married seven or eight months. I drank sometimes, but that only worked for me and my problems. It did little to change Paige, stop her worrying, stop her fretting, stop her changing and fixing. It bothered me. I just wanted a simple life, without the frippery or the politics. I'd give up everything just to undo half of what I'd done since moving to London. So I sought simplicity in the gutters, my natural habitat. I drank some and then I paid for sex from two women. It wasn't uncommon for wealthy men to visit their escorts, whatever they would have you believe, but I did not go to the fine establishments. I count myself lucky I made it home that night. I was drunk, but I remember getting in bed. Paige had been crying. She turned to me and asked for sex. And I remember telling her that the good stuff is worth paying for, which explained why she was free. Needless to say, at that moment, I had very little...

Self-control. I had little of anything. If I had anything in abundance, it was apathy and money. I went to the bank and did my work. I invested, diversified, increased our worth and our cash on hand. I made us richer. But my marriage was largely empty. After the bank closed, I would go home to eat, then retire to my study to do more work. Occasionally I drank, sometimes I went out to pay for sex. Sometimes I would go out and pay for sex, then come home and make love a second time to Paige.

In an odd sort of way, this arrangement got her to calm down, or else she just did not worry in front of me. She told me once that she knew men needed sex like fish need water. It was also a man's duty to provide for the family. As long as our finances were stable and I did my part to try and make a baby, she wouldn't complain about anything else that I might do. She would do her part to try and make a baby, start a family, and she would be a good wife.

After that, she stopped fussing over every inch of me, looking for any reason I might not be seen as a gentleman. She told me that if I couldn't pass by now, I never would. Furthermore, everyone knew well who I was, so it wasn't as if I would be fooling anyone. I just had to do my best to not embarrass the family.

That sudden burst of freedom sobered me up a bit, actually. I stopped going out to the brothels and I cut my drinking drastically, as it had grown over a matter of weeks. I tried to be a little more attentive to her, pay attention to her, without decimating our finances this time. I tried to be good again.

W hy couldn't I do it?" Owain lamented. "Why couldn't I be good? Why couldn't I give up all these things that had destroyed my life and were eating my marriage alive? How could I be so strong but so weak-willed?"

"I hardly believe that you are weak-willed," the priest stated. "You yourself have said many times that you brought yourself up from the gutters to the wealthy lifestyle. That takes determination and a strong will to keep going. Not to mention your other exploits in your life beforehand."

"Then what was my problem?"

"If you want my opinion, you lacked conviction, which is spiritual will. Your physical body and your physical life was doing very well economically, but your soul remained in the gutters. It never left. It still craved the alcohol and the sex and the pleasures of the flesh, also including dominance over other people. You lacked the conviction and the strength of the Holy Spirit and our Lord. Your physical body can accomplish many things, financially, politically. But as long as your soul is empty, you will never truly get anywhere in life; you will never be happy. And your demons will follow you. Indeed, they never leave."

"Why my periods of sobriety? Why did I go from bestial, drunken brawling to wealthy and married but still paying for sex?"

Forthill frowned. "Demons speak many languages, and perhaps it fulfilled some purpose of the Lord's that we cannot yet see."

"You keep saying that. I'm beginning to think it's church-speak for 'I have no clue.' "

"Because I don't. I don't know why or how or any of that. But the Lord sees and the Lord knows. All we are concerned with right now, in this chapel, is your soul. Focus on the present, the here and now."

He didn't want to. He'd spent a lifetime running away from his soul, and he couldn't even say why. No one had been able to answer that yet. Grown men may fight one another, seek to dominate one another. Money, power, those were concepts they understood and could be tangible. What evil had infected him in the womb? Had he not been evil, he would have had no reason to leave home. He would have been a good son, a worthy firstborn. He would have married a pretty girl from another farm, had children of his own, a good life. Not this. Why did it all start the way it did? Was he truly God's tool for something? Could God use a tool so deformed and misshapen?

He sniffed and wiped his eyes, even as he knew he was just smearing dirt across his face. He was damned. His beast, his demon had succeeded in driving his life into the ground until his soul was an irreparable mess, then left him to beg for crumbs of mercy from God's table. But he knew a thing or two about begging, and he would beg for the crumbs.

Our marriage wasn't all bad, really. There were days when Paige was the most beautiful woman in the world and I couldn't imagine life without her. I couldn't imagine not sleeping next to her, couldn't imagine sleeping with anyone else. I loved her smile, her laugh, her body. I loved her mind. She was intelligent, well-read, and she had a wit sharper than most knives. She could always keep me on my toes in a debate. And in that, she was spirited, not like the dull monotony of her father and his associates. She wanted answers, she wanted banter, she wanted information. She never let the pot settle for long before she was stirring it again with questions and scenarios sometimes preposterous and fanciful, but also thought-provoking. Often she was dismissed for her wild and free thinking, but I found it refreshing, on the days when it did not annoy me as well.

One thing we did share—something I did not realize until after my entrance into the more posh lifestyle—was a love for music. She played the violin, the cello, and the harp, and she was very good. She denied it and often compared herself to local quartets, quintets, orchestras, solo players, what have you. My fingers, well, you can see they're far too large for anything delicate, but I enjoyed listening to her.

On evenings when we entertained guests, she would bring out her instruments and rotate through them, serenading our guests after dinner. These guests were most often either her parents or associates of the bank. Applause was always polite, hardly what I considered appropriate for the occasion and the level of talent displayed. I told her as much.

"And what and where would you have me play in order to receive the appropriate applause?" she asked me.

"Perhaps you ought to learn some folk songs and play at an *eisteddfod,*" I suggested.

I was honestly confused why she was horrified by the suggestion, but my mind figured it out half a second before she explained it.

A pagan tradition," Forthill said.

Owain nodded. "Yes. But I would be willing to bet that even you, as a priest, still attend the *Eisteddfod* because it is a holiday tradition of your people."

The priest turned a bright red, but he nodded. "I do observe some activities, yes. It is great fun."

Paige would have none of it. She was a devout Catholic and would not be seen partaking of such barbaric, pagan rituals. I tried to explain it to her, the history, the activities, the traditions, but she would have none of it. She told me that if I ever brought it up again, she would have the Church brand me a heretical pagan and null our marriage.

Maybe I should have done that instead," Owain sighed. "I could have no more shame upon my head, and she would get off clean in the eyes of the Church and the community. Do you think that would have been better? Everyone would still be alive. She would have found a better, more suitable husband, and maybe I could have gone home."

"To what end, though? Do you think your beast would have let you just walk away? For how long? Did you feel any need for repentance at the time? If not, I truly think it would have only been a matter of time before you went back."

"You think this was all inevitable, then? Their deaths, me murdering them, me swinging at the end of a rope? What does that say about a loving, merciful God that He would plan for someone to die, to be butchered in such a...cold way? Why would He allow that? In what world does death make more sense?"

Forthill shifted position again. "Well, perhaps I will phrase it this way. When we first began speaking, you stated that if your parents had known who and what you would become, maybe it would have been better to drown you. Correct?"

Owain nodded sullenly. "I remember that."

"Do you still believe it?"

"Yes."

"Do you believe that if a man has more money that he is less evil?"

"No."

"Who is to know what events you have set in motion by your actions, but the Lord alone? He works all things for good. That we are here and you have expressed a desire for confession and repentance tells me that perhaps you are like Job. The Lord allows the Devil a little leeway of evil in order to accomplish a magnitude of good. At the end of the day, God Almighty still has the Devil on a leash and can call him to heel at any time. And here you are, perhaps fulfilling some purpose of the Lord's and being given a chance to confess your sins and so enter Paradise."

Owain nodded absently, then scoffed and looked at the priest. "Your choice of words is not lost on me, Father. You say 'maybe' and 'perhaps' as in, perhaps I am doing the will of the Lord. But what if I'm not? Where do free will and divine appointment intersect? How do I know that I've done God's will and not the Devil's? How do I know that I haven't done the Devil's will my whole life and this is God giving me my one and only chance for repentance?"

"Considering how much of the past you can change and how much hope for the future you currently have left, are you not grateful for this one and only chance?" the priest asked calmly.

I suppose so. And, really, it's hardly my one and only chance. As I said, Paige and her family were devout Catholics, and I partook of all the rituals with them, minus Confession as already stated. It was another reason our marriage was frowned upon, because I was Protestant, but I went through the routine. I took Communion, I went to Mass. But it was only routine, only ritual.

I confessed only what I wanted to confess, only what was proper for a man of my status to confess to. Despite the screen and everything, voices were telling, and everyone knew who everyone was. The priests knew the sins of their congregation. If it suited them, they knew how to leak that information to the gossip circles. As a Welsh barbarian, it was already assumed that I was unintelligent, a drunkard, and had sex with sheep in lieu of blood relatives like my mother and sisters—or my brothers, as some of the more scandalous circles liked to say. I didn't need to perpetuate any more rumors, say it that way. Every so often, I would confess to drunkenness, though I always played it down. Anything I confessed to I played down, tried to make it seem not as severe. Never did I confess to going to brothels.

Many times, I was worried that Paige would start those rumors, or our hired hands. I never heard anything, and the gossip circles were not what you would call subtle.

I asked her about it once. Paige told me that she was considering it, but she had one more thing she wanted to try before ruining me. That was easing up on her restrictions on me, trying to turn me into a gentleman and all that. If that hadn't worked, then she would tell everyone about my drinking, going to brothels, and she would say that I was a pagan heretic.

As much as I was grateful that she wasn't going to rat me out, it was also a bit of blackmail against me. I didn't like that. My beast certainly didn't like that. But as much as it wanted to neutralize the threat, I told myself to stay calm and stay clean. Eventually, enough time would pass that such accusations would be rendered moot. The problem was that the wealthy never forget. Few men do, but the wealthy have the means to make sure any past sins are paid for over and over again, with interest.

Instead, I told myself to be good to my wife, love her, lavish on her, essentially buy her silence. And at the same time, look for something to hold over her head, something that the women in the gossip circles would love to know about. I wasn't sure what I was looking for or how to go about it, really. I wasn't much for subtlety. But I tried.

It didn't need to be true, actually, just plausible and socially scandalous. If she spent too much time with the cook, I could say they were having an affair, even if they weren't. It was enough of a rumor to be devastating to Paige's reputation.

It wasn't so much that I wanted to hurt Paige as I wanted to defend myself, and the logic of it escapes me now. If it came out that I went to the brothels, my reputation would be tarnished, as would hers. Probably her father's name would be stained as well, which may be the real reason that it never got out. But even so, in hurting me which would hurt her, I now had a false rumor which would certainly hurt her which would also come back to hurt me, that I was insufficient for my wife and could not keep her under control. Whichever way it went, it hurt both of us. I just wanted to make sure that if she hurt me, I had some way of hurting her back.

I also considered that maybe it wouldn't be Paige to expose me, but her mother. Elizabeth Balk was not the wild horse that Paige was, but she was ten times as devious. Of the whole Balk family, it was my mother-in-law whom I feared the most. She could do the most damage to me and the least to Paige. She knew how to save the family name and her daughter. All she had to do was prove that I was a wretched, pagan sheep-shagger, claim that her daughter had been duped into marrying me, and with one well-placed rumor, she could destroy me and send her daughter off to be married to a better suitor.

There was almost nothing I could do about it. If I tried to start any rumors about her—it didn't matter if it was true or not—she could easily nip it in the bud with her own blackmail against the other gossip circle members. And that was if she even wanted to try or felt the least bit threatened. On the whole, it would be my word against hers. No, it would be my word against the whole Balk family. That wasn't even a competition. People would take their word over mine any day. The only reason I might have had any leverage over Paige was because I was her husband. Nothing more.

It was pathetic, and my inner demon told me so. I was a big man, a strong man, made to fight with my fists, not sneak around with pithy words like the gossiping hens. I was better than that. I had commanded respect once, and now I could be outdone by a bunch of women. How far had I fallen, really, when jailers would bow to me but not my own wife and mother-in-law?

It frustrated me to no end, but I was caught. If I did nothing about it, they could walk all over me, no matter what I did to improve myself and make myself a true English gentleman. If I did something about it—something violent, something akin to what my beast wanted me to do—I would only prove them right. There was no correct course of action for me.

Owain rubbed his face. "I realize now that it was all social stigma, peer pressure. There was no right way, only the least bad. I should have done well, made myself a better man, built a solid reputation for myself rooted in character and integrity. Why couldn't I see this before? It's one thing to examine a series of events when they happen quickly, where judgment must be made in only seconds. This was over weeks and months."

"Pride," Forthill replied simply. "I believe it all boils down to pride."

The convict nodded reluctantly. "I suppose it does. And you know, even when I was starving and sleeping on the streets, I still had plenty of pride to go around. If selfish ego alone filled bellies, I never would have wanted for food. If selfish ego alone could build buildings, I would have been living in castles long ago."

"Unfortunately, selfish ego only destroys. It's all it knows how to do. Selfish ego will fill your belly, but only by taking the food out of someone else's hands, causing them to starve. Selfish ego will build buildings, but only by tearing down the buildings of others so they have nowhere themselves to sleep. And in the end, it all comes crashing down anyway."

"I have learned that very well, thank you. I learned well the seven deadly sins, and I hit all of them at one point or another, sometimes multiple ones at the same time. Perhaps pride is the worst one of all. Pride and power, my demon fed on them. And you know what is one good way to feed a rich man's selfish ego, besides giving him more material possessions?"

Forthill tilted his head curiously, like a dog. "What's that?"

"Tell him he's going to be a father."

Chapter Eight

The Resolution

Paige not only wanted children because it was her duty as a wife to also be a mother, but because she loved them. She was not the only child her mother bore, but the only one who survived to adulthood. She talked about having many children. She wanted daughters, I wanted sons. About the only thing we could agree on was that a mix of both would be appropriate. And that our firstborn son would be named Walter Owain.

We weren't shy about sex when we were first married, and despite our many disagreements and problems, we made love quite often. Sometimes I could tell she didn't want it, but she wanted a child more and so she put up with it. Sometimes she forced me to, even when I didn't feel like it for one reason or another. For many months, nothing happened. She blamed me, blamed herself. Others blamed me. Some said it was just as well so that the baby wouldn't be defiled by my inferior blood. How they expected Paige to produce a child without me was beyond my comprehension, but such was the gossip and scorn.

We were married almost ten months when she announced her pregnancy. I don't know that she was ever so happy to be married, or anything else. It was as if her whole life's purpose had been fulfilled in that one moment.

Women are called to be mothers and caretakers," Forthill said calmly. "Our legacy is our children. I have none and so my name will fade into history until I am known but to God. But just think, the whole reason we have a history of mankind is because of women, women having children."

"Perhaps," Owain conceded, "but are there times when a man or woman simply should not reproduce? Should I have ever had children knowing they could turn out like me? My ma and pa had flaws, true, but I am no one to emulate."

"We are greatly influenced by our parents, but in the end, we are all our own human being and must take responsibility for ourselves. You did that yourself in your resolution to not be like your parents. It was flawed thinking, but you took your self and your life and your actions into your hands. Now you are reaping the consequences as your own man. So your child would have had to make the same decisions."

"That was assuming she lived so long."

Make no mistake, I loved Paige, I loved our unborn child, and I loved the thought of being a father. When I broke it down, business-like, into categorical assets, I had a lot to offer our child: food, shelter, wealth, education, prospects. Our child would have a good life, better than I would have had. And I was glad of it. I was not so obvious about it, but I was happy. I felt fulfilled myself, as if I had finally entered a life I had only been observing from the outside. I had run away from home, from a good life, and lived very selfishly for years. Now I felt as though I had come home again, accepted, respected, with a family of my own now. It was one of the few moments in my life where I felt true contentment.

Paige's parents were overjoyed. I think it was the only time I ever saw my father-in-law show anything resembling unbridled emotion. Most of the time, he was just a stoic observer of his universe, perhaps showing a little interest here and there as it served his goals. Certainly I had never seen him smile, and the closest to anger he got was a little annoyance. Sorrow did not even register as a concept to him it seemed. To see him react to the announcement with joy and even laughter, if I hadn't seen it for myself, I never would have believed an eyewitness, even if it was the Lord Himself. Even Paige and her mother were startled by it.

Naturally, the announcement was met with grand celebration, and it was one affair that did not seem to change much between Wales and

England. The biggest difference was how much money one had to spend.

Mr. Balk disdained me, to say it lightly. His associates weren't much better. But there were a few in the upper crust who liked me enough to want to treat me to a first-time father celebration. And what a celebration it was, or what I can recall of it.

Up until that point, almost all of the alcohol I'd ever had was cheap, even by poverty standards. Cheap ale, beer, mead. Even the more expensive stuff I got was still considered lower class. But it was what I knew, it was what I liked. One of the biggest chasms between myself and those born into the upper class, I did things because I wanted to, I ate and drank things because I liked the taste or some other more practical feature; in the case of alcohol, it was how fast I could get drunk. Upperclassmen ate and drank certain things simply because they were expensive and flaunted as more of a status symbol. The more exotic it was, the more influential you were. The newer and more innovative it was, the trendier you were. It didn't matter if you liked it as long as others saw it. This applied to private life as well because someone was always watching, and the help liked to gossip.

Now, this wasn't true one hundred percent of the time, maybe only ninety-five percent, but enough that I took notice of it and decided I didn't like it. I ate and drank what I did because I liked it. Paige often lectured me about status, but I think she secretly enjoyed some of the freedom my line of thinking afforded her. She was usually in charge of telling the cook what to prepare, and I noticed that, more often than not, it was good food, not just status food.

Anyway, the first-time father celebration was my first real introduction to the alcohol of the upper class. I'd had a brandy or a scotch here and there as was polite to entertain guests or associates, but mostly I just held the glass and occasionally took a polite drink. This party...I was expected to drink, and drink heavily. It was one of the few things I could do well. I was still more well-suited for ale and beer and mead, but I could get used to the brandy. At that party, I wasn't buying, so I acquired a taste for a number of rich liquors.

It was also where I had my first real cigar, again, very expensive. Despite my rampant alcoholism, I never cared for smoking, the smell, the taste, the coughing. I knew smoking was a vice and plenty of men smoked tobacco and other plants for various reasons, but it was never my vice. Even when I got rich, it never appealed to me as a status symbol. I still couldn't tell you why.

This celebration was the first time where I saw a rich man's party devolve into little better than a poor man's party. It was loud, the jokes were bawdy, and the booze flowed freely.

"There really is no difference between rich men and poor men, is there?" Owain interrupted himself.

"When it comes to alcohol, I daresay there isn't," Forthill said. "Similarly, we all come into the world naked and we take nothing with us when we die, save our soul. And it is the soul which the Lord judges. A penitent prisoner shall inherit more in the kingdom of Heaven than an unrepentant king. Mark my words."

"I expect I will find out soon enough."

It's somewhere in the rich party that my memory goes rather fuzzy. I don't know what I remember and what others told me, but the best I can gather, the others in attendance got loosened up, as I did, from the alcohol. They became less stuffy and a little more tolerant of my humble beginnings, my status as a Welshman. A poor Welshman who became a rich Welshman living in London and married to a wealthy banker's daughter. There was some joking around, some of it lewd, some of it ethnically charged and referencing the impending Blue Books. As drunk as I was, I don't remember if I was offended or delighted by it all. Probably delighted, seeing how I didn't assault anyone.

But it came to pass that some of the men wanted to know how the poor Welsh sheep shaggers partied. Could we celebrate as well as the rich Londoners? I told them I could show them how the Welsh partied and I didn't even need to go to Wales to do it. They challenged me to impress them and show them this grand lifestyle from which I'd come. Foolishly, drunkenly, I accepted the challenge.

My memory gets fuzzier and fuzzier, but I do know that we ended up going to at least two slum bars and a brothel. The brothel was last.

There was alcohol...and sex...and I don't remember anything else after that.

I remember waking up the next day feeling as though my head had been split open with an ax while I tumbled about at sea in a storm. Somehow I had gotten home. Paige was nowhere to be seen, but in the moment, with my head hanging over the chamber pot offering up several kegs' worth of booze, I wasn't all that concerned.

I stayed in bed all day, alternating between napping and being ill. No one came to check on me. At that time, I was grateful to suffer in silence and not be in jail.

I first started getting worried when it started to get dark and I'd seen and heard no sign of Paige. When I inquired after her, the maid said she'd gone to her parents' house. That was fine with me; at least there, I knew she would be safe. In hindsight, I should have gone after her, but I didn't. I stayed where I was, stayed home, and paid no mind to anything or anyone but me and my woes.

Paige returned home the following afternoon, as cold as the ice outside these walls now. It took some doing, navigating the maze that is the female mind, but I got part of the story that happened after my memory went blank.

I had stumbled home at some point in the wee hours of the morning before the sun broke the horizon. Paige had met me at the door, initially impatient, but in a loving sort of way. She tried to get me into bed to simply sleep it off. That was when I started unloading on her. She told me that I detailed some rather obscene sexual adventures in which I had partaken that night, told her that she could never measure up because she was a stiff-lipped hoity-toity wench, told her that her days of being sexually exciting were over once she had the baby and plumped up like a fat cow, and those were some of the nicer things I apparently said to her.

There had also been rants against her father, against the banks, against London and England, against a great many things I really had no business giving my opinion on. But give my opinion I did, and everyone in the house heard it, as well as in the neighboring houses I suppose.

Owain paused and put a fist to his lips, silent, fighting for composure.

"It's been said that a drunk man's words are a sober man's thoughts," the priest began softly. "You saw fault in everything around you and blamed your woes on them. You hadn't reached a point of acceptance for your actions."

"Why?" Owain asked, his voice breaking. "Why couldn't I? Why was I unable to see something so simple? Action, reaction. Cause, effect. Personal responsibility. What was I missing?"

"Sometimes, the greatest distance is between the head and the heart. Your head could do the math, run the calculations, compute the logic. Cause and effect is a very simple thing. Action and reaction is touted by scientists the world over. These are logical things. Personal responsibility is a matter of the soul, of admitting fault in minor cases and repenting of sin in major ones. It is not something we humans are naturally inclined to do."

"Why did God make man this way? Could He not give us free will with an inclination towards good instead of evil?"

Forthill's tone was gentle. "I cannot presume to speak for the Almighty. But I believe that our souls do long for the Lord. Our sin nature has simply burned the bridge between head and heart that will allow us to easily understand, as you said, cause and effect and personal responsibility. Repentance and a new life in the Lord helps to rebuild that bridge. You are rebuilding that bridge even now."

I certainly had a bridge to rebuild with Paige, but I don't know that I ever did. Actually, I do know that I never did. Whatever it was that happened at the party or in the immediate aftermath, it was another nail in the coffin of our marriage, second to last behind only divorce. I am certain that if Paige weren't pregnant, she would have played the pagan card and had our marriage annulled. I'm quite surprised that she didn't do it anyway, but I think the stress of a divorce and finding a new husband, plus the pregnancy would have been too much for her to handle all at once.

Her father had never held me in especially high regard, except now he all but openly despised me, denounced me as any relation to him, never mind his accursed son-in-law. I was relegated to meager bank work, no longer privy to management panels or investment meetings. I was simply an employee. He told me once that he considered sending me back to my wretched homeland under the guise of checking up on our business partners and arrange for a highway robbery, have me robbed, beaten, maybe maimed or killed. The only reason he did not do so was because of his future grandchild. But I should always keep the scenario in mind, just in case.

It was a threat, plain and simple. I understood. So did the beast.

My actions and their consequences had cowed me for a short time, but inside, my beast was raging, foaming as a wild animal. My beast enjoyed the carnal pleasures, wanted more of them again, hated anyone who looked down upon me for them.

The long-term goals were boring, unattainable, more trouble than they were worth. It was all numbers, banking, entertaining rich twits and pretending to be one of them. They weren't fooled. I wasn't fooled. Why did I continue along this path? Everyone hated me, and it was only going to get worse. Certainly Paige being pregnant didn't help things.

I remember my ma being pregnant with my brother and sisters. I remembered always thinking that she was never herself during those special times when her belly got big and then I got a new sibling. It wasn't until Paige that I really understood what was happening and why, and even then, I never understood. She got as angry as I did sometimes, but no one punished her for it. In fact, they doted on her all the more. She had staunch opinions she could not be swayed from, but no one punished her for that either. If they did anything, they politely agreed and changed topics.

I remember telling myself one day to stop being so selfish. I was going to be a father. I had to stop being so concerned with what other people thought of me. I wasn't the only one at the brothel. I wasn't the one who'd insisted on the celebration. Maybe I'd done some foolish things, said some awful things, but it was going to hang over my head only as long as I let it. I had to man up, move on, and try to be a good husband and father.

It was a war most days, if not with my beast, who wanted to return to the brothels and the bars and the slums, then with Paige, who barely acknowledged my very existence.

Gossip spread about our child, mostly in the women's circles. They worried about the pedigree of my child. Can you imagine? As if my child were a prized horse or hound! Several generations of fine English blood, suddenly disrupted by a Welshman. That was bad enough, but this particular Welshman was a drunk, whoring, brawling sheep shagger. Sure, he had money, but he offered little else of value. He was far cry from a handsome Englishman, with his broad shoulders, chest like a barrel, and massive arms and legs. His knowledge was ill-gained, scraps he'd gleaned from the wealthy, hardly anything he'd been born and bred into. He surrounded himself in finery, but he himself was not finery. Pearls before swine and all that.

It frustrated me, but it did not anger me until I heard that Paige was in on it and fueling most of the gossip. She told her friends that I was a hairy beast, that I mounted her like a dog and merely took my pleasure with her. She claimed I was a barbarian and had no manners inside the house; I was little better than a somewhat well-mannered beast.

I confronted her about it, and I was surprised to find her father agreed with me. We reminded her that she had been the biggest advocate for our marriage. She'd been the one with the idea to bring me in as a business partner. I was the one who would win the hearts and minds—plus the money and business—of the Celtic peoples in the British Isles, but it would only be accomplished through marriage. The whole thing had been her idea.

She tried to play the witchcraft card, saying that I was obviously an evil wizard who had duped her; I have stark blue eyes, after all. Her father told her that while paganism might work to annull the marriage, she ought to stop believing in fairy tales and take things like a proper English lady. Her choice of husband was unfortunate and barbaric, but she was only hurting herself and his grandchild—and he used those words, not her child, but his grandchild—by perpetuating all these rumors. If she must distance herself from me and still make a point, ignore me completely. The more attention she drew to my disgusting ways, the more the babe would be perceived as such, a copy of his barbarian father. Instead, the child ought to be known as the grandson of the valiant John Balk. A good, strong, English name with an equally good, strong, English family. The Welshman helped.

Again I was tossed to the sidelines, but in this instance, I was cast out and ignored. It was a slight improvement over being cast out and subsequently spit upon and mocked incessantly. At the very least, maybe such a lineage would protect my child. He or she would always have a Welsh father, would always be half-Welsh, but the association into a wealthy English family might spare him a lifetime of scrutiny and being looked down upon.

I endured. I warred with my beast but mostly kept that war internal. I didn't go out drinking, but I did drink, usually late at night after Paige had gone to bed. I always stopped when I started talking to myself, mostly because I wasn't always certain I was only talking to myself, and because I was afraid that someone else might answer.

Someone else, referring to the beast?" Forthill inquired.

Owain nodded solemnly. "Do other men have their own beasts that they wrestle with?"

"Everyone wrestles with temptation and the forces of darkness on a daily basis. In that, you are not alone. I will say, however, that you are the first person I've met who...whose beast sounds as if it has taken on a life of its own. You refer to it in the third person and describe it as a separate entity within yourself."

"Am I possessed? Was I possessed?"

"I don't think I would go that far. All recorded instances of true possession involve wild, uncontrollable behavior with no discernible thought or character. That's not to say that you weren't sitting at the same table as demonic forces, just not in the same chair at the same time. But please, continue. Did you and Paige never get along after that?"

Quite honestly, it depended on the day. Sometimes it depended on the hour. Pregnancy is unpredictable. There were times when she couldn't stand to even consider me a human being, let alone the man who fathered her child. Then there were times when she regained a glimmer of her old self, her fire and desire for adventure, and she wanted half a dozen more children by me. Wild children, she called them. The posh lifestyle of a wealthy English family with a little thrill and mischief from their Welsh father. I never understood the changes, never figured them out in any predictable way. Sometimes I could go along with it. Other times I endured long enough just to get myself a drink afterwards.

Except for the stress it would cause her, I never have been able to figure out why she didn't leave me. She had her excuse, if she'd chosen to use it. It wasn't as though there weren't other suitors waiting for her hand, even as she was married. Some couldn't even be bothered to be subtle. I think the fact that she didn't was what made it a little more bearable for me. She had the ability to leave, but she didn't. Maybe it was motivated purely by business and trying to bring the Celts into the investing and banking fold, but I like to think it was because she still found the idea of a rugged foreigner for a husband a splendid and slightly rebellious idea, simply thrilling, you know? Or do you think I'm simply deceiving myself and wishing for things that no longer matter?

The baby came due in October. I was at the bank working when she went into labor. No one came to tell me. I saw Mr. Balk leave, but he was so casual about it, I paid it no mind. He said nothing to me. I didn't hear any rumors or whispers around the bank, so I figured all was well, just the wealthiest banker in London off to tend more of his affairs; it wasn't unusual.

Naturally, I was blamed for a mistake I did not believe was mine. I returned home a few hours later, as per usual, and was barred from entering. It was rather chilly out, and I wanted in. Paige's mother would not let me in, explaining that there was a baby on the way and to close the door; I was letting in a draft. As if I cared. Obviously if I couldn't be bothered to be around when she went into labor, why should I care about the babe at all? I countered that it didn't seem to matter much if she was going to keep me from coming in anyway. She didn't like that answer. I had no desire to be around for the labor and birth, but I felt I had to get my point across. My mother-in-law suggested I go away for a bit. She didn't care where. Go back to the brothels as far as she was concerned because Paige wasn't going to be doing anything for me ever again if either of them had anything to say about it.

And, truthfully, that was exactly what I did. I gathered up a few of those who had been there at my first-time father celebration, found a few more friends of the shadier variety, and we went and partied again. I drank significantly less this time around, but there was still plenty of sex to go around. I ended up sleeping at the house of one of the men. I hardly knew him.

It was mid-afternoon when Paige's labor began and it was almost noon the following day before the baby was born. Thankfully I wasn't nearly as hungover as I had been before, and I managed to make myself presentable. I did not go to the bank that day, for I wanted to see my child. I was allowed in the house, but it was easily an hour before I got any news. Paige's mother informed me that it was a girl, and her name was Victoria Gwendolyn. I thought it was a lovely name. When I asked when I could see them, I was told in a couple hours once mother and child had slept off their ordeal.

An eternity passed before I was allowed in to see them.

F ather, have you ever seen a newborn infant?" Owain asked.

"That fresh? Can't say that I have, at least, not alive." Forthill frowned.

"And you have no children of your own, so you can't appreciate just how...awing...it is to hold something you helped create, something that's yours, something that you want to hold and cherish and protect and defend and never let go. You can't appreciate just how tiny and helpless they are, especially in huge hands like mine." He looked down at his hands, worn and scarred and calloused, a tear falling into the grime in the creases. He glanced back at the priest. "How could I let that go? How could I push that aside for my own selfishness? Was drinking and whoring and...and my own pleasure, was that really more important than my tiny newborn daughter?"

She had a full head of hair, thick and brown, just like mine. Her nose and cheeks were just like mine. Everything about her just screamed Fforidd. She even had my blue eyes.

"All babies are born with blue eyes," Paige told me. "Then they change."

But I just shook my head and said, "No. These eyes are staying blue. I can tell."

And I was just...content. I was so happy to be there, to look at my wife and child and know that this was my family. I had to protect them. I didn't know what from, but I did. It was my solemn, holy, God-given duty. I guess I never realized that the two biggest enemies came from within. The biggest threat to our daughter...was us.

Time's up," the gaoler Cassius growled.

"Please," Forthill said calmly. "Just a bit more time."

Owain shook his head. "No. That's enough for now. I don't know that I could take much more."

He was exhausted. He always was after he talked to the priest. His mind became sluggish, his eyes drooped, and he could almost fall asleep on command except for the things that lurked in the shadows of his cell. And yet, for all that, he did feel some clearing of conscience. He wouldn't go all the way to forgiveness just yet, but he did feel better for confiding in the priest.

That wasn't to say that it was easy revisiting his wretched life. His stomach dropped into his bowels and his heart wanted to burst out of his chest, twisting and bleeding and begging him to stop. Sometimes he thought about ripping out his own tongue just to keep him from having to say these words out loud. He was disgusted with himself and didn't want to shame himself more than he already had. Of course, it would do no good when he had the gaolers to heap plenty of shame on his head. This Cassius was the worst, and he seemed to take a certain pleasure in degrading Owain.

"You rich, wretched filth," Cassius growled. "Claim to love your family, but you love your drink more. Your drinking, your brawling, winning over weak-bodied men. But you have a weak mind. Can't focus on your own child for longer than, what, a couple weeks? Pathetic." He spat.

Ripping out his tongue would do no good. Perhaps he out to cut his ears off and try to silence the voices in his mind, even as he knew it wouldn't work. He wouldn't hear the rats anymore, but then the only company to keep would be his own conscience and the beast.

Yes, the beast remained within him. He knew it was the beast because he knew the beast, as surely as he knew Forthill and Cassius and the warden and anyone else. They were familiar. The beast was familiar. The only difference was that the beast was intangible, most likely demonic, as the priest said. But it was always there, ready with the shame and the guilt and a thousand ways to kill himself all lined up, just waiting for him to find the one that works.

Starving yourself takes too long, the beast told him. *And you're too susceptible to the hallucinations. But don't worry, we'll find some other way.*

Owain wasn't sure whether he was afraid of it or anticipating it even more. He put up no resistance as Cassius opened his cell door and pushed him inside. The other gaolers gave him a little shove, just enough to let him know who was in charge, as if he'd somehow forgotten. Cassius, though, he made a real effort to try and get him to hit the opposite wall.

The door swung shut, and Owain stood there in the darkness. He did not move for a long time. The rats began scuttling. He smashed one against the wall with his foot as it nibbled his toes; it let out a shrill shriek as it hit the wall and let go.

Eventually, he found sleep. The following day, the usual bowl of porridge came sliding through the door. He sighed, then reached for it.

INTERLUDE

THE DECISION

Forthill had to admit, he had come to enjoy his meetings with Fforidd. It was a bit like speaking to the Apostle Paul and hearing of his life before the road to Damascus. It was not pretty, it was not safe for children's ears, but it was beautiful when one considered that it showed the magnitude of God's love and the lengths He would go to in order to pursue His lost sheep. Millions had been saved because of Paul's letters to the churches and all the work he did. Maybe, somehow, millions more would be saved because of Owain and his transformation.

It was a bit of an idealistic thought, but what shepherd did not imagine a great flock, covering the hillside as far as the eye could see, all of them healthy? Yes, Worthington was right; he mayhaps daydreamed a little too much. Perhaps it was the scenery, the stone walls that caused his thoughts to wander to happier things.

He made his way up to the warden's office.

"Good evening, Father," Nathan greeted.

The warden did not look at him, but neither was his tone strictly formal or unfriendly. They had settled into a comfortable relationship. Neither really liked the other, but they respected each other, their jobs and positions. They understood that sometimes they might be at odds, but it was the job, not the man, that they were fighting.

Yea, we do not struggle against flesh and blood, but against poorly-worded job titles and vague job descriptions which leave far too much room for personal preference and leeway.

Forthill smiled internally as he sat down across from the warden. "Evening, Warden. Another late night, then."

"It is never not a late night. And you can speak; you're still here as well."

"That is true, and I have yet to make the journey back to the parish."

"Easier to do in the summer than the winter."

"That it is."

"It's been four months, Father," Nathan said, setting aside a paper and leaning back in his chair. "I expect you've gotten a very detailed story out of Fforidd by now and are preparing him to meet our Lord?"

"I believe that he is coming to his biography's conclusion, yes."

The warden raised a brow. "You're not a liar, Father, but you have a bad habit of not telling the whole truth. If I'm right, that's still a sin, whether you're Catholic or Protestant."

Forthill smiled and looked at his hands folded neatly on his lap. "Well, you are perceptive."

"It's my job to know these things, how guilty men think and act. What are you not telling me this time? You're not going to give Fforidd another stay on his sentence."

"Nor have I requested one; that I can assure you."

"Out with it, Father; you're infuriating me."

The priest shifted position and cleared his throat. "Fforidd has...I suppose you might say he has inspired me. He reminds me a lot of Saint Paul. There is hope of redemption for anyone, no matter their past."

"Yes...?" Nathan goaded.

"I have been telling his story to Father Worthington, whom you know I stay with at the parish. He was uninterested at first, but he has since come to see the same thing I have. He has been encouraging me to write down Fforidd's story and share it. Not to any congregation, mind you, not at this time, but to other pastors, priests, Catholic and Protestant."

The warden looked unimpressed. "Fascinating. I imagine it will come as quite a shock when he reaches the Pearly Gates and is admitted as a canonized saint."

Forthill barked a laugh and fished two letters from one of his pockets. "Yes, I imagine so."

"And what's that?"

The priest handed over the letter. "It is a formal request to stay

Fforidd's sentence until such time as his entire biography can be written and copied. One comes from the Catholic Church, the other from an organization of small Protestant churches and chapels all over the United Kingdom. They have been sent to the judge."

The warden read over both letters, identical save for the names of the senders. For a long minute he was silent. When he stood, his chair fell over, he threw the letters back at Forthill, and cursed righteously, not even bothering to excuse himself or ask for forgiveness. He was right furious.

"*Ydych chi'n ddeall beth chi'n gwneud?!*" the warden roared. (Do you understand what you're doing?!) "You are validating him! You are excusing him! You are telling every damned one of these prisoners that they can be a saint if they have a pitiful enough life and can dupe a priest!"

"I am doing no such thing," Forthill said calmly. "Only through repentance of sins is there salvation. I am showing them that there is no sin too great that the Lord can't handle."

Nathan shook his head. "He is a vile, heartless murderer. And he's duped you. You are going to regret this. If it were in my power, I would remove you from your position right now. Unfortunately, you have too much backing from both Catholics and Protestants that to do so would raise questions and cause them to press even further." Grudging pause. "You make my life miserable sometimes."

"Thank you."

"That wasn't a compliment."

"No, but I would be remiss in my duties if I did not make people uncomfortable at least some of the time."

"Get out of my office. Get out of this prison. Get off — this — island."

Forthill nodded graciously and saw himself out of the warden's office. He glanced down the corridor where he knew Fforidd's cell was. The big, mean gaoler, Cassius, was skulking around and did not appear to notice him. The priest turned away and headed down the stairs. He might have gone to Fforidd's cell to offer words of encouragement, but Cassius frightened him for reasons unknown and he could only describe as purely demonic. Something about him wasn't right. Perhaps, if

Forthill still had a job after Fforidd's execution, he would speak to Cassius.

The channel crossing was peaceful, but less than friendly with the patrols making rounds on the rocky shores. Forthill stepped on the far shore, thanked the boatmaster, and made his way up the road. When it was warm and if it wasn't too dark, he preferred to walk back to the parish, singing and praying and enjoying God's creation. Bandits were not a problem here; what bandit wanted to stick around so close to a prison?

He arrived at the parish to find Worthington still awake, sitting at his study. Hot water was just starting to whistle in the kettle on the stove. Forthill helped himself to a cup of tea and sat down on his mattress.

"So, do you still have a job?" Worthington asked, not looking at him.

"Oh, yes," Forthill replied, "though Nathan said as much that he wanted me removed immediately. But the backing of the Church and the chapels is too strong; it would only look suspicious if he were to remove me."

"There is that." The older priest brought out a few fresh sheets of paper. "And what of Owain?"

Forthill recounted the tale from the evening. As he spoke, Worthington dutifully scratched away with ink and paper. He had the speed to keep up with Forthill's train of thought; later, Forthill would copy everything in a more elegant hand.

When he was finished, the night's tale took up several pages, front and back. Worthington set it aside, next to the stack of finished copies which was becoming quite a novel.

"Am I doing the right thing?" Forthill wondered, sitting there with an empty cup in his hands. "I've no regrets about speaking to him and helping him cleanse his conscience, save his soul. But do you think perhaps, I'm making too much of it? Am I unnecessarily or even dangerously making a celebrity of him? What if Nathan is right? What if I am validating him to the other prisoners who will all seek to be saints in their own right?"

Worthington raised a brow. "Do the other prisoners even know what is going on? Has anyone told them?"

Forthill pondered this for a moment. "I haven't said anything, and none of the other prisoners have said anything to me during my rounds. I don't know that Nathan or any of his gaolers have said anything. All the same, Fforidd was supposed to have been hung months ago and he wasn't. That in itself must be news of some form among the convicts."

"Perhaps. But if the inmates thought that Fforidd was getting anything for speaking to you, they would likely already be bothering you about it."

He was still uncertain. "Maybe. But there is no going back now, I suppose."

"Indeed there isn't. Has Fforidd shown any signs of reverting back to his old ways?"

Forthill shook his head. "No. Recounting his life, I think he has finally seen his behavioral patterns and understood the error of his ways. It may be late, true, but not too late."

"As long as he breathes," Worthington agreed wisely. "Continue to do the work of the Lord and trust Him to provide."

"Not a few months ago, you doubted me as well." Forthill folded his arms and shifted his position. He wasn't really irritated with the older priest, but he sometimes gave him a hard time about it.

"Me of little faith, I know. And I have learned. Good things are happening here because you listened to the Lord's direction. As I've said before, I am sorry I doubted. Clearly the Almighty chose the better of us for this mission."

Forthill flushed with embarrassment but did not disagree. They could spend all night in a banter over who was more humble, and it would be only utter nonsense and highly Narcissistic, thus defeating the whole purpose. Instead, they called it a night. Worthington tossed a couple logs in the stove just to keep it going, hopefully, until morning. It was quite warm outside, but there was little worse in the world than having to wait for a fire to wait for the hot water to wait for the tea. Forthill had heard that in America they drank tea with ice. Sounded absolutely dreadful, to be honest. But it was an ocean away, and he was exhausted.

Being a prison chaplain had a way of aging said chaplain. He walked on the road during the summer to keep his body moving, but it was getting harder every year, and half of the strain came from the burdens he bore from the prisoners. Worthington still sprang about like a man half his age, but his flock was of considerably better stock and fewer problems. Well, that wasn't fair, really. Everyone had problems, and everyone was a sinner. But his flock in the prison had more egregious sins and they were not his flock by choice necessarily.

He took a calming breath and stared at the ceiling. The days were growing shorter, and the last of the light had disappeared shortly before he arrived. It would be returning soon, he knew. Another day.

He spent the next few days between prison visits copying Worthington's transcript of his dictation. The story came to life in Forthill's mind as his arthritic hand scratched out Owain's words. A tragic tale, really, but, if experience and the Lord were to be believed, there would be a happy end. Forthill had little doubt that one day (perhaps sooner rather than later) he would meet Owain again in Paradise.

But that was the future, he mused. Owain—and himself, for that matter—had yet to cross that threshold into eternity. Forthill would be lying to himself if no one else that the thought was still a bit uneasy. He was comfortable in life, and he was confident in eternity, but it was the threshold itself that frightened him, that instant of death as the soul departed the body. Would he know it, or would it be as falling asleep? Would it hurt? If all souls had to be tried by fire, and teachers were judged more harshly, in accordance with their actions to either direct or stray their flock...?

He shook his head and continued on his way, heading for the dock. It was Sunday again and he had service duties to perform. Attendance was not compulsory, but highly recommended. Highly. Recommended. Sometimes with the alternative of a good beating. For as uptight as Nathan was about this situation with Owain, he wanted his charges to find God and get out of his hair once they were released.

And, in all reality, most of the prisoners came to service because it was a break from the mundane, from the working and washing. It was a chance to hear a voice other than the gaolers' or the warden's, and a chance to hear something other than cursing, crying, or commands.

But when Forthill entered the chapel that morning, he was stunned to find Owain in the front row. In the early morning light, he looked impossibly wretched, but there was a shadow of hope, a mouse putting a nose out of its hole to test the air. Owain's gaze met his, and the prisoner gave him something almost resembling a smile, and Forthill saw a glimmer of gratitude flicker over his countenance.

He couldn't remember what he preached about that morning. Might have been one of the parables. In fact, he was fairly certain it was a parable. The one about the talents. Yes, that was it. The talents and the greedy servant. One servant invested his master's money and received a grand return. Another servant invested the master's money and received a decent return. But one servant buried the money and did nothing with it, so the master sent him away. Someone in the audience had made a comment, said maybe next time he was caught stealing, he would say he was just investing the master's money so he wasn't sent away. He received a heavy-handed cuff from one of the gaolers with a muttered threat about more later if he kept up his stupid antics.

Forthill waited until the chapel had been cleared completely before excusing himself and making his way to the warden's office. Nathan was nowhere to be seen. Despite professing to be Catholic, Nathan was a bit of a stranger to Mass, preferring to spend his time ensuring the attendance of his convicts to chapel service and then to work afterwards. Forthill found the man in the women's work room, giving a hard time to a girl who couldn't have been twenty years old, a baby on her hip.

"Warden," Forthill said, just loud enough to make himself heard.

Nathan abruptly bit off his sentence, head whipping around so hard Forthill could heard his neck crack. His expression was unreadable, but surprise was certainly in there. He said something to the girl in a low voice, then stalked up to Forthill.

"Yes, Father, can I help you? Aren't you supposed to be making rounds?"

Forthill smiled pleasantly as if he couldn't guess what the warden was up to with the women. "Yes, of course. I was just about to when I found you. Curious thing this morning in the chapel service: Owain

Fforidd was present. He's not been present since he's been here."

Nathan clenched his jaw a second and huffed a sigh. "Indeed. In the interest of keeping peace between the prison and the churches you've rallied behind you, I made an allowance for Fforidd to come out on Sundays. Only for chapel. I still will not put him in the work room or the yard with the other prisoners."

The priest nodded once. "Of course. Small steps. He did seem grateful this morning."

The warden was not impressed. "Yes. Grateful. He can reminisce on this gratitude while in his cell. If you are making your rounds, you know the routine. Just let the gaolers know when you need to see him."

It was not unusual for Nathan to be in a bad mood, but he seemed uniquely eager for a fight. Perhaps it was because Forthill had interrupted him with the women. The priest waited until he was out of the room before letting out a breath. There were many problems here. One at a time, one at a time...

He made his rounds. Most of the prisoners were not interested in talking to him. Some felt as though they had been unfairly targeted by his sermon. Many of them were thieves of one form or another, so it made some sense. It was still early in the afternoon when he returned to the chapel and waited for Owain to be brought out of his own personal hell.

The man had seemed so eager, so alive, sitting in the service. Even now, he retained a ghost of that energy and hope. And yet, there was a familiar fear and resignation creeping over him, bending his back, that it had been only temporary, perhaps a trick of the Devil, giving him false hope. But in the end, he still had to return to his black cell. He was returning again to recount a miserable, unhappy life he would rather forget.

"I saw you at the service this morning," Forthill began conversationally.

Owain nodded and did not look at him right away. "How could you not?" A faint smile. "I was right there in front."

"Indeed you were."

The man turned serious again, but there was a certain genuineness to it that gripped Forthill's heart as Fforidd said, "Thank you. For helping me. If nothing else, you helped me see the sun again."

Forthill smiled warmly. "Well, to make a play on words, I think I've also helped you see the Son for the first time."

"Yes. There is that as well. I still thank you. I worried that I would only see the sun again on my last day."

"Always glad. Now then, where were we?"

Chapter Nine

The Outsider

I couldn't stop looking at her and saying her name. Victoria Gwendolyn Fforidd. Socially she was known as a Forbes, but her legal name was Fforidd. I wrote to my parents to let them know the good news. It was the only time they ever wrote back, congratulating us. Maybe they hoped I really had turned my life around and I was going to be a good father, good husband, shed my demons and become a family man, wealthy and successful. I had those same hopes, at first.

Paige was still a bit idealistic, and in the initial magic, she loved me again and said she wanted to raise our daughter like how my parents would have raised me. (I didn't bother to correct her on anything.) Now, obviously, there were vast differences between my parents and their situation raising children, and our situation raising children. Country, city, farmers, bankers, those sorts of things. Paige's idea of raising our daughter like my parents raised me amounted to feeding the babe herself from her own breast. And that was about it. I suppose it was just her trying to recover from the birth, being pregnant and then not, but I digress.

As for me, I was too stunned to do much more than watch and consider that this infant in our house was mine. I had helped to create life. And she looked so much like me, as I said. It was astounding.

O wain looked at his hands. "I could go on for days just about the awe and the love I felt for this child, and I still would not be able to articulate it well. It's not something you can just put into words; it is more than just a feeling, it is an instinct, a part of your being that is as natural as breathing."

"Stop there," Forthill said gently. Owain looked at the priest. "Now consider this, that this feeling you are describing is the same love that Creator God holds for us. Actually, I believe that we can feel only a fraction of that love. You loved your child. You wanted the best for her. You wanted her to be as astounding as you felt astounded. You wanted her to have the best of everything. You wished that she could feel that soul love that you felt for her, to know that she was special to you. And in that, you wanted her to love you back."

Tears were streaming down Owain's cheeks into his dirty beard and he managed a small, almost inaudible, "Yes." He choked a sob and wiped his face. "Yes. That is everything I felt and wanted. But I couldn't do it."

"Now imagine a Father Who can do it, Who can continue to love that way at all times, Who never turns away to His own pursuits because you are His pursuit."

For a long moment, Owain said nothing. A flood of emotion had bubbled up in his body and he fought to keep himself from choking, although that did not sound like a bad thing at the moment. The priest was keeping him alive so he might tell his story. Who would want to hear such a thing? Finally he was able to take a breath and compose his thoughts, distance himself from the tragedy it was about to become.

I couldn't do it. In the short-term, neither could Paige. Infants can be rather demanding. Within two weeks, Paige hired a wetnurse to feed the child and take care of it when she was busy, which was quite often. Our investments in Wales had begun turning a noticable profit. Mr. Balk wanted to both solidify what he had and expand even further while we had the chance.

I know I said that Paige wanted to be a mother. And she did. Before the baby, she talked about it often, having children, being a mother, having a wealthy family to rule London as little lords as it were. Part of me wondered how much of it was her dream and how much of it was a dream her parents had instilled in her, their goals impressed onto her as if it was her duty to fulfill them. I don't doubt that Paige loved our daughter, but there was suddenly a great chasm of time between having the children and seeing them grown and successful.

In the meantime, Victoria was only an infant. She did not talk about family. She did not consider business. She did not want to go here or there or meet with this or that person. She ate. She slept. She vomited and soiled herself and wanted to be held for no discernible reason. And she wanted to do it at the most inconvenient times, when we were busy, when we were sleeping, at all conceivable hours.

It was exhausting, and frustrating. It was frustrating for Paige who wanted to be involved in the bank as she always had, but she also wanted to be a mother. With Victoria still being a baby and doing all that stuff I just mentioned, she didn't want to deal with that, but she also felt guilty about leaving her with the nurse. She was confused and angry, and she often took it out on me. She would claim that I had no interest in our family because I was always at the bank. I told her I *was* interested, interested in keeping us financially stable. Plus, with everything going well in the investing world, Balk was considering sending me to Ireland to secure some investments there while the market was suffering from the Famine. Paige almost lost it, demanding to know whose idea it was to exclude her.

It was actually her mother who gave her a stern lecture about family and business. Paige was a mother now, she said, and it was in everyone's best interests for her to step out of the bank for a while and be a mother. Let the men handle the bank.

That only enraged Paige more. She declared that she could travel, and so could Victoria. We would all go together. We could present ourselves as a family bank, which was a much softer approach than a bunch of stuffy Englishmen in expensive suits. It might win over the Irish who were also family-centric.

After some arguing, I suggested Mr. Balk send a different associate. Better to keep the peace in the family or else the family name means nothing. It was one of the few times her parents wholeheartedly agreed with me on anything, and her mother again gave her a lecture, this time on actions and consequences.

This got her sore at me again. We argued. We argued a lot during that time. Generally, we were good about keeping it to ourselves so as not to disturb Victoria. But after that series of events, the lectures—even though they weren't even aimed at me—the business, the baby, I felt that I couldn't do it anymore. So I went out drinking. It was only a half-hearted thing at the time. My mind was so muddled and confused, I couldn't focus on anything long enough to make me want to drink. Considering how little it actually took, once I got going, that should say something about my state of mind. I returned home, woke up with a hangover, and carried on.

As you might expect, nothing much changed. Paige and I still disdained each other. Victoria continued to be an infant and do infant things. The bank was prosperous and investments were doing well. But my beast...my beast seized on the discord, fed my rage all the things it had stored up over the course of my marriage, seized on the drinking I had done, mixed it all together in a cauldron of inevitability.

D o you think things could have turned out any other way?" Owain wondered. "Where do free will and fate collide? At what point had I crossed the barrier from one into another?"

Forthill frowned. "Up until the time we make a choice, we always have one."

"Yes, but once you jump off a cliff, you have no choice but to fall. You can choose to jump, but you can't choose not to fall. Where had I jumped off the cliff? When we had Victoria? When we got married? When I started investing? When I went to London? What point would I have to go back to in order to make it all better? And does it matter?"

The priest sighed. "I'm afraid not. The past is the past. It is the future that matters, how you choose to spend your time from here on."

A t that time, I began spending more and more of my time anywhere but home. Some days I didn't even go to the bank, but just went out. Walking, to the pub, it didn't matter. Paige's parents agreed with me only that one time, but it was an occasion, not the norm. They still hated me. They hated that I was from a lower class of a lesser people, yet dining with their perceived royalty. They hated that my daughter looked like me and not like her mother. They hated that I drank, yet they did so just as much—though they preferred the refined liquor versus the poor ale and beer of the lowly masses.

And still life went on.

When I was home, Paige and I argued, and I began to notice that her words were very reminisce of her parents, especially her mother. She would use the same words and phrases to describe me or my behavior. Not a few times I could have sworn I was talking to my mother-in-law. I knew women tended to take after their mothers, but she was just...identical. I don't even know if it was intentional or not.

Whatever the case, I didn't like it, and my beast had a supply of rage at the ready, feeding the fire of my hatred, of my selfishness and self-loathing. When we argued, at first, Victoria's crying could put an end to it as Paige went to tend to her, mostly to get her mind off of me, I think. Then she stopped doing that and had the nurse see to Victoria so she could keep arguing with me. When that happened, I started out by just leaving, often going out to a pub. But the funny thing is, while I went to the pub, I didn't drink, or I didn't drink a lot. I could still remember everything, could still walk well, but the excess had dwindled away. I drank enough to fuel the rage, but not so much that I forgot my actions.

I don't know where my beast ended and I began, to tell you the truth," Owain said. "What was it that kept me from overindulging? Did it help, or just make it worse? Would I have been here six months earlier if I had going back to excessive drinking to the point where I couldn't remember anything?"

"I'm afraid there's no way to really know that answer," Forthill said haltingly, unsure whether the questions had been rhetorical.

"And it goes back to the jumping off the cliff scenario. Was God trying to stop me from getting close to the edge, or was my beast accelerating my fall by having me do everything sober? Was I even in my right mind? I know all men make choices and are responsible for their own actions, but when do men become mere puppets? What is it that causes a puppet to cut his own strings? Does he cut his strings or just hand them off to some other cosmic entity to control?"

The priest shifted uncomfortably. "You're asking some very big questions."

"I know. And asking them won't make me feel better about them, nor will it change the past any." Owain frowned.

"Why don't you keep going?"

It was a long moment and several strangled sighs before the prisoner continued.

I hit Paige. I don't remember the exact date, I don't remember the argument. I just remember standing there, feeling as stunned as she looked in that split-second after my hand met her face. I remember the hurt in her eyes. I remember thinking that it was all over, that things would never be the same. They couldn't be. I remember the silence that followed as she stared at me for a long minute, then quietly left the room.

I remember not caring.

I remember the astonishment fading quickly, only to be replaced by apathy and smug self-righteousness. In bestial terms, I had defended my dominance and my territory. My challenger had backed down and returned to her proper duties. It felt good. It felt right. Or so said my beast. Once I regained control of my body and could move again, I went out, went to the bank, and resumed my work as though nothing had transpired.

My pa had switched me plenty growing up. And my sisters had never been exempt from punishment of some form, though my ma usually took care of that. But never had my pa hit my ma or any of my sisters. Never. Not once, not even as a warning. He never threatened to hit them. He always told me not to hit anyone if I could help it, but never ever turn my hand to a woman. If he caught me or even heard about me hitting a girl, he would flay my body and rip the skin from my hands. I didn't fear him, as you know, and I did not care much because I already hit girls and robbed them.

As I mulled this over, I was overcome with guilt. That night, I tried to apologize to Paige. She wanted nothing to do with me. It took a few days before she would accept my apology, even if it was just out of formality.

I didn't tell the priest at my next Confession, because I knew it would hit the gossip circles like a spark to dry tinder. I just had to do better.

Destroying myself through my drinking was one thing, but I shouldn't drag Paige into my destruction as well. To say nothing of all the people I had wronged in my youthful days. But I had to do better. I was married and had a baby girl. It wasn't about me anymore.

Except my beast did say it was all about me, and it didn't take much to relapse. Many times, when we were arguing, I had to presence of mind to simply storm out before I did anything drastic, go out and drink enough to relax my muscles even if my mind was still fuming. But there were other times when I would hit Paige once more, then wait for her to slink away before going out and doing the same. I can't even remember what we argued about, honestly. The bank, maybe. Finances, maybe. I don't even know.

It all seems so petty now. I don't understand it. Why couldn't I be grateful and happy? Why does it feel like my whole life has been about anger and ingratitude? What started it?" Owain took an even breath. "I know I've asked this before, and I know that even if there was an answer to be found, it wouldn't change anything. But just knowing would be nice."

"Would it?" Forthill asked innocently. "Or would it only frustrate you more that you couldn't see it before? I'm not saying I have the answer, nor am I implying that it is not a worthy question. But do you really think it would help?"

A long moment passed before Owain finally replied, "No. It would only serve to frustrate me more."

Another long minute stretched into five minutes or so.

"Are you finished for the evening?" the priest inquired politely.

The prisoner sighed.

I went out to drink, but I didn't always do so. I would go to the pub, I might eat, but I didn't always drink. Or if I did, it wasn't much. It didn't interest me as much. In my mind, the drinking was about the rage and the power. In my mind, Paige was the enemy. Paige was not an enemy I needed to prepare to fight. I could overpower her with only half my strength. And as we argued and fought more and more, my beast wondered why I didn't overpower her, show her once and for all who was dominant. If she just calmed down, sat down, and did what I said, everything would calm down and go well.

Even my beast knew that was a fantasy. Paige was constantly going to her parents for everything, agreeing with them on everything. I'd become more distant from my father-in-law—not that we were ever very close, mind you, but I was much less involved in investments and other business dealings—and I didn't know a lot about what went on behind closed doors. I do know that she never told her parents that I was abusing her. It would have meant admitting that they had been right all along, that I was a barbaric, country Welshman. Her pride demanded she stay silent.

Owain couldn't stop himself as he broke into sobs. The sudden move startled Forthill and earned Owain a cuff from the gaoler. The priest waved the gaoler off and gingerly put a hand on the prisoner's shoulder. A good five or ten minutes passed before Owain could control himself enough to continue speaking.

"She broke her silence the day I turned on Victoria." He sucked in a breath and held it, wiping his eyes and nose and making a mess.

"What happened?" Forthill asked gently.

I had gotten home from the bank late and Paige was upset. Most of our staff was ill, so she'd had to take care of Victoria all day by herself, or near enough, I suppose. And she'd spoken to her father recently and there was some issue at the bank. She wanted to know more about it, what was happening, how was business, were the investments still good. She barraged me with questions. I'd had a hard day and I just wanted to sit down but she kept pestering me and pestering me. Nagging, always nagging.

So I got upset with her. We argued. I hit her. But instead of backing down, she met me head on. She said things. Vile things. But that didn't mean they were untrue. I was a horrible husband, a poor father, a sorry excuse for a human being. She said she never should have married me, and she couldn't even remember why she'd ever thought I'd had the potential to become a wealthy Englishman. Clearly I would never be anything more than a Neanderthal, and such an accusation was insulting to Neanderthals.

I hit her again, more forcefully this time. She stumbled backwards. Again with the accusations, this time with threats of divorce. She was going to have the church null our marriage and everyone was going to know that I was a barbaric pagan who had no place in polite society.

We were yelling by now. And at some point...Victoria had gotten close. She was crawling now and experimenting with walking. I remember she sat on the floor. She was crying because she was afraid and we were shouting. At that moment, I didn't care who or what she was; I just wanted the noise to stop. So I turned...I turned and...I kicked her. I ended up lifting her and sending her back a few feet, and she started squalling.

I made some kind of move, and the next thing I knew, there was a knife in the back of my shoulder. Paige had stabbed me. Stunned, I just stopped and tried to figure out what was happening. Paige took that moment to grab Victoria and run out the door.

I didn't know if she was going to tell her father or the authorities, and in the moment, I didn't care. I was injured. But more to the point, I was astonished. She had not only stood up to me, but she'd attacked me. She'd injured me. If I hadn't moved at the last second, there is no telling where that knife would have gone. It could have gone through my back into my heart. I couldn't comprehend it.

It was hell trying to get the knife out, and I did a poor job of stitching and bandaging myself. She'd hit my shoulder blade, but missed anything debilitating like a lung or an artery. In the end, it was more of a flesh wound, but that didn't mean it didn't hurt. But the pain still took second place to the unnerving realization that I hadn't won that fight. My inner beast felt all the rage it needed to, but as I stumbled outside, I managed to keep it quiet. I had to get somewhere safe, somewhere familiar. So my beast changed tactics, exchanging rage for soothing temptation.

Owain sniffed. "That's the last concrete thing I remember. I know I wobbled off down the street and got to the slums, looking for the dirtiest, slimiest pub I could find. After that, it all gets hazy and then cuts out. Next thing I know, I'm in jail."

Another long silence followed. Finally Forthill said, "Why don't we call it a night? I think this has been very trying for you today."

The gaoler grunted. "How so? He lived it. He reveled in it."

"As you revel in your own self-importance, watching another man suffer," the priest said sharply. "Do you presume to be on the moral high ground simply because you are on the legal high ground? The Lord will judge us all equally."

"And so He shall."

Cassius jerked Owain up by his chains. Unprepared, the prisoner was little better than a rag doll and he ended up slumping to his knees on the hard stone. He grunted but had little time to consider his predicament before the gaoler simply reached down and hauled him to his feet. No sooner had Owain gotten his feet under him than Cassius delivered one punch to the stomach and another to the face. Owain went down a second time, but he managed to make it to a pew to sit down.

"Honestly!" Forthill barked, standing suddenly. "Have you no decency?"

The gaoler turned to the priest. "No. I don't. Nor do I fear for my soul."

He did not wait for Forthill's response. He grabbed Owain's chains a second time and started walking away. Owain lurched out of the pew, tried to stand, fell, was dragged a short distance, then got his feet under him and managed to hobble along after Cassius. His face was streaked with muddy tears and his whole body ached. He had a difficult time getting up the stairs, and he collapsed into his cell, grateful for the privilege of just lying down and not being bothered. He couldn't even be bothered to startle when the door slammed shut behind him.

He lay there, and he wept. He did not weep for himself, for he was beyond redemption. He wept for everyone whose lives he'd ruined because of his selfishness. He wept for his parents, the scorn and humiliation they had endured for their unruly child. He wept for his siblings, whose first sensation in the world was love from their ma, and whose second sensation was utter terror of their eldest brother. He especially wept for his brother, forced to be the caretaker and unable to do that. Owain wept for all the people he'd wronged and sinned against, from those he'd robbed on the street, to the prostitutes he took advantage of, to those he'd intimidated in jail, to the jailers who'd had to deal with him in all his moods, most of them bad. He wept for those he'd wronged in his quest for riches and success, those he'd stepped on in order to elevate himself.

But most of all, he wept for his wife and child. His wife, while her own motives may not have been pure, still tried to help him become a gentleman, worthy of his riches and of his place in high society. His child, entirely innocent and desiring only the love of her family, something he could not give because he held none for even himself. Self-love was a misleading term. When you got right down to it, self-love was actually an oxymoron. Even the most Narcissistic people did not truly love themselves. They hated others, but they feared being exposed as being less than perfect. They really hated themselves and all their flaws, whether real or perceived, and worked hard to cover them up.

Owain had no love. Not for himself, not for anyone else. He loathed himself and had only indifference for the rest of humanity. The gaolers were giving him what he deserved, so he couldn't hate them. The priest really was trying his hardest and doing what he believed God had called him to do, so Owain could not hold that against him. But it was all useless. Eventually, the courts would rule that he had to die, and no one short of Jesus Himself coming back was going to stop it.

That was fine with him. He needed to go. There was a funny little quirk in the justice system, however. The law said he needed to die. The church may have stayed his sentence for a time for their own pet project, but he was sentenced to hang eventually. Owain himself was not against this. But he was supposed to die on the law's terms. Any one of the gaolers, Cassius especially, would be happy to beat him to death, shoot him themselves, even. He probably only had to ask. Maybe the warden would help them disguise it as a suicide or some such thing. Except, fundamentally, he couldn't die until the law said he could die. How strange was that?

But as it happened, he did suffer several beatings from the gaolers over the next few days. They fed him every day like they were supposed to, but it was always preceded by a beating. Sometimes they left him only half-conscious, and by the time he got around to his food, it was almost gone, eaten by the rats. Or maybe they didn't give him much to begin with. Or both. His frail, condemned body wouldn't need sustenance for much longer anyway, so why waste resources?

His hunger strike felt like so long ago, but he knew he couldn't try that again. Hunger did things to a man. Made him sick in the head. Made him see and hear things. But was it really much different from what inevitably awaited him in death? Darkness, fire, torture, eternal torment. What was a little hunger-induced hallucinating, really? Not that he was looking forward to Hell or anything, but his body wouldn't let him try another hunger strike.

He slept fitfully anyway and woke in the familiar morning gloom, a sliver of light giving him just enough to see his hand in front of his face. That was the best it got that day, and the gloom quickly devolved back into darkness as the sun moved around the gaol. His meal came that day, but no beating. When he counted off the days, he realized it was time for another visit from Forthill. The gaolers couldn't deliver a dumb man to Confession, after all. That would just be in poor taste. To say nothing of the bruises he was sure he had, his swollen cheek and painful breathing.

He looked forward to the visits, not because he enjoyed recounting the tale, but because he would take any chance he had of getting out of his cell, if only for a short time. The darkness was suffocating, though he breathed it every day.

The gaoler was not Cassius this time, but he was in no better a mood. This gaoler was largely apathetic as to the welfare of the prisoners, and he rarely stepped in to separate two prisoners in a tussle. As far as he was concerned, they could kill each other and he would have two fewer prisoners to look after. His attitude was no different this day than any other day as he retrieved Owain and marched him out of his cell, down the stairs, and to the chapel.

Forthill looked at Owain, looked at his wounds, then looked at the gaoler.

"And what is this?" the priest asked, his tone firm.

"Your bi-weekly visit," the gaoler replied smartly. He shoved Owain into the front pew where he normally sat.

"And the bruises?" the priest inquired, almost sarcastically. "Are the rats here the size of dogs, or are you beating him?"

The gaoler made a dismissive motion. "I suggest you two get talking. You only have a limited time here. Both of you."

The priest did not budge an inch. "I will speak to the warden about this," he said sternly. "There is no reason this man should be treated this way. And before you lecture me on all the people he hurt, ask yourself if you're much better. Vengeance is the Lord's, and who are you to be assuming that duty?"

The gaoler appeared unimpressed, and he'd had far more practice in stare-downs than the priest. It didn't take long for Forthill to give in, though Owain could see he was still a bit disgruntled. The priest took a calming breath and looked at him.

"Are you all right?"

Owain shrugged meekly. "As well as I can be, I expect. I am still alive and walking this side of the grave, but I don't know whether that's a good thing."

"Don't talk like that."

"It's true."

Forthill frowned. "Well, we still have some story left to go, I think. Would you like to continue?"

Owain shrugged again. "I suppose. Where did I leave off?"

CHAPTER TEN

THE BUM

Let me just say that after several years of not going to jail every few months, going back to jail was almost a new experience, and yet, it was all too familiar. I knew my surroundings. I knew the code, the hierarchy. I knew how things worked. Sure, they might have been a little different from place to place, but fundamentally, it was the same as I had always known it. Maybe that was why I was able to survive as well as I did, because it was something I was familiar with.

When I first woke up in jail, it was, as I just said, familiar, but also very out of place. I knew I had a bed and a home, and I couldn't figure out where those were. I couldn't remember how I got where I was. I will say that I had a wretched hangover, so that may account for some or most of the confusion.

It didn't take much to figure out that I was in jail, but it did take a little time to figure out that I was not automatically the head inmate. In Wales, I was known the country over as one tough guy. I did things my way, and you did things my way, too. That was just how things worked.

In London, I was known as a bit of a drinker, maybe a little shady when it came to how I acquired my wealth, but the point was that I was wealthy. I had nice things. In a word, I was soft. It didn't matter that I was a big man or that I still had my strength. My wealth and my high standard of living meant I was soft, easy pickings for the more desperate in society, those I'd been associating with recently in my quest to escape from home. They'd never taken me for anything but a sleazy rich man.

I quickly showed them that I was no lightweight. But where my younger years had been spent fighting for dominance and total control, this time around, I fought just to keep them off my back. Enough to send a message but not enough to gain more attention than warranted. Maybe I had sobered up a bit, but mostly I think I was still just stunned by this turn of events. I was back in jail. All my work and all my wealth, and I was back behind bars. I couldn't comprehend it. It scared me.

Then I began to consider why I was there. Honestly, I still wasn't sure what had actually landed me there. I had no memory of the night before, which told me that heavy drinking was involved. Maybe I'd assaulted someone. Maybe I'd robbed someone. Maybe I'd destroyed the pub. Maybe it was a combination of all three, or something far worse.

It was only then that I considered that maybe Mr. Balk had sent the authorities after me. It only stood to reason that Paige had fled to him and told him what happened. She held her tongue when it was only her pride, but...but turning on Victoria was too much for her to bear. And I don't blame her one bit. But as one day turned into two, then three, then a week, I knew that no one was coming for me. Something had happened out there, and I was no longer wanted.

I think I confused the others in jail. I was wealthy, but hardly a gentleman. I was getting older, but I was still ruthlessly strong. I'd had a fine life and yet I understood very well how the criminal underground worked. I knew the slang, I knew the body language, I knew how to function. I didn't break down over my loss of status, I didn't beg to be freed, I didn't try to bribe my way out with money or favors. I took my situation and I rolled with it, the same way I had done for years.

The jailers were confused, too, I think, and while I was not confused by their confusion, I was still confused within my soul. I'd always hated jailers, always blamed them for a variety of things going wrong in my life. I'd held no respect for them, and I'd fought them at every turn, whether I was drunk or sober.

This time around, I felt no such hatred for them, not even a petty annoyance. I wouldn't say that I respected them, individually, because they could still be pricks, but I knew now that they were just doing their jobs. By and large, their actions were actually reactions to our behavior. Some were still pricks drunk on their own power, but on the whole, they just did a dirty job overseeing wretched people, all so they could take care of their own families. They weren't out to get us per se; they had no real vendettas of their own. They just went to work and did a job. The same way I went to the bank to do a job to take care of my family. I didn't care about the regular patrons.

It was about two weeks or so before I learned of my fate in the outside world. First of all, I had been arrested for drunken brawling. I'd destroyed most of a pub and delivered severe bodily harm to half a dozen men, one of them a constable, before they could get me down. In the past, such a thing would have delighted me to know that I was that strong and so feared. Listening to the tale while speaking to one of the jailers, I just felt sick. It hurt me to know that any human being was capable of such a thing, but it twisted my stomach to know that *I* was that human being. I had always been that human being. I had no redeeming qualities in my life. Or if I did, I'd never used them for good, only my own selfish gain.

But aside from that, Paige had taken Victoria and run to her father. She'd told him the whole story. When word got to him that I was in jail, he'd bribed the courts and the jail warden to keep me here until such time as Paige's divorce could be finalized—with blessing from the Church, I might add—and all my assets could be redistributed. I will mention that Mr. Balk bribed the courts with my money and Paige would get everything she wanted. Everything else was being auctioned off or disposed of. I knew in advance that when I walked out of jail, I would be no better than when I'd first entered England, with nothing but the clothes on my back.

The big difference now, though, was that there was no chance of me regaining my wealthy status. I knew Balk would have eyes and ears out for me everywhere. If he even got a sniff that I was crawling my way out of the gutter, he would be on me like a cat on a mouse. While bankers and investors competed, there was also a certain brotherhood among them, so that if I tried anything, even in another man's territory, he would know, and I would incur the wrath of all the bankers. Plus, with how much Balk had expanded his influence—due not in small part to my efforts—it was likely that I wouldn't be able to go anywhere in the British Isles without him knowing about it. He was also starting to gain influence in world markets: Paris, China, New York. I couldn't go anywhere in the world without his knowledge. It terrified me, that all my hard work...I'd lost it all, and it was all my fault. I had no one to blame but myself.

I wept. In jail, crying is reserved for women and men who wish to be beaten or sexually assaulted. With my known strength, the other inmates weren't sure how to treat me. The one who did try anything was...well, I shall only say that he was dealt with and I had no further problems for the duration of my stay.

But still I wept. I am ashamed to admit that I did not weep for Paige or Victoria, or if I did, it was not in sadness. They were better off without me, without living in fear of me and what I might do. As much as I despised the man and the man despised me, Mr. Balk would ensure their health and well-being, and he would be able to more stably and predictably support them financially. He may not have been able to show love—indeed, I wonder if he knew what such a phenomenon even was—but for the bare necessities of life, he could provide for them without the terror I had exercised over them.

Instead, I wept for myself, wretched man that I am. I wept, not because I had lost everything, but because it was my own stupid fault. I wept because everything that had led me to that point was entirely preventable, if only I'd had more self-control. If only I'd been less selfish. For years I had justified myself, saying that I had no control over it, that my beast left me no choice, but I knew, always, deep down, that it wasn't true. I always had a choice. It may have been more difficult for me than, say, for my pa, but I always had a choice. I was responsible for my own actions. No one forced me to do anything, and my body did not move of its own volition. It was all me. Every time.

Owain paused and took a breath. "If God is all-knowing, then He must have known it would come to this. Why didn't He stop me?" He continued before Forthill could speak. "I know, we've talked about this before, but I have little else to think about in my cell. I understand His ways are mysterious, but do you really think any good could come of this?"

"The Lord works all things together for good for those who love

Him," Forthill recited.

"But what of the rest of us? I obviously didn't love Him. At this point, I wouldn't know how. I don't know that Paige or Mr. Balk or anyone loved Him. They went to Mass, but is that the same? They always seemed more interested in the bank than the Church."

"God will judge their souls."

"And you think there is still a chance to save mine?"

"If you choose it, yes."

"Would God already know whether I would say yes or no? If He already knows that I would, does that count if I were to fall over dead right now? Or would it simply be like tripping at the finish line of a race? I was obviously going to win, but then I fell and broke my ankle. Oh well, it doesn't count. Does God judge that way? Would He extend that last bit of mercy upon me, knowing that I was heading in the right direction and almost there?"

Forthill frowned. "I think you are making it more complicated than it needs to be."

"As I said, I have little else to consider in my cell."

I spent a little over three months in jail, almost four months. When I walked out, I had only a handful of change and the clothes on my back. I had no name, no titles, no home, no family, no contacts, no wealth, no assets of any kind. I had only what was on my immediate person. In a way, it made things very simple, because then I knew what I had. Which was nothing.

I'd been told that Balk had a blanket restraining order on me. I couldn't get close to him, his family—and by extent, my family, though Paige had divorced me and taken Victoria with her to her new husband, who was now listed as Victoria's father—any of his banks, and some of the major businesses he was invested in. If I did get too close, I would be taken back to jail. In a way, that almost sounded pretty good. I already had an impressive criminal record, so it was nothing new to me. I couldn't go anywhere, had nothing to my name, so I wasn't losing anything. At least in jail I would have a roof over my head, and meals, while few and far between, were more regular than trying to steal on the streets which would only land me back in jail anyway.

For a while, I considered returning to Wales and seeing how my parents fared. I didn't know quite what I would tell them. Maybe that Paige had gone to another man. Maybe that she'd divorced me because of some pagan ways. I came up with a number of vague lies and half-truths, but I always discarded them. For one, Paige knew who they were and where they lived. I had little doubt that Balk would threaten them in some way if necessary. I wasn't sure why he would pay them any mind at all, but such was the state of my own mind.

For another reason, it was dishonest, and it made me ill to think about. I was still a bit leery of my pa, but the thought of lying to my ma and causing her more pain was more than I could bear. To that end, I decided to just not go back. Maybe I would stay away forever, maybe my thoughts would clear up later on, I really couldn't know at the time.

I suppose, deep down, there was one strain of my rage that fed off of my economic circumstances. Farming provided, but it was not a glamorous lifestyle. One good drought or the sweep of disease could ruin a family. Hell, the Irish are still living it. A bit of my rage fed off that prospect, that delusion, of being poor. There was always a part of me that thought more money, better stuff, could make some of it better. Not all of it, because I still enjoyed the dominance and the fighting and the drinking, but having the wealth to fund my blasphemous lifestyle and maybe have enough to pay to turn a few heads, that was not entirely out of the question.

I'd worked my way up. I had practically been given the keys to a great banking empire, or a fairly good portion of it, anyway. But my rage was not satisfied. That line of hunger simply redirected to some other thing to brood about. It found some other thing to cry foul upon, cry that it was unfair, that I was somehow a victim. I had everything I needed, everything my parents and my siblings could have ever wanted, and I squandered it away like...like the damn Prodigal Son. I'd lived like a king, and soon I found myself dining with swine.

I didn't understand it. I didn't like it. I hated myself with such fervor, I picked several fights that I thought would kill me. Apparently I'd either become too good or else I hadn't gotten as old as I thought because I still won. And I carried on.

I'm sure there are official documents out there that could tell you, but I don't know how much time I spent on the streets. Couldn't have been more than a couple months, when all was said and done. It felt like longer. A lot longer.

Years had gone by since I'd been unsure of where I was going to sleep, or what I was going to eat. Years had passed since I'd had only one option to choose from—whatever I could find. I slept in alleys, on the street itself if I had to. I scavenged for what I needed, stole the rest.

Several times, I considered finding work. Maybe I could at least go back to digging ditches or sewer pits or something, make some money and rent myself a room again. The problem was, in just the few years that I'd been rich enough to not need that work, there had been such an influx of immigrants that there was no work left for me. Worse than that, most of those whom I'd worked for remembered me, and they didn't like me very much. Even if they'd had openings, they said, they wouldn't give me a job.

I was able to get some work, a few passing day jobs, nothing concrete. Most of it was the dangerous, life-threatening stuff. As I said, a lot of employers remembered me, and not in a good way. They gave me a task hoping I would fall to my death, be crushed, or otherwise perish. When I didn't, they only gave me half the wages they promised, and the starting wage was a pittance to begin with. I couldn't save much, between what I needed to eat and my alcoholism. Shelter seemed like a distant memory.

O wain rubbed his eyes. "Sometimes I wondered if I didn't simply dream up my entire rich life. Perhaps I'd passed out drunk, hit my head, and just imagined this lavish lifestyle I'd thought I'd lived."

Forthill nodded slowly. "It is rather stunning how quickly we humans forget where we have come from, and it goes both directions, rich to poor or poor to rich. It is also stunning how quickly we can adapt to various circumstances, if we allow ourselves to. Clinging too tightly to a particular lifestyle can be a form of idolatry."

"Well, then, I must be a saint because I just...went with it. I had no other choice."

I had no choices, no steady work, no friends. No one even really feared me anymore. I mean, they did if I turned on them for some reason and got physical, but my mere presence no longer inspired fear or submission. No one listened to me. No one cared. I was poor and weak even among those who are, by and large, poor and weak. It was humiliating. More than once I considered killing myself. Not a few people told me to do it.

I f evil people kill themselves, is it still a sin, or is it a mercy to the rest of the world? If God was orchestrating to kill a man, but he took his own life instead, does God get offended?" Owain wanted to shift his ankles, find some way to relieve the pressure of the shackles, but could not find a position that worked.

Forthill sighed resignedly. "May I confess something to you, Owain?"

Owain gave the priest a look. "It would be the first time anyone has ever asked. I feel obligated to say yes."

"I have heard many confessions in my time. I must say that I find you to be very thoughtful, introspective, and curious about the greater mysteries of our world—"

"Took me long enough to get there."

"—and I must confess that many of your questions challenge me. Honestly, I am often uncertain how to answer them. Some of them I really don't know an answer, for the simple fact that it would mean knowing the mind of God, which I do not. But your curiosity and desire to know, I believe, is a good thing. It makes you aware of greater things, even as you face your own death. Your soul has not rotted nor disintegrated, but only the Lord can make it fresh and new again before you die."

Owain searched the old priest's gaze, looking for some indication of mockery. He found only sincerity. "I want to believe you."

"Don't believe me," Forthill said gently. "Believe the Lord. Trust in Him. Don't waste an opportunity that may not come again. You understand that we are not guaranteed tomorrow."

"I know," the prisoner murmured. "And maybe the warden and the gaolers are right, that I am still selfish and arrogant. But I think even you might have something more to say about me once I finish my tale. Because now we've come to the part where I murdered six men. And I was completely sober."

The priest did not respond for a long moment, and when he did, it was with a change of subject. "I understand that the tale becomes more difficult to tell, the closer it comes to this point. I can see plainly that you are ashamed and uncomfortable with it. Perhaps we ought to save this part for the next time we meet. We will have more time then, as the hour now grows late. You will also have time to reflect and pray and consider your words."

Owain knew the priest probably meant well, but he wasn't so great at hiding his feelings himself. Forthill was equally as uncomfortable by the prospect, intimated even. Many bad men came through Beaumaris, but few stories were as chilling as one man killing six, especially considering the details.

He nodded. "Perhaps. I'm afraid I don't know too many prayers, though."

"If you are sincere enough, pomp and circumstance are not necessary, and God will hear you regardless," Forthill assured him.

It was small comfort as the gaoler took his cue to descend upon Owain and jerk his chains a bit. Owain stumbled to his feet, ankles aching, feet numb. He could barely lift his feet and almost could not walk up the steps. Still the gaoler pushed, prodded, pulled, and cursed at him. Owain tripped on the top step and went to all fours, palms slapping painfully on the stone. He went to the ground as the gaoler stepped on him to get over him, then forcibly pulled him upright and dragged him the last short distance to his cell.

Mercifully, all of his shackles were removed. When the door slammed closed, he wept silently just out of sheer relief, his sliver of happiness in the darkness. He could feel his wrists and ankles—especially his ankles—begin to swell, but they were free nonetheless. He pulled himself onto the small bench he called his bed and forced himself to relax. He closed his eyes and slowed his breathing, though his mind remained active, as it usually did.

But this night, he did not pay mind to the rats as they scuttled in the shadows. He did not pay mind to the darkness or the imaginary layout of his cell. He did not pay mind to the aching of his body. He did not pay mind to any of the noises outside and hope against all hope that a slant of light might find its way in. All of these things, which normally swirled through his thoughts in an endless torrent of demonic torture, were now but background noise. Not silent, but dull to the senses.

Grunting and groaning, Owain slid to the floor with less grace than the rats, collapsing to the ground, almost unable to catch himself but for the sheer strength of his arms. His feet were useless, knees sore, hands limp. Gradually, he got his body back under him in some semblance of a kneeling position.

"God?" he began, then stopped.

Would God listen to him? Did he have to wait in line or wait for God to answer in some way to let him know He was listening? Would his prayers end up on the bottom of a stack of other prayers from other people? Was he just not important? If Forthill was already praying for him, did that make his prayers unnecessary? Surely the priest had a better in than him. Should he just not interject himself and let the priest bargain for his soul, tell God how sincere he was? Was he sincere? Would God know whether he was sincere even if he himself wasn't sure? Would he get credit for trying, or would that be selfish and arrogant? Was it proper to pray for himself? He wasn't asking to be delivered from the noose; he knew he well deserved it. But everything else...

Hell, what else was there? He was in prison sentenced to hang. There was nothing else. He had nothing else. He had nothing coming but death and whatever lay beyond.

"God, I don't know how to do this," he began again, finding that he was moving his lips and thinking his prayer more than saying it out loud. "I don't know how to pray. I don't know how to talk to You. Paige and her family recited prayers, but I don't think they really believed in them. My ma and pa tried to get me to pray, to memorize prayers. I still have the story of Cain and Abel memorized, and I remember my ma saying something about praying Scriptures. I don't know if Cain and Abel would be the best choice, though. Maybe it would, since I killed a man. Six men, actually. If I'm praying, no use trying to lie. You know what I did.

"And God...God I did a lot of things I'm not proud of. You've probably got a whole list of things up there. The murder was just the finish line, but my whole race was filled with lying, cheating, stealing, drinking, beating up as many men as I could just to prove my worth, as if it mattered. I'm not worth much now, I think, except whatever it costs to make a short length of rope. Maybe the cost of the daily meals. And that's just because they have to.

"Did You pull any strings when I got sentenced here? Because I know I shouldn't be here. As far as prisons go, this is pretty nice, actually. Or so I'm told. The better prisoners get to go outside, but at least I get food once a day. But the amenities don't matter too much to a dead man. Maybe you brought me here to meet Father Forthill. Is that it? He seems to think he can save my soul. I don't know, maybe he can. I'm talking to You, aren't I? Never thought I'd be doing that. Never thought You'd listen.

"So did You really go through all this trouble just to save my soul? Surely there could have been other ways. I don't understand what demons possessed me as a child, but couldn't You have stopped them? Teo turned out all right; I know I would have, too, if I'd been a normal son, the good firstborn that my ma and pa always hoped for. Was it really necessary for me to hurt and kill so many people just so I could kneel here to talk to You and ask forgiveness? Forthill says You work in mysterious ways, and I have to agree because I am lost and confused. I don't understand."

Owain stopped. He wasn't sure if his eyes were open or closed, and he blinked intentionally several times just to be sure. He didn't know where he was going with this, honestly. He sounded like a mad rambler, even to his ears. Was it better to be a sober murderer or an insane one? Would he walk up to the gallows, babbling like a lunatic? Had his last meeting with the priest truly been his last opportunity to save his soul before madness overtook him?

He shook his head. "I don't know where I'm going with this," he went on. "I kind of feel like I'm having a one-sided conversation, just talking to the darkness. I'm not asking for a miracle. I'm not asking for an earthquake to split the walls and splinter the doors that I could walk free. I am beyond that now. I am no wrongfully-imprisoned saint. I am a rightfully-imprisoned sinner. And, once Forthill is done with me, I will walk up the steps to the gallows and be hanged for my crimes.

"I'm not asking for a miraculous deliverance, though dying in my sleep does sound more appealing than a short drop and a sudden stop. If I did have one request, it might be that my death is painless, that I don't struggle." He let out a breath. "But would it really matter, if I am only destined for eternal torture and the lake of fire? I don't know.

"I don't know how anyone could say that You still love me, that this has been some elaborate plan to win my soul back from the Devil. Or maybe the Devil has had me all along and this really is my only chance to save myself. Is that selfish of me? Is it Your will?

"Anyway, I don't know what I'm asking for. I don't know why I'm talking to You. Escape is out of the question, I think. But we're all destined to die eventually, are we not? Forgiveness, maybe? Perhaps, if I could believe that You would want me after all that I've done. Maybe just one last drop of mercy before I go."

He ended abruptly, confused and annoyed with himself. That was no way to talk to God, rambling on like a fool. God had probably turned away from him halfway through and gone back to the more important prayers, like Father Forthill's. Those were easily more sincere and more well-articulated. Those were prayers worth listening to; even Owain could see that.

"Amen, I suppose," he sighed, electing to end his pseudo-prayer before he embarrassed himself even more, though the only one to be embarrassed in front of was God Himself, and that was probably the worst part. But that was assuming God was paying attention to him at all.

Limbs still weak, Owain managed to crawl back onto the bench, pushed several rats off onto the floor in the process. He couldn't quite stretch out all the way, so he turned on one side and brought his knees up. As he lay there, he saw that there was some form of light sneaking in under the door. It flickered and waved a bit. It wasn't bright enough to be a torch or a large lantern. If he had to take a guess, he might have thought that someone had lit a candle and put it outside his door.

CHAPTER ELEVEN

THE MURDERER

Owain felt sick to his stomach as he walked into the chapel and saw Forthill waiting there as he always was. He hadn't needed to stay up at night thinking about what he was going to say, trying to put the memories back together. Indeed, he'd never forgotten. The memories had never left him, hadn't faded or distorted with time. It took only the tiniest bit of effort for him to pull that night to the forefront of his mind. And as he lay in his cell, dreading this encounter, it hadn't taken any effort at all. Indeed, the memories had come back unbidden, haunting him all night, waking and sleeping.

"I'm told that you were permitted to go outside for a spell this afternoon," Forthill greeted amiably, though his posture spoke of uncertainty and a touch of anxiety. Owain knew how he felt. Still, he nodded.

"Yes. It was...nice. To see the sky."

"You don't sound overly enthusiastic."

"I am a small man in a cage. What right do I have to behold God's creation?"

"Because you are part of it still. And you are His child, whatever anyone tells you. Just as your daughter may have had her name changed, but she would always be your daughter."

"Would," Owain murmured. "Because she's gone now."

Forthill frowned. "You knew this day was coming."

After a long moment, the prisoner sighed and said, "Yes. Maybe I'd hoped it wouldn't. Maybe I'm still clinging to some feeble hope of life. If the story kept going, maybe I would be allowed to live. But it's not going to happen. A day, maybe two or three, to finish the tale. And then I hang."

"That's right. But you shall suffer no more, and you will be with our Lord."

"Yes, but for how long?"

"Forever, if you choose it."

"After today, do you think He would still accept me?"

The priest tilted his head. "Mr. Fforidd, we are only reciting the past. Telling the tale again will not change the Lord's mind."

"No, but it might change yours about whether or not I can be saved."

Forthill said nothing to that, just made a motion for Owain to begin.

I'd learned very quickly that Paige had remarried. His name was Frederick Travis. He was a close associate of Mr. Balk and his banking business. Now, I knew banking well enough, but I knew people better. My gut always told me that he was looking for a way to dethrone Balk from inside, take over the business and inherit his own empire without having to do any work. I think Balk knew that, too, and that was why he let me marry his daughter instead of Travis. I was less of a threat to the business.

That wasn't to say Travis wasn't a threat in other areas. He was physically imposing, not quite as big as me, but he could give me a run for my money if he put his mind to it. I can tell you now that he never did. He also enjoyed alcohol, but like most fine men, he only drank fine alcohol. You would never see him in a common pub, but he had a drinking tray in every room of his home and a bottle in his jacket at all times. His nose was always cherry, and I don't know that his eyes were ever not red. But still, he did his work and he did it well, or well enough for Mr. Balk I suppose. Look at me, and you might think his standards weren't too high.

But I digress. Travis only kept up on the latest fashions because either his mother, his sister, or his new wife badgered him about it and told him how to dress. It wasn't that he couldn't afford it or that he didn't care to keep up with the fashions, but his attention was often focused more on the bank and his money and how he could acquire more of it. Everything else was secondary. I daresay that his list of priorities went as follows:

money, alcohol, everything else. The only real difference between me and him, other than he was born into money and I had acquired it, was that my priorities put alcohol first and money second.

I can't say how long I'd been out of jail when I got the news. It wasn't so much that anyone sought me out to give me the news, so much as the news was so big that it was inevitable that I would hear it eventually. And of course, there were variations and contradictory details and any number of little rumors that sprang out of it before it reached me. It took me a while to piece things together, but I did. I don't know whether I would have been better served not knowing.

Ultimately, it came down to the fact that Frederick Travis was no better than I. He'd been born into money, I had acquired it, but we both loved alcohol and money more than anything else, even Paige. Travis hadn't waited a week before hitting Paige. She'd denied him sex because of her cycle and she was in pain. I'd gotten that excuse often enough, and most of the time it was true. But he hit her and went to have a drink. The next time she denied him, he hit her and then forced her to pleasure him. The third time, he simply raped her.

Paige went to her parents and tried to tell them, but they dismissed her. For one, Travis was a born and bred Brit, not some country ruffian from a filthy, pagan people. She ought to have more respect for him. And on that, she also ought to learn to rein herself in and her wild, outlandish attitudes, and attend to her family. She would do well to have a child by him. Clearly one child wasn't keeping her busy enough since she still felt the need to cause trouble.

Now, I have to pause here and say that...just this news alone was enough to infuriate me. In a way, I did still love Paige. Quite honestly, I still do love her, if that is even possible. I know that it is wretchedly hypocritical of me to say so, but any man who touched my wife like that deserved a good thrashing by my hand. I wanted to make him squeal like a pig. I wanted to break every bone from his shoulders to his fingertips and then break his cock. I wanted to do unspeakable things to him just as he had done unspeakable things to Paige.

But then the news got worse. One night, they had been arguing something fierce. Both the cook and the maid attested to vicious screaming that should have only belonged to fighting alley cats. Both of them were yelling and throwing things; Victoria was utterly inconsolable, screaming despite the staff's best efforts to keep her quiet.

Finally, Travis—who was wildly drunk—got fed up with the arguing, and he'd run out of things to throw except the broken pieces of everything that had been hurled and broken so far. So he grabbed Paige around the throat, mid-scream, and squeezed. She choked. She jerked. She tried to pry his hands off her. Then she went limp. According to the maid, even after she went limp, he gave another final, definitive squeeze and crushed her windpipe. Then he opened his hands and just let her slump to the floor.

Victoria was still crying. The maid even had a rag pressed over her face to try and muffle the sound, but to no avail. Travis turned his sights on her.

Owain choked a sob and stared at nothing for a long moment. Another sob. He wiped his eyes and took a shuddering breath. He put one hand weakly out in front of him.

"He snatched Victoria out of her arms, put one hand around...her throat...and he just...squeezed." Another sob. "And he just held her there. For over a minute." He sniffed. "Then he squeezed again, just to be sure." A shuddering breath. "And he let her fall to the floor. The maid ran. All the staff did. They ran and reported the incident to the police."

He broke down. His chains echoed in the chapel as his whole body shook. He couldn't stop, and he wasn't sure he wanted to. He'd always known what had happened, and yet it was the first time he'd ever really grieved. For them. He'd wept for himself plenty of times, but never for Paige and Victoria. He'd never actually cried over his wife and child. Until now. That realization only renewed his sorrow and he continued to weep until he couldn't breathe and became light-headed. When he looked up, chest heaving, he could hardly bring the room into focus. Something was held out to him and he blindly reached for it. A cup of water. His first instinct was to guzzle it down, but his first drink ended up in his lungs and he spent another few seconds coughing it back up.

At long last, he was able to drink the water and calm down. The chapel was dead silent for a long minute.

"Tell me, Father," Owain whispered, barely audible, "what good purpose does this serve in the Lord's mysterious plans? Is my soul really worth their lives? Was there no other way to get my attention? What purpose does this all serve?"

Forthill's cheeks were wet, Owain saw, though the man had wept silently. He did not appear to be done, either, as his words were also soft. "I don't know. I wish I did. I wish I could tell you what the Lord has in store, what He sees, but I cannot. I wish I understood it myself. If I did, maybe I could explain it to my superiors and —"

"And commute my sentence? Keep me from hanging? To what end? Why do you bother with mercy? There is no mercy in the world. And the only justice is the justice we make for ourselves. No one was going to prosecute Frederick Travis for the deaths of his wife and child. Why? Because he was rich. He was influential. Mr. Balk wouldn't have it, however much he may have wanted it."

"And why not, I wonder? You've portrayed Balk as a very shrewd businessman, but he was still a family businessman, was he not?"

Owain might have shrugged, but his shoulders were too tired.

The common folk always know what's really going on, but the upper crust have to save face. If Balk went wildly public with the story and made a show of prosecuting Travis like he had me, it would be more of a taint on his business. It would mean his associates were insane, drunkards, brawlers, heathens, volatile, and untrustworthy. No one would want to do business with him. And, without an heir, he had nothing left but his business. If that went under, he would be a pauper on the street in no time. Furthermore, with his daughter marrying two insane men, he would be viewed as senile, too easily fooled to have given his blessing to these marriages. How much better could he be in business? What if he took foolish, unnecessary risks? And you can see how it all goes back to his reputation.

The official story came through the newspapers about a week later. First, it derided the entire staff as insane liars. They didn't know what they really saw and they'd made the whole thing up. They were paid a handsome sum to keep silent and quietly released of their employment. Of course, they only stayed away from the newspapers, but the common folk heard the true account, which is how I heard about it.

Second, the story stated that I—the drunken, pagan ex-husband—had broken into their residence in a fit of drunken rage, looking for my wife and child whom I was supposed to stay away from. Things got heated. The yelling everyone heard actually came from me and Paige having an argument, and her calling for her new husband. I killed her, strangled Victoria to keep her quiet, and there was only a minor scuffle between me and Travis before I ran off.

I think what makes that the hardest to bear," Owain said, "is that it is entirely plausible. I was a drunkard, a fighter. I'd beaten Paige multiple times. She'd only come forward because I turned on Victoria, so who is to say what could have become of that if we had stayed together? It wasn't what really happened, but it would be so easy for the upper crust to believe."

Forthill's brows knitted together. "And was Balk going to really continue to employ the man he knew for a fact—even if he tried to hide it publicly—who killed his only living child and grandchild?"

Owain shook his head. "That was the third part of the official story. Frederick Travis was so grieved by the incident that he would be taking a leave of absence from Balk Banking and Investing, perhaps pursuing other employment opportunities elsewhere."

The priest shifted position. "I still have a hard time believing that Balk would just let him walk away, reputation or no."

"You want to know my opinion? I think he would have waited a couple weeks, then set him up to be murdered. He could hire someone and then blame it on me, say that I had come back to finish what I'd started. With that, he would be rid of his daughter's murderer and then he would use Travis' murder as the launching point for a manhunt for me to lock me up for good so he wouldn't have to worry about my whereabouts anymore, if he even was. He could have done it immediately, with the publication of the official story, but the fact that he didn't told me that he wasn't done using me—or at least my name—just yet."

Owain studied Forthill for just a second. The priest seemed slightly intrigued, as if he hadn't considered such possibilities. Owain had spent too long looking out for himself, and too long learning the inner workings of the elite social class, not to believe that someone was always going to use you for something. There was no such thing as a free dinner.

"I'm curious," the priest began slowly, "did you consider all of this...?"

"Before or after I killed them?" the prisoner finished. "Honestly, I did consider this all beforehand. I got my information and sorted it all out over the course of a few days. And I thought it was a little odd that I hadn't already been apprehended. I didn't make myself known, but I was not actively attempting to hide, either. And it wasn't as though I had many friends who were willing to lie for me and help conceal my whereabouts. A few questions would have brought the police right to me. So when the 'preliminary' official story came about, I was able to piece things together."

Your next question is going to be, why did I do it then? Well, there are a few reasons. One, it was only a theory. I considered it a very educated guess, but it was still only a guess. I had no way of knowing for sure whether Balk would hire someone to kill Travis. That leads me into reason two, which was, as far as I was concerned, the only person who had that right to vengeance, was me. Travis killed my wife and daughter, so I wanted to be the one to kill him. That leads into reason three which was how disgusted I felt about the whole thing. Travis was going to skate public humiliation and a hanging because Balk didn't want to lose face. He was more concerned about his business than seeing his daughter's killer receive his due.

You may have already guessed that Balk was not as clean as he would have anyone believe. Of course, few people trust bankers. Balk was not above dirty tactics when it needed to be done. Most often, it was just a little political and industrial maneuvering to squeeze his opponents. I looked away for the simple fact that I was hardly in a position to lecture Balk about morality and interpersonal or business relationships.

But now it really bothered me. The man was going to help Travis slip through the cracks of justice. Even if he did exact his own revenge in some way, it just wasn't right. And no, the irony is not lost on me. But this was my wife and child. If anyone was going to avenge them, it was going to be me. And I was going to make sure that they could not harm anyone ever again—in bad business practices, in normal life, criminally, in any way ever again. If I did nothing else in my life, I was going to stop them.

As I said, the irony is not lost on me, and you can save your lecture about vengeance belonging to the Lord. I am fully aware now, and I was fully aware back then. But I had never been so sure of anything in my entire life, as I walked down that street toward Balk's house, that I needed to kill him. I needed to kill them both.

How can one distinguish between righteous killing and murder?" Owain wondered. "The Bible is full of people killing each other. Sometimes it's blessed and sometimes it's not. If it is God's will for a man to die, is the executioner still on the hook for murder? Is that still a sin? If we reach Judgment Day and discover that by killing Balk and Travis and all of them, that I saved millions of lives in the future, am I still condemned for those murders? How does God judge man so?"

"I'm afraid I don't know," Forthill answered honestly. "I do not presume to know the mind and the workings of the Almighty, only that they are pure and just."

Owain let out a breath.

"What happened next?"

I walked down the street that night. It was late, dark, candles in some windows but most dark. In the slums, the night life was in full swing with pubs and brothels, much drinking and carousing. But in the upper class neighborhoods, everything and most everyone had settled in for the night. The streets were empty and the night was peaceful and even clear, one of those rare nights it wasn't so foggy you couldn't see your hand in front of your face.

I walked up the steps of the Balk household. I knew how many steps there were, knew that there was a loose stone on the second step and so I avoided the spot where one might naturally step, instead sliding my foot to the left. I knew that Balk's butler, Brigsby, was fiercely loyal to his employer and would not only alert Balk to my presence, but undoubtedly send for the police at once. I knocked on the door and heard the butler's purposeful stride approach the door.

Before the man even had a chance to recognize me, I punched him first in the throat to shut him up, then cracked my forehead into his. It dazed me momentarily, but it knocked him out. I could have killed him, but I had no reason. He simply did his job. And he always did it well.

I didn't actually know the men were having a meeting that night. I'd thought I was going to have to hunt them down one-by-one, go to each house individually and take them out. And, honestly, I'd only intended to kill Balk and Travis. The others I had no qualms with. But once the blood started flowing, I couldn't stop myself.

They were in Balk's study. Six of them. Balk was at the head of the table. He was a fine man, and his wife always kept him dressed just as well. He was slight, not very strong, shorter than me. He kept his mustache neatly trimmed and impeccably groomed. I always thought his nose and cheeks a bit misshapen, his jaw a bit too prominent. His shoulders were too sharp, chest too narrow, hips too skinny, knees too knobby. He just wasn't a handsome man except for his money.

Travis, as I said, he was one of the few who might have had a chance against me if he had any clue how to use his size and strength. He was not a particularly handsome man either, his eyes and cheeks a bit droopy on account of the alcohol.

His lawyer was Dan Smith, a beak-nosed man who was all limb and...nothing more. His fight came from his intelligence, but he was physically poor, at least as far as I was concerned. I'd only met him once and seen him a handful of times at the bank. Bankers and lawyers have a bit of a love-hate relationship.

The other three men were simply associates, bankers like Mr. Balk. If he trusted anyone, it would be these men. George Willis, Thomas Taylor, and Henry Billings. While they worked very closely with Balk, they still understood that he was the one in charge, and they worshiped him. Whatever he bid them, they would do, without question, without hesitation. Likely, they were included in the meeting so they knew what story was going to be perpetuated in the home bank itself, but also the branch banks, the smaller banks he owned, and all his investing partners, his clients, everything. When the little men started asking around and maybe started questioning their decision to do business with Balk, those three would be ready to answer all questions, assuage all fears, and win their loyalty even more in some way.

Balk was the closest to the door. He was not the first one to see me, but he was the first to make a motion, standing and calling for Brigsby to throw me out or call the police.

I'd brought a knife with me. The next thing I knew, it was buried in Balk's throat. Blood gushed from the wound, from his mouth and nose, over my hand and arm. I ripped the knife out and watched Balk slump to the floor. You know, I still remember his face. No, not his face. His eyes. Those sightless eyes, staring at me. I swear to Almighty God Himself that Balk's eyes still saw me, still watched me. In the moment, it was just a detail, but now it haunts me and makes me nauseous.

The rest of the men began to panic and tried to flee. Smith, the lawyer, had been sitting directly to Balk's right. I caught him by the collar of his shirt. He was so small and so light. I smashed his face into the table then cut his throat, blood pouring out over the table. I can still remember the pattern it made on the wood.

George Willis was the only one who actually tried to stand against me and brought a weapon. He had a knife, but he was clearly unskilled in how to use one. He made a wild swing at me, but I caught his arm. I wrenched his arm out of place at the elbow and the shoulder. He screeched in terror, but it was almost completely silent. I could see in his face that he knew it was painful and could probably feel it, but it hadn't fully registered yet. In his moment of shock, I twisted his body around and drove him forward into Thomas Taylor who may have also come to assail me. The knife pierced Taylor's chest and he went down. Then I took my knife and cut Willis' throat.

Henry Billings was cowering in a corner. I probably could have let him live, but in the moment, I didn't care. I already had four bodies. I was already going to hang. Billings was one of Balk's biggest boot-lickers. As far as I was concerned, he had to go. There was no greater punishment for me than what I had already incurred. I kicked him and he went sprawling onto his back. I cut his throat, one clean slice. He was dead before he could spit blood.

All that was left, then, was Frederick Travis. He wasn't cowering in the corner, but he was afraid, standing with his back against the wall. I could see from his darting gaze that he was trying to judge the odds of him making it past me and running out the door. His odds weren't looking so good, and we both knew it.

He didn't fight me when I plunged the knife into his chest. He never raised a hand to defend himself, even instinctively. He made no move whatsoever. I'd like to think that he understood why I was there, why I was doing this. I'd like to think he understood that this was justice coming for him and he couldn't escape it. But I'm probably being fanciful. If one murderer kills another murderer, is that justice, or a second murder?

I wrenched the knife out of his chest and cut his throat, just to be sure. He slumped to the floor, lifeless. And I stood there, in a room with six dead men. Six men dead by my own hand. Only one had really tried to stop me. The one who had a chance had never lifted a finger. And there I stood, drenched in blood. I was covered in it, all down my front, my arms. I took a white cloth and wiped my bloody face.

Those moments right after the murders are so vivid, but they feel like a dream. I remember suddenly feeling as though I could see the end of my life. I knew I had done something inexcusable. My life had ended. I would never return home to Wales. I would never see my parents again. I would never see London again. My whole life, my entire miserable existence, this soul of mine, wretched and battered, never amounting to much, was going to end in a cold stone cell. But this time around, it hadn't been some disembodied inner demon or other perceived or projected rage. I had deliberately chosen this. I had done this completely sober, in both body and spirit. Perhaps my beast knew my soul was now beyond saving and so it had left me to my own devices, uncaring of my fate as I was irrevocably damned. Who can know?

But it was with these thoughts in mind that I sat went to the desk and poured myself a glass of brandy and sat down at the table, right where Balk had been sitting not five minutes before. The chair was still warm.

A heavy silence settled over them. That was it. The story was basically over. Everyone pretty much knew what happened after that. His next stop, then, was the gallows.

"It's been a long day," Forthill said finally. "I think we should get some sleep."

"I've not gotten sleep since I got here," Owain commented absently.

"Is there more you wish to say about the matter?"

He shrugged. "There was the arrest, the trial, all of that. Hardly a story; it's fairly common knowledge, I should think."

"Perhaps. Did you want to speak of it anyway?"

Owain took a breath and slowly let it out. "I suppose. I will continue to narrate my story, perhaps even as I am walking up to the noose."

"Perhaps," Forthill echoed, his voice breaking. He cleared his throat. "Even so, try to sleep. And if you have not done so, pray to the Lord for salvation. As you draw breath, He hears you."

Owain did not respond as he stumbled to his feet and limped along behind the gaoler. This gaoler was not Cassius, but he had no illusions: they were all out for his blood. Might be that they would cast lots to see who would be the one to send him through the floor. A short drop and a sudden stop.

He was exhausted from the day, between going outside and recounting the story of tragedy and revenge. His heart twisted and his stomach lurched as he hobbled up the stairs and saw Cassius waiting for him outside his cell. This was unusual, and unusual almost always meant something bad was about to happen. The vengeful gaoler unlocked the cell door and heaved it open.

Neither Owain's wrists nor his ankles were unbound as he was pushed inside, falling on the floor on his side. But instead of the door swinging shut behind him, the smaller gaoler who had brought him from the chapel suddenly kicked him. Because of the angle at which he lay, it was little more than a harmless kick to the back of his thigh. Cassius, though, was not so merciful and instead gave him a kick to the stomach. Owain made an odd, strangled sort of sound as the air was forced from his lungs. Each gaoler got in one more kick before someone barked a command. In seconds, the door was slammed shut, the lock clicking.

The small gaoler had aimed his second kick right for Owain's balls, and it had struck true. Cassius then followed this with a kick that sort of glanced off his stomach and went up but couldn't quite hit him square in the jaw. It was just as well because the glancing blow hurt enough. A solid strike would have possibly broken his jaw.

After recovering somewhat from the kick to his manhood, Owain dragged himself onto the wooden bench. His movement was restricted because of his shackles, but that was fine. He could manage to curl up somewhat on the bench. He closed his eyes, knowing that sleep was far away.

BEAUMARIS GAOL

INTERLUDE

THE BEGINNING

Father Forthill waited a couple minutes before following the gaolers and Owain out of the chapel, making his way up the stairs, heading for the governor's office. He stopped abruptly when he got to the top. At first he couldn't process what he was seeing. Then he realized two of the gaolers were taking turns beating Owain in his cell.

"Stop this at once!" Forthill barked.

The gaolers immediately ceased their attack, slammed the door, and twisted the key in the lock. For a moment, the priest was afraid they would turn on him. Instead, they turned and walked away quickly, muttering loudly and laughing. Forthill wanted to say or do anything, but his tongue had been stuck to the roof of his mouth, and he simply stood there dumbly. He considered going to Owain's cell and speaking kind words through the door, but refrained. For one, he did not know what he would say. For two, likely Owain simply wished to sleep. He had a lot to think about. Forthill judged it best to leave it between him and God.

And the third reason, the one he elected to hide behind, was that Dillon emerged from his office at that moment.

"Something going on here?" he asked.

Forthill faced him. "Two of your gaolers were beating Fforidd in his cell."

"Ah." The warden seemed less concerned that the gaolers were beating a prisoner, and more concerned that the priest had witnessed it. "It will be dealt with." It was an empty promise, Forthill knew. "I presume it was me you were actually looking for up here?"

Forthill nodded and followed the warden back into his office. The fire had burned low and the tea had been replaced with whiskey. Nathan poured himself a glass but Forthill refused when offered.

"Are we nearing the end of this drama?" the warden inquired. "Can I set an execution date for him yet?"

"Just a few loose ends to tie up," the priest answered. "He did describe the murders to me tonight."

"And were they as grisly as I warned you?"

Forthill hesitated but nodded. "They were. It was chilling to listen to. I cannot imagine what demons torture him at night."

"Likely the same ones that will torture him in Hell."

"You do not believe he can be saved?"

Nathan raised a brow. "You believe that he can?"

"All who call upon the Name of the Lord will be saved. Not 'some,' not just those belonging to a particular people, but 'all.' Everyone. As long as Fforidd draws breath, he has another opportunity to be saved."

The warden frowned and shifted position in his chair. "I appreciate what you're trying to do, Father. And there are some instances where the Church has done a lot of good intervening for a convict. But don't you think you are taking things just a little too far in this case? Confession is good for the soul, but you've made this man practically a saint! Is that wise?"

"I am simply doing as the Lord has asked. Nothing more. Nothing less."

"I thought you would say something like that. Very well. How much longer do you think you'll need?"

The priest ran his tongue over his teeth. "Hard to say. He seemed to indicate that there was more he wished to say, but I don't know how much further he wishes to go. If he goes all the way to the end, he shall be reciting our first meeting and so begin the story over again in an endless loop."

The warden did not find this amusing. "Wrap this up quickly. The courts don't like how long this has gone on, regardless of what the Church and the chapels may say, and they're bringing it down on me. They, and the public, want Fforidd executed by the end of the year. And that's a lot more time than I thought they were going to give me."

"We're going into autumn, Nathan. Once the ground freezes, where will you bury him?"

"We won't. We'll sink him."

"But that's a wretched, disrespectful way—"

"We make do with what we have, Father. Once the soul departs the body, what is the body but a husk of dead flesh? Do you not teach that? Does it matter whether he is buried, sunk, or fed to the dogs? We will all rise again with our glorified bodies to be with the Lord, right?"

Forthill was stunned into silence. On the one hand, he was furious that the warden would disrespect a body. On the other hand, the warden wasn't supposed to use his own words and tactics against him. *Lord, forgive me, but...damn him!*

"Was there anything else you wished to say to me, Father?" Nathan inquired, his tone bored. "I'm almost finished with my paperwork, and I would appreciate getting some sleep. You likely need rest as well. It can be just as trying, listening to Fforidd's story, as it is telling it. I also hear a storm is supposed to move in this morning, so I would suggest you return to the chapel before the crossing gets choppy."

There was little the priest could say to contradict the warden. Forthill thanked Nathan for his time and saw himself out of the office, out of the gaol, and down to the ferry. The nights were becoming chilly as they turned the corner into autumn, and Forthill wished he'd brought a jacket instead of relying on the warmth of the day.

The water was calm when he got on the ferry, but even as they made the narrow crossing and reached the far shore, he could sense the shift in the weather. The water was just a little rockier, the wind just a little harsher. The ferryman made a comment about getting home quickly, which Forthill was obliged to do. The priest wished the ferryman safe travels before turning and departing for the chapel, now severely wishing for a jacket.

By the time he reached the chapel, the wind had picked up and the first drops of rain had just begun to fall. He ducked inside and immediately reached for the tea on the stove. He poured himself a cup and sat down at the table across from Worthington who merely watched him for a long minute.

"So, how was the story this evening?" In front of him, Worthington had set out his paper and ink.

"Frightening," Forthill confessed. "A tale of vengeance and blood, not safe for women and children to hear in detail. But as much as it frightens me, I can only imagine how fearful Owain must be...of himself. To know what he is capable of, what he has done."

"Sometimes the most frightening monster is the one we see in our reflection. But it also provides the opportunity to watch the transformation the Lord can work in our lives."

Forthill frowned. "I fear Owain still believes he is too far gone, that he did what he did because the Lord abandoned him to it and there is no redemption for him."

"We can only do our part," Worthington told him calmly. "It is the Holy Spirit who leads men to change, not any persuasive words from us." He picked up his pen and made a calligraphic loop on the page, testing the nib. "Now then, why don't you tell me everything?"

As soon as Forthill opened his mouth, words began pouring forth like a waterfall that could not be contained. Words and sentences, memories and experiences, all bubbling up like a spring from his mind and soul. Things he never thought he would remember he explained in vivid detail, just as Owain had. By the time he was halfway through, he spoke as though the memories were his own, as though he'd lived it, experienced it. As if he had killed those men.

It was a terrifying prospect to consider. As a boy, Forthill had helped his pa dress wild game or butcher the animals on the farm, but that was simply a task to be done so they could eat. There was little emotion involved. But to take the life of another man...for Forthill, it was simply unfathomable on any level. Even the thought of killing a man in self-defense was enough to make his stomach feel ill. Now he was recounting the tale of six murders, as if he himself had committed them.

He looked down at his hands, expecting them to be covered in blood, warm and sticky, mixed with dirt and grime from the streets, a knife in one hand, dripping with more blood. At some point, he stood and was walking about the room, calmly, slowly, reciting everything as if performing at an *eisteddfod*. Then he sat down and poured himself a drink. When he brought it to his lips, he expected to taste fine brandy, but instead found tea.

It was the taste of tea that dissolved the illusion. Forthill looked around. He was in the parsonage of the little country chapel, the one he shared with Father Worthington. The stove was in one corner, their mattresses moved to the far corner. They each had their own desk, and they sat at the table between them.

Worthington sat across from him, face as white as a new Catholic robe. His hand was clenched around his pen, knuckles also white. His eyes were huge and he was just staring at Forthill.

"And that's how it was," Forthill said. He wasn't sure what he'd just been saying, but he knew the story was done.

"Are you quite well?" Worthington asked, though he seemed to be asking himself as much as Forthill.

He nodded. "Yes, I suppose I am." He took a nervous drink of tea.

"And he told this story with a straight face," Worthington stated.

"He wept for his wife and daughter, but the murders...yes, he told it with a straight face."

The older priest let out a breath. "I'm sorry, but I...have a hard time reconciling it in my mind."

"I understand. And I would be remiss if I did not say that I did not have my doubts as well."

"Doubts about what?"

It wasn't as if Worthington couldn't guess, but he wanted Forthill to talk it out and put words to his thoughts.

"Doubts about whether he could really change, truly feel remorse and repent of his sins," Forthill said. "Whether he really is trying to just buy himself time by fooling me into thinking he had changed, that he really is like Saint Paul."

Worthington nodded. "I understand. But as everyone has seemed to enjoy pointing out: his soul will be judged by the Lord. We will not know how that conversation went until the Last Day when we see him again, for ill or for better."

Forthill sighed. "I know you are right, but the doubts remain. I don't want to see him walk up to the gallows without knowing I did all I could to bring him back to the light."

"You have talked to him, listened to him. You have advocated for kindness when he does not deserve it. You encourage him to repent of his sins, to accept responsibility for them but to also accept that there is no sin too great for the Lord to erase. These things are the Way of our Lord. The rest lies only in his own heart."

"I know you are right, but I still feel there is more I should be doing."

The older priest leaned back and folded his arms. "Is this coming from some prodding by the Lord, or your own ego, that you wish to say that you were the one who saved the vile murderer's soul?"

The younger priest blushed. "Perhaps my own ego. But I do not believe this is over just yet. I know for a fact that something has been left uncompleted. Some action undone or some words unsaid."

"Well, you have until the end of the year to find out, it seems. Perhaps there will be some new revelation as he finishes his tale."

Forthill opened his mouth to speak, but a yawn came out first. "Yes, perhaps. But I think sleep is of greater importance at the moment."

"Indeed."

Worthington gathered up his papers and added them to the pile, as he always did. Forthill's hand began to ache as he thought of having to transcribe them the following day. His heart twisted at the thought of the words he would have to write. He shook his head and tried to push it from his mind. He needed to get some rest and process everything that had transpired today.

It took him two days to transcribe Worthington's notes, and not because of the man's shaky handwriting. Forthill didn't remember explaining things in such gruesome, vivid detail, but here it was. He described the news of Paige and Victoria's deaths, and the dichotomy of stories that the bank circulated. In a way, he couldn't help but share Owain's sentiment toward the bank, or Balk anyway, that the man would be so much more worried about his business and public image that he would let his daughter's murderer go free in the public eye, then later have him killed to be rid of him and to frame his ex-son-in-law. It was utterly repulsive.

But it would do no good to get emotional about it now. Even if it might be considered righteous anger that justice was not done, it was in the Lord's hands now. All six of those men would have their souls—their actions and motives—judged by God Most High. There was nothing more for Father Forthill to do regarding them except to tell the true story.

Although, another thought occurred to him. What if Owain was lying? What if he really had killed his wife and daughter and blamed it on Travis?

Forthill mulled this over for a moment. What reason would Owain have to lie about it, though? Half the people already believed he did it. He already had six bodies behind him and the gallows in front. Did it matter if two more bodies were added? He would already be judged by history as a heartless killer. Would it really be that important to lie about killing his wife and child? Unless he thought that vengeance would justify him. Except he'd already admitted that four of the men didn't have to die; it was a matter of convenience.

No, he decided at last. Owain didn't kill his wife and daughter. He was telling the truth on that. Of that, Forthill was certain.

He finished transcribing the papers and leaned back from his desk, one arthritic hand rubbing the other. How he wished he could have a youthful body like Worthington, and the man was over a decade his senior. Forthill sighed. Well, there was little he could do about it, he supposed. If wishes were horses, beggars would ride. And prisoners would be free, and families would be reunited.

He sent his pages to a chapel in Caerdydd where they had choirboys and altar boys who could make more copies to send to the other chapels and the Church, all of them who were interested in Fforidd's tale. The number seemed to be growing each month. Well, the words this week were certainly a story to behold. Forthill briefly wondered whether the priests would let their younger choirboys read and transcribe these pages. Would this part of the story even reach the masses? If it did, how watered down would it have to be in order for it to be even mildly palatable?

But, he figured, the hardest part was over with. They'd gotten through the murder of Paige and Victoria and covered the murders of the six men. All that was left now was the trial and the sentencing. As

Fforidd had said, everyone knew that part. It had been the biggest news in all the United Kingdom. But Forthill was still interested in hearing Owain's side of the story. There was something left undone; he was sure of it. Maybe this would bring it out.

He slept fitfully and woke up Sunday morning feeling as though he hadn't slept at all. Grudgingly, he dragged himself upright and joined Father Worthington in morning prayers before breakfast. Then Worthington began preparations for Sunday service, and Forthill departed for the prison. This time, he remembered to bring a jacket. The day was slow to warm up, and he had a hunch that it would be chilly by the time he left.

For the moment, he simply enjoyed the walk. He did not particularly enjoy the cold that he knew was ahead, but he enjoyed watching the seasons change. Lush greenery turned into a sea of gold, and a placid sea transformed into a frothing monster beating upon rocky shoreline. Forthill found himself whistling as he approached the dock, and the ferryman gave him an odd look.

"A man who whistles his way into prison ought not to leave, methinks," the man said.

"Perhaps," Forthill said, taking his customary seat, "but what prison can contain a light heart that is filled with the joy of the Lord, awed by His creation?"

The ferryman said nothing, just raised a brow, loosed the line, and shoved off. The two of them rarely spoke beyond greetings and common pleasantries. The ferryman had his job to do, and he would do it. Forthill never thought the man took any pleasure in it except that it was steady, predictable work. Fishermen were at the mercy of the tides and the migration of fish. Ocean sailors were at the mercy of the weather and liable to never be seen or heard from again. But the prison ferry, well, that was something he could count on day in and day out. Forthill did not hold it against him.

They reached the island and the priest disembarked. There was only one dock here, and it was in sore need of repair. He made his way up the slope to the stone behemoth, hips and knees protesting the whole way. Maybe after Fforidd was hanged, he would voluntarily resign from this position. He could assist Worthington and take over once the older priest passed away. He just wasn't sure he could continue making this trek twice a week, especially through the winter.

He had no problem getting in, but then, that was never a problem. It was easy to get into prison. Getting out was much harder. Ignoring the smells and the sounds and the shadows that seemed to come from no solid body, Forthill proceeded to the chapel where he got himself set up and situated, then nodded to the gaoler to let the convicts in.

Chapter Twelve

The Defendant

I sat there in Balk's study all night. I drank some, slept a little, but mostly just sat there. I don't know that I felt anything or thought anything; I guess I was in shock. It was Mrs. Balk who found me in the morning. She screamed. I didn't move. She went and managed to rouse Brigsby and send him for the police. Knowing that this was the end for me, I took the brandy and went to sit on the front step. I drank until the police arrived and shackled me.

You know, one of the things that stands out the most about the immediate aftermath is that the brandy had no taste. I mean, I could physically taste it, but I felt nothing for it. I did not feel any fire in my belly, did not get drunk. I could have been drinking mother's milk for all I knew.

And I know what you are going to say. Revenge has no taste and is not satisfying. I know. And I won't say that after killing those men that I felt like things were going to be better in the world. Maybe they will, maybe they won't—as you said, only the Lord knows. But just for me, in my life, in my world, things were better. I felt as though something had finally been accomplished, brought to an end. All that remained was for me to discover my fate.

I've repeated many times how I was feared for my strength and brutality, but other than fighting in taverns, my criminal record was fairly tame. Trespassing, theft, things of that nature. I'd never really done anything violent, certainly nothing while I was sober, at least not until recently. And now I'd killed six men. After my last sentence for beating Paige and Victoria, perhaps it was only a natural progression. Say it this way, the only one who seemed surprised by it was me. The police, the jailers, they all sighed and nodded and resigned themselves to the case, like seeing a man hit the ground after jumping off a cliff. The result is inevitable.

Do you think that?" Owain wondered. "Was I just always destined for this? Has my life always been a waste?"

"I don't believe so, no," Forthill answered.

"What you believe and what is, may be two different things. What good have I contributed to society that says I was worth something?"

"You brought investment and industry to Wales."

"But is that a good thing? It's all English investment and English business. Have I only succeeded in bringing more English influence where it is not wanted? Am I traitor to my own people?"

The priest did not answer.

Because of my crimes, I was not placed near the common criminals while in jail. I had been strong and violent before, obviously, but murder somehow made me more dangerous than I had been. I was placed in my own cell and forgotten. I was given food maybe once or twice a week, water every other day if I was lucky. I don't really know how long I was there like that. Quite frankly, I don't know very much about the passage of time at all after the murders. I know it's been over a year, maybe closer to two years.

Finally, I was taken out of my cell and to another room to meet with the man they said was my lawyer. At first, I really couldn't understand why I got one or needed one. Lawyers only defended innocent men, tried to prove their innocence in court. I'd been found in the room with the men I killed. I was obviously guilty. Why was I meeting with this man?

Of course, this only speaks to my state of mind at the time. During my time as a banker, I met with plenty of lawyers, both as customers and on a professional level if the bank ever got into trouble. I knew that lawyers also defended guilty men and worked to get them off, or at least get the charges or sentences reduced. But in the moment, I didn't understand.

Another reason I didn't understand was because I was a Welshman, and this was an English lawyer. Why should he want to defend me? Why shouldn't he be pushing for greater charges and a more severe punishment? I don't know how much worse a punishment you can get beyond death, but I'm sure he could come up with something.

He asked me what happened that night, and I told him, similar to how I told you. I remember he turned pale and then he turned green, as if he couldn't handle a simple narrative of events. But I suppose not everyone is suited to the more unpleasant aspects of life. Maybe it was just me.

He left me alone after that, told me not to say anything, not a word. He left the room for a bit. He came back and said I would be taken back to my cell. We would be going to court in the near future. I did not say anything.

I didn't want to go to court. I didn't want to go to trial. I knew I was guilty, and even in the best circumstances, I was still going to die in prison. I would never be a free man again. I would never see the outside world again. The only thing left to me was my memories, few good ones though I had. But I had nothing coming. I still have nothing coming. Even the good memories have begun to fade, and I wonder whether those times even existed or if maybe I simply dreamed them up. I really can't be sure anymore.

Do you know how frightening that is? To not know if something was real? To have gaps in your memory, enough to make you wonder whether your mind is just playing tricks on you? To decide that it all must have happened somehow only because of the consequences?"

Forthill shifted position. "I have heard stories that heavy alcoholics suffer amnesia above and beyond the standard drunk fare."

"I don't know that I've reached total amnesia," Owain said. "I just can't remember what's real. Or else I don't want to. Do you think it matters at this point? Who cares what a dead man does or does not remember?"

Again, the priest did not answer.

I went to court. Following my lawyer's advice, I didn't say a word. I did not speak in my own defense. I had nothing to defend. I was caught drinking when they found me, but I'd had nothing to drink beforehand. I'd been completely sober.

The prosecutor had a week's worth of witnesses against me. Everyone knew who I was. I was a drunkard, a thief, violent. I was accused of trying to undermine Mr. Balk at one point, depose him and take over the business. A lot of what was said about me was very true. Some were lies, but they were plausible lies. Again, I said nothing in my defense. I had intentionally gone to Balk's house with the desire to kill. I had planned on going to Travis' house and killing him, too. There was no passion, no spark of rage in an argument. The other four were just in the wrong place at the wrong time. There was no way I was getting out of this alive. Quite frankly, after my experience, I would very much like to be hung than spend my days in the black cell.

That can be arranged," the gaoler growled off to one side.

"Please," Forthill said, casting him a look.

Owain did not look up, but he was willing to bet that the gaoler paid the priest no mind. As he was oft reminded, God had no jurisdiction here. This was man's precursor to Hell. Purgatory, if you like. This was where the Devil got his first look at all the souls coming his way, some more quickly than others. Probably Owain's seat in the lake of fire was already reserved. And the Devil didn't enjoy his reservations canceling on him.

"Why do you say you would rather hang?" the priest inquired gently.

"Because it's the truth," Owain told him. "I'm not Saint Paul, Father. I'm not Saint John, either. I'm not a saint at all. I don't even know that I'm something as redeemable as a sinner. I am a sorry excuse for a human being who has no redeeming qualities and has done nothing in his life worth having his name attached to. I am a failure and there is nothing more that I can do to make myself good."

"That may be true, but why do you think it has to be you that does something?" Forthill shifted in his seat, almost eagerly. "Owain, that's what I've been trying to tell you. It's not about you. It's about Christ on the cross. There is nothing you can do or need to do. Jesus already did something. He did everything. One single act is what redeems you. A single price, paid once, paid forever. A gift if you choose to receive it. That's all. No ceremony, no pomp and circumstance, nothing but a choice. You don't have to do anything; He already did." The priest sighed. "I know you feel your sin is too great. But consider this: Christ was asking His father to forgive His own killers. He can rescue you, too, from the fiery pits of Hell."

It didn't take long for the jury to find me guilty of all charges. Actually, I was surprised they didn't interrupt the proceedings and render a verdict in the middle of the trial. I was surprised they left the courtroom at all to even deliberate. But I suppose there were rituals that had to be observed in order to ensure a fair trial. Or something.

Now, don't get me wrong. As much as I knew as I was guilty and I thought the trial unnecessary, in a way, I suppose I was grateful for it. There is justice in the world for those who can't buy their own verdicts, or there is the hope for justice, anyway. Sometimes I suppose that is all we can get.

It sounds ridiculous, I know. While I was sitting there in my cell in London, I remember thinking that Mrs. Balk was getting exactly what she deserved, and I mean that both ways. On the one hand, she was a witch. She hated me, hated anyone beneath her station or anyone she perceived as being beneath her station. She was cunning in her own right, crafty, knew how to get her way or help her husband get his way. Or their way, as I have every reason to believe their goals often coincided. I suspect she was as guilty as anyone when it came to dissociating from me, having Paige marry Travis, and helping Travis escape public justice. My pa always told us boys to be kind to women, but even had I been a good man, I think she got exactly what she deserved. She finally reaped what she and her husband sowed. But on that same token, I derived no pleasure from the suffering I knew she would endure, and continues to endure, I imagine. All the same, she was very good with money, so I imagine she will survive on her late husband's finances.

On the other hand, she also got the justice she deserved, and I don't mean just me. Even if she was helping to orchestrate Travis' initial release and subsequent murder, at least this way, she doesn't get her hands dirty. She can't be implicated in any way. She is free to go about her daily life as she sees fit. Maybe she remarries. Maybe she takes over the bank herself. Maybe she simply withdraws from all of it and settles down into her own routine. I don't know. But her daughter and granddaughter's killer is now gone, and her husband's murderer is almost gone.

Well, I feel that this is as good a time as any to mention that she has been perhaps the most vocal opposition to your sentence being delayed," Forthill stated.

"That doesn't shock me," Owain said, almost smiling. "She'd hang me herself if she could. Half of London and most of Wales would surely enjoy lining up to be my firing quad."

The only thing I can think is that God must have intervened in my sentencing. Initially, the idea was to simply hold me in a cell until the executioner could be roused from his own drunken stupor to hang me. And I will say that I think I have a better understanding of what Jesus went through when the crowds were calling for his crucifixion, because they did the same to me. If words could kill, I would have dropped dead on the spot—or perhaps years before.

No one was more shocked than I when the magistrate ordered me returned to Wales, but the crowds did not get truly violent until it was announced that I was to be sent here to await my hanging. The people could stomach sending a barbarian back to his barbaric homeland to be dealt with; they didn't need his kind mucking up London more than it already was. But to send him to such a lavish prison? Unthinkable! He should not enjoy the luxury of time outside and a meal every day. He ought to be locked up and left to die in a cold stone cell. His hanging would be seen as a mercy.

As I said, I was stunned. Before I could protest myself, my lawyer simply told me to keep my mouth shut and not say a word. This was a huge mercy, so don't speak out against it or things could get ugly. So I did as I was told and said nothing.

Later I learned that my lawyer was working as much for himself as for me. He didn't like me too much either, but he was less intent on murdering me in the most brutal way possible, and more focused on simply getting me out of London, out of England entirely if he could. He proposed the idea of sending me back to Wales. The English judge agreed and got a hold of a Welsh judge who agreed to take me. But they would not be so brutal against their own. Hanging, yes, but I would spend my time here, in Beaumaris Gaol. I think it might have been different if I had murdered other Welshmen, but considering the venom that the English wrote about us Welsh and sour relations, I think this was a small slap in the face to the English. How polite men and judges fight without fighting.

Owain could see the wheels turning in the priest's mind. He'd been sent here as a slap in the face to the English, an unspeakable crime in itself that he should see sunlight and be fed once a day. So then, why wasn't he permitted these things? Owain didn't know, honestly; the warden had never told him. But as he had been reminded often enough, these things were luxuries. No prison had ever tried this before. If he got any of these things, he ought to be grateful, because he could easily be sent to one of the common prisons where he had no hope of any niceties.

Suffice to say, Owain didn't complain too much. Actually, he didn't complain at all. He just elected to keep his mouth shut and await his fate. Problem was, his fate seemed to be pretty slow in coming.

It wasn't a long trek from London to here. I was the only prisoner coming out of London, but once we crossed the border into Wales, we picked up a few more here and there. A hog thief. A tax delinquent. A prostitute. All of them less damned than me. We were not allowed to speak on the journey, yet they knew well who I was. Word of the murders of Balk and his associates had spread far and wide. Even if we could speak, no one wanted to talk to me. No one wanted to associate with me. Some still remembered me from my younger days and wanted even less to do with me, spitting on me, kicking me, tripping me, yelling insults when they could get away with it. And they could often get away with it because the guards would join them, or at least not stop them.

I suppose I have reaped exactly what I have sown as well. In the end, no one loves me. No one cares. And even if they did, I don't know what I would expect them to do. I am justly imprisoned, and I do not know that it would do anyone any good for me to miraculously go free. I would not know what to do with myself. I have lived on both sides of the law, both sides of poverty and wealth, and I have failed at everything. What is there left for me?

Owain sighed. "I think you are the first person to want to listen. And you've not passed any judgment that I can recall. Perhaps you are the first person who has cared about me. Except, I think, for my ma. But I fear it is too little, too late. I've been running away from God and doing my own thing for so long, I have run right off a cliff. And I cannot choose not to fall."

Forthill shook his head. "You have not fallen off the cliff until you cross the threshold into death. Until then, you can still be saved."

There was a certain pleading in his voice. They were now at the end of the story. There was nothing left to stall the executioner from coming and carrying out the sentence. The warden only needed the word. Personally, Owain gave himself two weeks, maybe a month if the priest could continue to sweet talk the warden.

"What have you been doing with my story as I've been telling it?" Owain asked. "Do you tell it to other priests for their use? Am I an object lesson for wayward youth?"

"You were an object lesson for wayward youth long before you got here," Forthill told him honestly. "But to answer your question, I have been diligently recording it and sending it to other chapels, even the Catholic Church. It's how you earned a temporary stay of execution for six months."

"My earnest confession in order to be right with the Lord."

"That's right. I have been keeping them abreast of our meetings and circulating your testimony."

"Testimony," Owain echoed. "Whom shall I tell? And what will you say of me? Am I a martyr? Or simply a condemned man who did not receive the Lord until he had nothing left?"

"Those who worked in the vineyard for an hour received the same pay as those who had labored all day," Forthill reminded him.

"Yes, I know the story."

"Do you doubt it?"

Owain opened his mouth to speak, then closed it again. After a long minute, he answered, "I don't know. I don't know that I can be saved. If I can, I don't know that I am so worthy as to even receive such a mercy. If I can't, I simply wish for all of this to be over. Perhaps the Lord will consider me as low as the beasts that my soul will merely return to the earth and not be tormented for eternity.

"And what if I go to speak to Saint Peter and Mr. Balk is there as well? What if, through some improbable circumstance, we are both admitted into Heaven? What shall I say to him? 'Please forgive me for murdering you in cold blood'?"

"I think there are many things about Heaven that we do not understand," Forthill said, his tone mildly amused. "And we shall not be the people we once were, either. Here we are faced with demons and temptations. Such things shall not exist when we are with the Lord. Balk will not burn with bitterness or vengeance because such things do not exist in the same way they do here. Vengeance belongs to God alone, and I see not room for any form of bitterness. All tears shall be wiped away. It is a difficult thing for even my mind to grasp, I admit."

The prisoner took an even breath. "I don't know that I have said it, but if I have, I will say it again. I find your honesty refreshing, that you admit when you don't know something. How many years did I spend under a Catholic priest who had an answer for everything, even if it contradicted himself or the Lord? But there was nothing he didn't know, and he knew that my pagan, drunkard soul was irrevocably damned."

Now the priest managed a small chuckle. "Well, I don't know a lot of things. I don't know what death is like. I don't know what it is like to walk beyond this life. But I do know that you are drawing nearer to those doors and must make a choice. As long as you breathe, you can still choose the narrow road." He went on before Owain could say more. "God has not given up on you, Owain. He has given you many chances, intervened a number of times as you yourself have admitted. Don't give up on God. And don't give up on yourself. You can be saved."

Owain frowned. "And what happens once I am?"

"Then the angels rejoice, and you can step forth into Heaven with confidence."

"Right through a hole with a rope around my neck."

The gaoler evidently took that as a cue that their time was up, for he moved and took Owain's chains in hand. The prisoner struggled to his feet.

"I will speak to the warden," Forthill promised.

"And tell him what?" Owain wondered.

"I will be here for my midweek rounds, and then again for chapel next week. I would speak to you at least one more time after the next service. If that's all right with you."

After a moment, the prisoner nodded. "I would appreciate a midweek meeting as well."

"Of course."

So that was it. One week to speak with the priest and make one last push for salvation. Another week until he entered Heaven by way of a rope around his neck. He'd known this day was coming for a long time, and yet, it made his stomach churn to think about and dwell on for any length of time. He'd become accustomed to the story, and he'd enjoyed meeting with Forthill if only because it got him out of his cell. A few times, he'd even been able to go outside. Granted, the scenery wasn't much, but he saw blue sky again, and the sun darting in and out of the clouds.

He thought back to an old chapel service from his childhood, one of the few he could be dragged to. He remembered something the preacher said. "Here today and gone tomorrow" was a modern proverb in the era of fast banking and consumerism as the Industrial Revolution took off around the world. "Here today and gone tomorrow" was how everyone lived their lives (or they did in the cities, so saith the preacher). But one day, that attitude will come to an end. And you, your body and soul, will be "here today...and gone today." Everybody dies. No one knows when that will be. Got to get right with the Lord today because there was no guarantee that you would live to see tomorrow. Only the Lord knows when you're going to go.

Condemned men seemed to have an advantage then, Owain figured as he was marched back to his cell. His execution date was going to be set here pretty quick. Then he really would know when his day of reckoning would be.

And the door to his cell slammed shut, the whole room suddenly felt like ice, and a boulder of fear dropped into his stomach. The first time around, he'd simply accepted his fate with a sullen resignation. He knew he deserved it, and he still deserved it. But now he was overcome with unholy fear. Something in his mind clicked into place.

He was going to die. He was going to meet the Lord God Almighty who'd merely uttered words and brought about all of Creation. Everything he saw around him had sprung forth from the very imagination of God, when he himself could not presently imagine his way out of a box. He was going to meet that God and be judged for his sins, countless and heinous though they were. Worst of all, he'd murdered six men, beings created in the very image of God Most High. He'd stolen life from them when they were not his to take.

Owain soon found himself on the floor of his cell, gasping for breath but unable to make his lungs work. His stomach lurched and he got sick, but his muscles were so tense, he couldn't get it all out. He began coughing and gagging, muscles finally working but now he had only vomit in his system. His body heaved again. Fluids dribbled from his nose, and even with his muscles fully tensed, he did not close his mouth or allow himself to inhale until he was sure everything was out.

Thoroughly exhausted, he slept where he lay.

The following day, he was permitted to go outside. This small miracle proved to be a joke amongst the gaolers as it was raining heavily. Thunder rumbled in the distance. Owain did not care. He took the opportunity to give himself a crude bath, wiping away dirt and grime and the remnants of his episode the previous evening. It would probably be the last wash he got before his execution, and even then, his lifeless body would only be modestly wiped down before it was buried. This was as clean as he was ever going to get.

The gaolers did not like that he did not appear to mind the rain. Might be he even enjoyed it and tried to freshen himself up a bit. Whatever the case, they left him out there for the full hour allowed him. It wasn't because they were nice, Owain knew, and cared about hygiene. Likely they were hoping he would contract some disease from the filth and a chill, save them the trouble of having to take him all the way to the gallows. It was all a joke to them. They cared nothing for him. They saw him as merely a being. A creature.

He'd looked upon other men like that. That was why he'd beaten them, robbed them, killed them. Because he thought them insignificant, beneath him. He was the king and other people just got in his way of what he wanted.

He was going to face Almighty God with a lifetime of an attitude like that. How could he? Now that he recognized his sins for what they were, he could not even begin to come up with any kind of reason or excuse. He was a wretched, filthy man. He was going to die like one, and he was going to be eternally tormented like one.

He was returned to his cell. The early autumn rain had still been somewhat warm, but the stone gaol was rapidly beginning to chill. With no shoes or stockings, by the time he returned to his cell, Owain was shivering. He curled up as best he could, but when he finally got somewhat comfortable, the latch clicked and his daily meal was given to him. It wasn't hot, but even room temperature felt good against his cold skin. He ate greedily and sent the empty bowl back through the port in the door.

Owain spent the next few days curled up in a ball of utter dread. He knew his time was limited, that he would be dead and buried before Christmas, before the ground froze solid. He could hear Forthill in his mind telling him that as long as he drew breath, there was still hope for his soul. He could still be saved. But the dread overrode any capacity for actually feeling hope. It existed only as a word, a distant concept, not anything tangible he could access and cling to.

He ate like a man starved, as if he might never eat again. Sometimes he managed to consume the whole bowl of bad porridge in just a few bites. He knew it was only a few days between his meetings with the priest, but it felt far longer. Weeks, even months, passed in those few days. His fear only grew, and hope became a distant memory.

When the door finally opened and he was told that Forthill was waiting for him, Owain almost wouldn't come. Not because he was trying to be difficult, but because he almost couldn't comprehend the sight of another human being. Another wave of fear rolled over him and he had to be forced out of his cell, hardly a difficult feat.

His shackles had been undone when he'd been returned to his cell after the rainstorm. In that time, his ankles and wrists appeared to have healed almost, but that couldn't be right. Something wasn't right here. It couldn't be. There had to be some trick here. Perhaps the demons were already torturing him, too excited for his arrival to even wait for death.

Forthill waited for him as he always did, in a small wooden chair near the front pew of the chapel. When Owain saw him, he began to weep. The priest waited patiently and did not interrupted, did not make any move. It was a long time before Owain managed to gather himself enough to speak.

"So, my son," Forthill said softly, "what do you have to say to me?"

CHAPTER THIRTEEN

THE PRISONER

They brought me over first in the boat. They were afraid that if they didn't, I might try to escape. It was a windy day, and the snow had turned to ice. I had to close my eyes to keep the ice from stinging, and then, suddenly, we docked, and the gaol loomed large over us.

I wanted to turn and look around, to get a last look at the world before I died, except...between the wind and the snow, and the fog that was forming over the water...everything just disappeared. There was nothing for me to see, no memory to hang onto. I guess this just reinforces the point that I have no good memories to cling to in my solitude. Maybe I'm just not allowed to have any.

We didn't wait for the others to come across. I had to be taken inside and locked up just as soon as possible, or I suppose that's what the guards told themselves. Though I had caused no trouble at all during the journey, I was still the most dangerous one in the group. I had to be kept separate from the rest of them still. I don't really blame the gaolers; they were just doing their jobs with the information they had.

Jail was not new to me, and I knew the procedures were generally about the same wherever you went. But walking into Beaumaris was a completely new sensation. I don't know if it is this place specifically, or if the realization finally hit me. There was a sense of finality when I walked in here. The end. This was where I would be spending the last weeks of my life. Once the doors closed behind me, they closed for good. There was nothing left for me. Everything about me, my life, it all got cut off. The only thing I had coming was my execution.

It terrified me in a way that nothing in my life had up to that point. These stone walls were all that was left. These gaolers and the other prisoners were the last people I would see on God's green earth. Not my family, not a crowd of strangers, but a group of men who were in power over me, who hated me, who wanted to see me dead and would send me to the grave themselves. Any rights I had as a human being hadn't made the crossing with me on the ferry.

Do you know what it's like to realize that there are birds in the trees and on the water that are more highly regarded than you?" Owain wondered aloud.

"Only in the eyes of man," Forthill told him, almost predictably. "You are still a child of God, His very own creation."

Just walking in had invoked that sense of finality. When the main doors closed, however, I almost lost it. I was overcome with such fear, I wanted to kill myself right then. I wanted God to strike me down and send me to Hell. I wanted to tear my clothes and rip my heart out of my chest. But all I could do was stumble after the guards.

They took me to a small room where I surrendered my clothes and any worldly possession I had left—which wasn't any because I'd been kept in jail and they already confiscated everything. After they doused me with several buckets of cold water, I was given this common garment, just something to cover me, hardly enough to keep me any semblance of warm.

Then they took me to meet the warden. He took my file, read through it, and then regarded me with such contempt. Even my father-in-law had not disdained me so much, or if he had, he never let it show through completely. I thought for sure he was going to have me executed on the spot. Truth be told, I would have welcomed it. I did not want to be here, and he obviously did not want me here.

He informed me that my execution was scheduled for six weeks hence. He told me that Beaumaris was a controversial prison because of its policy on feeding inmates daily and letting them out for exercise, as well as permitting some to work. However, that did not mean that such things were an automatic guarantee. Because of my history and the nature of my crimes, he deemed me too dangerous to be among the common population. I would be placed in my own cell. The condemned cell, for obvious reasons. He informed me that because of how dangerous I was, I would not be permitted to work, and it was unlikely that I would get out in the exercise yard during my time. If I did, it would not be with the other prisoners, but by myself once they had all cleared out. He told me that I would probably get my daily meal, as long as I didn't cause trouble.

I was made to sign a paper just saying that I had arrived in the prison. By habit from the bank, I signed as Walter Forbes. Before I could correct it, the warden ordered me taken to my cell, which, as you know, is hardly a stone's throw from his office. My shackles were removed and the door locked behind me. I did not get food that day, but the next day, it was delivered. And the day after that. I caused no trouble, said not a word. Indeed, I'd hardly spoken since the trial. I'd decided that my lawyer may have had the right of things. Say nothing and no more trouble will come.

After a few days, the gaolers came for me. They shackled me and took me back to the warden's office, made me sit down. He informed me that the day was Saturday. The gaol held chapel services on Sunday mornings. However, I was not permitted to partake in them with the rest of the prisoners. But, if I wanted to, I could meet privately with the chaplain after the service or during the week when he made his mid-week visit.

W as Dillon really that afraid of you, or afraid for the other prisoners?" Forthill inquired.

Owain shrugged. "I don't know. He would certainly have reason to be. Mostly, though, I think he just didn't like me. Still doesn't. I think he just wanted to keep me contained in my own cell, not to be brought out until execution when he could wash his hands of me."

He could see the priest was displeased with the answer, not because it was somehow unsatisfactory, but because he did not like imagining the warden as being so callous about his prisoners. What use was a controversial prison with such lavish amenities when they were not afforded to all of the prisoners in hopes of making them better people?

Or was it simply because this particular prisoner was condemned? No need to waste resources on a dead man. But were sunshine and fresh air really such limited resources?

I refused at first. I had little desire to speak to a Catholic priest who would only reaffirm what I already knew, that my soul was already damned and there was no hope of gaining enough righteousness in such a short amount of time. I had little desire to speak to a Protestant preacher, either, knowing that I had failed my countrymen, turned my back on everything I knew and had grown up with. If I did not receive equal condemnation, then surely they would only look upon me with pity that my soul was damned, a waste from the very beginning.

Instead, I sat in my cell. Sunday morning came and went. I could not even hear a service from where I was. Indeed, it's difficult to hear anything in the condemned cell. The farthest I believe I can hear is the warden's office, and even then the sound is muffled.

I tried — still try, to be a good prisoner. I try not to cause trouble, and I don't speak to the gaolers often. I don't complain. Once a week, I scrub out the latrine. It's not something I enjoy, but at least the door is open and I see some light, even if it comes only from a small lantern.

Then the gaolers started counting down my days. With every meal they brought, they would tell me the number of days until my hanging. The thing is, though, they did not seem to understand that, at the very least, I know how to count. And I can do math. Six weeks is forty-two days. It was at least two weeks before they started counting down for me, which would be a maximum of twenty-eight days. They started counting from thirty-five. I think they did that on purpose, so that I would cling to the hope of having another week to live, and then they would come for me and tell me that I was going to be taken for execution.

Whatever the case, the counting made me nervous. In my mind, it was like walking toward a stone wall, and somehow I knew that there was nothing behind it. Everything beyond the wall just ended. It was as if I'd walked and walked and finally found the edge of the world. At the same time, though, the wall had a door. I don't need to tell you what the door symbolized, but I had no idea where it led. And I was getting closer and closer to that door every day. One step closer with each day they counted down, plus all the days they weren't telling me about.

I got scared. Finally, one day when they brought my meal — and they really hadn't been entirely consistent in bringing it every day; most days, but not every day — I told them that I wanted to talk to the chaplain.

It was another day or two before I was taken out and back to the warden's office. He initially said that I was in there for harassing the gaolers. I denied it and said that I merely wished to speak to the chaplain. I didn't know how to go about it, so I simply told the gaolers at meal time. I couldn't really tell the warden's reaction, whether he was displeased with me or the gaolers, but given the choice, it was probably me.

In any event, he told me that the chaplain would be present at my hanging, for last rites and if I wished to confess or otherwise receive prayer. I told him that my list of confessions was far too long for an afternoon summary. I had many things on my mind and wanted to speak to him beforehand if possible. Seeing how I could not go to chapel, I would have to meet privately with him, as the warden himself had told me only a few weeks before.

I don't think the warden liked that very much, being reminded of what he'd said, that he had offered something nice and I was taking advantage of it. Nevertheless, he said he would attempt to honor my request. The day we met was an off day. The warden said he would speak to the chaplain the next day he came and see what could be arranged. The chaplain usually had a set schedule of things, so I would have to be worked in separately. I did not have much faith that he would actually honor my request before my hanging, but I could only try.

Owain paused and sighed, looking at the priest. "And I think you know the rest."

Forthill nodded graciously. "Dillon took me aside after my rounds that Wednesday and told me that a prisoner wished to confess his crimes. I inquired as to which prisoner, seeing how I'd just made my rounds. He told me it was the condemned man, Fforidd, locked up for six murders. I had a vague understanding of who you were, or why you were here. He said you had more you wanted to say before you were set to hang. And so, the next week, we met for the first time, and you began your story."

"I began my story," Owain echoed. "And now it looks like it comes to a close. This is my ending. At the end of a rope."

"And how do you feel now? Compared to when we first met?"

He paused and considered this. Then, "I'm glad someone listened. I'm glad someone knows. I don't know that my soul is cleansed or that my conscience is clean, but at least the story has been told. I feel better for it, I suppose."

"How has your time been since we first met? Two weeks has turned into quite a long time."

Owain nodded and forced an empty laugh. "It's the longest six weeks I've ever spent in any prison." He shook his head and wiped his eyes. "The gaolers beat me, berate me. You know I've only come to chapel a handful of times. I've seen the outside less than that. I spend my days in darkness, and my nights in terror. You know I've tried to kill myself at least once. Sometimes I have a mind to try again. At this point, I don't know that it would be worth it."

Forthill frowned. "The warden has informed me that Sunday after chapel, the three of us will meet to discuss what will happen the day of your hanging. Then Dillon will leave us to speak privately. Anything more you have to say to me, that would be the time. You are free to take all the time you need, even if it is half the night."

"Do you know when the execution is scheduled?"

"He has pushed for next Saturday. I admit that it may have been a bit at my behest. Winter is closing in quickly. If the ground freezes before you are hung, they will sink your body in the sea. I confess myself that I advocated for a Christian burial in the ground, but did not consider my words well in that it would mean speeding the date."

Owain shook his head. "You say that as if I would wish to spend another winter here, freezing in my cell. I do not. There is nothing to be gained by waiting until spring. The gaolers will yet beat me, the warden will ignore me. Best to hang me and rid the world of my curse." He hesitated awkwardly. Then, "But I thank you for the consideration."

The priest seemed uncertain how to respond. Owain stood even before the gaoler moved to take possession of him. "Thank you, Father, for listening. Thank you for advocating for me. I expect I shall see you Sunday after service."

Forthill did not say a word as the gaoler took Owain's chains and led him along, out of the chapel, up the stairs, and around the corner. The drama was over. The delay had pressed on long enough. It was time to get back to how things were supposed to be, where he was set to be hung, now in less than two weeks.

The same fear he'd felt just a couple days before enveloped him again as his cell door was shut and locked behind him. This was the end. No more delays, no more bargains, no more confessions to tell. He was going to be executed and then stand before the throne of Almighty God, Whose creation he had defiled. His soul was irrevocably damned.

Could he really hope for forgiveness? Could God really overlook the lives he'd taken? Did he dare hope for mercy? He couldn't even overlook these things in his own mind. But was that because he was eternally guilty, or because it was one of those things the demons did to torment people? No such thing as bitterness in Heaven, the priest had said. Mr. Balk would hold no contempt for him because it would not matter. Forgiveness was forgiveness, and with no bitterness to smolder in his heart, Balk would only be glad that Owain had found salvation.

Owain could not even fathom such a situation. He could not imagine Balk smiling or being joyous about anything, certainly not anything unrelated to his business. And salvation for his ex-son-in-law whom he'd hated from the beginning and called a pagan destined for Hell? Not even part of the question.

But Balk hardly mattered, when Owain considered that such a reunion would be after God judged him. He had to get past that part first. Was it really as simple as asking?

Owain thought back to when he was a child, bedridden after being trampled by the family cow. His ma doted on him, but it was his pa he feared. He, Owain, had almost killed his brother, and had been nothing but trouble from the very beginning. Lying there in bed, completely vulnerable, though his parents cared for him and his mother obviously loved him, could he really expect any forgiveness from his pa?

That was a bit how he felt now. The priest cared for him, but it was God whom he would be answering to and asking forgiveness from.

Running away and getting into worse trouble hadn't worked for him the first time, and it seemed as though he had little choice but to ask for forgiveness. He wasn't getting away from this meeting. He had roughly ten days to get right. He'd already made his confessions to the priest. Was it enough, or was there more? Simply asking for forgiveness sounded too easy, a way for the pious in society to make themselves look holy in public. Like a snake oil salesman showing off his wares. There just had to be more to it.

Owain lay down but couldn't come up with anything. He didn't remember anything growing up, no prayers or rituals, and he was loathe to indulge in any Catholics practices. Maybe he'd missed that chapel service. Maybe he really was eternally damned, and had been since he was only a child.

INTERLUDE

THE MEETING

It wasn't even his execution and yet Forthill felt a certain sense of terror shaking his soul. He'd felt it since his last meeting with Owain and it had only gotten worse as the days went on. Thursday, Friday, Saturday, the dread and the fear and a measure of uncertainty, heavy on his heart and in his gut as though he'd swallowed a bag of rocks. By Sunday, he almost expected to be walking up to the gallows himself, and there was yet a week until the actual hanging.

He'd confided in Worthington the night before, expressing his dread and dismay.

"It's not an easy task, walking a man up to the gallows," Worthington told him, and for the first time, the older priest looked his age. Forthill saw the folds of his skin, the liver spots, stiff hands, and when had his hair gone white? How had he ever looked upon this man and thought him half his age? Perhaps in demeanor only, for his body was rapidly succumbing to the effects of time.

"Have you ever done it?" Forthill inquired.

To his surprise, the old man nodded. "Once. A younger man than Fforidd, killed a man and raped his two teenage daughters. When the wife came home, he raped her, too."

"Did he repent?"

"Not at all. He showed no remorse and had little interest in confessing his sins. He questioned himself once, but that was as far as it got before he was hung."

Forthill shifted in his seat. "So you think there is hope for Owain?"

Worthington's expression was unreadable. "There is always hope, as long as he draws breath, but every man must make his own decision.

God knows what is in his heart. He knows what demons torture Fforidd's mind. If what you have told me about him is true, I fully believe that we will see him in Heaven one day. It's just going to be getting there that is hardest, both for him and for you, I think."

"I saw a man hung once," Forthill sighed. "When I was a child, I saw a man hung for adultery, among other crimes. He, I think, was repentant. I will never forget the man's face right as he dropped. He knew what was coming and had prepared for it with the priest who was with him, and yet he still looked so surprised. And then afterwards, just that slack, vacant expression, eyes glassy, his soul gone. This happened years ago, and I can still remember it so vividly.

"That wasn't even the worst part. The worst part was hearing the snap of his neck. I remember gagging when I heard that sound, and my ma warned me not to get sick on my new stockings. The man's face was unnerving, but the sound of his neck snapping was more than I could bear. How can I do it again?"

"You can do it again," Worthington told him severely, "because Owain needs you to."

And that was that. Sunday morning, Forthill was up early and on his way to the ferry. He did not know what he was going to say or do. He had only his Bible and a hope that God would put words in his mouth. Autumn seemed to have blown in overnight. The last tendrils of summer warmth had gone and winter was beginning to work her icy claws into the blowing winds. The first frost was coming soon, and the first snows would not be far behind.

Forthill did not recall saying anything to the ferryman, but that was not unusual. He did remember nodding politely to the gaolers who let him in and escorted him down to the chapel. He felt woefully sluggish and unprepared. His mind was fixated exclusively on Owain and his predicament so that he could hardly focus on all the other prisoners contained within these stone walls. It was a little embarrassing to consider, but all the same, Owain's days were literally numbered. He had less than a week to make right with the Lord if he hadn't already. Forthill prayed silently that he had, or that he would do so today. This would be their last meeting before Saturday.

He always prayed before he left the parsonage in the morning, and he always opened the chapel service with a prayer, but now, rather than immediately allowing the gaolers to bring in the convicts, he sat in the front pew himself and bowed his head.

"Lord, I don't know what I'm supposed to do here. You've given me a mission and I feel like I'm failing. Give me the words, Lord, to get through this chapel service and to speak to Owain one last time. And I don't know if it will help, but I'd like to pray for his forgiveness. Let him see kindness just once. Just one more time before he goes."

The Lord did not reply. Forthill did not feel particularly enlightened, but the bag of rocks in his gut slowly dissipated. When he stood up, he found that he was able to focus on the present moment. He looked around. He was in the chapel at the gaol. This was Sunday service. He had an hour with these prisoners. He had to tell them something. Taking a breath, he looked at the gaoler at the door and nodded. Send them in.

He wasn't sure exactly what he told them, but he knew the words had not been his. God came through for him as He always did, speaking through him so his own tongue could not muck things up. For this, he was grateful, that he did not have to rely on his own silver tongue and superb speaking skills, neither of which he actually possessed.

The convicts were always slow to leave the chapel. Forthill knew that most came just to get out of work or to add some excitement in their day, more than just the same-old, same-old. A few were repentant and wanted to reform their lives before they got out and returned home. Regardless, it was like herding slow-moving cattle, getting them all to leave.

Then Forthill was left alone, save for one gaoler who watched him with mild disinterest. They all knew what was happening. Forthill wondered if they really derived such pleasure from torturing Fforidd, or if it was just a select few. Was there any way to find out? Nathan did not appear too interested in reining them in, even if they did take pleasure in such things.

It was a good five minutes before Nathaniel Dillon showed up. He took a seat in the front pew, crossing an ankle over a knee, perfectly at ease.

"Father," he greeted civilly.

"Warden," Forthill acknowledged.

"Have you any more surprise letters for me?"

"No, sir, I do not."

"Very good." His tone was difficult to judge.

A minute later, Owain Fforidd was led into the room. He looked almost as haggard as he had the first time Forthill had seen him. No doubt he had a lot on his mind even as there was only one thing on his mind: death. This would be his last Sunday alive. Tomorrow would be his last Monday. And on and on until Saturday, his last day on Earth. Was he still considering his story, thinking that he could not be forgiven? Forthill wondered if there was anything more he could say to tip the scale and help him make the right decision.

You have said all you can.

He let out a breath he hadn't realized he'd been holding. His part was finished. His piece had been said. The rest was between Owain and the Lord.

Owain took a seat in the front pew across from the warden. He stared at the floor and did not look at either the warden or the chaplain.

"Mr. Fforidd," Nathan began formally.

"Sir," Owain responded, raising his head but still not looking at anyone.

"Father Forthill has informed me that you have concluded your confessions and other religious rites."

"Yes, sir."

"To my knowledge, no further appeals have been made for clemency or commutation."

"I understand."

"To that end, your execution by hanging will take place Saturday afternoon."

Owain sighed and studied his hands. "I understand."

"What will happen is you will be brought out in the morning. You may be permitted to walk the exercise yard. Then you will be given a last meal. If you choose, you will meet with Father Forthill for about ten minutes before being taken out to the scaffold."

"Then you will put a rope around my neck and I shall plunge through the hole into the abyss," Owain finished.

The warden faltered for half a second. Then, "That's right."

The prisoner sighed. "All right. So it will be."

Nathan glanced at Forthill, but Forthill said nothing. After a moment, the warden said, "Do you have any questions for me?"

"None that would matter, I'm afraid. What questions could be so pressing that they would overshadow my own execution?"

The warden had nothing to say to that. He cast an almost bewildered look at Forthill before standing and saying, "Very well. I will leave you to speak with Father Forthill for a time."

And he left. It was one of the few times Forthill had seen Nathan less than completely confident and in control. He waited until after the warden and all but one gaoler had gone before moving to sit next to Owain.

"I'm afraid that on Saturday, we will only have perhaps ten minutes to speak. If there is anything more you wish to say to me, perhaps something I can write down and take to your family, your parents, now would be the time."

For a moment, it seemed as though Owain hadn't heard as he stared at the floor, countenance sullen and resigned. Finally he said, "If my family has heard of this, they will want to hear no word from me, for I am shameful. If they have not heard, I will not burden them with the knowledge that their eldest son met his end on a rope, nor what he did to be there."

"Not even a short letter, just to say you love them?"

"They would never believe me. No, better to keep them removed from this."

"Would you prefer I visit them afterwards, just to inform them of your death?"

Owain opened his mouth as if to answer, then reconsidered and closed it again. Finally he said, "That would be acceptable. Appropriate, I think, just to let them know. So they can stop waiting and praying for my soul."

"I won't tell them the why or how."

"Thank you."

They sat in silence for a long minute, enough for the gaoler to make his presence known.

"Was there anything else you wanted to talk about? Anything else on your mind?" Forthill inquired, hoping to spark something in Owain that would save his soul.

Another moment of silence passed. Finally, Owain stood. Forthill could see his cheeks were wet, but his voice was soft as he replied, "No. At this point, I have nothing more to say. Thank you, Father."

On this cue, the gaoler approached and took Fforidd away. Forthill could envision it almost perfectly: out of the chapel, up the stairs, to the left, just around the corner, and there was the condemned cell. He heaved a sigh and studied his hands, folded neatly in his lap. Owain was not the only condemned man in Beaumaris, but the other man had an excellent lawyer who was appealing right and left and pushing back the sentence constantly.

Forthill was not looking forward to Saturday. He was not enthusiastic about being up there on the scaffolding when Owain took his plunge into the abyss, as he'd so eloquently put it. Maybe, once it was done, Forthill would talk to Dillon and resign from his position. This was hard enough. He couldn't do it again if and when Richard Brown's appeals ran out and he was sentenced to hang.

Eventually, the priest stood and made his way out of the chapel, up to the warden's office. Nathan was nowhere to be seen, so Forthill helped himself to the seat this side of the desk and waited. Forthill could hear yelling coming from somewhere. Judging by the snaps, he might guess someone was in the whipping room.

It was an hour or so before Nathan appeared in the doorway.

"Father," he greeted. "You should have sent for me. I don't mean to keep you waiting."

"No trouble," Forthill assured him. "My knees were grateful for the rest."

"Yes, it was not the brightest idea to put the governor's office on the first floor." The warden took a seat, appearing confident though he still seemed slightly dazed by his encounter with Owain. "What can I do for you?"

"I haven't decided."

"Haven't decided?"

"Once this...deed...is done, with Mr. Fforidd, I'm considering resigning from my position here."

Nathan nodded. "I can understand that. It's taxing work. Your companion — Worthington, isn't it? — he meets with people who tell small lies, maybe take the Lord's name in vain while dealing with stubborn mules or broken tools. You talk to men who make those sins look laughable. Thieves, rapists, murderers. It can be difficult to come to terms with the dark side of humanity."

"And this drama involving Fforidd has not been the most kind, either," Forthill agreed.

"I understand. Unfortunately, we do need a chaplain. They can be kind of hard to come by here. I'll accept your resignation on the condition that you find me a replacement."

"I will do my best."

"Good man. Was there anything else?"

"No. I don't believe so."

The warden raised a brow. "You look like you're the one about to hang, Father."

"As I said, this drama involved Mr. Fforidd has been trying."

"Of course."

Pleasantries were brief, and Forthill was on his way soon enough, making his way down the stairs, out the main gate, and to the docks. He did not speak to the ferryman except for a brief thank you. The sun was falling quickly and the wind was picking up. With any luck, Saturday would be a fine day, sunny with bright blue skies, something spectacular to behold, something beautiful to hopefully push Fforidd in his last moments to find salvation.

It is not your place anymore, the small voice told him. *Your help is no longer required here.*

While Forthill knew well that he ought to trust the Lord that all things would work out for good, and while he felt a certain measure of relief that he was off the hook, he couldn't help but feel as though he had still failed somehow, that there was still something more he could do to persuade Fforidd.

It's not about persuasion, else men would be converting in droves. It is about faith, conviction in the heart and the desire to change.

It didn't make it any less frustrating.

He returned to the parsonage where Worthington was just putting on water for tea. Forthill was still amazed at how the older man seemed to have aged overnight. He now looked his age, moved like it, too. It could be that Forthill would be taking over for him.

"How did it go?"

Worthington's tone was reserved. He knew well that today hadn't been just an ordinary chapel service. More had gone on. Forthill did not answer right away as he removed his slippers and sat down at the table.

"I don't know if he's saved, Peitr," Forthill said. "I've explained it to him every way I know how. I see that he craves redemption and acceptance. I just don't know that he's made that final leap into salvation."

"There is nothing more you can do for him, Arthur. You get ten minutes with him before he walks out to the scaffolding. Maybe it will happen then. But it must be his decision."

Forthill groaned and put his head into his hands. He huffed a sigh and shook his head. "I just can't...something about this...there's something missing. I don't know what it is. I just don't think things are going to happen the way we planned."

"They rarely do," Worthington chuckled.

"I'm serious, Peitr. Call me fanciful, but I don't believe that this is over yet."

"It won't be over until Fforidd is in the ground."

"Speaking of things being over..." Forthill told his fellow priest about his intended resignation.

Worthington listened patiently and solemnly agreed, saying, "I think in that you are making the right decision. It has been a difficult road for you."

"Thank you. At least I feel as though I've done one thing right."

"Be patient, my friend. You forget, we are not far behind Fforidd in death." The older priest laughed, but it was nervous, and his hands shook.

Forthill slept fitfully that night, and every night that week. He did not go to the gaol for his midweek visit. If anyone asked, he would claim illness, for he did feel ill. His head throbbed and his stomach was uneasy. He'd been the chaplain for some years now at Beaumaris, but this would be his first execution. He'd done many last rites, and he'd assisted Worthington with countless funerals, but there was something far worse about this impending execution.

He felt as if he'd really gotten to know Owain, understand him. He hated to see a life thrown away. He hated to see such despair on a man's face as he faced death with perilous uncertainty.

He did not sleep Friday night. He told himself it was the storm outside, but he'd slept through many a storm in his day. Finally, as the sky turned from black to gray, he conceded defeat and pulled himself upright. Worthington was still asleep. Forthill forwent tea and food, knowing he would not be able to keep it down.

All the way to the ferry, he could only see the man's face as he hung on the rope. Sometimes it was patience, as he had been when he was still alive. Sometimes it was surprise in that split second as he was falling. Sometimes it was slack emptiness, the soul departed from the body. The whole time, even through the wind that persisted from the sea, he could only hear the snap of the man's neck as it broke. When he finally set foot on the island, he felt ill once more.

He did not fully understand the finer details of the day's events, so when the gaolers at the main door informed him that the warden wanted to speak with him, he did not argue, nor did he suspect anything was amiss. Indeed, he remained rather passive all the way to Dillon's office. It was the warden's expression that first tipped him off to mischief.

"We have a problem."

CHAPTER FOURTEEN

THE SORROW

The gallows was broken.

Autumn storms were nothing new. It was just part of the yearly cycle of weather. Soon enough, rain would give way to snow. But the one constant was the wind. In this instance, the wind had taken a branch off a tree and carried it so it struck the scaffolding. The strike, combined with high sustained winds, had destroyed the entire structure.

There would be no execution today.

Truthfully, Owain wanted to scream his frustration. He may have, actually; he wasn't entirely sure.

Was it really so difficult to die? Why was it that most men seemed to have no trouble at all, while he sat in his cell, fully deserving and expecting to die, but it just wouldn't happen? First the priest got the date pushed back, and now nature had given him another extension. What seemed to be the problem? Was he perhaps already in Hell and the demons were tormenting him already?

Even as he thought this, he was also forced to wonder what his hurry was. He fully expected and deserved to die, but there was still that sliver of anxiety, that will to live that had kept him going through impossible situations. There was also a touch of fear in there, knowing that he would be going before Almighty God, not with mud-stained robes, but quite possibly no robes at all. He was that vile. It was that last anchor keeping him tethered to this world, wretched and filthy as it was.

Actually, the world was quite beautiful. He'd never been able to fully appreciate it before, but the world was a beautiful, remarkable place, even in some of the more questionable areas. But there was a way of life even in those places. There was no way of life here, in the prison, in the black cells. Perhaps the other prisoners had carved out a meager, temporary existence as they whiled away their time, waiting for release, but he had no such luxury. He had nothing coming, no freedom, no hope. Only death. And they couldn't even seem to get that right.

He'd been informed of the gallows' fate early this morning by a very disgruntled warden. Then the priest had met with him briefly, prayed for him, and also departed. When Owain had inquired as to his fate, they simply told him that they were trying to figure that out. So he was left to consider his other options for execution.

Option one, firing squad. It was quick and easy, providing the gaolers had any kind of decent aim.

Option two, stoning. It was Biblical, after all, but hardly painless. But then, the gaolers might enjoy it more.

Option three, beheading. Again, quick and easy. The problem was inevitably the cleanup. There was a lot of blood to be found in the head and neck, and it would only attract flies.

Option four, torture. Owain had little doubt the gaolers would enjoy torturing him to death. Start with the whip, break some bones, pull out his fingernails, take a hot poker to his eyes, all very carefully, very slowly, until his body simply couldn't take any more and he passed out or died from blood loss.

Option five, drowning. Also a Biblical option for those who curse their parents, as he had no doubt done in the past, even if he couldn't remember it. Tie a millstone about his neck and toss him into the sea.

Option six, push him from a height, with or without a rope. The first floor of the gaol was tall enough for this to be an option. They could push him freely and hope he broke his neck, or tie a rope around his neck and ensure it. Sure, he would hit the side of the building, too, but it was still a viable option for hanging.

Option seven, poison. Yes, it was a woman's weapon, but there were some poisons out there that could cause grisly side effects, enough to perhaps satisfy the bloodlust of the gaolers.

Option eight, starvation. Just like he'd tried to hunger strike his way to death some months ago, they would only have to intentionally stop feeding him. He would suffer some wretched pain as his body tried to cope, but the end was the same. Similarly, they could also withhold water from him and watch him die even faster.

Option nine, infection. This would not necessarily be an intentional murder by the gaolers, but it would be just as effective. There were any number of diseases he could contract if he was wounded, and some even if he wasn't. The infirmary could only do so much, and their purpose was arguably aimed more at the gaolers if they got injured than the prisoners.

Option ten, fighting. If he picked a fight with the gaolers and gave it everything he had, it might warrant the use of deadly force. It would be a hell of a way to go, too, more than just meekly walking to the gallows.

So then, ten good options for how he could still be executed. Maybe not today, since they all seemed pretty flustered about the whole gallows thing, but soon enough. He supposed he could hold out for one more week, if that was what it took. It wasn't as though he hadn't been pressing on against his will for the last six months.

He wasn't ungrateful for it, though, the priest pushing back his sentence so he could talk and get things off his chest. He still wasn't sure that his conscience was clear or his soul was cleansed, but it was nice to have someone listen and care. A simple kindness, as Forthill put it. He wasn't asking for clemency or commutation, just simple kindness.

Although, the way things were going, maybe Forthill would ask for clemency for him, claim he'd changed his ways and just wanted to go home. The destruction of the gallows was clearly a sign from God that this man was not supposed to die, not here, not this way.

It was a fanciful notion, one Owain was loathe to entertain for even a moment. He'd heard over and over again that God was just and fair. Why should He not want a convicted murderer to hang? Or maybe the gallows was a trick by the Devil to keep him alive in his misery even longer. How could he know, really?

He was given the usual bowl of porridge at feeding time. The gaoler did not mention anything about his execution, or say anything to him at all. No one came to retrieve him, and no one came to visit. He was simply left alone in his cell like any ordinary day.

The following morning, he was not retrieved to go to chapel, nor did the priest visit him afterwards.

It was Tuesday before anyone seemed to remember his existence. The gaolers came for him and took him to meet with the warden and the priest.

"Notice anything unusual, Mr. Fforidd?" the warden inquired.

"I'm still alive?" Owain guessed.

"Indeed. I know you were informed that the gallows was unfortunately destroyed the night before your scheduled execution. I'm sure it broke your heart."

He elected not to say anything to that and the warden continued, "So, the question then becomes, what are we to do with you? There are any number of ways we can kill you, and I'm sure you've considered at least a few over the last couple of days, am I right?" Owain nodded. "However, there is the matter of legal procedure that must be observed. It is what separates judicial execution from common murder." Was there a difference? "Certain rules must be followed, such as who may and must be present, and how things are to proceed. The magistrate cannot simply come here on a whim, much as I wish that could be. However, we are pressing close to winter, which makes travel that much more treacherous. Furthermore, I have a written request from certain high officials to have you dead by the end of the year.

"To that end, it may be that we cannot honor Father Forthill's request to have you buried properly. Speaking to the magistrate, it will be November before your execution can be carried out. Between shipping the lumber needed to rebuild the gallows, getting the magistrate out here again, and other logistics, it will be a couple more months. Forthill wanted to push it back further into the spring, but as I said, orders are orders. Unless the Good Lord sends a snowstorm to bury it or knock it down again, we're looking at November."

"Is a firing squad out of the question, then?" Owain inquired.

"As I said, there are rules that must be followed. The magistrate must be present to oversee everything, and we would need a court order to just change your method of execution like that. All of this comes from lawyers, little devils in their own right. Otherwise, yes, I still would have had you executed on Saturday. It's not out of the kindness of my heart that I am informing you of what is going on."

"I understand."

"Good. With all that being said, would you like to continue to meet with Father Forthill at your regular times?"

Owain considered this for a long moment, but ultimately shook his head, deliberately ignoring the wounded look that crossed the chaplain's face. "No. I have nothing further to confess."

"Very well."

The warden made a motion and Owain stiffly rose to meet the gaoler. Father Forthill also rose and opened his mouth as if to speak. Everyone in the room paused, waiting for him, but finally the man closed his mouth, nodded mostly to himself, and sat down again. He gave Owain an unreadable look as he was taken away.

His shackles were unlocked and he quietly sat down in his cell. November. He wasn't going to be executed until November. It was only just September now. He was going to be stuck in this hell for weeks yet.

Panic set in. What did it really take to kill a man? Why was this so difficult? Even when everyone in the prison wanted to see him dead, they still had to follow rules and procedures. Needed a court order, needed the lawyers, needed the magistrate, needed everything to go exactly as planned. Wasn't the plan to just kill him? What was so difficult about that? If he'd gotten a court order to murder Balk and his associates, would he still be in this predicament? One of the men had been a lawyer, so that aspect was covered, right?

He couldn't stand the thought of spending so much more time in this cell. No light, no day or night, no work, no exercise, no one to care. Just him and his demons. Sometimes it was the shadows, taking on a life of their own. Sometimes it was sounds, whether real or imaginary, he did not know, which made them all the more frightening. The worst was the hallucinations. Seeing his pa or his brother, yelling at him, telling him how worthless he was. Sometimes it was his ma, weeping over what he'd become. Paige, Balk, any number of people he'd associated with over the years. Other times it was a faceless, drunken brawler, an opponent he'd bested years ago in his quest for dominance.

Dominance over what, he wondered. He'd gained nothing and was now set to lose the last thing he had, his life. And they couldn't even get that right, it seemed. God, the Devil, whoever was preventing his death, could they not just leave things alone and let nature take its course? Everybody died. Some just went sooner than others. Did it matter if he died in prison today or tomorrow? It was all the same. If he died sooner, then the warden and his gaolers could get back to their normal lives more quickly and everyone would be happy.

He paced anxiously in his tiny cell. Finally he ripped off the meager garments he'd been given. Gritting his teeth, he got up on the narrow bench alongside the wall. The cell was not especially tall either, and he could reach the ceiling easily. If he was right, there ought to be hooks in the ceiling. In the event the whipping room was occupied or a prisoner could not be safely removed from his cell, the gaolers could chain him up right where he was to administer punishment.

His fingers brushed something metal and round. He gripped the hook and tugged on it a bit. It did not budge from the stone. Heart pounding in his chest, he rolled up his garments and pushed them through the hook just enough that he could tie off. If the prison couldn't manage to kill one measly prisoner, that prisoner would have to do it himself. He couldn't stay here anymore. He couldn't wait to be hanged and make sure it followed the rules. He got a rope around his neck, he went through the hole, and his neck snapped. That's all there was to it. Nothing more, nothing less, and nothing that couldn't be improvised if necessary.

By now, his whole body was shaking, and not from the cold. As a matter of fact, he was sweating profusely. He was taking matters into his own hands. That had resulted in destruction often enough in the past, he figured he could rely on it now. Clothing was not an ideal material to try and tie a true noose, but if he made the loop small enough and the knot tight enough, and if he managed to jump quick enough, it should still have the same effect, same result.

He swallowed hard, feeling his Adam's apple pulse against the dirty fabric. As he stood there on the bench, he looked out and saw everyone he ever knew, standing there, watching him, waiting for him to take the step. At the front was his pa, arms folded, expression cold.

This was everything I ever amounted to, Owain thought, feeling his stomach twist. He did not dare look at his ma.

He met his pa's gaze as he moved one foot forward, felt the edge of the bench, felt the open air beneath. His stomach knotted tighter and he was afraid his bowels would give even before he'd finished killing himself. Wouldn't that be wretchedly embarrassing. And what an odd thing to consider at the moment.

Finally, he put one foot out past the edge of the bench, and slid his other foot out beside it. He felt a moment of sheer terror as he hit open air, the falling sensation as he had no control. Panic set in again as he felt the cloth around his neck tighten, squeezing his neck, cutting off his air.

Not a long enough rope, he remembered thinking. *Too long and the victim's head will rip off. Too short and he'll suffer, strangle himself before his neck breaks.*

The moment of fear lasted only a second before he heard the tearing of cloth. Then he felt cold stone under his feet. His muscles turned to water and he could not catch himself as he went down hard on the floor.

As it turned out, the darkness that followed was actually him being knocked unconscious. When he woke, he found himself on the cold stone floor. His head was murky with confusion, his senses turned to thick mud or maybe soaking wool. He was naked and shivering. He tasted blood in his mouth. He tried to spit, but it was pitiful and merely dribbled down his chin into his beard. When he tried to move, searing pain shot from his knee to his foot and then all through his body. He tried to gasp, but the cloth was still around his neck and made it difficult to breathe.

Beating down another wave of panic, he managed to get up on his elbows, then his hands. His knees were throbbing and would not cooperate. His back was sore and his shoulders were stiff. When had he become such an old man? What happened to the young man who could drink and fight and drink and fight, sleep for only a couple hours, then drink and fight again? What happened to the young man, newly married, eager to sleep with his new bride as often as he could, sometimes twice in a night? What had happened to him? When had time turned against him, bent his back, aged his bones, stolen his youth? Had he really spent a majority of his life doing nothing?

Wheezing and feeling light-headed, he blindly reached up and pawed at the cloth around his neck. He managed to get one hand between the two, and he took in several gasping breaths. He spit blood again. He stayed like this for several minutes. His head was still aching and murky. He wasn't sure how much time had passed, or even what day it was. Hell, he could hardly remember his own name.

He wasn't sure how long exactly he stayed like that, nor could he recall whether he'd been considering anything of importance. But the next thing he knew, the lock in the door was grinding with the twist of a key, and orange light spilled into the tiny cell. He instinctively squeezed his eyes shut and looked away.

The gaolers may have said something; he wasn't entirely sure. His head was still thick with wool. He did remember them dragging him to his feet where he cried out because of aching knees and a sore ankle. He remembered them fussing with the knot on the cloth around his neck. He remembered them debating whether to finish the job themselves and claim he'd been successful. Then one of them brought out a knife.

Option eleven, common butchering, he thought lazily. Simply draw a knife across his throat and be done with him.

But they just cut his garment off. He took in several breaths, but it initially only made the light-headedness worse. He could not stand, never mind walk, and the gaolers had to drag him out of his cell.

Mercifully, the infirmary was on the same floor, just down the hall, actually. He was dragged in and deposited on one of the hard beds that may have been better used as a table.

"What's the story here?" the physician inquired.

"Evidently tried to hang himself," one gaoler answered. "Tied off to one of the hooks in the ceiling."

Not a lot of care was afforded the prisoners, and a man condemned to death received even less. What was the point of trying to save his life when he was only going to lose it in a couple of months? If his leg was broken, it might not even be healed by the time he walked up to the gallows; there was no point in spending a lot of time and resources to heal him.

The physician knew this as well and even made a comment on it.

"Then why did they bring me here?" Owain found himself asking, words slurred a bit, throat stinging.

"Propriety," the man answered. "It's the rules."

More rules. Why did death come with so many rules? Who made these rules? Whose job was it to make rules on how people were and were not allowed to die? Everyone was permitted to die of old age or natural diseases. No one was allowed to be murdered, but the murderers were to be executed, unless that condemned murderer tried to kill himself, which wasn't allowed. Then he had to be kept alive so he could die according to the rules set forth by those who made the rules of death and execution. It sounded absolutely bonkers. Owain said none of this out loud, of course. If he didn't speak, he wouldn't get in trouble.

The physician was not gentle in his examination, but he was able to determine that Owain had likely not broken his legs. He had, however, twisted one ankle and busted up his knees pretty good. Probably not broken, but even so, there was little that could or would be done for him. The most he got was a small splint for his ankle—a broken one the physician had been ready to discard, but could be salvaged for use on a dead man—and a couple strips of cloth to wrap around his knees. It wasn't much, but Owain wasn't going to refuse them.

After a few more minutes, the gaolers came back with a new garment for him to wear. It wasn't really clean, but it was fresh from the laundry, anyway. It was a little heavier material than his last one, or maybe just not so threadbare, and there were considerably fewer holes. This one might actually keep him remotely warm at night, at least for a little longer, before winter really set in.

As with any inmate injury, especially with suicide attempts, the warden was called. Dillon was markedly displeased by the whole affair, but if he had to hazard a guess, Owain might say that the man was more upset that he failed than that he tried at all. Nevertheless, he delivered a scripted lecture about it. He mentioned that he might order a good whipping or other punishment for the attempt, but that was probably exactly what he was looking for. So instead, Owain would not be punished at all as a form of punishment. Again, this was all rehearsed, and Dillon probably would not have been too upset if he had been successful.

Dillon offered the call the priest back before he left the island, but Owain declined. He had nothing more to say to the priest, and there was nothing new that the priest could tell him. The warden left.

Seeing how he did not work or have any other special privileges, there was nothing he could do in the infirmary that he he could not also do in his cell. So, with a gaoler on either side of him, he was made to limp painfully back to his cell. Even limping was difficult when both knees were sore, but seeing how his left ankle was the one that was twisted, it made him favor that side even more. The only good thing to come of it was that he was only shackled at his wrists, but his ankles were left alone. He plodded along. Suddenly, the infirmary that was so mercifully just down the hall from his cell was now a great deal farther from his cell than he remembered it being. The corridor may as well have spanned across the island if it was a hundred paces.

The gaolers grumbled and groaned about the slow pace, but they did not abuse him physically.

"How did you know what I'd done?" Owain wondered breathlessly.

"We were coming to make sure you scrubbed your latrine," one told him.

"You're still doing that when we get back," the other informed him sharply. "Don't think you've gotten out of that just because of your little escapade here. Latrines are filthy and have to be clean so we don't all die of infection."

Because his day really couldn't get any worse, Owain mused silently. Perhaps it was God who had destroyed the gallows, but only so He could punish Owain a little more while on Earth. After all, once he crossed the threshold of death, he would be sent to lie with demons, and God would not be able to carry out any more punishment upon him.

Owain suddenly felt very foolish for his suicide attempt. He would not say he did not understand what he was thinking at the time, for it only took a whisper of a thought to bring back the terror he had felt, the crowd of people before him, waiting for him to hang. But all the same, he could not do it this way. He could not take matters into his own hands. As he had just proven, it turned out disastrously every time. And furthermore, it would only rob the people of the justice they craved. It wasn't fair.

He arrived back at his cell where his wrists were unshackled and the door propped open. He was given a bucket and a brush and told to scrub his latrine.

He never enjoyed it. He liked the light, liked the break from the darkness and the routine of merely waiting for food. He did not like scrubbing the latrine itself. Despite being cooped up with it every day, it still stank horridly, and made him gag. He did not dare vomit, because he would be smelling and cleaning that up, too. He clenched his jaw, turned his head, and did his chores. What made it even worse this time around was having to be on his knees to do it. He could not stand to do it any day of the week, his ankle was out of the question entirely now, and kneeling was almost as bad. He tried to get on the bench and lie on his stomach, do it from above, but the angle was hard on his arms and shoulders as he tried to scrub, so it was back to his knees.

Afterwards, he was permitted to wash his hands in fresh water before being locked in his cell, back in the darkness. But at least it didn't smell as bad, and he'd been given a little fresh straw. The fresh straw, freshly scrubbed latrine, fresh garments, it was almost enough to give a condemned man hope, but he knew better. He'd learned that the first day he set foot in Beaumaris Gaol. He had nothing coming, so he might as well save himself the trouble and discard any hope he had left.

He sat on the bench, about the most comfortable position he could manage. His ankle was sore, but it was his knees that arguably hurt the worst right now, after all the work he did on them. Gingerly, he touched them, winced. In the infirmary, he had seen that the skin was broken, but it wasn't much worse than a scrape. The damage was deeper, then. Maybe he had cracked his kneecap or something. A simple skin wound wouldn't hurt this much, wouldn't hurt so deep.

It didn't matter, he supposed. Internal wounds were almost preferable. Bone might heal wrong, but it would heal and be perfectly contained. Broken skin allowed for infection and greater disease. He would end up on the cold floor, shivering but looking for some way to alleviate the heat sweltering in his body.

He sighed and lay down, curling up as best he could with his injuries. Once upon a time, his ma had doted on him, hovered over him whenever he had any kind of injury. Most of the time he'd brushed it off, but there had been times, such as when he'd been trampled by the cow, when he'd been forced to accept help. At the time, he'd accepted it grudgingly, maybe brushed it off, only remotely appreciated any form of help. Humiliation was not the same as gratitude.

How he wished he could go back, tell his ma thank you. Tell her he loved her and appreciated everything she ever did for him, even when he rebelled. Tell her he wanted to be a good eldest son and make his family proud. Tell her he wanted to make things right.

But that wasn't going to happen. He couldn't go back in time and change anything. He couldn't send his parents a letter, either. Forthill had offered, but there was nothing the priest could say to convey all that Owain felt, his guilt and shame and all that came with it. He wasn't even sure what words he would use to describe them, and he was the one feeling them. He even had the experience and education to use bigger, more nuanced words—in two languages, no less. Still these feelings seemed to transcend everything he knew about emotion and language.

He couldn't go back and change anything, he couldn't write to his parents. He wasn't going to leave this island until he died, when his soul departed his body and he went to stand before the throne of God above. After that, he would be cut down off the gallows and taken out by the undertaker. If the ground could still be worked, he would be buried, per Forthill's request. Considering it now, Owain was grateful for the priest's intervention. A small measure of kindness. But if the ground was frozen, then he would likely be sunk. They would take his body out on a dinghy, a short distance from the island, and heave him over. He would be wrapped in a cloth with a bunch of stones, enough to keep him weighted down.

It was a strange thing to consider, the fate of one's body after death, Owain figured. Oddly enough, he found that even as he could not quite wrap his head around it, it was not a scary thing to think about. Maybe it was just the knowledge that life here would continue after he was gone. He just wouldn't be around to see it. His door was coming up quick. He would make a detour to Heaven to be judged before being sent to Hell.

The only thing he could think was that his mind was just numb with shock. He'd gone through so many emotions in the last week or so, he had nothing left to give but shock and emptiness. He shifted uncomfortably on the bench and tried to relax. Now that he was lying down, his whole body ached from his failed suicide attempt.

At some point, he came flying awake. He'd had nightmares before, but this was not the same feeling. It felt almost as if he'd been struck by lightning. Divine inspiration, perhaps. Or, more likely, demonic inspiration. But in his desperation, he would seize on anything.

He had an idea.

Chapter Fifteen

The Plan

He lay on the cold floor, unmoving, breathing shallow. His eyes were open, but he did not blink. He'd been debating that back and forth, about the blinking. If he kept his eyes open, then he had to keep them open. Expecting the gaolers to close them was a bit much to ask in his opinion. If he kept his eyes closed, it would be easier on him. It would also be difficult to see what was going on exactly, when he would have to make his move. He had a general idea of when he wanted to do it, but it would be easier if he could see his surroundings, even just a little bit.

Breathing was the hardest to control, he thought. If he stopped breathing for too long, he started getting light-headed, then there was a sense of odd euphoria, and then his body started twitching right before he felt like passing out. Once he passed out, he started breathing again. He had to, else he wouldn't wake up again.

He had to learn to control his breathing, to be able to take in minimal amounts of air without his body moving. The only time he had to truly stop breathing was when they put the glass over his mouth to try and get him to fog it up with breath. He hadn't quite gotten to that part yet.

The plan had come to him in the night a couple weeks ago. Once he died, they would have to dispose of his body. It was required, to keep disease from spreading. If he could get out of the gaol, maybe he could escape.

That was as far as his plan had gotten. Beaumaris was an island, and he couldn't swim. His only chance would be by boat, and he didn't understand the ferry schedule. From what he understood, the ferry docked on the far shore for the sole purpose of ensuring prisoners could not escape and hijack the boat. There had to be some kind of signal the priest or other visitors used in order to get the ferry to come over, but he wouldn't have that much time. In the time it took for the ferry to row over, the gaolers would be on him. No doubt the ferryman would see the commotion and turn around midway across.

His only hope, then, was the undertaker. The ferry did not dispose of bodies; he didn't want the filth and the disease aboard his vessel. That much Owain knew for sure from gossip from the gaolers. Therefore, there had to be a second dinghy that the undertaker used to take bodies out to sink them. Whether he came over on that dinghy or it was permanently stored on the island was unclear. On the one hand, the undertaker might come over on the ferry if all he was doing was burying a body. This posed a significant problem if Owain could not get to the ferry before he shoved off again. On the other hand, if the undertaker brought his own dinghy or there was one stored on the island, then the ferry wouldn't matter.

And what were they going to do to him if they recaptured him, anyway? Kill him? He was already condemned, and there was no punishment they could deliver that he did not already mentally inflict upon himself. Physical punishment might come as a relief.

His knees were aching something fierce. In the days following his failed suicide, he did not dare stand up, instead stretching his legs out on the bench. By about day five, his knees were almost back to normal, and he politely returned the cloth wraps used to bandage the scrapes. His ankle was still a little tender, but in two weeks, he could hobble along here or there if he needed to.

The key word here was "needed." He didn't need to. At all. He still did not go to chapel. He still did not go outside, though for that he was grateful this time of year. Nor did he do any kind of work. He simply stayed in his cell, waiting for the day of his execution. Or so they thought.

Instead, he spent his days pretending to be dead. He'd spent half a night with six dead bodies, and now he tried to call up that memory. Well, the memory wasn't hard, but the details were a little more elusive. There had been plenty of blood to obscure anything truly vivid, but some things he remembered. The vacant, unfocused stare. The pale faces. How the bodies went stiff. He wasn't sure about the stiff part, but he knew that the stiffness eventually went away, when the body began to bloat. He'd seen it a time or two in the bodies in the slums of London. It was a grotesque thing to behold. At the time, he'd simply been grateful that he wasn't one of them.

Now, he would have to become one of them, or else he was going to become one of them. No matter what, he had nothing to lose but his life.

So he lay there, ignoring the pain in his knees, the throbbing in his ankle, the unholy desire to claw his eyes out as he refused to blink. And above all, he focused on his breathing, counting out the seconds that he could go without breathing at all, pushing himself further and further until he danced at the edge of unconsciousness. Even when he did allow himself to breathe again, they were calm, measured breaths. He forced his body to remain calm and not twitch uncontrollably. Every thought he had, it had to be focused on being dead.

It was not an easy thing to do when the hallucinations started, but he figured it was good practice for when the gaolers came to check on him. He could not look. He could not react. No matter how annoying, outrageous, or emotional their words or actions caused him to be, he could not let it reach the surface in any sense. Not a muscle twitch, not a shifting of the eyes, not a sound. He could not gasp or draw sudden breath, could not do anything at all.

Doing nothing was the hardest thing he'd ever done in his life.

The port opened, and the bowl of porridge slid into the cell. Joints aching something fierce, Owain started to breathe again and sat upright. Stiffly, he reached for the porridge and began to eat. He had to keep up his strength and not let on that anything was amiss. That meant eating his daily meals—delivered five or six days a week—and dutifully scrubbing his latrine every week. He had little face to keep up with the gaolers, for he did not speak to them, and they did not hold him in high regard, so all remained normal in that aspect of things.

He did not meet with Father Forthill. He knew that if he did, he would spill everything and confess to plotting escape. As much as he foolishly hoped that the priest might aid him in his escape, he knew it wouldn't happen. For one, there was always a gaoler right there who would hear. For two, the priest was bound by holy oath to be an upstanding citizen, and he was a decent person who would uphold the law to the best of his abilities. He would surely tell the warden of the plan.

He sent the empty bowl back, stretched his body as much as he dared, then settled in for another round of pretending to be dead. He had little else to do while in his cell, after all. He would do this for hours at a time, or what felt like hours. Sometimes it was hard to tell. Sometimes he fell asleep while pretending to be dead, and he would wake up, initially confused and once thinking he had actually died. That was enough to send his heart into his throat and make him almost call off the whole plan. Once he got his head back on straight, he reasoned again that he had nothing to lose by trying. Hell, they might even kill him in his escape attempt. He could only pray they did it right the first time so it was a quick death. And the magistrate wouldn't even have to be present. Ha!

He wasn't sure that he would call this feeling hope. Hope was something you felt when things might be looking up. So far, he had only a plan. A desperate plan. A literal last attempt at freedom.

He wasn't even sure what he was going to do if he even did make it to the far shore. The warden would no doubt have all of Wales looking for him. When word got out, if the police didn't mobilize on their own, Mrs. Balk would surely have all of London, England, maybe even Scotland and Ireland looking for him, too. He couldn't stay here on the Isles. But where could he go?

The magnitude of his plan looming over him, he almost sat up and gave up right there, but he forced himself to remain still. He couldn't allow himself to get overly emotional. He couldn't react. The problem was very real, that he had no clue what he would do if he did indeed get off the island, but he couldn't freeze with fear. Then he would surely be caught and what little progress he did manage to make would be gone instantly. He had to do what he'd always done, just roll with things and take opportunities as they came.

That wasn't the end of it, not completely, but he couldn't be too rigid in his plans. He'd learned that a long time ago. Be smart, but be flexible. Go with the flow and always try to think a few steps ahead. That was how he'd worked his way from a slum-living ditch digger to one of the most powerful bankers in London.

He worked on his methods and his acting for weeks, but the problem was, he had no idea whether he was actually getting any better. Wasn't as though he could just pull a gaoler aside and ask if his playing dead was improving any. True, they might take it as a sick joke and give him a snide answer, but he couldn't tip them off to anything.

It could be that his whole plan was for nothing, that they would see right through. Might be that they just thought he was lethargic, ill, maybe contracted an infection, but they would hang him all the same. He didn't need to be perfectly healthy right before he died. Actually, having him ill and lethargic might be preferable; he would be less likely to try and fight them on his way to the rope.

The strange things he thought about when his only goal for the day was to play dead. A month after his failed suicide, he was able to keep his body still, and he'd figured out a method to allow for minimal air into his lungs without obvious chest expansion. Or at least, he thought he had. Once again, it was very difficult to see in the dark, but he'd become very attuned to his body's movements—or lack thereof—over the last four weeks or so. He was fairly sure he'd gotten it down.

He'd also relaxed his eyes to a position where they weren't wide open, but they weren't closed either. It allowed him to see, but his eyes didn't strain or ache or twitch from needing to blink. It was about as close to dead as he was going to get, but he wasn't going to waste his only attempt on a foolhardy test. It was all or nothing in this.

It was mid-October when the warden summoned him to his office. As he'd come to expect, Father Forthill was also present.

"Your new execution date has been set," Dillon informed him.

"When is it?" Owain asked sullenly.

"November 19th."

"The ground will be frozen by then."

"The ground is freezing as we speak. I'm sorry. It's the best I can do." He almost sounded sincere.

Owain looked at the priest. Their twice-weekly meetings seemed so far away now, a separate lifetime lived over the summer, now come to an end. They were little more than familiar strangers now. He could see the priest still felt strongly about saving his soul, but Owain had a hard time meeting him there. He had a plan, a chance for escape. He expected Forthill might have some lecture about him and Jonah, but Owain just wasn't ready. He wasn't ready to go. He couldn't meet God yet. He had to try one last time to be free.

He was returned to his cell.

He had a little over a month before he was scheduled to be executed. How close did he want to cut it with his escape attempt? It stood to reason that in the days leading up to his execution that there might be some kind of heightened security. He was dangerous after all, so dangerous he wasn't even allowed to see the outside world.

That in itself presented a significant problem. He didn't even know where he was going once he got out. He didn't really know what the island looked like. He vaguely remembered coming in, but he wasn't sure where the undertaker was going to take him to sink him. It could be on the back side of the island. Then he would be in real trouble, trying to get all the way back around.

But, once again, what were they going to do to him that they weren't going to do already? He had only his life to gain.

He tried to count off the days as best he could. The best he could figure, it was somewhere between November 3rd and November 7th that he started tapering off on the food he ate, pushing back more and more of the porridge in his bowl until he sent it out just as soon as it came in. He got up on the bench and gave himself a cut on his palm. With all the training he'd been doing to not react, he didn't so much as gasp when the skin broke and blood flowed. It was a decent cut, too, probably needing stitches. In hindsight, that probably wasn't the best place for a cut since he was going to need his hand to row the boat. Well, it was done now.

He waited another day, pushing back the porridge as he was given it. The gaolers grumbled something, maybe something about not giving him anything the next day if he was just going to keep pushing it back. Another gaoler said something about Owain trying to starve himself before being hung, and good riddance.

The next day, what he believed to be November 10th or 11th, he began his charade. The porridge came, and he ignored it. The gaoler came back and demanded that he send it back. He demanded it a second time or he was going to come in, take the bowl, and stick Owain's head in the latrine so he could scrub it with his teeth. Owain did not react, just like he'd been training himself. He did not say anything, did not move, even to look around. He relaxed his eyes. He allowed himself more comfortable breathing while the door was closed, but as soon as he heard the key in the lock, he diminished his breathing as much as he could.

The gaoler took one look at him on the floor and cursed righteously. He shouted for another gaoler who came reluctantly and with plenty of words of his own. Those words turned even more sour when he looked upon Owain's unmoving form.

Owain made sure to keep his injured hand out and obvious, hoping to dissuade any touching of a body and giving them a plausible cause of death.

The gaolers cursed again. Then one turned to the other and told him to run and get the physician.

He hadn't thought about that. The physician would want to do an examination. That could take hours. He couldn't hold out for hours.

The door closed, but not all the way, as the first gaoler stood watch. A minute later, both the physician and the warden showed up. Close behind was the priest. The warden cursed. The chaplain prayed; it sounded like he was weeping also. Guilt tightened Owain's chest, but he dared not react. He'd been through this with his hallucinations, seeing his mother weeping over him, seeing his father cursing him. He had to remain dead.

"I'd say he contracted an infection in his hand," the physician said. "Let me examine him quickly."

Owain could tell the physician approached and knelt in front of him. A quick examination he might be able to suffer through, but he wanted to avoid it at all costs. He'd intentionally urinated on himself, as he'd noticed the six dead men had done. He had to come up with something else now, something —

Only at the last second did he clamp down on outward muscle movements as he belched and farted at the same time. He did this twice and allowed himself to relax just a bit more, as if settling. The physician made a strangled sort of sound and stood up without ever touching him. He took a few steps back.

"He's dead," the physician said. "His body is releasing its gases, and in no pleasant manner, either. I suspect there will be plenty more of this over the next few hours."

"God Almighty," the warden said, coughing.

"Indeed," Forthill murmured.

There was silence for just a moment.

"Very well," Dillon sighed. "I will send for the undertaker. A bit early, but it will save him the trip in a few days."

"If I may, Nathan," the priest began.

"Yes, you may perform whatever rites you deem necessary."

"Thank you. And, with your permission, I told Fforidd that I would inform his parents of his death."

"Of course. Do what you feel you need to."

The cell was soon emptied of everyone but Forthill and Owain posing as a dead body. The priest did not touch him, but he knelt very close and said several prayers, most of them for Owain's soul. Owain felt his whole inside twisting with grief and guilt and other emotions he had no good names for. It was all he could do to not react, not give any indication that he was only pretending.

He was too relieved when the priest finally left, closing the door behind him but not locking it. Owain allowed himself to breathe, but he still did not move. Dead bodies did not move. That was one aspect of his plan he hadn't fully considered until now, but he was glad he'd always carried on as long as he could. Maybe a few open wounds from lying down would help to convince them he was dead.

After some time, the door opened again and a threadbare blanket was laid over him. Well, at least that might allow him to breathe a little easier, for a short time, anyway. He did not relax his body completely, but once the door was closed, he wiggled stiff fingers and toes. He so badly wanted to flex knees and elbows, but did not dare lest he was unable to return to his dead position.

He thought for sure the gaolers would be a little more intent on getting rid of a dead body; it felt like days before anyone came for him, long enough for his stomach to protest, anyway. The protest was weak, seeing how he'd been minimizing or skipping meals for several days beforehand, but he was fearful that someone would hear the rumbling.

So he lay there, forcing himself to stay awake. If he fell asleep, he would shift position, and he would start breathing normally. He had to stay awake. Had to stay dead.

His resolve was beginning to seriously waver and his eyelids were drooping when he heard the door open again.

"This is the one," the warden said. "Poor bastard was scheduled to hang in just a few days. Guess the Lord decided to have mercy on him."

The warden's tone was different now, almost pitying. Well, no one spoke ill of the dead, after all, even if he was a dead murderer.

Owain hoped his racing heart could not be seen or heard as the undertaker peeled back the blanket a bit, glanced over him, then put a glass to his mouth. Only when the man nodded and replaced the blanket did Owain close his eyes and send up a silent prayer of thanks. Was that the right thing to do? Must be. If God did not want him to escape, then He could have ended it all right here.

"Very good," the undertaker said. "Wrap him up, get him down to the dock, then."

Wrap him up. Owain hadn't even considered that. They were going to tie him in the blanket with a bunch of stones. What if he couldn't break out? He would be sunk and he would drown! Maybe that was his punishment for trying to escape, a slower, more painful death than hanging. Still, he did not break. There might be a chance yet. If he couldn't break out, they would surely know he was alive just by his movements, and they couldn't sink him then. Right?

Several gaolers were called in. With their jostling around, Owain was able to at least flex his joints a little bit before he was deposited on another blanket. Stones were placed at strategic points around his body and the undertaker mercifully closed his eyes. Owain wondered if anyone had noticed his eyes getting tired and his eyelids drooping. Then the blanket was wrapped around him.

"Don't tie it tight," the undertaker warned. "I may have to adjust the stones a bit before putting him over. Just enough to get him down there."

The gaolers did not argue, grumble, or complain in any way, just did as they were told. Cassius must not be among them, Owain thought. He was usually the instigator of grumbling.

The ties were loose, but kept the blanket around him and the stones in with him. Then he was hefted on a stretcher and taken down to the ground floor. Everyone seemed to know his job, and there was little talk among the gaolers or the undertaker. There was only a brief mention of opening the gates to the outside.

There was a creak, and a cold blast of air buffeted Owain through the blanket. It was cold inside the gaol, but it was wretched outside. At least inside his cell, the walls blocked the wind. Outside, there was little to hide behind. And he had only his meager garment. Whatever he did and whenever he did it, it would have to be soon and fast, while he still had some strength in his limbs. He didn't want to end up freezing to death while escaping a death sentence by playing dead. The irony in it was too strong, and he wasn't going through all this trouble just to die halfway to freedom.

Now one of the gaolers cursed as he tripped over something in the frozen ground and lurched forward. The rest almost went down with him, and there was plenty of cursing to go around. Even the undertaker had a few choice words for them. Then he turned his attention to someone else—who Owain could only assume was some sort of assistant or apprentice—and told them to go get the boat ready.

Owain's heart was pounding. He was outside the gaol for the first time in over a year. Granted, it was less than ideal circumstances, and it was frigid cold, but for a moment, he was just glad for the freedom, the chance to be outside. His resolve only hardened as he considered what he was going to have to do. He slowly let out a breath, hoping he wouldn't fog up the air outside the blanket. No one said anything.

The gaolers stopped, shifted position and their grip on the stretcher. The next thing he knew, he was being slid into a small boat across the seats. The undertaker was giving orders and moving things appropriately. Owain wished he could see what was going on. As it was, the best he could tell was that it was daytime, and he could see vague shadows on the blanket as someone moved within his line of sight.

The water was wavy, but not overly treacherous as the undertaker and the warden exchanged words for a moment. Then the boat rocked as the undertaker got in. The boat was pushed off, away from the dock, and out they went into the channel. Owain didn't think his heart could beat any faster, but apparently it could. He wasn't sure if he was grateful for skipping his meals as the water got a little more rocky away from the shore.

"All right, this spot's as good as any," the undertaker said finally. Some time had passed, but with the waves, Owain had no way of knowing just how far they'd actually gone. Were they at least halfway between Beaumaris and the mainland island?

"Hold the oars, Henry, while I get everything situated. Keep us steady as you can."

There was some shuffling and shifting of goods and people. The undertaker moved about on the small craft with all the grace of an elephant. Owain felt his stomach turn, but he knew he had nothing to give. As the ties began to loosen even more, Owain slowly worked every muscle methodically, in small movements, trying to time them with the waves and the string. The undertaker growled a bit about the knots being too small for his big, stiff fingers. Finally he took a knife to them, starting at the feet, saying something about tying them tighter once he was finished anyway.

The last one over Owain's chest was cut. The blanket was peeled back from his chest. As the undertaker lifted the fold covering his face, Owain made his move, springing to life.

The motion startled Owain as much as the undertaker. His body was cold and stiff and did not want to respond, but he'd forced it to, and now it was trying to figure out what was going on. The undertaker, an older man of between fifty and sixty years, startled with a silent yell. He stumbled back, hit the side of the boat just as it heaved, and tumbled into the water. The assistant, a boy of no more than nineteen years, sat, huddled where he was, hands tight around the oars. He only stared at Owain, mouth open but saying nothing.

Just as the boy made a move—whether to start rowing for shore, to jump over himself, or to attack Owain, was unclear—Owain grabbed him by his shirt and lifted him up. As soon as the boy let go of the oars, Owain tossed him overboard.

That was likely two more murders on his record, but what was two more when he was already suppose to hang for six? He wouldn't say he didn't feel a little guilty about it, because he really did want to be good. It was just necessary, he supposed, taking the boy's seat and taking up the oars. Grabbing onto the old wood with his wounded hand sent knives of pain running through his hand and up his arm to his shoulder, but he gritted his teeth and looked around, trying to get his bearings.

Well, he wasn't halfway between the gaol and the far shore, but he had a decent head start, anyway. At the very least, he was on the right side of the island and only had to continue the direction he was going; he could see the ferryman's dock.

Wrapping his death blanket around his shoulders, Owain steeled himself against the discomfort in his body and the pain in his hands, gripped the oars as tight as he could, and began rowing. Not three strokes in, he knew he'd lost a lot of strength, which wasn't entirely implausible. Combined with the cold, and he was having a hell of a time. His arms burned, his hands hurt. Still he forced himself in, falling into a rhythm as he fought the waves.

At the center of the narrow channel, he thought for sure he was going to capsize. He allowed himself only a brief moment to reflect on the irony of a failed escape attempt now, and then he reined himself in. He could not succumb to doubt or fear. He would not.

Water crashed over him and he nearly lost hold of the oars. Cold wind chilled him, but he pushed himself harder, feeling the sweat on his body begin to freeze. And still he was only just halfway across. If the warden or the gaolers suspected anything amiss, they would be waiting for him on the other side at this rate.

He pressed on, forcing his limbs to work. The pain in his hand had become an icy fire, as odd as that sounded. He gritted his teeth and told himself to keep going. He glanced over his shoulder every once in a while to ensure he was still heading for the far shore. The ferry got smaller and smaller as he was pushed away, but he was still heading in the right direction, at least.

Then he hit rock. He jolted and lost his left oar. Owain turned and found he'd bumped against rocky shoreline. He really didn't feel like traipsing around in the water and then running around in the cold with only a sack for a garment and a frozen blanket, but he had little choice.

The rocks were slippery, but jagged, and they afforded him good hand and footholds. Grunting and growling and occasionally crying out as more skin tore, he pulled himself out of the boat and onto the rocks. He stayed as low as he could on his belly, crawling over the rocks like a crab.

The boulders ended suddenly and he found himself on a gravely shore covered in snow. He'd done it. He'd escaped. He was free.

He stood and started running.

Chapter Sixteen

The Fugitive

Owain didn't get half a mile before he was on his knees, shaking with cold. The blanket had frozen stiff. It chilled him, but being solid, it helped to keep the wind off. The day hadn't been too bad, all things considering, but the water and the cold were killing him. Literally, they were killing him. He had to find shelter and some sort of warmth, or else he could still die in his attempt to escape from prison by playing dead.

He forced himself to keep moving, acutely aware of the sun setting behind him. The days were short, and the cold was rapidly intensifying. He shivered. Pain tore at his fingers and toes though he could hardly feel them otherwise. His joints were stiff and his face was numb. It hurt to breathe. Where he'd once trained himself to breathe minimally to avoid chest rise, now his chest almost would not rise. His breath puffed out in front of him in short bursts of steam.

He paused as he crested a small hill overlooking a valley. The forest below looked young, but all he cared about was the house squatted at the edge of the tree line. All hope of survival funneled into a single thought of getting inside that house. He wanted to drop the blanket and run down there, but he did not do either. He would need the blanket later, he was sure.

The house was abandoned. He could tell that from a distance when he saw no smoke coming from the chimney and no candles in the windows. No matter; it was shelter. With woods nearby, he might gather a few sticks and start a fire. He trudged onward, forcing his way through the snow until he reached the front door.

Whoever had lived in the cottage hadn't left it too long ago. The framing had only just started to show signs of rot, and from what Owain could gather, it had been a fairly wet autumn. Inside the house, dust coated everything, but it still looked merely unkempt versus full-on abandonment.

Owain's gaze first fell to the fireplace, and then to the wood box beside it. He fell down in front of it and pried open the lid with frozen fingers. The box was full, and there was even a flint starter set on top of the pile.

He fumbled miserably with the wood, his fingers refusing to respond, but he got a small set-up going, arranging the larger sticks and stuffing dry grass and pine needles in the middle. It took several tries for the flint to catch, but the fuel was dry enough that it only required one spark. Owain sat back on the dusty floor, tears streaming down his cheeks. He couldn't recall a time when he'd been so happy. Just to be outside in the world, just to be alive, it was almost too much to bear. His heart twisted and he felt light-headed. He couldn't even describe it; he was just so happy.

Building up the fire got easier and easier as his hands thawed, and soon he got it big enough that he could leave it for a few minutes to look around and see what else the former occupants had left.

The best he could tell, it had been a couple who'd had at least one, maybe two children. They'd been terribly poor. Even accounting for vermin getting into their remaining things, most of the possessions were broken, ripped, moldy, rotting. Owain managed to find a set of clothes that fit. Well, they didn't fit perfectly, but they covered his body and kept him warm and dry. He peeled off the prison sack and laid it out by the fire to dry. As much as he wanted to throw it in the fire, it was still another layer he could wear against the cold.

He found a razor quite by accident, and with his foot. He cursed as he bent to examine the wound, but it was not deep, not even needing stitches. But at least he knew the razor was sharp. He had no razor cream, but a little burn from a razor was the least of his problems right now, and hardly the worst thing he'd sustained recently.

So he sat there in front of the fire, shaving as much hair as he could. He sliced off his beard which had grown remarkably long and tossed it in the fire to burn. Then he drew the blade down his cheeks until completely smooth. After the shorter beard hairs had been gathered up and tossed in the fire, he sliced off his long head hair and did the same. He did not dare shave his head smooth on account of the cold, but he got it short and as neat as he could manage doing the work blindly.

He set the blade down and just sat there, staring into the fire, mesmerized. Had today really happened? Had he really broken out of prison? It felt surreal, as surreal as the knowledge that he had once been a wealthy banker. Two completely different lives for a single man. How many more lives would he live before he died? Would he be able to remember them all?

Involuntarily, he broke into a yawn. He was exhausted. He'd been about ready to fall asleep when they'd finally dragged him out of his cell. The panic and the need to escape had seen him across the channel. Running around in the cold and snow had seen the return of his fatigue in full force. Getting warm again had pepped him up a bit, but now that same warmth was relaxing him, causing him to doze off.

Did he dare try to sleep? How long before they came for him? Maybe they would find the empty boat and assume he'd fallen into the water. Likely the wind had already obscured his tracks, but what if it hadn't? They probably knew all the houses in the area, knew where an escapee was likely to run to for immediate food and shelter, maybe threaten a few locals. If this cottage hadn't been abandoned for long, they might come looking. If they knew about this place at all, they would probably come looking.

But he couldn't keep running indefinitely. He had to sleep at some point. He needed sleep, and he would have to find food.

It was the last thing he remembered thinking before drifting off.

The following day, he awoke, initially confused, then suddenly panicking. Why wasn't he in his cell? Had he died? Was this Hell? Was it Heaven?

As he looked around in the gray predawn light, the events of the previous day filtered back into his mind, and he relaxed a little. So they hadn't come for him in the night. Good. And he felt rested. For the first time in months, he felt truly rested. And he was just sleeping on the floor in front of the fireplace.

He coaxed the fire back to life, then went outside to relieve himself and observe his surroundings.

It was still cold out, but he hardly felt it with the new life flowing through his limbs, and he went out a bit to explore.

A fast-flowing river, maybe as wide as he was tall, perhaps thigh-deep in some spots, was situated a good hundred yards down from the cottage and flowed west, deeper into the trees. Most of the trees around the river were pine, and the young growth appeared to be maples and other deciduous varieties. He found a dead pine and broke off a few of the low-hanging branches, taking them back to the house where he snapped them into smaller pieces and fed them into the fire. He couldn't remember the last time he'd felt so alive.

He found the root cellar easily enough. It was harder to find anything to eat. Any jars left behind were spoiled. A poorly-braided cluster of onions had sprouted from one side and rotted on the other. He did manage to dig up a few potatoes which he took back up to the fire. Rummaging around in the kitchen produced only a single cracked pot, but it worked well enough to somewhat steam and cook the potatoes. Again he was overwhelmed with happiness, just at being able to taste something other than porridge. He didn't remember the last time he'd had potatoes, but it had probably been years. And cooking them up with one of the small onions that hadn't quite sprouted yet, he may as well have been dining with the king himself.

Owain finished off the potatoes and onions and just sat back on his elbows, simply basking in the warmth and the simplicity. He didn't need much. He'd never needed the wealth or the status. He'd never needed that kind of cutthroat ambition. He didn't need to dominate or conquer or try to prove anything to anyone. He simply had to be. That was all there was to it. Just life. Living life as it was meant to be lived, for the joy of being alive.

Which he wouldn't be if the warden ever caught up to him. He was still dangerously close to the gaol. He had to act as if they were out hunting for him. Otherwise he may as well walk right back there and announce himself. They may not have done anything the previous day because by the time they realized something was up, it was already dark and cold and their chances of finding anything were minimal. Today was turning out to be a very nice day, which meant they would be coming after him with everything they had.

He didn't know where to go. His first thought was to go home, but that was decidedly not an option. His pa would turn him back over to the authorities, assuming he didn't shoot him on the spot. And besides that, there was no way he could face his ma, not after all the pain he'd caused. Granted, the last time he'd seen them had been years ago when he was still a happy newlywed, but there was no way they couldn't have learned about his treachery. On top of that, seeing how he had no friends, it would make logical sense that he would return home. Might be that the warden was already sending a small group of men to his parents' house for that very reason, to try and meet him there, or even intercept him on the road.

He would have to take to the road, travel cross-country, at least for a little while. He looked outside and shuddered at the thought. He would have no food, and his clothing was hardly ideal. It wasn't even sufficient. He had no idea where the nearest town was, and he couldn't just hope to happen upon an abandoned house every night, or even an occupied house. His options were sorely limited. All the same, he couldn't stay here.

His best bet, then, would be to follow the river. Civilization was built around water, after all; he would come upon a house or a town eventually. On top of that, animals were drawn to water as well, which meant he had a chance of finding small game. If he could remember how to rig a few simple traps, he would at least have meat which would keep him going for a while. If he was able, he might be able to tan the furs and attach them to his clothes. It was wilderness survival at its finest, but people had been doing this for hundreds, thousands of years.

He had two options: die in the forest a free man, or return to the gaol and die a condemned murderer. But he couldn't stay in the cottage.

After giving it some more thought, Owain stoked the fire, then got up and did a more thorough search of the house. He found a knife with a broken handle and a slightly bent blade. A little dull, but it would work in a pinch. A length of rope that was a little dirty and moldy. It wouldn't hold as much as it used to, but it could still snare a rabbit. He found a swath of burlap with moth holes in it. He dusted it off and managed to bring it up into a sort of bag. As long as he only kept large items in it, he shouldn't lose anything.

He'd laid out his blanket the night before. It had gone from frozen to soaking wet once the fire got going, but it was dry now. Inspecting it more closely, the holes were not as bad as he had feared. Certainly a far cry from an ideal winter cloak, but he could only use what he had.

A last check of the cottage yielded nothing of use, but he didn't want to leave having overlooked something of extreme importance. For a minute, he considered taking the flint with him. He would certainly need fires to keep him warm at night. All the same, he knew from experience that fire and smoke would attract attention to him when he did not want to attract attention. If he could make it to a town, gain a head start on the authorities, he would buy his own flint. He wasn't sure with what he would purchase it, but he would obtain one the honest way.

He was just about ready to spread the ashes in the fireplace and head out the door when movement through the window caught his eye. Instinctively, he ducked and inched his way toward the window. There, coming down the hill, was the warden and at least four gaolers, maybe six. They stopped about halfway down the hill. He could see the warden was saying something, saw him point here and there, making more gestures. Judging by the way they were moving, they were fairly confident that he was here, or could be. They were going to surround him so that if he tried to bolt, someone would always be waiting.

The cottage had three doors, one on the east and west side, plus the root cellar which was also accessible from a hatch in the common room. But he couldn't let himself get trapped down there. There was a lot of spoilage down there, yes, but there was also a lot of flammable material. They might try to smoke him out or just burn him alive and call it a day.

Owain nearly went through the wall at a knock on the door. All right, so maybe they weren't entirely sure he was here, but they probably had a pretty good suspicion. Might be they were going to try a peaceful resolution before a fight. Problem was, the only resolution here ended in death.

There was a second knock, but he heard no shouting. Taking a breath, he went to the door and opened it.

"Hello, Owain," Father Forthill said.

"Father," Owain greeted, his voice cracking.

"Is this why you didn't want to meet with me? Because you knew that you would tell me of your plans?"

"That might have something to do with it."

The priest looked at his feet and sighed. "Tell me, Owain. Was it all fake? Did you feel no remorse, all those days you wept while speaking to me? Or did you simply seek to use me?"

Guilt gnawed at Owain as he shook his head. "I never had any ill intentions toward you, Father. I meant every word I said, and everything I felt was real."

"Including this apparent fear of death."

"I understand it now, better than I ever have. And yes, it scares me."

"You know this only ends one way. You attempted suicide twice. You are bound for the gallows. At this point, they're ready to hang you just as soon as we return. Is it death that you are afraid of, or meeting our Lord?"

Apparently Owain's hesitation was enough of an answer.

"Oh, Owain," Forthill sighed, his tone putting Owain instantly in mind of his ma. "Owain, Owain. There is nothing I can say to convey how greatly the Lord desires fellowship with you, which includes grace and mercy and forgiveness of sins, if only you ask. It is not complicated. It is not a contract with terms and conditions. It is love at its finest."

Owain ran his tongue over his teeth. "Now tell me something, Father. Let's say I'm hanged today. Let's say they shoot me dead right now. Will it really satisfy justice? Will the world really be a better place without me? Or could it be better if I am allowed to be better?"

"By escaping from prison by pretending to be dead?"

"Semantics."

The priest frowned. "The Lord grants mercy. Men are a little more hard-nosed."

"And whose example should we follow?"

"You suggest clemency. Owain, only God knows the heart. It could be that the Lord sees a pure heart in you. Men do not see such things. And as you have just proven in the last day or two, some men seek only to exploit the merciful and the peacemakers. You have exploited my kindness. I may believe that you had no ill intentions toward me, but who else will believe it? Words mean little, and your actions are not the most imitable. It would take a lifetime of good deeds to prove that you have changed. Unfortunately, you don't have that."

"And does the Lord only forgive once? Or is it seventy times seven time that he forgives?"

"Do you suggest that there be no punishment at all? No justice whatsoever?"

Owain shook his head. "Of course not. But some men learn. It may take us all the way to the moment of our deaths, but some men learn. And justice has been served. Let a changed man be changed."

Forthill closed his eyes and may have said a quick prayer, judging by the minute movements of his lips. Finally he opened his eyes, expression almost regretful. "I'm sorry, Owain. I don't have that kind of power. The warden is not here to negotiate. He is here to return you to the gaol to be executed. Or he will execute you here."

By now, the gaolers had closed their circle around the cottage. The warden stood about fifteen paces behind the priest.

"Very well," Owain said quietly. "I'll go back peacefully, but I have one request."

"What is that?"

"I want to sleep here tonight. Not in a dark, cold, stone cell with dirty straw and rats. Here, on the blanket with a warm fire. They can shackle me and keep a watch on me. They can take me back in the morning and hang me in the afternoon, but I want to sleep here."

Forthill nodded graciously. "I think that can be managed. Give me a moment."

Owain waited patiently in the doorway while the priest stepped back and went to speak to the warden. The warden clearly was not pleased as his flagrant gestures and raised voice indicated, but the priest remained calm and stoic. The gestures were soon contained and the voices lowered. Forthill returned to the step.

"Dillon has agreed to allow you to stay here for the night. He and the gaolers will be here, as will I."

"I expected nothing less," Owain said graciously. "I hope they brought their own food because there is little more than potatoes and a few onions here."

The warden sent two of the gaolers back to let those back in the gaol know what was going on. That left four gaolers plus the warden. Dillon tried to get Forthill to return, but the priest refused. In fact, he offered to take first watch, that he might have words with Owain. While Owain greatly preferred the priest's company to that of the gaolers', he was also terribly afraid of the conversation.

The gaolers made themselves at home in the cottage, placing Owain's blanket in the center of the room so they could surround him. The warden took up a position near one of the doors.

They had brought a little food, but not with the intent of staying out overnight. Portions were small, even considering that two members of the party had left. Owain was given potatoes and onions from the cellar while the gaolers doled out pieces of jerky, a few pieces of cheese, and a handful of nuts each. Their breakfast would be a similar affair.

Outside the prison walls, the gaolers were a rather rambunctious troupe. Jokes were loud and bawdy, and the warden didn't do much except for give them a warning here and there if it started to get a little too out of hand. Their drink of choice appeared to be mead. Owain rather enjoyed mead, but he found himself uninterested in it. Maybe it was just his mindset at the moment, but he did not crave the alcohol they unscrupulously indulged in. Of their group, only Forthill did not partake in the merriment, instead sticking to a flask of wine that he only took nips from.

The mirth lasted long into the evening. Considering how early it grew dark, Owain estimated the hour to be about ten o'clock before the last of the gaolers fell asleep, warden included. Only the priest remained awake, and he was dozing. By ten-thirty, he, too, was asleep.

Sitting there by the dying fire, shackled, Owain considered a number of escape attempts. He knew a thing or two about being silent and stealthy. The problem became dealing with the damn chains. Anyone who saw him would know him for an escaped convict. No one would help him. He had to get rid of these shackles.

They weren't extraordinarily tight so that they drew blood, but they were shackles for a reason. He was not able to slip his hands through. At least, not as they were. His fingers were fine, it was just his fat thumb that got in the way.

Owain was no stranger to death, and he wasn't even referring to the men he'd killed. There were plenty of bodies to be found in the slums of London, or those who were passed out drunk and looked like dead bodies. One time, he'd seen a couple of feral dogs tearing into a body that couldn't have been more than a week old, drug up from a ditch. Owain had seen plenty of bones and gotten an important, if gruesome, anatomy lesson. It wasn't just the joints in the obvious thumb that made things difficult. There was also the joint that connected the thumb to the hand.

Looking around and making a few intentional sounds to check the wakefulness of his guards, Owain put his hands down in front of him and started pressing down on his thumb with his foot. If he could somehow dislocate that joint and push his thumb over, more into his palm, maybe he could make his hand slender enough to slip the shackles.

Being a veteran of many fights, Owain knew a thing or two about breaking bones and dislocating joints. Most of the time, he was doing it to other people, but that wasn't to say he hadn't experienced it himself from time to time. He still remembered breaking his leg while breaking into someone's root cellar. The difference was, this time around, it was utterly imperative that he be totally silent. He could afford no mistakes here.

That being said, he tasted blood in his mouth as he bit his tongue long before he heard and felt the pop of two joints in his thumb. He strangled a yell in his throat and froze completely. All around him, the gaolers and the warden still snored like a bunch of hibernating bears. The priest was still seated with his chin tucked into his chest, leaning just slightly to one side.

Knowing that the swelling would begin immediately, he got his limp thumb where it needed to be and carefully slid his hand through the shackle. Hot tears streamed down his face. When his hand was finally free, he gently lowered it to meet his other hand where he carefully popped the joints back in place. That was ten times easier to do, and proportionally more painful. He choked down another cry as the joints went back in, but after the momentary flash of agony, the pain subsided almost completely.

Time to do the other hand.

Owain took a breath and resolved to do this one quickly, thinking it would be a little easier since he would have his free hand to help instead of just his foot. Just one good thrust and it should pop out.

He went stiff a second time as he fought back any and every sound and movement that might come out of him or be caused by him. The pain was not so bad the second time, probably because he basically knew what to expect. After a moment of forcing himself to be still and not make noise, as well as calm his breathing, he slipped his right hand through his shackle and popped the joints back in. Again, the pain subsided fairly quickly. He took deep, calm, quiet breaths, then looked around again. No one appeared to have stirred. Now he just had to plan how to get out.

The warden was sleeping in front of one door, and a gaoler slept in front of the other door. Those weren't good options anyway because of potential noise as well as the sudden blast of cold air that would blow in. But no one was on the hatch to the root cellar, maybe because it was still covered by a small rug. He did, however, still have to get over one gaoler.

That proved easier than anticipated, even with his blanket and bag that was sitting next to the rug, but it was not without its share of anxiety. Owain's hands still hurt, the one with the deep cut especially, and that was even before his thumbs which were starting to ache. They didn't hurt, but it was a deep throb in the joints that made any movement stiff and painful. Nevertheless, he pushed the rug back just enough to reach the hatch. He did not lift the hatch all the way, just enough for him to slip into the darkness. This proved to be a fairly large opening that he needed; he'd lost some strength, but very little size it seemed. He was careful to time any squeaks with the snoring of the gaolers and lower the hatch just as carefully.

He dropped into the darkness. Panic flooded over him, and he froze for just a minute as he told himself that he was in a root cellar, not a prison cell. The two had a lot in common, however. He reached out and touched the dirt wall just to remind himself where he was.

He had to get moving before one of the gaolers woke up to take watch.

In a way, his time in the black cells proved to be advantageous. He knew how to memorize the layout of a room from only the briefest glimpses in bad light. He knew exactly where to find the potatoes, stuffing a couple in his bag before making a beeline for the outside door. He was careful when opening it, trying not to let the wind rip it out of his hands, even as he knew it would take a substantial wind to take it from him, as heavy as the door was. But, to that end, he couldn't let it slam open or shut, either. He eased it open and closed with the same care he had with the interior hatch.

"Where will you go?"

Owain nearly came out of his skin at a voice behind him, and he whirled to see the priest standing there in the snow. He'd come around the corner of the house and stood hardly three paces from Owain.

"What?" he asked dumbly.

"I asked where you will go." When Owain did not answer, Forthill continued, "Owain, if I wanted to, I could go back in and raise the alarm. Dillon would rouse his gaolers and they would have you recaptured within the hour, if that. Do you know why I don't?"

Owain shrugged. "Why?"

"Because this is not where your story ends. I don't understand it, but I believe the Lord has shown me at least part of your path. And it does not end here."

"Where does it go?"

"I can't say for sure, but I believe it involves a cave in a far off land."

"A cave?"

"As I said, I don't understand it. It's not my business to understand it. All I know is that you don't go back to Beaumaris. Not today."

Owain frowned, the guilt returning to plague him. "I never had any ill intentions toward you, Father."

Forthill nodded. "I know. I believe you. And I think you're right when some men have to be brought right up to the moment of death before they can change, before they will change."

"You think I've changed?"

"I don't know. Have you? How are you going to prove it? Words are meaningless unless you deliver; surely you learned that at least as a banker, if not in other situations."

"I don't know. But I'll find a way."

The old priest smiled gently. "I know you will. If I could, I would offer you sanctuary at my parish, but I fear that would not go well." He slowly approached Owain, bringing out a small pouch. "Instead, the best I can do is offer you my faith, my blessing, a prayer—" He held out the pouch. "—and a few provisions. These are mine that I give to you, so don't worry about them finding out."

"Oh, they'll find out."

"But they won't know that I helped you." The priest returned to the cellar door and opened one side. He looked at Owain. "Go, now. I'll wait a bit before I tell them."

Owain met the priest's gaze. "Thank you."

Forthill nodded. "Thank me by becoming a better man."

Interlude

The End

Father Forthill waited about an hour or so before sounding the alarm. The gaolers, wretchedly hungover and in a crankier mood than normal, scrambled to find their missing prisoner. Forthill did not deny that he had fallen asleep, and he earned a severe rebuke from Nathan for it, and was dismissed from his post on the spot. He showed them where Fforidd must have escaped through the root cellar. Forthill had come out to relieve himself when he found the door open and tracks leading away.

Being the middle of the night, Nathan figured it would be fairly easy to find Fforidd; he was hardly dressed for the cold. They followed the tracks to the river where they disappeared. They could only conclude that Fforidd had gone in the river and was traipsing through the water to cover his tracks and his scent, in the event they brought dogs to search.

"He'll freeze by morning," the warden declared at last, after they followed the river for a short distance but found nothing. "We'll return to the gaol, gather food, supplies, and send letters to the surrounding authorities to bring dogs."

And so it was. By the time they reached the cottage, the sky was beginning to lighten. They gathered up anything they may have forgotten, then set out for the gaol. It was not a pleasant trek. Everyone was tired. Everyone was hungry. Everyone but Forthill was hungover. Plus it was cold and snow had begun to fall. By the time they boarded the ferry, the gaolers, who just the previous evening had been making merry, were about ready to murder each other. Once they reached the island, Dillon dismissed them to get some food and rest up for a bit. They could alleviate their anger by torturing some of the other prisoners later in the day.

"I suppose I will ensure that I have left nothing here, and then be on my way," Forthill said meekly once the gaolers had departed.

"Come with me," Nathan ordered.

The priest followed the warden at a respectful distance, through the gaol and up to the first floor, around the corner to the governor's office. Nathan bid the man close the door and sit. The two men stared at each other across the desk for what felt like an eternity.

"Tell me honestly, Father," Nathan said finally. "Did you help him escape?"

"I did not help him," Forthill answered. "I simply did not stop him. I did fall asleep, and when I woke, he was gone. I went outside and just caught him before he took off into the woods."

The warden nodded. "That's what I thought." He gave the priest a look. "You know, that sort of thing could land you right here among the prisoners yourself."

"Then I suppose I shall be quite intimate with my flock."

"Indeed you shall. But I am not going to do that to you."

"If I may beg a reason?"

"For one, you're an old man. Prison is no place for you, as you have proven in more ways than one." He shifted in his seat. "I respect you, Father. I really do. But you are an idealist. You want to see the good in everyone. It's an admirable trait, but not one we need here. You are better suited, I think, for the more meek and mild members of the flock, the country parishioners such as your companion Worthington is in charge of. I think you know that as well, which is why you asked to be relieved after this debacle was over with anyway. I think this endeavor with Fforidd has proven to be more taxing than you realized, more than you can handle."

Forthill sighed and nodded. "On this, we can agree."

"However, some of the inmates do like you. Genuinely like you. Short of the Lord taking you in the night, I think it would be unfair and unwise to simply remove you from them with no warning."

"What are you saying?"

"Come back next week. One last Sunday chapel service. You can tell them what's going on. Among the other letters I need to write today, I will also inquire after another prison chaplain to lead service and hear confessions."

The priest nodded graciously. "Of course. Thank you, Nathan."

"Don't thank me just yet. This still isn't over with Fforidd."

"I understand. All the same, thank you."

The warden's expression said he didn't understand why he was being thanked, but he accepted it anyway, saying, "Make one last round around the gaol. Talk to your inmates, clean up anything you may have left behind, as unlikely as that sounds. But know that if I can't get a replacement chaplain in time, I expect you will come back to deliver last rites as needed."

"I expect I shall come for that purpose, anyway."

"I thought you might say that," Nathan said, nodding. "Well, I have work to do, and so do you."

The priest grimly agreed and departed the warden's office. He took a particularly long time making his rounds. Prison chaplain was not a job for everyone. Not everyone could handle it, being stuck in a massive stone gaol with a bunch of criminals. While he had been able to do it in his younger years, it was certainly a good idea to retire while his reputation was still in tact. And not having to climb up and down stairs all day was something he would admit to looking forward to. His knees agreed.

But while the job wasn't for every pastor, for those who could it well, it was a somewhat rewarding experience. Watching the hardened criminals accept humanity as a real entity and take responsibility for their lives, watching and praying with them as they repented, it was a marvelous thing, in his opinion. These marvelous times were few and far between, however. And after everything he'd gone through to grant Owain a small measure of kindness, only for him to turn around and run away...it was hard. Forthill knew that Owain's life couldn't end here in this gaol, but there was still a feeling of betrayal, that Owain had used him in some way.

It was strange, after six months of making rounds and then speaking to Fforidd afterwards in the chapel, he'd become accustomed to the routine and wasn't prepared for their meetings to come to an end. He'd expected their last conversation to be just before the hanging, not while Owain tried to escape.

Forthill faithfully made his rounds, telling some of the prisoners that he would be retiring after the next chapel service. Many had an opinion. A few were sorry to see him leave and thanked him for talking to them and being kind. A few were all too happy to be rid of him. He didn't let it get to him, though. It did no good in any situation, but especially here, where he would only be here for one more service.

From his present vantage point on the first floor, he saw the warden and a few fresh gaolers depart the island. The gaolers looked ready for business, but the warden just looked tired. Forthill didn't blame him, really. He was just doing his job. Withholding yard time was a bit unfair, the priest mused, but when it came to escapees — or, as is most often the case, attempted escapees — that was something even a priest couldn't argue, especially when the escapee was a murderer. All the same, he was certain that Fforidd would not be returning to Beaumaris Gaol, dead or alive.

Forthill finished up the last of his rounds, then went to wait patiently for the ferry to return. It didn't take long, and soon enough, Forthill was on his way back to the chapel. He didn't really realize it until later, but the whole trip back, starting on the ferry and ending at the parsonage, he'd been praying. He couldn't remember the words specifically, but he did recall that most of them had to do with keeping Owain safe and well wherever he was, and wherever he would be going.

"I was beginning to worry," Worthington said, looking up from where he was just taking a fresh loaf of bread off the top of the stove and delivering it to the table. "Hungry?"

Forthill shrugged. He wasn't really hungry, but he accepted a slice of bread with some butter.

"So," the older priest said. "What happened? You've never stayed overnight in the gaol. I was beginning to think something must have happened."

"You might say that." Forthill recounted the tale, including the part where he indirectly helped Owain to escape.

Worthington regarded him with a stone cold gaze. "You do

realize—"

"That I could be thrown in a cell right alongside Fforidd if he is recaptured?" Forthill finished. "Yes, I am very aware. Nathan and I had this same discussion."

"And?"

"Obviously I'm not in a cell alongside Fforidd."

"But you were deposed."

Forthill nodded solemnly. "Yes. I made my last rounds today. Sunday will be my last chapel service. Nathan allowed me the dignity of telling the inmates that I am leaving. There are a few that I have come to know, though not so great as Owain."

"It's a mercy," Worthington told him seriously. "I suggest you take it."

"I understand that, and I am. I am pushing my luck no further than I already have."

"Good, because someone is going to have to take over for me when I'm gone."

"Me take over for you? I thought for sure you would be taking over for me!"

The two old priests shared a laugh, but that was the reality of things. They were both too old for what they were doing. Well, they were never too old for the Lord's work, but the time was coming when they would die or have to stand aside for the next generation of priests to come through.

It was an odd thing to consider, Forthill thought, helping himself to another slice of bread. Someday he would be gone, and yet the world would keep going until the Lord judged it time to return. One day, perhaps soon, he would see his last snow, his last rain, his last sunrise, his last sunset, his last moon and stars. Then he would die.

Perhaps, he thought, climbing under his blankets, that was what scared Owain enough to try to escape. The man had oft proclaimed himself a coward, and once a coward, always a coward. Maybe it was the thought of death itself, that he would fall asleep and perhaps not wake up. Would he ever know it? Maybe it was the thought of going to stand before Almighty God. Most men spoke of such things as if it were a distant possibility, not a definite reality that may come sooner or later to each man. For Owain, it had certainly be a very rapidly-approaching possibility. For a man with his past, and a mindset unable to comprehend and accept mercy and forgiveness, the prospect must have looked terrifying to an unimaginable degree.

If that was the case...there was every chance Fforidd was going to return to his old ways. He may have been terrified by the thought of death so close, but it would only drive him to avoid it at all costs. Forthill would have liked to imagine that it meant Owain would turn from his ways and become a law-abiding man. The problem with that was that there was nowhere in the British Isles he would not be recognized and turned over. Dillon would have Wanted posters sent out all over the countryside, in the hands of every man, woman, and child. Casting a net and bringing it in ever so slowly.

Depending on how long the chase lasted, the warden probably wouldn't even bother trying to drag Owain back to the gaol; he would order him executed on the spot. It was a tragic and lonely prospect to consider. Had Nathan been right all along? Was there really no hope for Owain Fforidd? Should he have focused his efforts elsewhere, on a different prisoner?

Well, it was too late to do anything about it now, though Forthill slept poorly the next few nights. With his chaplaincy coming to an end, Forthill took up other responsibilities under Worthington. He'd never seen a man age so quickly in only a year, and never had he imagined it would be Worthington. To go from a springy youth, old by time only but young in every aspect that mattered, to withering away, bent over, constantly fatigued, plagued by the pains Forthill had been dealing with for years now, it was almost enough to shake his faith just a little, though it was a foolish notion. It was appointed unto all men to die once. Peitr Worthington would not live forever. Arthur Forthill would not live to see the new century. Owain Fforidd was unlikely to live past his sixtieth year except for some sort of Divine Intervention.

And in a hundred years, a hundred and fifty years, their little drama would be but dusty memories. No one would know. No one would care except to say, "Such a fascinating tale" and move on to the troubles of the day. Maybe it was better that way. Who wanted to bother with the trials and dramas of years past? Holding a grudge for a minor offense was bad enough, but to dwell on events of the past over which no one had any control? Utter folly.

Forthill did not receive any news about Fforidd that week, which he found somewhat odd. Nathan had told him that he was to be present when Fforidd was executed. Of course, if Owain had been killed trying to avoid the law, what need was there for a priest? Forthill expected he would find out soon enough as he crossed the narrow channel for the last time.

The ferryman was impossible to read, whether Fforidd had been brought back or not, and the man did not volunteer any news. The gaolers, likewise, were in the same bad mood they were always in. A few greeted him with some variance of wishing him well in the future, but most were commonly bad-tempered.

As the priest set up in the chapel, he was momentarily overcome by light-headedness and confusion. He knew where he was, who he was, and what he was doing, but some part of it just felt strange. Maybe it was the realization that this was the last time he would be here. Maybe it was that he would not see Owain again until either his execution if he was brought back, or Judgment Day if the Lord took him elsewhere. All this despite the fact that they hadn't been meeting for some time now. Maybe he was just getting old and sentimental. As much as he would not have chosen this career except for the Lord's guidance, he'd become accustomed to the work, grown fond of his unique assignment. He would not have traded it for a sea of jewels.

He announced to the inmates that he would be retiring. Most expressed varying degrees of indifference, but some approached him after the service and wished him well. A few told him that he'd inspired them to be better, more godly men when they were released. It was those sentiments that made his job worth it, Forthill decided, watching the last of them leave the chapel.

And that was that. His last chapel service in the gaol. He was now retired from this position. Well, might as well speak his last greeting to the warden before he left. It was only polite.

He heard the raised voices long before he reached the top of the stairs. By the time he touched the first floor, a door was slammed shut, but the raised voices persisted. The voices came from the warden's office. Two of them, it appeared. Nathan was definitely one of them. The other was familiar, one of the gaolers, but Forthill could not put a name to it. He considered making his presence known, perhaps quell the angry sea merely by the presence of a man of God, then decided against it. A time for peace, and, apparently in this instance, a time for anger. He did not want to be the old man caught in the middle.

"Fforidd has disappeared," the gaoler was saying. "All the gaolers have been called back, and the local police have sent out their fastest runners to every corner of the Isles. No one has seen him. Even his parents claim not to have seen him for some years, and a search of their house and land says the same. He is nowhere to be found."

Nathan made a frustrated growling sound. "The magistrate is coming in less than a week. I promised him Fforidd would be hanged. What do I do if I have nothing to give him?"

The gaoler said something Forthill could not catch.

"Hang someone else, are you insane, Cassius?" Nathan hissed. "Who would you even suggest?"

"Richard Brown. He's also a murderer, also condemned."

"His appeals have not been fully processed yet. To hang him and then have one of his appeals go through...it would cost me my job. Having nothing for the magistrate would be far easier to handle than hanging the wrong man."

"Then don't hang the wrong man," Cassius said lowly. "Put a bag over his head. Say that because of his escape, he does not get to see the sun on his last day. If and when Fforidd is captured, then say that it was Brown and he got belligerent, so you had to kill him. Gets rid of both men."

"That's a flimsy plan and you know it. We claim to hang Fforidd, then he turns up in London. What are we to do then?" Nathan went on before Cassius could speak. "No. Our only choice is to tell the magistrate what has happened, and hope that the local authorities somewhere on these godforsaken isles find, capture, or kill Fforidd. We'll wait on

Richard Brown until his appeals have passed or rejected. Dismissed. I said dismissed."

Cassius left the office in a huff, nearly trampling Forthill underfoot. The priest waited a moment before calmly entering. The warden was at his desk, leaning back in his chair, considering the drink in his hand.

"How much of that did you hear?" Nathan wondered, not looking at him.

"Enough that my faith in you and your integrity and character has strengthened," Forthill replied honestly.

The warden just grunted and downed his drink. "Well, at least someone has faith in me right now. And it comes from the man I have belittled and defied for most of the year on account of this one prisoner. Have you ever wondered whether the world has gone mad and just forgot to tell those of us on the fringes of society?"

"Frequently."

"I thought so. So then, you're leaving us for the last time."

Forthill nodded. "I am."

"Good for you." The warden sat up, then stood and held out his hand. "It's been—well, I won't say it's always been a pleasure having you here, because it really hasn't. Sometimes you have annoyed me, irritated me, and enraged me. But for all of that, you have remained true to your calling, and I respect you for it."

"Thank you, Warden."

Their conversation was comparatively brief, but Forthill left with the feeling that everything was going to turn out just fine.

America

CHAPTER SEVENTEEN

THE RETURN

After saying his farewells to Father Forthill, Owain made for the river. Wet and cold did not go well together, but with snow on the ground, he would be tracked anywhere he tried to hide. One of the easiest ways to get around that was with water.

His luck held as the day grew somewhat warm, enough to melt snow rather than freeze it, as he trudged laboriously upriver, heading east. He followed the river for most of the day until it ended in a spring bubbling up from a rocky formation. He found himself in the woods with very little clue where he was, whose land he was on, or how far he was from the gaol. Not far enough, in his opinion. But he couldn't just stand in the river all day. His feet were freezing and he couldn't feel his toes at all. He'd bunched up his blanket around his shoulders and kept his bag high, but there was only so much he could do with what he had.

At last, he got out of the river and headed north. It wasn't even a mile until he found a rocky cliff. The next best thing to water for covering up his tracks was stone. The problem was, not only was the rock slippery, but he was completely exposed. All the same, he had to keep going somewhere.

Eventually he came to a point where the cliff rocks began falling away and he managed to get down to sea level. Here he was able to find seaweed and other small plants to eat. It was hardly a meal and did little more than take the edge off his hunger, even when he dipped into the small pouch of provisions the priest had given him. But it was food, and he was grateful for it.

He spent the night in a tidal cave, easily walking in at low tide, but having to huddle on a small ledge when at high tide. For a time, he was afraid the water would fill the cave completely and drown him, but then the water started to recede, and he could go down to collect more seaweed to eat.

Owain stayed in the cave for several days. It was out of the wind, which was a big help, and between the water and his own body heat, he was able to dry off without freezing. Still, the seaweed wouldn't last forever, and he didn't want to get trapped in the cave when the water began to freeze. Either the rocks would become too slippery to navigate, or else an ice wall would form and he would be completely walled in. Just another kind of cell, he mused.

He followed the coastline as much as he could, heading even farther north. He avoided people as much as he could, but near as he could tell, no one set the dogs on him. Actually, he came upon several fishing villages having trouble with their nets in the strong, late autumn tides. He helped the fishermen bring in their nets and boats, helped them with some repairs. In return, he was given food and clothing. While some offered shelter for the night, he always refused. He wasn't about to stop and nod his head just yet, not until he knew he was in the clear. When that was going to be, he did not yet know.

His English accent got him through the English coast. His Welsh accent was more acceptable to the Irish living along the channel between Ireland and England. Scotland was also a little more tolerant of his Welsh accent, holding little love for the English.

It was around Christmas when he arrived in Scotland. His clothes still held up, but always being on the move meant he had little chance to settle down with a fire, dry himself off, dry his clothes, take a bath, and get a decent meal beyond what he was able to quickly scavenge or barter for. Now winter was in full force and he had little chance of surviving if he couldn't find anywhere to stay and rebuild his strength. At the same time, if he spent too long in one place, someone was likely to recognize him and turn him in. Then where would he be?

He found a spot in the woods one evening, when he could go no farther, and simply made a makeshift camp where he sat. In his travels, he'd acquired a bigger, better bag for his things, several blankets, and survival necessities like flint and even a book of matches. He'd also traded work for a small cooking pan, on the rare occasion he had anything to cook.

He set out a trap that night and was pleasantly surprised to find a hare in it the following morning. Perhaps it was dumb luck seeing how he hadn't really had any bait, or maybe God was looking out for him in some small way.

Owain dressed the rabbit with a deft hand and soon had it over the fire. Not five minutes later, he was on his feet, looking around as he heard something moving in the trees.

"Calm down, friend, I mean you no harm." It was a man's voice. He emerged into the small clearing a minute later.

Considerably shorter than Owain, a little soft around the middle, wearing a robe and sash of some form with different designs and small trinkets dangling here and there. While it looked warm, it also seemed very out of place, even for Scotland.

"Is this your land, sir?" Owain asked politely, trying to sound amiable. "If it is, I mean no harm and will leave if you wish."

"The land belongs to the land, not to any man," the man said, seeming completely at ease.

Owain studied the small man. "Who are you?"

"You may call me Phillip, but others call me priest." The man, Phillip made a motion toward the fire and the roasting rabbit. "May I?"

Owain nodded and moved to sit himself, feeling very conspicuous. *"Paganiaeth,"* he stated, indicating the robes. (Paganism.)

"That's right. And you are a Welshman, are you not? I can tell by your accent." The fat priest stretched out his legs before the fire. "You're a long ways from home in the middle of winter, just past the winter solstice. Ill fortune has brought you this way."

"I don't know whether it's good fortune or ill, honestly," Owain sighed, turning the rabbit on the spit. "It may be good fortune that I'm here, but I could still die before the spring comes."

Phillip nodded. "Indeed you will if you camp out here and rely on rabbits to wander into a trap with no bait."

"How much father north does this land go?"

"If you continue walking, Scotland will end in a day's time or so.

There are some outlying islands, but the land is done. You can cross the sea east to Scandinavia if you wish to proceed farther north, but all the land ends eventually." The priest shifted position. "Where is it you are going?"

Owain opened his mouth, but said nothing for a long moment. Finally he let out a breath and answered, "I don't even know anymore. At first, it was just...away. But the Isles stubbornly remain islands, and I don't know that I can cross to the mainland."

"I see." The way the priest's tone changed set off alarm bells in Owain's mind. "And what is it you are running away from exactly?"

"Myself, I suppose."

Phillip frowned. "I see. Trying to run away from oneself is like trying to run away from the land. You cannot run from yourself any more than you can run from a storm. Your best option may be to stand your ground and whether the storm, face yourself and make peace. Live with the land rather than manipulate it. If I recall, most Welsh are Protestant, yes?"

"That's right."

"Well, it's better than Catholic, I suppose."

Owain managed a small chuckle. "You're not wrong there."

"Do you know what the biggest problem with either of them are?"

"What?"

"They seek to be conquerors just as their God is a conqueror. They seem to think that because their God tamed the land and sea, that they can do so as well. They do not understand that they are still part of Creation. Part of it, not masters of it. Myself and those who remain pagan, we live with the land, as part of it, giving thanks to that which has power over us."

"Catholics and Protestants do the same."

"I have seen very few genuine examples of this, but I will take your word as your experience, for I admit I have very little outside of Scotland. Perhaps all the Welsh are perfectly devout, save you. But all the same, you see yourselves as being separate from the land, separate from Creation. Are you not subject to all the laws of nature, the same as any tree or any animal?"

"Well, yes."

"In fact, are you not subject to more laws because you elevate yourselves above the land and the beasts?"

"Um..."

"And what of the folk tales of fairies of the forest and other creatures? Are they not part of Creation also?"

"Well..."

Phillip grinned and laughed. "I do not mean to make you uncomfortable. I am sure you have heard your own tales. The English hold little regard for any of us Celtic peoples. The pagan heathens as they like to call us. I merely like to provoke thoughtful discussion. Surely the pagan gods of Scotland are known among the Welsh, just under different names, for the simple fact that it is nature. We cannot separate ourselves from the land any more than we can run from ourselves. It is always the same, wherever we go."

Owain shook his head. "No. The land is not always the same. People are not always the same. People can change."

"Anything can change. A field can become a forest. Or a forest can become a field. But this only illustrates the bigger picture of a collective, not the individual. Does a tree ever stop being a tree? Does its spirit ever become anything other than a tree?"

"Maybe not, but a tree is confined to being only a tree. A man may never be more than a man, but he is free to move and think and exercise the free will that God gave him. To take action and take responsibility for those actions. Man is made for a higher calling which is why we are subject to greater laws, the same way that more is expected of a leader than his followers. Yes, a leader and his followers may be part of the same group, but there are defined roles within the group, and some may be in positions of greater power and authority than others. Just as you are in a position of power in your community. More is expected from you."

Phillip was a master of disguising his thoughts, Owain thought, but the man was not unkind.

"Indeed," the priest acknowledged. "It appears as though the seeds of wisdom are within you. Now then, what are you going to do? Stay here in the forest all winter debating philosophy?"

Owain huffed a breath. "I don't know. The winter is only going to get worse, and it will be too difficult to travel."

"As you are currently are, yes, it will be difficult to travel." Phillip stood. "The question then becomes, do you simply wish to take your chances here in this sacred wood where you have angered the goddess with your talk of the Protestant God and his contradictory teachings, or do you wish to humble yourself and ask for help from Scottish pagans?" He went on before Owain could answer. "Mind you, it doesn't take a Christian to see that your spirit is darkened with misdeeds and doubts. If you believe in any god, the Christian God or otherwise, they cannot help you in another god's sacred wood."

Owain had never been terribly argumentative when it came to religion, and the Catholic and Protestant feud merely wore on his nerves, but everything he knew about paganism—the Welsh version, anyway—and Christianity said that God could go anywhere and save anyone, but that dark forces could keep angels at bay. On the other hand, had any angels really been fighting to get to him when he was in prison?

And so it came to be that Owain stayed with Phillip the pagan priest for most of the winter. They had many theological discussions while they were snowed in his tiny cottage. Owain wasn't sure if it was just good fun to have the discussions or if they were trying to convert each other. Either way, they were exhausting as they revealed what Owain did or did not know, what he did or did not believe. And Phillip mentioned on several occasions that Owain challenged him as well, and he was grateful for it. He'd met numerous Protestant and Catholic priests who did not seem to know or understand as much as Owain did. This was probably some form of flattery, Owain was sure.

He came to learn that, despite there being numerous pagan gods and goddesses to choose from, Phillip and his community primarily worshiped two: the goddess of the forest, and the horse. Everyone had a horse. Every learned to ride from the day he was born, even the women. And while the English proclaimed a heavy handed rule over the Scottish people, Phillip's community still learned to fight on horseback as well. So it was that Owain also learned a bit about horsemanship during his stay, on those rare days when the sun came out from behind gloomy gray clouds.

Owain's past came up every once in a while, but he always skirted the issue. He never gave out his last name. He never admitted to having a family, simply said they were all dead. He did admit to being an alcoholic when he was younger, but said nothing about being a wealthy man or a murderer.

No one ever came looking for him or asked after him. He never heard any rumors about him or his past. Not once did he see any kind of local policeman. The pagan community had been effectively ostracized after Christianity became widespread, Phillip explained, so they were pretty self-sufficient, with the goddess' help and the horse's provision, of course. Owain had never heard better news coming from a pagan.

It was March when he spoke of leaving. Phillip convinced him to stay until the vernal equinox, that way the community could send him off with a blessing. Owain wasn't sure he wanted to be seen off with a pagan blessing, but they had been nothing but kind to him so far, and he didn't want to insult their hospitality.

Would their blessing somehow negate Father Forthill's blessing? Would God be mad that he allowed it? Would it have any effect whatsoever? Would it set demons upon him, to hound him all his days? He really wasn't sure, but there was a distinct lack of Protestant preachers in the area to ask.

Owain did not understand the ritual the priest performed, but he was assured that it was a blessing of fortune and prosperity. In addition to the ritualistic blessing, Owain was also given a horse. One blessed by the gods themselves, he was told. He could ride this horse anywhere in the British Isles and he would always return home, so don't worry. If he did leave the Isles, simply let the horse go and he would find his way back.

It was cloudy when Owain said goodbye to the priest and left the pagan community with mixed feelings. In spite of all his antics, he'd been raised Protestant. Sure, he heard some of the tales of fairies and goblins and the like that lived in the wood, but not once had he ever seen or heard from any of the old pagan gods or goddesses. Thinking back on some of the better times in his childhood, he remembered a few songs and dances, but they had likely been changed from old pagan names to the names of the Saints or whomever.

He really wasn't sure how he felt about it, maybe because he'd never really embraced anything. God and Christianity and Protestantism was all a very distant ritual compared to his shenanigans in the present, whatever they had been at the time. All the same, it was all he had really known.

Owain rode for three days before realizing he had little clue where he was going except south. South was where London was, and all the people who hated him. South was where Beaumaris Gaol was, where they were surely awaiting his bumbling return.

South was where home was.

He hadn't realized it until just then, but he was terribly homesick. Living in a strange land with strange people and strange gods had made him long for home. But why should he return? No doubt his parents knew of his escape, and, by extension, his crimes. Why should they do anything other than turn him in? He'd managed to successfully hide through the winter. Now that summer was here and food easier to come by, why shouldn't he wait a little longer?

Because he had nothing to live for here. No one cared for him. It was only a matter of time before he was apprehended. At the very least, he wanted to see his parents again. After that, he didn't know what he was going to do. He had no plans, no hope, no future. He was just a man on the run...on an island.

Again Owain avoided civilization as much as possible. With the onset of spring, it was easier to find food. The only thing that really slowed him down was finding sufficient food and water for the horse, which he still hadn't named, nor had the pagans told him the horse's name. Mostly he just called it Ceffyl.

The problem with traveling cross-country and avoiding people was that he really didn't know where he was or which way to go. Sure, he'd criss-crossed the countryside when he was out causing havoc, but things changed over the years. He hadn't been home in nearly five years, and he hadn't traveled cross-country like this in nearly a decade. He expected it to be easier to run into a bounty hunting party looking for him than to stumble across his parents' farm.

It was May before things came into focus. He couldn't say just when it happened. He was plodding along the roadside, one of the few times he did, eating something from his small pouch of provisions, when he looked up and suddenly he recognized everything. It was as if a dream had come to life. He knew exactly where he was, where the road led, where it twisted and curved, and where he had to turn off to get to a familiar little cottage.

The horse seemed to sense his change in attitude, his excitement, and started to step a little livelier. Owain urged Ceffyl on until he was practically cantering, turning off the main road to a little-used trail. Just up the hill would be a grove of trees, acting as a windbreak for one side of the cottage. Just out the back side of the cottage was the garden and down the slope was the barn. From a distance, Owain could see one figure in front of the house. Judging by the shapes as he bounced along on the horse, his ma was out doing laundry. He did not see his pa.

His ma looked up from her work, set aside her current piece of clothing, and wiped her hands on her apron. Owain reined Ceffyl in back to a trot.

As he neared, his heart sank and his whole being twisted with guilt. When had his ma grown old? When had her back bent and her hair turned silver? When had her skin become wrinkled and her body thin? Even the last time Owain had seen her, she'd still been youthful and excited and ready for life. To see her now was to see someone awaiting the end of life. When had that happened? Had it just been one more thing he'd overlooked in his selfishness? Or had it happened suddenly, perhaps when she learned of her eldest son's wayward ways, going from mere drinking all the way to murder, taking the lives of God's children?

He brought Ceffyl down to a walk, hoping that a slow approach would convey a nonthreatening demeanor. Finally he stopped and dismounted, a short distance from his ma who watched him with a curious gaze. As he turned toward her, he saw the spark of recognition in her eyes. Then she did something she hadn't done in all the times that he'd come stumbling home: she ran.

She did not come to him and embrace him, did not bring him food, did not offer him a place to sleep. She ran. Back to the house.

Guilt such as he'd never felt before crashed down on Owain and he fell to the ground weeping. The guilt went beyond the fear of God turning His back and condemning him to Hell. This pain was far greater, knowing that his own mother, who had stood up for him time and time again, had finally reached her breaking point and was now running away from him.

A sob caught in his throat as cold metal touched his chin. Owain coughed and spat to the side, then looked up. The barrel of a gun rested under his chin against his neck, and at the other end was his pa. His pa had grown old, too, and Owain was reminded of that night in the barn when his pa first threw him out, how he'd looked in the lantern light. That was the man standing before him now, back bent with age, skin wrinkled, hair not quite gray. But he still retained his strength and determination, if the gun in his hand and light in his eye was any indication.

"What the devil are you doing here, murderer?" Teo Forbes demanded, spitting out the last word.

Owain had imagined any number of scenarios when he'd decided to return home. His pa having a gun was prevalent in most of them. In his mind, he'd always known what to say, had planned out some sequence of words that might allow him to express his sorrow and his desire to change. But all that came out now was, "So, you know."

"We heard," Teo growled. "When the police come a-knockin' on our door, telling us what our son been up to, ask us if we seen him. They tear up our house, our barn, our land, looking for you. Say you killed six men and escaped from prison right before your hanging."

Owain could not meet his pa's gaze. He would have lowered his chin if he'd been able to. As it was, he could only say, "That's right."

"So why are you here?"

"I don't know. I have nowhere else to go."

"You can go back to the noose where you belong, or I can send you to Hell myself in the name of the king," Teo said.

"Teo, no!"

Owain's ears rang as the gun went off, but it did not touch him. When he opened his eyes, his ma had knocked the barrel away into the air and the shot fired off harmlessly.

"He is still our son," Gwyneth pleaded, and it seemed to Owain that it took every ounce of her strength to get flustered anymore.

"He is no son of mine," Teo stated.

"He is still my son. And I will not let you harm him."

Now Teo put the gun down and faced her. "What do you want, Gwyn? He's a murderer."

"And how will you be any different if you kill him?"

"How is the executioner any different? He's a murderer and he was supposed to be hanged. You yourself ran from him when you first saw him. You, who always gave him food and shelter whenever he came stumbling home, drunk and running from the law again."

By now, Gwyneth had tears in her eyes. "And I'll do it again."

"To what end? Why do you continue to shelter him when you know he's just going to run off again?"

"Because he is my child. Is that not enough of a reason? If we abandon our children, what hope do they have? Where can they go that they know is safe and loving no matter what? I'm his mother. It's my duty to care for my children."

"It's true," Owain said quietly. "I tried to kill myself twice in prison but couldn't even manage that. I have no hope, nowhere to go."

Teo made a motion. "What do you want, Owain? That's the one thing I was never able to figure out. What in God's green earth do you want? Money? Power? You've had both and lost them, so that can't be it."

"Teo, honestly," Gwyneth hissed.

But Teo pressed further. "Freedom, well, maybe. Family? Well, I think we all know where you stand on that issue."

"I don't know," Owain cut in before his ma could speak. He sighed. "I don't know what I want. I never have. And maybe that was the whole problem. It wasn't about what I wanted, but why I didn't want what I had. And I don't know."

Gwyneth knelt in front of her son and gingerly placed her hands on his shoulders. "What did you hope to find when you came here?"

Owain could not meet her gaze either. "I don't know. Like you said, I just knew that this was a safe place. Or I thought it was."

"You thought wrong," Teo said.

"You thought right," Gwyneth countered, giving her husband a look. She looked back at her son. "Come inside. We'll get you something to eat and then we'll talk. All right?"

Owain hesitated for a moment but nodded. He really didn't know what he'd been expecting when he came home. The gun under his chin was certainly deserved, but why he was so surprised at his ma's kindness was a mystery he was unprepared to solve. She took his hands in hers and got him to his feet. She seemed to have shrunk a bit in her age, he thought. How old were they? He was in his mid-thirties, near forty, so they had to be fast-approaching sixty.

Sixty years old, waiting almost forty years for their prodigal son to change his ways and come home. But was this really the instance he changed? He could feel the question racing through both their minds. His pa initially did not want to join in lunch, but his ma made him, saying he wasn't going to sneak off to the police behind her back. They were both going to stay where she could see them, and all three of them would share a meal together.

"We heard you escaped last fall," Gwyneth began awkwardly after Teo had blessed the food. "Where did you winter?"

"I actually stayed with a community of pagans up in Scotland," Owain answered, feeling the blood rush to his face. "They'd been ostracized and no one bothered them. Just six weeks ago, they gave me a horse so I could return home. I got lost a few times."

They did not ask about his escape or his time in prison specifically, but he knew the questions were there. The closest they ever got to that discussion was his ma asking, "Were you treated well? I hear Beaumaris is a kinder gaol, where they give you food every day and let you go outside."

Owain could not bring to tell his ma of the horrors of Beaumaris, so he simply mumbled, "Yes." It wouldn't be entirely untrue. Forthill had treated him well at least.

"Why did you escape?" Teo asked. "Did you not think you deserved to hang for murder?"

"*Dw i'n gwybod boddi'n ei deilyngu o,*" Owain said, making sure to emphasize the present tense. (I know that I deserve it.) "I know I took the lives of six men. I know I've ruined plenty of others. I know perhaps no one will ever believe me a changed man, or that I want to change. I don't know that I would even deserve that chance because of my escape. But I do know that a bad man who has changed his ways can do more good than a good man who is dead."

"And what good do you propose to do in the world?" Teo sneered.

"I don't know. I don't know that I've ever done any good except for that which benefits me." He shook his head. "I just don't know."

They sat and ate in silence for several minutes. Owain ate but did not taste. Gwyneth mostly pushed her food around, looking rather sullen. Teo ate angrily, his demeanor like that of a hunting dog straining against his master's lead to chase after some prey.

"America," Gwyneth said finally, looking at her son.

"What?"

"Go to America. It is the land of opportunity. It will be a chance for you to start your life over fresh, where no one knows you or what you have done. It's a chance to get it right."

"But what will I do?" Owain asked. "I have no skills."

"You have your strength, and farming is certainly an industry over there. You will find work. If nothing else, your brother has already gone ahead. Seek him out."

Owain almost said that he didn't want to, but then he stopped himself. What other choice did he have? If he stayed in the British Isles, it was only a matter of time before the law caught up to him. He really didn't want to go to America, really didn't want to be a farmhand or seek out his brother. But it wasn't about him this time. Selfishness had seen him almost all the way to the noose. It was time to take responsibility for himself and take this one last shot at freedom. Finally he nodded. "All right."

Chapter Eighteen

The Departure

Owain was permitted to sleep in the house that night, though he couldn't have slept if he'd wanted to. He heard his ma and pa argue all night. It wasn't the argument that kept him awake, but the arguing itself. He knew his parents had disagreements, but never in his life had they had an argument like this. Never had he heard his ma take such a strong stance on something that she would be the rock that defied the waves of her husband. Never had he heard his pa take such a strong stance on something that he would even consider defying her so strongly. Most often, even when their arguments had been about him, they just held their tongues until he wandered off again to get in trouble. Now they were arguing over whether to help him escape the law, escape justice, and flee to another country. It was certainly a serious discussion to be had, but it was astounding to hear.

It made him feel ashamed in a way, made him feel like a child, but he kept his mouth shut. His silence had caused him fewer problems than his words.

What sleep he did get that night was fitful, and more than once he woke up confused and certain the gaolers were coming for him. He ended up pulling himself forcefully out of bed just before sunrise, if for no other reason than to escape the confusion and the nightmares. He made his way to the kitchen where his ma was also just getting up and around.

He helped her cook breakfast and do the morning chores. Neither said a word for a long time, until the bread was just about ready and Gwyneth was preparing to set the table. She had shrunk, Owain decided, as she reached up to take his face in her hands.

"You're a good man, Owain," she told him softly. "Confused at times, maybe, but deep down, I've always known you were a good man. We all go through the Lord's fire to be refined into pure gold. I think you started out a little more impure than most, but I also think you're just about there. Pure gold. My son."

His hand completely dwarfed hers, and he could find no words to convey his gratitude. The moment was broken at the sound of his pa entering the room, and they settled in for an uneasy breakfast.

"We'll help you get to America," Teo said, his tone as begrudging as Owain had ever heard it. "We'll get you some papers to take over there and get you established. After that, it's up to you to decide who you're going to be."

The way he said it told Owain that once he was gone and heading for America, they didn't want to hear from or about him ever again, good or ill. Maybe his ma wanted to know, but his pa wanted nothing more to do with him. Probably he was going along with this only to please his wife and had nothing to do with hoping his wayward son would truly change his ways. It was a small hope, and Owain seized on it.

"I'll give you a token of some form to give to your brother," Gwyneth went on. "That way he'll know that we spoke and you're as good as your word." Her look silenced anything Teo had to say to that. "And maybe you can start a new life for yourself by helping him."

"How long will it take to get papers?" Owain asked. "What do I have to do?"

Again, his ma answered before his pa could speak, waving a hand and saying, "Don't you worry about that. The less you're seen around here, the better. You let us worry about that. Actually, you let me worry about that. Your pa will help you learn or re-learn some skills you might need when you get over there."

It was her way of keeping both of the men home. Owain would be kept out of the eye of the neighbors as much as possible, which would help to quell any rumors. It would also keep Teo home, keep him from running off to tell the authorities of his whereabouts. Whatever his ma was going to do, it would be easier for her to do it alone as an elderly woman, far below suspect level. When had she become so cunning? Or had it always been part of her nature and he'd just never been around to appreciate it?

How much he didn't know about his own family.

Teo Fforidd was just a few years shy of sixty. Owain was several years short of forty. The difference between them was that, despite his age, Owain still maintained his strength. Maybe he wasn't as monstrous as he'd been back when he was in his twenties, but he was still quite capable of heavy lifting. Teo was not so fortunate as he began to succumb to his age.

Maybe that was another reason Gwyneth forced them to spend their days together. Owain had much to learn, and Teo could teach him. Teo was beginning to struggle with the farm labor, but Owain was still strong enough to help. Teo was by no means pleased with the arrangement; his every movement, his every word, conveyed and amplified this attitude. All the same, he honored the arrangement and taught or re-taught some of the most basic farming skills Owain might need to find work in America.

Butchering was fairly straightforward, and Owain had dressed a number of animals in his trek home, but tanning he was less confident in. It was a smelly, messy process, but he did everything exactly as his pa told him. Given that he frequently helped his ma prepare the meals, at least breakfast, he obviously hadn't lost his talent or love for cooking. After months of porridge or gruel or nothing at all, Owain was more than happy to cook his own meals.

Horse care he'd become well-versed in from the Scottish pagans, but there was an art to it when it came to farming. At least, that was what Teo said. Maybe there was an art to it and Owain just couldn't quite see it as he copied his pa in everything he did, or maybe his pa was trying to spook him, try to provoke him back to his old ways, get him to run so he'd have an excuse to alert the authorities. Whatever the case, Owain was determined to stick it out.

It was a little more difficult to expound on planting and harvesting when they were stuck between the two seasons now, but Teo could take Owain out and show him healthy plants, common weeds, a few diseased plants laid out to dry so they could be tossed in the fire.

"Don't let them rot and go back into the ground," Teo told Owain sternly. "They carry disease with them. You have to burn out the disease. Once a plant's gone to waste, you can't bring it back."

Owain was uncertain whether his pa meant the comment as a stab at him, but he felt it nonetheless. As had become the norm, he simply learned, agreed, and generally kept his mouth shut. In the event he did have a question, he tried to make it a thoughtful one, one that might lead into another lesson or a discussion. It rarely happened. Teo Fforidd was not happy about his charge, and he was not about to let his guard down.

That was when Owain realized that his pa didn't really hate him. Well, all right, there was a strong possibility he did hate him. Hated him a lot. But the fact that he was helping at all was indicative of some kernel of hope in the old man's heart. Owain had hurt his pa time and again, brought shame to the Fforidd family, made a mockery of his pa and his grandpa and everyone who ever bore the name. He was the black sheep in the flock. His pa was tired of being hurt, tired of watching the family be hurt. He was tired of seeing his prodigal son hurt his ma every time he went off and did something stupid. He'd put up walls to protect the rest of the family. If he continued to allow Owain to run free, it could destroy them all. It was for the good of the family.

So for the good of the family, I must leave, Owain mused as he lay in bed. About a week had passed. He'd learned a lot but knew there was so much more he was missing. His pa had decades of experience behind him. There was still no word on his departure, but his ma assured him all was going well as long as he stayed put and didn't try anything too daring. No one had said anything, and life was going on as normal. There were no rumors about any strange folk hanging around, and she wanted to keep it that way.

That hope lasted only maybe five more days before the quiet illusion of normalcy was broken. Missy, Owain's oldest sister, stopped to visit after chapel service to help prepare dinner. She froze when she saw Owain in the kitchen with their ma.

"Honestly, Missy, come in and shut the door," Gwyneth said calmly. "You're letting in a draft."

"O-Owain," Missy stammered, quietly shutting the door behind her.

He did not say anything, simply looked away.

"I heard you were in prison," she went on, her eyes still enormous. "I heard you escaped."

"And that's all you'll hear," Gwyneth told her daughter, fixing her in a gaze Owain knew very well, one that clearly hadn't diminished with age.

"What's going on?" Missy asked. "Why is he here?"

"He's not. He's escaped from prison and we don't know where he's heading."

"What do you..." Missy lowered her voice to just above a whisper. "What are you doing? Are you helping him to escape? Is that why you've been quietly collecting funds for some unknown reason?"

"Your pa is getting older and we may need to hire some help for the harvest. Last year's harvest was less than we would prefer, so we don't have enough extra to hire a hand."

Owain had never heard his ma lie, but the way she did it so calmly told him she must have had some practice at it at some point.

It was also the first time in over ten years that Owain had seen his eldest sister. She was only a couple years younger than him, and was the spitting image of their ma when she was that age, long, curly brown hair, narrow face, beautiful brown eyes. Like their ma, Missy had gained weight since having children, but she still looked good. Or maybe that was because Owain was only really seeing her for the first time that he cared to remember, and he also didn't interact with too many women since the murders.

Despite their ma's calm words, Missy was still skittish around Owain, always maintaining a fair distance from him. It wasn't until supper was almost ready that Gwyneth managed to slip away for a minute and leave the two of them alone in the room.

"I know I've done a lot of wrong," Owain said before Missy could sneak away as well. "And I know every memory you have of me is wretched and terrible, and I've done awful things to you."

"I almost didn't get married because of the reputation you brought on our family," Missy told him, her tone carrying more heat than Owain was prepared for. Another thing she inherited from their ma, he was sure. "I almost had to wait until Teo got married."

"I know. As I've said, I've done a lot of wrong. There is not enough time left in the world for me to make it up to anyone I've wronged, especially my family. As much as I want to say I'm sorry and start over, that's not an option for any of us. And it's all my fault. No one else's. It's not our parents' fault, not yours, not Teo's, not the law, not anyone but mine."

Missy sighed and ran a hand through his hair, her expression conflicted. "You're right. Every memory I have of you is tainted. I wish I could just open up like ma and extend a hand of mercy. But I don't know that I can except that the Lord commands it. All the same, if you are so intent on making things right, why did you escape from prison?"

"You mean, why don't I turn myself in and die?"

She did not respond.

Owain sighed. "Because a bad man who changes his ways can do more good than a good man who is dead."

"But are you still a bad man who has changed his ways...if you continue to run from the law?"

"I don't know. Only God can judge that. Considering everything I've been through since my escape, I think maybe He's judged me worthy of a second chance."

Missy paced the room a time or two, obviously distressed. "I want to believe you, Owain. I really do. I just don't know that I can."

He nodded. "I understand. And that's why I'm leaving. I have one last chance to get it right. If I mess it up, I am only guaranteed death. But if I get it right, maybe I can do some good before I die and completely waste the life our ma gave me."

His sister was silent for a long moment, but she still paced. Finally she paused and looked at him. He forced himself to meet her gaze.

"All right," she said at last, letting her hands drop to her sides. "All right. You escaped prison and we don't know where you're heading." She folded her arms. "I won't tell."

"Thank you."

"I'm not doing this because I like you, or because I believe that you're going to change your ways. Those you can only prove through actions, which so far have been rather despicable. I'm doing this because I can't bear to think of my brother being hung or sunk or put down like a dog. If you're going to ruin your life, I would rather you do it on your terms."

Owain nodded. "I understand. It's more than I expected."

He was fairly certain their ma had been hiding within earshot, just waiting for them to come to some kind of truce. It was the only reason he could think of that she happened to reappear at that moment. Not long after, Teo walked in. He greeted his daughter warmly, ignored Owain entirely, and took his seat at the table.

Dinner was a tense affair. It had been tense before, since Owain returned, but with the addition of Missy, it was only worsened. Gwyneth could order, bribe, or negotiate with her husband to keep him quiet about Owain's arrival. She had no such power over Missy, not once she left to return home to her family. She could easily tell her husband of her wayward brother's return.

Gwyneth knew of this very real possibility, so the two women "went for a walk" once the table had been cleared, and Owain and Teo went out to continue chores and other errands.

"If you had known what I was going to become, would you have let me live past infancy?" Owain asked meekly as they reached the barn.

His pa gave him an odd look, one of the few he'd seen that was not outright anger and disgust. After a moment or two, he answered, "Of course I would have let you live." Owain was hoping for some admission of familiarity, that Teo would recognize him as his son, but he received no such blatant admission. Instead, opening the barn door, his pa went on, "If I had known, I may have done things a little differently. Said things differently, doled out punishment and reward differently. I probably would have prayed differently, too."

Owain just nodded. His pa gave him another strange look. Finally Teo stopped and turned to face him. "I hope to God you are sincere. I hope that this is finally the answer to all the prayers your ma and I have put before the Lord since you tried to stone your brother. Maybe it was a different path than either of us would have chosen for you, but I suppose if it works out in the end, I have no quarrel with the Lord. But there is nothing you can say to me now to undo everything you've done. You are beyond words, Owain. You have escaped justice and danced with death. Words mean nothing without action to back it up.

"This is the last time we will be able to help you, and I hope you understand the risks we are taking for someone who has never shown the proper respect or gratitude for the life he's been given. I want to believe that I will get my son back in the end, that we can rejoice in Heaven together one day. But if you want my opinion...I'm not holding my breath. You must show us that you have changed. Your ma and I exchange letters with Teo every so often. I expect we'll hear about you at some point, and I want it to be good. Do you understand me, Owain?"

Chastened, he nodded. "I understand. I do more than that, I feel it."

"Well, at least you're feeling something, even if it is only guilt." Teo sighed and looked away, hands on his hips. "I don't know what else to do for you. Maybe your ma had the right of things, always offering an open door. I just kept telling myself that you're not my son, and it made it easier to bear when we heard of your terrible antics, whatever they were. No, not my son. I only got one son, and he's named for me. Murderer, killed six men? No, not my son. My son left for America. I don't know who that is. Some no-account criminal who's going to hang and burn in Hell."

Teo sniffed and quickly wiped his face. "And then you show up, asking for forgiveness, looking for help. And your ma..." He trailed off.

"She convinced you to let me stay," Owain said quietly.

His pa nodded. "One last chance. The only chance you'd have left, seeing how far you'd pushed your luck. Either this works or it doesn't, but it's all we have left to give you."

"I understand."

"No. I don't think you do. But it's a start."

When they returned to the house later that evening for supper, Missy was long gone. Gwyneth informed them that she promised to keep Owain's presence a secret as long as he didn't cause any trouble. The instant something happened, that was it. Gwyneth said she assured Missy that if anything happened, Teo would have Owain turned over to the police and bound for the noose before she ever heard about it. Owain wasn't sure how to take that comment, but he stayed silent.

But nothing happened over that next week. Owain continued to follow his pa around the farm, helping with this or that as needed. He did not go to Sunday chapel. If there were visitors, he made himself scarce, scrounging up a dozen different hiding spots he remembered as being a lot more concealing as a child. Nevertheless, no one knew of his presence, or so he believed.

It was a little over two weeks after his arrival, after the table had been cleared of supper plates, when Gwyneth called both Teo and Owain together. She handed Owain a parcel which he opened. Inside, he found travel papers. Among other things, they indicated his status as a skilled migrant worker with no criminal history and no family. The most intriguing part, however, was that the name on the papers was Walter Forbes.

"I never legally changed my name, though," Owain said.

"I know," his ma replied. "That's why I did it. All the court documents for the murders and all your other convictions list your real name."

"The prisoner entry log in the gaol listed Walter Forbes."

"Those records are hand-written by the warden as an unofficial account to satisfy the governor and control inventory. This is a legal document. No one is going to take this legal document which says Walter Forbes and compare it to a legal document listing Owain Fforidd and think they are the same. Besides, who is to say that there isn't another Walter Forbes in England somewhere?" She went on before he could speak. "Your brother and his family got their names changed when they went to America. American customs didn't like the sound or spelling of their name, so they changed it to Forbes. Records are fickle things."

Owain wanted to argue and point out the many flaws in the plan, but he refrained. His ma was trying to help him. As poor Welsh farmers with no influence and a son wanted for murder and escaping prison, this was the best they could do.

Also included in the parcel was a good bit of money and a bill of receipt for one passenger aboard a ship.

"It's not the most comfortable way to travel I'm afraid, and you may be put to work some, but you'll get to America one way or another," his ma told him.

"How do you know how to do this and where to go, who to talk to?" Owain wondered. "I'm the one who was involved in illegal escapades and ran with the wrong crowds."

Gwyneth got a sparkle in her eye that suddenly made her look decades younger, far more mischievous. "I know. I remember some of the friends you used to run to town with. Most of them shaped up. Not all did. A couple of them had an idea of who to talk to. It was similar to how we helped Teo and his family get to America, except they could use their real identities so everything was as close to true as possible."

Owain had no idea his ma could be so crafty. He could name no reaction other than stunned. She clearly saw this in him and she giggled, again sounding decades younger. Looking at his pa, Owain could see he was trying to be angry but having a hard time of it. The fires of passion were no longer roaring between them, but had settled down into warm, comfortable coals, an elderly couple still in love.

"Where can I find this ship?" Owain inquired.

His ma told him the name of the port. "It is not the most reputable place," she warned. "You must be on guard. Go only to this ship and speak only to the captain. And do not rest until you have reached the other side."

Just from this, Owain knew that he had a better chance of being robbed of his goods before being accepted onto the ship. All the same, he couldn't very well go to a reputable port. People there were honest and would turn him in, but only after robbing him of his goods. This port of ill repute would conceal his identity; it was part of the criminals' code, after all, to stick together as much as possible, not give each other away, in hopes that the favor might be returned later. If he used his size, strength, and reputation to get on the ship without getting robbed, he might be able to count on a certain measure of secrecy.

"It would probably be best if you left at first light," his ma went on, her youthfulness disappeared as she looked down at her hands, folded neatly on her lap. "You can reach the port in a day and depart by night, I should think."

Owain shook his head. "Too dangerous for ships to navigate the rocks and shoals. Too dangerous for me on the roads. Better to travel by night and depart by day." He noted her expression. "But because this news and gift have come late, I suppose I shall have to stay one more day and leave tomorrow evening."

That notion cheered his ma some, and they retired contentedly to bed. Well, that may have been too bold of a statement. His ma was the only one who seemed content. His pa was conflicted at best. Owain again found himself dreading what lay in store for him.

Up until he was sent to Beaumaris, Owain had never considered a future in which he couldn't return home. It was just something he'd always done, or known he could do. Suddenly he was faced with the possibility of that not being an option. He was always heading toward this point, he figured, because his parents were growing old and would not be around forever. That was one of those things he'd always known but never really took to heart. Now, on top of that reality, he was going to cross an entire ocean. It was going to be a little harder to return home for an occasional dinner.

There was every chance that he would never see his ma and pa again. The notion was terrifying, even as he scolded himself for acting like a little boy. How long had he spent, growing up, longing to be free of his parents? But that was when he was young and naive and impulsive and violent. Now he wanted to stay with his parents, to learn from them, to appreciate them, to be a good son. The problem was, he'd squandered so much of his life already that it was no longer an option. He'd always wanted to take control of his life, well, now here he was, taking control. He had no other options now, except the noose.

He slept little that night, which was probably just as well. He helped with the morning chores as he had been the last couple weeks, then took an afternoon nap. Again, he slept poorly, but he couldn't recall too many nights when he'd slept well. If he got to sleep at all for more than an hour or two, he considered it a night well spent.

Even after he woke, the sunlight gradually dimming, he spent some time just lying in bed, looking around. This was a room he'd known since childhood, yet it held almost no fond memories. It was a room he'd shared with his brother for many years, but there was little bonding time that he could recall. He had no relationships with anyone except his ma. At his age, he ought to have been married with kids, maybe had grandkids or near enough.

His ma had told him that the last time they exchanged letters, Teo had four children, two boys and two girls. Their youngest boy had just turned two. They lived in the mountains, his ma said. They'd been planning to go farther west as the United States expanded, but when they found their little valley, it reminded them so much of Wales that they decided to settle down right there. Theirs was a loose community of Welsh immigrants, scattered over hill and dale. If he could find it, they should be very accommodating.

Gwyneth held out more hope for her son than even her son thought she had a right to. He loved her for it, and hated himself. She deserved better, always had.

At long last, Owain roused himself and went out to the kitchen. His ma was just tying off a knapsack which she said was full of food to see him over for a few days if he rationed it out. As she went to hand it to him, he pulled her in a full embrace. Any staunchness she was maintaining in order to see him off crumbled and she began weeping into his chest.

"Oh, my son," she whispered. "Where did I go wrong? How did this happen?"

"It was my own stupid fault," he told her. "It had nothing to do with you."

She took a gulping breath and pulled back just enough to take his head in her hands. "Promise me something, Owain. Promise you'll try and do good."

He nodded, fighting his own emotions. "I promise. I'll do better than that, I'll actually do it."

His ma sniffed and managed a small laugh. "I know you will. Come on, then. Your pa got your horse ready."

Owain facing his pa was considerably less emotional, but not completely emotionless. Teo had walled himself off from his eldest son in order to protect the rest of the family, but that didn't mean he did not weep behind that wall or question himself. Owain caught only glimpses of this man here and there over the last couple weeks, and their departure was one of those times.

"You know we've lost a couple children over the years," Teo said. "Flu or fever or whatever it was. A long time ago, I thought we lost our oldest boy to the sins of the flesh and the pleasures of the world. So far, none of the children we lost have been brought back to life." He took an even breath. "But I'd like to be proven wrong."

And, just as unceremoniously as he had greeted his son two weeks ago, now he departed, shoving his hands in his pockets and wandering off toward the barn. Gwyneth and Owain watched him go for just a moment. Then she pulled a handkerchief from a dress pocket and handed it to him. When he unfolded it, he found such fine stitching as only she was capable of, a house that looked like theirs, a barn, plus the names of all the children she'd ever borne.

"Give this to your brother," she said. "Then he'll know that we've talked, and maybe it will open a door between you."

Owain looked over the cloth one more time before folding it neatly and tucking it safely away. "I will. And I'll do good this time."

She smiled and nodded vigorously, wiping tears from her face. "Yes. I know you will."

With that, Owain kissed her on both cheeks before climbing on his horse and turning back toward the road. He stopped only once to look back. His ma was still standing there, watching him. Always.

Chapter Nineteen

The Journey

Truth be told, Owain actually preferred traveling by night, and it wasn't even because of his inner criminal taking advantage of the dark. Well, not entirely. He preferred the peace and quiet, listening to only the sounds of nature around him. The crickets, the frogs, the wind in the grass or the trees. In this case, the addition of the plodding of horse hooves. He enjoyed the solitude without the confinement. As he traveled along, he found that this time around, he appreciated it a great deal more. He'd expressed his gratitude to the Scottish pagans when they gave or loaned him the horse, and he had enjoyed that ride south, but there was just something even more refreshing about this particular ride. It felt almost as if he were riding for the first time. He was already homesick, but he just felt free, free like he'd never been before. Not escaped from prison free, but as if his soul had been freed.

Maybe he was being fanciful. Until he set foot in America, any number of things could happen to him. He could be apprehended on the road. The ship could sink in the Atlantic. The ship might be randomly searched by the Royal Navy or attacked by pirates. Until he was safely on the other side, he was not taking anything for granted. And that included the journey, which he was growing to love the longer he rode.

He alternated between a walk and a gallop, but tried to stay at a trot as much as possible. It was an even, steady pace, a steady rhythm he could get used to.

Having been all over Wales, Owain knew about where this port of ill repute lay. It was not widely advertised, they claimed, because it was treacherous to approach, by land or sea. Rocks everywhere. It was true. The harbor itself was as ideal as any seaman could ask for, but the channel in and out was not suited for large craft with a deep draft, and if one did not navigate it just right, the rocks would tear a ship to splinters. Similarly, the road leading to the small town was a maze of rocks and narrow passages, winding down a rocky cliff. On a pleasant summer day, any idiot who was paying half attention to his steps could get up and down just fine. After a rain or especially after a snow, everything turned terribly slippery. In winter, the whole track became ice, and even the most knowledgeable of the road could slip and fall to their deaths.

But it was May now, nearly June, and the weather was fine. Owain's biggest obstacle was the darkness, but with the days as long as they were, he knew he would not need to wait long for good light, assuming he arrived at any point in the dark.

The sky was just beginning to lighten from black to gray, and Owain was still a few miles out from the port. By the time he reached the turn-off in the road that led down the treacherous trail, more colors streaked across the horizon but the sun had not yet peeked over the hills behind him. Owain considered riding the horse down, then thought better of it. If Ceffyl stumbled or tripped and fell, he would be at the mercy of the great beast and they could both go tumbling to their deaths. Owain wanted at least a slim chance of being able to get out of the way if something happened to the horse. So he dismounted and took the reins. The horse snorted as if reading his mind, but obediently followed.

The harbor really wasn't very big, enough for six docks plus a few more ships waiting a polite distance off. The docks were crude but sturdy, the surrounding buildings less so. Some businesses had been erected in various caves carved out in the cliffs by the water, and they were arguably the most sturdy, and quite possibly the cleanest as well. The rest of the buildings, those that had been constructed of wood or whatever the builder had on hand, they were far more questionable, but no less frequented.

The jolly atmosphere of drink and sex and other merriment was beginning to wind down by the time Owain set foot on the shoreline. He let out a relieved sigh and looked around. Now it was morning, with ships wanting to get in and out as fast as possible. The authorities could come by at any moment. But, with pretty much everyone hungover, work was often slow, the workers bad-tempered, the overall atmosphere was far from friendly.

It was exactly the kind of place Owain might be expected to frequent, but it was also a place where no one wanted to snitch lest they reveal their own sins. It was a perfect place for him to find illicit passage to America, and he was still a little wary at how his ma knew where to go, who to see, and what to do. Bad friends aside...

Could it be a set-up? Had she turned him in and this was just an elaborate scheme to drive him to a place and arrest him? Maybe she hadn't turned him in, but maybe the authorities had gotten to her anyway. Maybe the police had threatened her in some way. She didn't want any trouble at her home and didn't want to appear to be betraying her son, so they concocted this elaborate ruse to capture him and keep her in the clear.

Owain wasn't sure how far he wanted to follow either line of thinking. After all his ma had done for him in the past, he had a hard time believing that she would give him up at the last minute. And besides, if any pursuers had wanted to, they would only have had to corner him on the rocky road down to the port and somehow get him to fall to his death. Their hands are clean, he's dead, and life goes back to normal. Gwyneth and Teo don't know anything is amiss until weeks or months later when they hear nothing from their other son in America who knows nothing about Owain's visit.

Paranoia was a terrible thing, Owain thought as he forced himself to approach the town. Instead he focused on other things, like what he was going to do with the horse. He couldn't take it with him, but he felt guilty about selling it seeing how it had been a gift. Could he really set it free and it would make its way back to the pagan community? Either way, they had reached the end of their friendship, and now he had a choice to make.

In the end, Owain took the saddle and reins and everything else off the horse. The provisions and his meager worldly possessions he kept. The rest of it he would sell and maybe have a little money on hand when he got to America, or in case he had to engage in a little bribery here. But the horse he would turn loose. Maybe it really would find its way back to

Scotland. Maybe it would be captured by a farmer. Maybe it would die. It was no longer his concern.

Oddly enough, the horse seemed to understand what was going on. It nudged him once in the back and snorted, then turned and started back the way they had come, starting up the rocky trail and not looking back.

A chill creeping up his spine, Owain took everything and started into town.

He knew he got ripped off as he sold the saddle and the reins, but all the same, he didn't exactly have time to argue and bargain. He still had to find his ship, for one. And for two, this was a harbor. A smuggler's harbor. They had little use for horses on the water. Even on land, it was another mouth to feed and water and keep quiet, and they could be difficult to hide in a pinch.

Still, he was relieved to be rid of a majority of the weight and bulk, leaving only his bag with the remainder of his provisions and his smaller bag of supplies and other possessions. Everything he owned and everything he had to his name was either on his body or in the bag. It was a sorry reminder of his lot in life, the results of his own stupidity, but it made it easier to travel, anyway. The cash and his mother's kerchief he kept on his person. If anyone wanted those things, they would have to fight him for it, especially the kerchief. A thief could take the money, but if anyone touched the kerchief, there was every chance Owain Fforidd was going to make another body to put in the ground.

He tried not to think such thoughts, even as he was fairly certain that they might fall under the category of righteous anger. Everywhere he looked in the little harbor, he saw everything as though it came from his own soul. The morning grew brighter, promising a fine day, but he only saw darkness. Sex and alcohol was rampant. Every man present was clearly a veteran of many fights; he didn't see a single person without scars of some form. Some were missing limbs, some eyes, many had few or no teeth. All were armed as if they were about to face an entire army in single combat. Tattoos were everywhere as well, denoting naked women, various forms of death or torture, and numerous good luck charms for the sea. Owain saw card tables that had been overturned, several pubs with years of damage and multiple patchwork layers to fix it up. There were no alleys that didn't have at least one body, and few storefronts didn't play host to diseased folk, many with open wounds. Naked children ran to and fro. Owain came around a corner and saw one little girl, couldn't have been older than nine or ten, wearing a tattered dress, one sleeve down to show off a breast that didn't even exist yet.

"Excuse me, sir," she said, walking toward him with an awkward saunter, "may I pleasure you?"

Years without sex earned an instant reaction from Owain's groin, even as his mind could hardly comprehend what he was seeing. He quickly did the math. Victoria would be right around her age, maybe a little younger. How could this happen to such a young girl? Probably she had known no life outside of this harbor.

His mind jolted back to the present as she touched him and began unlacing his pants. He grabbed her hands and moved them away. Then he knelt in front of her and handed her a note for a full pound.

"That's not necessary, dear," he said. "Get yourself something to eat."

She looked at the note for a long moment, then back at him. "You're looking for a ship, aren't you, sir?"

He nodded, fully aware that other young eyes were watching him. They'd rob him blind if he wasn't careful. "I am. Maybe you can point me in the right direction. Take me there, and you get another pound."

The girl readily agreed to that, taking him by the hand and starting toward the docks. Work had increased dramatically in just the last hour, and everything quickly turned into a crowded maze. Owain kept one hand on the girl and the other tight on his bag. The last thing he needed was some percussive pickpocket stealing his things. More than once he ran his fingers over the place where his money and papers were hidden, just to assure himself they were still there, which they were.

"*Mermaid's Tear*, sir," the girl said, pointing to a small ship that looked just this side of ocean-worthy. But the stern of the ship was painted with the appropriate name. True to his word, he gave the girl another note. He wanted to give her some kind of advice, but felt sorely unqualified. Maybe not unqualified, but certainly hypocritical. By the time he even thought of anything mildly encouraging, she had disappeared.

Owain straightened and turned to the ship. He was hardly knowledgeable about ships, but compared to the rest of those in the harbor, this one seemed to be undertaking a rather long voyage and was getting ready to cast off. He approached a sailor he'd seen walk on and off multiple times.

"Your captain," Owain said, stopping the man. "Where is he?"

The man did not answer right away, nor did he cower. He straightened and met Owain head-on. Owain had met several men who were as tall as he was, but never before had he met someone who matched him in both size and strength. In fact, this sailor might be the first one to appear bigger than him. Maybe his problem, then, hadn't been his lust for power, but because he'd simply been born into the wrong family and made the wrong career choice. He clearly could have thrived as a sailor.

But that was neither here nor there. After a long moment, the man grunted and jerked his head toward a man about thirty paces away. He did not wear anything fancy, but he held some kind of ledger and was speaking to another man. Both had some air of authority about them.

Owain did not thank the sailor he had stopped. It would not have been proper. It would have only pegged him as weak. For as much as Owain wanted to change himself and be a better man, he wanted to be a dead man even less. So he simply turned away and approached the man he perceived as being the captain.

"This your ship, sir?" he inquired, bringing out his best disinterested banker's attitude.

"Might be," one of the men replied. "What's it to you?"

He only reached Owain's chin, but he walked as though the reverse were true.

"Going to America any time soon?"

"Might be. What's it worth to you?"

Owain ran his fingers over the spot where he'd hidden his papers and his money, a subtle gesture he'd picked up long ago, a way of saying he had money without actually bringing out the money. "That depends. What are you offering?"

The man snickered. "Does my ship look like a luxury passenger vessel to you? If you want comfort, your better bet is go to and find yourself one of those ships, because I'll be charging you double for it. If all you want is passage..." The man gave Owain a once-over. "I might be able to put you to work to cover some of your fees."

"Do those fees include no questions asked?"

"That's complimentary, long as there's no trouble."

"I do my best."

The second man snorted a mild laugh. "Then you're already doing better than half our crew."

"A thousand pounds if you're willing to work," the captain said. "Another five hundred if you're not. Another five hundred if you cause trouble."

"I don't have that much."

"Unfortunate for you, then."

"I have a receipt for one hundred pounds received," Owain said. "And another hundred pounds cash. Plus I can work."

The captain gave him a look. "Ah, so you're the one. I thought it a little odd that—well, never mind." He folded his arms. "I don't normally like lowering my price that much, but I'm doing this as a personal favor to someone who is apparently a mutual friend of ours." He nodded. "Very good, then. Williams."

The captain moved off and the second man took Owain onto the ship, barking orders at the crew as they passed by. Owain was momentarily overcome by waking nightmares of the gaol, and he numbly followed the man into a small cabin at the rear of the ship.

"What have you here?" The man indicated the bag.

"Some personal affects. I also have papers, if you want."

"Keep those to yourself," the man warned. "Don't show them to anyone, don't tell anyone about them, and always keep them on your person. You're not the only one we're taking across, and few of them have papers. Desperate men would kill for what you have. Understand?"

"Perfectly."

"Good. What's your name, then?" The man brought out a ledger and readied a pen.

"Walter Forbes," Owain answered, remembering himself at the last minute.

"My name is James Williams. I'm the quartermaster on this vessel. Captain is James Martin." He rattled off a list of other higher ranking crewmen Owain knew he would forget. "You have any experience on a ship before?"

"I've rowed a dinghy once."

The man, James Williams, gave him a look. Then, "Well, better than nothing, I suppose. You any kind of strong?"

"I'd like to think so."

"Well, you certainly look bigger and stronger than some of our other passengers, so I don't want to put you in the galley. You'll be working as a bo'sun's mate."

Williams went through everything the same way his pa could ramble off a list of chores for the farm. This was the man's whole life. He knew what was expected of him. He knew how the ship operated, he knew his men, he knew the sea. Put simply, the man knew what he was doing. He expected everyone under him to have at least a vague idea as well so things would go smoothly. Owain inquired about signing on as a crewman, but the quartermaster said no. He was going to be completely invisible. It was at that point that Owain turned over half his fee, the receipt for a hundred pounds already paid.

"Well, I expect we're about ready with the cargo," the quartermaster said, looking at a pocketwatch. "Tide's just about perfect, too." He looked at Owain. "Find Bo'sun Andrews and tell him you'll be his mate for the voyage."

"Aye, sir," Owain said, and ducked out of the cabin.

He found Andrews easily enough. He didn't look like much, but he certainly knew his stuff. He unloaded a whole ship full of terms on Owain, maybe to try to scare him or test his resolve. When Owain did not budge, the bo'sun commended him and told him to go below and find a place to string up a hammock. Then get back up on deck for departure.

Owain was thrilled and terrified at the same time. No one had come to haul him back to Beaumaris, but at the same time, he was leaving the only home he'd ever known, and it was unlikely that he would ever return. He was glad to be getting a second chance, but he still felt as though he were running away without making proper amends. At the same time, the only way he could make proper amends was by going to America and becoming a good man.

Their departure was smooth, the sailing far less strenuous than the movement onboard the ship as the signed crew barked at each other and snapped at the passengers working their way across. Owain was on the receiving end of several snarled commands and corrections. He didn't appreciate it. His beast, still dwelling in the far corners of his mind, lifted its head, wondering if it was time to come back out. Owain quickly beat it down and submitted to the work. It was always stressful to get underway. If it wasn't done right, the ship could be damaged, people could be hurt, and an entire voyage could go to waste. That meant a lot of wasted time and money, something sailors didn't have in abundance, especially transatlantic sailors who only made a few trips a year.

It took the better part of the week before they were clear of the British Isles and all the surrounding hazards, when the captain declared them out in open waters, and it was another week before they cleared the invisible wall, where Royal Navy vessels patrolled for pirates, enemy nations, and smugglers. By all accounts from the veteran crew, they'd made out swiftly and surely, a rarity in their business, and were well underway.

Owain hadn't really been too anxious about the water—leaving, yes, but not the water itself—until the day he woke up and discovered that all signs of land had disappeared: Wales, all the outlying islets of the Isles, every vague shadow that could have been greater Europe or just his imagination. All of it gone, leaving nothing but sky and water and, at certain times of day, nothing to distinguish the two.

With the greater threats largely behind them, Owain was better able to sit down and learn his duties as bo'sun's mate which was primarily seeing to the sails and rigging. According to Andrews, Owain had been stationed there because he had the strength to climb the rigging, to hang on when the ship teetered in the waves, and to catch and hold the sails and ropes.

It was not Owain's favorite job he had ever done, and he frequently joined some of the other passengers to offer up his lunch to the sea gods. Not until about week three or four was he able to climb here and there with little or no trouble. It may have also had something to do with the other passenger who was working as a bo'sun's mate who had gotten nauseous and fallen to his death.

They were beset by a storm on week five of their voyage. It was not a hurricane, but it may as well have been the end of the world as far as Owain was concerned. He didn't mind the rain or the thunder and lightning or even the wind, powerful as it was. What he didn't like was all of this beating on him while the ground shifted beneath his feet. He hated the rocking of the boat, not because it made him sick, because it didn't anymore, but because he had no way to anchor himself and keep moving. All the wood was slippery, and with the boat rocking like it did, even if something was strapped down, it was still hard to get to because he was not.

It was a very frustrating endeavor, one that Owain did not come through happily. He was sore, he was exhausted, and he really just kind of wanted to be on land again. Didn't matter which land, he just wanted to be on solid ground.

While the veteran crew did not share his sentiments about wanting to be on solid ground, they were in an equally bad mood about the whole storm, which only brought about Owain's greatest temptation while on the high seas, something he could not easily run from: alcohol.

Captain Martin forbade open air drinking or drunkenness for the simple fact that he didn't want his crew stumbling about drunk and either fall over the railing into the sea or else stupidly climb something and fall to their deaths that way. At least belowdecks, everything was fairly contained. Owain knew when the crew began their nightly drinking because most of the passengers would come out on deck to avoid them.

There were twenty-four passengers in total, about the maximum that the ship could carry, and that was with severe rationing of space and provisions. Fifteen of them worked with the crew in some fashion to reduce their fees. Most were families. A few were couples. Owain was the only single passenger he knew of. Someone once said something about a couple children supposed to have been on the ship but didn't make it. Owain thought of the young girl he'd encountered and had a pretty good idea of where those children might have ended up if they talked to the wrong people.

Most of the passengers did not partake in the drinking with the crew. Owain was one of them, but that didn't mean he didn't want it. He wanted it. He wanted it bad. He wanted to feel the fire in his belly, the strength in his limbs, the youth in his body, and the comradery of the crew. It had been a long time since he'd had any friends, and at sea, friends were found around the bottle. Gambling was also forbidden, but that didn't mean the men didn't still play cards. Owain knew a few games, a few tricks he'd picked up from wealthy men who gambled a thousand pounds at a time.

The desire to belong was the lie Owain's beast told him to try and get him to go down and join. And maybe, once they reached America, he wouldn't disembark. Maybe he would sign on with them. This was his crowd. They got drunk, they slept with women while in port, and they constantly skirted the law. Might be that he really had chosen the wrong career as a child. The things that had gotten him excised from the community and thrown in prison could have won him promotion on the high seas. And it wasn't too late for him to join them, either. He still had his strength, and he was learning quickly. It would be so easy. Maybe the ship sank. Maybe he met some other misfortune on his way to see his brother. No one would ever have to really know.

He found himself in the crow's nest that night, mulling over his life's choices, the ones he'd made and the ones he would have to make. It was a dull thing, and he knew he would be bad company if anyone spoke to him before he got to sleep. He really did like the work, and it wouldn't be a bad way to make some money. Maybe it wouldn't be this ship, but another that he could work on for a time. He could make some money, build an honest reputation for himself.

He shook his head and felt for his ma's kerchief. No, he couldn't do that. He had a promise to keep. First and foremost, he had to find his brother. He had to establish a connection with family and prove that he could make himself better, that he could be a good man. He owed it to them to try. If his brother drove him off or some other misfortune prevented him from seeing Teo, then he could always return to the sea. That sounded like a promising alternative, a backup plan.

There was little to do in the middle of the Atlantic. Certainly there was nothing to look at. Captain Martin was fairly permissive of his men's behavior, but one rule that was always enforced was no mistreatment of any female passengers. Even being caught looking at one wrong could be grounds for a few lashings just as a reminder. All that left was the watch schedule, meals, drinking, cards, occasional merriment from a crewman who could play the fiddle, and many hours of boredom.

The weeks blurred together. The days were hot, even surrounded by water. They saw no ships, but Andrews explained that it was because they were not taking the standard shipping routes. They were slightly off those shipping routes in order to avoid any confrontations. As such, their voyage would last a couple weeks longer than it might if they followed the straight shipping lines. Owain had ceased to care somewhere around week six.

Storms swept through fiercely and departed just as quickly, most of the time, leaving the crew frustrated and soaking wet. It was around this time when Owain began to question himself regarding his desire to work on a ship in the event that things with his brother turned sour. For one, he didn't hear the call of the sea like the veteran sailors did. They talked about it as if they could actually hear something, hold a conversation with the waves, like a bunch of lunatics escaped from a nuthouse. Their talk could easily make Owain believe that the sea was a mistress, considering how often he saw — well, never mind. He'd slept with a lot of women and he'd done a lot of things, but sailors were truly a different breed.

But another thing he was beginning to notice was that he couldn't keep up with the sailors, and not just because he was unfamiliar with the tasks and what his duties required of him. He was actually starting to notice his age. He was still strong, no doubt, but not as strong as he had been in his younger days. He'd gotten off shift the other day and had to retire to his hammock because his back was hurting. His back had hurt before for a variety of reasons, but it was the first time that he'd actually taken time out of his day to rest and relax and hope the pain went away. His knees and wrists were starting to ache as well. When had that happened?

He couldn't waste too much time looking for work when he got to America; he would have to find his brother posthaste. He was getting old. Probably he would never marry or have children. He would be living on charity the rest of his life, at least once he couldn't work well anymore. He had to find his family and restore that bond. Rephrase, he had to forge a new bond where there had been only pain and suffering for decades.

Fear began to creep into his mind. If he failed, he not only ran the risk of being alone, but he would not even have his strength to fall back on. Eventually, he would not be able to care for himself.

The more he considered where his selfishness had gotten him and the trajectory he'd been on and could easily fall back into, the more Owain was able to quiet his inner beast, to the point where he might believe it was gone, or almost so. He no longer had the luxury of time or strength or wealth or anything at all. He had to pull himself together, take responsibility for himself, and work harder than he ever had in his life to try and forge a new life as a better man. Hopefully with his brother's help.

He didn't know how much time had passed after that silent resolve—all the days tended to blur together while at sea—but the next thing he knew, there was a shout from above.

"Land, ho!"

CHAPTER TWENTY

THE NEW WORLD

Owain had never been so happy to see land, but then, he'd never been too far from it before this voyage. Land started out as just a little blur on the horizon, enough to break up the endless stretch of sky and sea. Pretty soon, the break filled the horizon. More ships began to appear, small dots moving here and there, gradually getting bigger until sails and flags started coming into focus.

Buildings began to appear, and how numerous they were! An irrational feeling of dread formed in Owain's gut as he wondered if they hadn't somehow turned around halfway across and returned to London. What if Mrs. Balk was waiting for them, waiting for him? Owain knew his ma meant well, but what about this mutual friend of his and the captain? How far did he really want to trust invisible acquaintances from a time in his life he was working hard to forget?

The land kept growing and growing, until Owain thought it couldn't grow any more. How was it that he'd somehow forgotten just how big the world was? How could he have forgotten just how vast the land was, how small he was compared to it? Was it his arrogance, or was that more related to all the weeks he'd spent at sea? Considering many of the other passengers had similar reactions, he was willing to bet the latter.

He fingered his papers, still safe and sound. He was amazed that they'd survived, actually. All the storms and the labor and everything else he'd been through the last few months, he thought for sure he would have lost them, or that they would have been otherwise destroyed. They were by no means pristine anymore, but they were readable. Made it more believable, Owain supposed. He'd handled plenty of papers as a banker, and not a few times, someone tried to pass off a fake account or false bookkeeping. One of the ways to spot a fake was that it looked too good to be true. Paper went through wear and tear, ink faded or got smudged or blotted. If it looked utterly pristine, question it.

"All right, listen up!" Captain Martin barked. "If you are a passenger—doesn't matter if you've been working or not—if you're a passenger, assemble here now!"

Owain and the remaining twenty-something passengers assembled as ordered on the open deck.

"As you may have noticed, we are approaching New York City," the captain began. "I expect that at any moment, we will be intercepted and possibly boarded. There is only one rule which I will emphasize and the rest of the crew will enforce. No—talking. You do not say a word. I will deal with the authorities. It won't be a particularly long or difficult process as long as you let me do my job. This is what you paid me for.

"Afterwards, you will be taken to a boardinghouse on the mainland and given further instructions from the authorities there. Let me also emphasize that once you leave this vessel, I am no longer responsible for you. Anything you leave behind will not be returned to you. And perhaps most importantly..." He met the gaze of everyone in the crowd. "This never happened. You and I do not know each other. We are not friends. We are not acquaintances. We are not business partners. We are not mates. We are total strangers. Getting you across the Atlantic is the only favor I am doing for you or will ever do for you, and even so, you pay me for it. End of transaction. Is that understood?"

Heads bobbed, some more reluctantly than others.

"Very good. And make no mistake: this is not the first time I have done this. You've been a pretty agreeable lot, so this should go over very smoothly. But if it doesn't, my crew and I have no qualms about throwing you into the harbor and fleeing. So if you're thinking about trying anything, at least have the decency to wait until you get off my ship. If you're smart, you'll wait until you make it through customs and into the city so you at least have somewhere to run.

"And finally, those of you who have been working for the crew, you are now released from your duties. Good job. Get your things packed and be prepared to disembark. All of you, Mr. Williams will be around to collect the rest of your fees, if any are owed. If you don't have the money, you can either sail back with us and work it off, or take your chances in the water."

Captain Martin unceremoniously ended his little speech, leaving the passengers to speak amongst themselves while the quartermaster made his way through the crowd with the ledger book, collecting fees as necessary.

"Mr. Forbes," he began, approaching Owain but still with his nose in the ledger. "You worked hard on this trip. If you weren't so intent on getting off and making your fortune here, we might have offered you a place in our crew."

"Seeing how that is not the case, you decided to go with the next best thing and waive any outstanding fees," Owain countered.

"You're a funny man, but that's not the case, unfortunately. Already you're paying less than most here, so don't be greedy. You still owe a hundred pounds, according to this."

They were nothing if not honest, sometimes brutally so. Owain had fully expected them to pocket the initial hundred from the receipt and claim he still owed two hundred pounds, which was why he'd kept an extra stash of bills. But he merely handed over the hundred and settled the account. Williams thanked him politely enough, then moved on to the next person owing money.

And still they neared the harbor. Now that they were almost upon it, Owain's sense of scale and depth perception was realigning itself and he no longer felt so overwhelmed by the sheer size of the land, never mind the city.

It wasn't long before they were intercepted and half a dozen men boarded their vessel. Owain had learned an American accent, but even this sounded foreign to him. Maybe it was just him. Nevertheless, he did as the captain said and remained silent. But then, not speaking was not the same as not listening.

Mostly it was formalities. *Mermaid's Tear* was late by a good two weeks. Poor fortune in wind and weather, Martin told them, and even more so for his unaccounted passengers, it seemed, whom they had found shipwrecked after a storm. His ship had managed to skirt the edge of the system while their vessel was drawn right in and torn to pieces. Only a few spoke any English, and information was limited. Nevertheless, he did his righteous duty before God, took them aboard his vessel, divided his ship's already sparse rations even further, and brought them safely to the land of opportunity. Only a few had papers of any kind, and fewer still had any skills that he knew of.

Owain hadn't heard so much crap since his time as a wealthy man, when the wealthy would brag and boast and try to politically and economically outmaneuver one another with fine bluster. Coming from the captain, knowing all that he did, it almost made Owain laugh. As it was, he was careful to beat down even a smile. He was a shipwrecked passenger and his fate, his chances of getting into America, all hinged on these men here.

He looked around at the other passengers. A majority of them were Irish, fleeing the Famine. They'd taken a small boat from Ireland down to the shady port in Wales where they boarded Captain Martin's ocean-going vessel. Most, if not all of them, spoke English to some degree.

There were a few other passengers, however. A family from eastern Europe with English so limited and so bad it was fair to say they spoke none at all, and a couple who spoke no language known to any of the crew, so it was impossible to say where they were from.

"Are any of them criminals?" one of the authorities asked.

"How should I know?" Martin wondered. "Do you think they would admit to it if they were? In my experience with them, none of them have caused any trouble or been accused of any wrongdoing."

"Have any shown signs of illness, scarlet fever, yellow fever, sores?"

"None, sir."

The authorities did a quick inspection of the rest of the ship, including the cargo. Owain never did learn what the reported cargo was supposed to be that they were hauling—the official documents, not the smuggling portion—but whatever it was, it was all properly accounted for, nothing missing, nothing added.

The authorities still found it odd that after a terrible shipwreck, whole families had managed to stay together, but with little more than a suspicion that something wasn't right, they could do nothing about it.

Besides, they were only trying to keep diseases from ravaging the city. True, no one really wanted the Irish in America, but the shores were open, New York City awaiting their arrival. Captain Martin thanked them for their consideration and saw them off.

A collective sigh of relief went up from the passengers, but the crew just looked annoyed. Then they were moving again, maneuvering into an open dock and laying the gangplank. They were directed to a customs office, and from there to a boardinghouse that would serve as temporary immigrant inspection.

More terrifying memories of Beaumaris Gaol roared to life as Owain descended below decks for the last time, grabbed his meager bag of possessions, and followed the others toward the squat building that would serve as their home for an undetermined length of time. They stood in a line while a desk worker took information and gave them instructions. When it was Owain's turn, he handed over his papers.

"What's this, then?" the clerk asked.

"Papers, sir," Owain told him.

"Yes, I see that. Why are you giving them to me?"

"Don't you need them?"

"What for? I'm simply recording who you are, that you're here at all. Keep those on you, though, if you ever go before a judge or talk to the police. Now then, your name?"

It's right there in front of you, Owain thought, pocketing his papers. "Walter Forbes."

"How old are you?"

"Thirty-seven." That may or may not have been a lie. He honestly couldn't even remember his own birthday anymore, not that it had ever been of great importance.

The clerk looked him over a bit and jotted down some more information. "And what country are you coming from?"

"Wales." The word was out before he could remember to lie and say England.

"Like Ireland, but you prefer the comfort of your sheep, don't you? Or so the bloody English say." The man shook his head. "Doesn't matter to me, I suppose. Good luck in New York, though." He scribbled down some more information, filling in boxes on the form, a whole book of names and assorted information. Finally he set the pen and inkwell aside and leaned back in his chair. "Do you have any family knows you're coming?"

"Sorry to say, they don't."

"All right. Listen good, then. You go down this hall into the main room, take a left. There's a desk there with paper and pens and ink and whatnot. You write a letter to your family, tell them you're here. If you can't write, you can ask someone to help. If your family comes, talks to the people in the office, you get to go with them. Otherwise, you stay here for ninety days."

Owain wanted to argue and ask questions, but he knew it would do little good. Just like the clerk at a bank, he was only here to do a job at the behest of his superiors.

Nevertheless, he was hesitant to take another step into the building. It was far too reminisce of prison. Sure, three months was a pretty light sentence, comparatively, but it was a nightmare just being awake; how much worse would it be when he did finally close his eyes?

He found himself moving down the corridor as if in a daze. There were several large rooms, but he was relegated to the largest one of all, the catch-all of incoming immigrants. He had no family with him, no children, he was not a woman, and he was not expected by anyone important.

He found the alcove with the paper and pens. There was precious little paper for the crowd that was coming in, and certainly not enough pens. He took a single sheet of paper, then found a spot on the floor to sit and wait for a pen and ink, as well as consider his predicament.

All he knew about his brother was that he'd gone west and settled in some mountains, and that his last name had been changed to Forbes as well. He hadn't thought to ask his ma how or where she'd sent her letters to Teo. Maybe she thought that someone here could help him. Maybe she didn't realize the sheer size of just this one city, never mind any mountains out west.

A pen opened up and he jumped on it, almost literally. He took it and slid off to one side, then paused. He turned at a tap on his shoulder.

It was a man, maybe twenty years or so, dirty, but looking no worse for wear.

"*Is féidir leis an bhfear sin ansin cabhrú leat,*" he said, indicating a guard. (That one there can help you.)

"I'm sorry, I don't speak Irish," Owain told him

The man raised a brow, but gestured again and said in accented English, "He can help you."

I don't need help writing, Owain thought grudgingly. But he thanked the man and approached the guard, catching him just before he left the room.

"Need help writing a letter?" the guard asked, looking and sounding bored.

"I can write my own letter," Owain informed him. "I don't know how or where to send it."

"Good for you that you can write. We can help you with how to send it. Where, though, that's a bit of a problem."

"I know my brother is here, in America. He says he went west to live in the mountains."

"Which ones?" At Owain's apparent confused look, he continued, "We got the little mountains of Appalachia right close here. But if you go out farther west, into Indian country, toward California, you find even bigger mountains. And there's a good stretch of distance between them."

"He was supposed to go out west, but then he stopped in his first mountain crossing, in a nice green valley."

"All right, that's helpful, I guess. Do you know what state or territory he's in?"

Owain felt his hopes sink. "No, I don't. I have his name. And he's part of a Welsh community."

The guard shifted his stance and gave Owain a look. "We can't just send a Pony Express rider out running around them mountains looking for a particular man with a particular name, no clue where he might be. Got the Indians out there would butcher him before sunrise if he strayed too far from a trail, and if your brother lives too far north, God help the rider if the Iroquois catch him. If your brother's living too far south, got them crazy Southerners might get him, too. 'Confederates' they call themselves, might think he's sending secret government transmissions." He went on before Owain could speak. "Point is, without knowing even what state he's in, any letter you write is going nowhere. So put the paper and pen back where you found it, and let someone who knows what they're doing have a chance."

Time was, Owain would have had a serious problem with the man's attitude and how he treated, not only him, but all the immigrants. Unfortunately, he had no standing and no leverage to force anyone to treat him better. It seemed that his best bet would be to simply sit tight and wait for his ninety days to run its course. Then he would have to track his brother down the old-fashioned way.

The first day was a terrible mess of people as the rest of the passengers from *Mermaid's Tear* plus passengers from another larger vessel fought for space in the cramped boardinghouse. Owain tried to keep to himself along one wall, just enough space for him to lie down, but it didn't always work. Apparently, the larger one's actual size, the less space others were willing to give. He was a big man who was relegated to space fit for a child, while a little girl no older than six got a space more suited to someone his size. It might not have been so bad, he thought, except the cramped sleeping position on a threadbare blanket and tight quarters was just too reminisce of Beaumaris. At least he was on a blanket instead of straw, and he didn't see any rats, but still the memories came to him unbidden.

He didn't sleep much that first week. When he did, it came in fits and starts, with half-remembered images and occasional yelling, as his disgruntled neighbors informed him. Not a few times he took his things outside the door into a small yard area so he could sleep in the open air and ponder a new conundrum.

It had been late spring, early summer when he left Wales. A many-month journey brought them into the beginning of September. Staying here for ninety days meant it would be December before he would be permitted to leave. Traveling in the winter was not a smart thing to do even in your own familiar town, never mind in a foreign land you knew nothing about and, if you listened to the authorities, where danger and enemies lurked around every corner. He would have to find a place to stay and a means of work through the winter.

He didn't like to be delayed. Owain wanted to find his brother as soon as possible. But he also had to be smart, or else he would never get where he needed to go. He had to make a plan, then. While he was holed up in New York City, he needed to gather information about where he would likely be going, learn the geography, the people. The more he knew, the better prepared he would be to navigate unfamiliar territory.

It sounded like a swell idea, up until the day he woke up and found all his cash stolen. He never felt a thing, never had any inclination that something was wrong until he did his daily inventory and found it missing. All of it. Over a hundred pounds, gone. He could have lived in New York City for a month on that, once he got it exchanged.

He tried to tell the guards, but they could do little about it. No one saw anything, and no one was saying anything. Owain spent some time moving among the people, asking, interrogating, demanding, but no one was going to give it up. If he had to hazard a guess, it was probably a child who'd robbed him, small hands slipping inside his shirt to grab the cash. After a while, he was forced to concede that, in their desperation, whoever had robbed him was more afraid of starving than they were of him.

He sat outside in the growing cold. Frost had covered the ground in the night but had since burned off. He stared across the street at the city. Just at a glance, it greatly resembled London, the hustle and bustle, the movement of people, rich and poor. Business and theft.

"'Tis a shame," one of the guards, whom he'd come to know as Bill, said, stepping outside and standing beside Owain, pipe between his teeth. "Lot of theft goes on in here. I hate to see one man's fortune get stolen before he has a chance to make his way with it."

"Don't remind me," Owain grumbled.

"Well, you need not fret too much. If it happens that you leave by yourself with no one to see to you, you'll get a small bit of change. It'll be enough to see you through the night so you can find work in the morning."

"That's the first good news I've heard since I got here."

The man gave him a look. "Can't imagine the news you got back home that made you leave, then."

Owain wanted to say something slightly witty but a bit ominous, something about the noose, something about prison, something about murder, but he refrained. They didn't need to think him a dangerous criminal on the run, even if he was. He didn't need them to send him back to Wales in chains. Moreover, he didn't need to drag that life across the ocean with him if he didn't have to. And he didn't have to, because he was going to be an honest, decent, hard-working man.

The money never did turn up, as the days got even colder and snow began to fall. At first, it just fell during the night but would usually melt by the afternoon. Then it began to stick and accumulate. The days grew ever shorter. Toward the end of November, sickness began to spread rapidly among the immigrants huddled in the house. The guards tried to keep it contained by quarantining anyone who showed symptoms in another room, but it got out anyway and continued to spread. The whole place echoed with coughing, sneezing, and crying. For as cold as the air was, the boardinghouse was quite warm as nearly everyone ran high fevers.

Owain was no exception to the sickness, but he refused to let it get him down. He'd been ill while on the road before, and he knew well that if he stopped, if he rested for any good length of time, it could easily mean certain death.

For some, that prophecy came true. By the time the illness began to really wane from the population, nineteen people had died, twelve of them children. Mothers wailed, fathers beat their fists against the cold walls. Owain simply took his blanket and his bag of things and went outside.

It had taken a little longer for him to recover than he thought it should, looking out over the yard toward the street, ice beginning to crust over the water. Used to be that when he got sick, he might have to slow down for some days, maybe a week, but then he would be back on his feet in no time. This time around, it had taken several weeks for him to fully recover, and there had been a few days, when it got really bad, that he'd had to simply stop and lie down and rest. When had that happened?

The same time he'd had to sit down and rest because his back was hurting, he concluded. He was aging. He was no longer a fit young man in his physical prime, poised to take on the world, conquer Wales and England and anyone who stood in his way. Now he was simply a man sneaking past his prime into old age, coming to America on a smuggler's ship with no money and only a vague idea of where his brother might be.

He was pathetic.

A few weeks before Christmas, when the clerk came around calling names, Owain was pleasantly surprised to hear his name called. Walter Forbes. Yes, he was still here. No, he hadn't found any family to contact.

Having recovered from his ordeal with the sickness, he returned to the customs office for another interview and inspection. Once he was deemed healthy again, given a handful of change, mostly pennies. It would get him a meal and a room for the night, but everything else was on him. Welcome to America.

And there he was, standing in the biggest, busiest city in North America, an entire ocean separated from everything he had ever known. No one here knew him. They didn't know he'd been a drunken brawler in his youth. They didn't know he'd been a wealthy banker and investor with a wife and child as a younger adult. They didn't know that he was a reviled murderer who had taken the lives of six men, including his father-in-law. They didn't know that he had escaped from prison with the help of a priest and smuggled over to America with the help of his parents whom he would never see again. They didn't know anything about him.

In a way, it was wonderfully freeing, and if the cold hadn't prompted him to get moving and find someplace warm he could get a meal and a bed, he might have broken down right there, kissed the ground and pledged his allegiance. This was a land of opportunity. But as it was, it was too cold even to see the sights. The day was fast ending and he had work to do.

To say that the people of New York knew nothing about him was only slightly untrue. They knew one thing about him: he was a damn foreigner. He knew immediately that it didn't matter to the Americans that he was technically from Wales. There was a massive influx of Irish into the city right now, so anyone who came from the British Isles and wasn't strictly English—be they "technically" Welsh or Scottish or anyone else—they were automatically Irish.

Owain learned within ten minutes that American opinion of the Irish was not very high. Some restaurants refused to serve them, much the same way they might refuse to serve Negros, or else they would have separate rooms and services. Random graffiti was everywhere in paint and posters, depicting the Irish as lazy, starving, greedy drunkards, and much fun was made over the Famine with more caricatures of potatoes than Owain had ever seen in his life or even thought possible. The farther one ventured into the poorer parts of town, the more bawdy the graffiti became.

Owain was no stranger to being disliked because he was Welsh. He'd endured that every day he was in England, twice as much when he was in London. Honestly, he was a bit disappointed that he couldn't find relief here in America. He really wanted to be able to just be himself, be a good, honest man. Was that really too much to ask? Why should he have to continue to jump through these hoops?

After several attempts at finding a good meal at a decent price and polite conversation failed—every time being told to go home, *boyo*—he decided that if he had an advantage, he was going to use it. And he did have an advantage, in that he had learned to speak with an American accent. It might take some doing because it had been some time since he'd used it, but he would give it his all. Compared to the rest of New York City, it still sounded foreign, but hopefully the locals would recognize it as being from America somewhere.

Apparently, he was a Virginian, somewhere close to Washington, D.C., or so he learned. As soon as he brought out the American accent, he was treated ten times better than he had been. He got a hot meal, and someone offered to buy him a drink, which he cordially turned down. He was not treated perfectly, as Virginia was a southern state, and tensions were straining something fierce between the North and South, but all the same, he was an American and permitted every convenience possible.

In a way, it annoyed him. He knew it wasn't just about how he spoke, but the way he spoke and what it said about who he possibly was, where he was possibly from, and what he was possibly bringing to America. All the same, that his standing in public opinion could change that dramatically just over his accent, he may as well have moved back to London and brought out his English accent. If only everyone in London didn't already know him and want to skin him alive.

Nevertheless, he managed to get a hot meal and directions to the nearest hotel he could afford. It wasn't much, but it was a roof over his head and the sheets appeared to be mostly clean. He was directed to a nearby pump to bring water for the washbasin beside his bed. As far as he was concerned, it was a lot better than being stuck on the ship for months on end.

He washed everything that could be washed, every nook and cranny on his body and every fiber on his clothes. Then he hung everything up on a line and lay in the bed, naked under several blankets.

He wished he could write to his ma and tell her he'd arrived safely. As it was, he had just enough money left to get a small breakfast before going out and looking for work in the morning. Maybe once he'd worked a few days and had a penny or two to spare, then he would send her a letter, telling her that he'd arrived safely, had food and shelter, had a job, and was just waiting out the winter before going to search for Teo. Maybe he ought to ask for his brother's mailing address and make the search that much easier. Then he would have not only his ma's kerchief, but a handwritten letter that he could give Teo.

These were the last thoughts he had before he drifted off to sleep.

Chapter Twenty-One

The Traveler

Like London, New York City was seeing a time of expansion and economic growth, which meant plenty of jobs. Unlike London, America was undergoing a massive ethnic shift with a resulting increase in political tensions as Negros fled slavery in the South, searching for the same opportunities as the Irish fleeing the Famine. Depending on who you asked, the Freedmen might be welcome but the immigrants not, or the immigrants might be welcomed but the Freedmen not. Or both might be welcomed, or neither were welcomed. It was a wildly tumultuous time, and Owain's job prospects might have been non-existent except for his American accent. And even then, because it was a Virginian accent, and Virginia being a Southern state, it could still be hit-and-miss whether he got a job that day.

By the time the new year rolled around, marking the coming of 1850, Owain had rented a small room not far from the Irish slum known as Five Points. It was about all he could afford at the time, working a variety of menial labor jobs. He did eventually write to his ma, but it would be months, maybe a year, before he ever got a reply.

As much as he wanted to pack up and start searching for his brother just as soon as the weather allowed, he quickly came to realize that it was hardly a realistic plan. It wasn't just the Confederates or the Indians or any of that, either. He'd never realized America was so big. Great Britain, he'd crossed and recrossed and criss-crossed time and again. The news he got from travelers and those who liked to gossip about impending war, America could not be crossed in a day or a month or even a couple months. North to south was a good year's journey. And to get from New York to California? A couple more years, and that was being generous depending on the time of year you tried to cross the two mountain ranges in between.

There was no way he was just going to pack up his things, take off one day, and find his brother in a month. At the very least, he had to wait, hope his mother sent a response to his letter, and gave him a better idea where he might start his search.

So he stayed put in New York that year. It was October before he received a reply from his mother.

"My dear Owain,

"It brings me such joy to know you have arrived safely and are working hard. It certainly eases my fears that something may have happened to you on the way over. For as much trouble as you get into, know that a mother always worries. A letter is a very welcome thing.

"I am also pleased to hear that you are finding a place where you belong. It may be that your time in London did you some good, as only the Lord knows. Please continue to do good work in New York City.

"As for your brother, his letters come addressed to me only as Appalachia. I don't know what that means, sadly. It could be the name of the mountain or mountain range. It could be the nearest town. I received your letter after I sent one to him, and I do not wish to send out a second to him and so always have one letter chasing another, just out of reach in time. I will wait for his response and then ask him in my next letter to him. I shall let you know just as soon as possible.

"Take care of yourself, Owain. Be a good man; I know you want to so desperately. Keep these letters to remind you of why you are there and what you hope to achieve.

"Love,

"Your dearest ma"

While Owain was more than happy to get a letter from his mother, it frustrated him to no end that she didn't have much of an answer for him as to how to find his brother.

The year turned 1851.

Owain wouldn't say he never drank, but he never ended up in jail, anyway. He worked various odd jobs here and there, but steady employment was hard to come by. As an "American," he was afforded first pick of jobs. But when it came time to cut costs, labor costs were the first to be cut, and an Irishman was willing to work for half or a third what Owain made, so he ended up with the job in the end. A few times, Owain went out of his normal stomping grounds and presented himself as himself, an "Irishman" (he'd given up on correcting those who didn't care one way or another) hoping that even if he took a pay cut, he might have steadier work. That never paid off and he came close to being evicted from his little room.

It was basically like living in London all over again, trying to make himself a better man. You had your slums, your upper crust, and the only thing standing between the two was sheer determination.

This time around, however, Owain did not seek to advance his social station. He always remained light, able to pack up and travel at a moment's notice. He did not bank, he did not invest. He did not walk among the wealthy, he did not buy himself fine clothes and other expensive possessions to impress anyone. Except for his accent, he did not pretend to be something he was not. He told himself to just keep his head down, don't get overly involved in anything, and just be patient.

And, most importantly, he did not seek a woman. He did not pay for sex, he did not approach courtship. He barely made friends with the women in his neighborhood or, sometimes, at his present place of employment. It wasn't that they weren't nice or that he didn't appreciate the favors they sometimes did him—wash his clothes or clean his room, all the while tsking that he was nearly forty and unwed—but he was still reeling from his failed marriage. He still felt a bit betrayed by Paige, trying to force him to be something he wasn't and threatening him when he couldn't do it. He felt betrayed by himself, that he couldn't have been a better husband. The whole debacle still haunted him, and he couldn't bear the thought of looking for another woman. He had to find his brother first.

He received no letters from his mother, and the year turned 1852.

His beast hated him, often kept him up at night. Yelling at him, shaming him, haunting him, torturing him, trying to goad him into behaviors that had caused nothing but trouble in the past. Owain had many sleepless nights as he tossed and turned, wrestling with his sins and his guilt. He would jolt awake in a cold sweat, shadows and demons swirling about his mind, and that was assuming he could wake up at all. Sometimes he would become trapped in the nightmare so that only the grandfather clock chiming in the common room would wake him.

He wanted to start traveling, but he also wanted a starting point. He collected information about the Appalachian mountains, but the more he learned, the less he wanted to just wander off and hope that he might stumble upon his brother. The mountains were vast and dangerous. If you didn't die of starvation or exposure, the local Indians were more than happy to send you to see your Maker. The government was having a hell of a time getting them all rounded up and moved west, and any man with white skin was fair game as far as they were concerned.

He also had to learn to time his journey, assuming he got a better idea of where Teo was hiding. He could end up spending one year just trying to get close and then have to winter somewhere while he waited for the mountain passes to open back up.

It was nearly Christmas before he finally got a letter from his ma.

"My dear Owain,

"I admit, I had hoped that you might write me for the sheer joy of it, the comfort of having family to write to, and not just for help and information. It also crossed my mind numerous times that perhaps something awful had happened and perhaps my letter will arrive to no one. If nothing else, please write and let me know that you are doing well.

"I have been exchanging letters with your brother still. I have not told him you are coming. I feel that this is something you will simply have to work out between the two of you. You both know I have always believed the best in people, so my word will mean little without you to demonstrate to your brother that you have changed. I pray it is still true.

"Your brother tells me he lives in the state of Virginia, the western portion, in the mountains. I can't say that I know where this is in relation to New York City or anywhere at all, but I trust you have not been idle in your time. In fact, I expect you to drop everything and make for Virginia posthaste.

"Your father sends his greetings and reminds you to be good.
"With love,
"Ma"

At first, Owain was just stunned that his pa had said anything about him, let alone anything good. On the other hand, his ma could have written that in there just to be polite and make it seem as if his pa cared, give him some encouragement.

Whatever the case, it looked as if he would be heading to Virginia. It was a start, anyway. From what maps he'd seen, Virginia was a fairly large state, stretching from coastline to mountain range. He hated asking for information about it, since he was alleged to have come from that state, his accent and all. Instead, he tried to ask for recent news. Two years in America, he was becoming well-educated on current events.

His inquiries earned him plenty of suspicious or hostile looks. Was he secretly a Confederate? Why was he in New York, anyway? He lived in close quarters with plenty of Irish scum; where did his loyalties lie? He tried to play it off as curiosity, thinking of friends and family back home, what they might be experiencing, keeping abreast on the news, anything but being a Confederate spy or sympathizer.

1853 rolled around. April could not come soon enough, and soon Owain found himself on the road, heading south. He figured his best course of action would be to move along the coast first until he reached Virginia, then figure out the best way to reach the mountains.

This was easier said than done. America was huge, and, as he quickly found out, it was far more advantageous to move south to north and follow the progression of planting seasons. Plenty of work for any willing hands. Going against the grain, following the harvest, was the better option for him, but he couldn't wait that long. Owain could hardly grasp the concept at first. In Wales, if the south was planting, there was a good chance so was the north. As he quickly learned, Georgia could plant almost the year round, while New York and even farther north had to begin harvest in late August, early September.

Even so, work was also much harder to come by in the South, especially in farming, or any sort of agriculture. That was what slaves were for, after all. He would need a plan. For a time, he dropped the charade, lost his American accent, and tried to be an "Irishman" willing to work just for a bowl of soup and maybe a place to sleep in the barn. Few took him up on the offer. His progress was woefully slow. By the time he reached Virginia, it was September, and things would only get harder, he knew. Slaves were the great debate in the North, but in the South they were as numerous as the flies. There was no need to hire anyone to do any farm work, and it was a damn shame to employ a white man next to a Negro.

Owain stopped in Richmond, exhausted, hungry, and having only a couple pennies. His clothes were ragged from the road, and most of his worldly possessions also had some manner of wear and tear. He stopped at a restaurant and managed to get a small meal, leaving just enough for a cheap room at a run-down inn.

"What's the news from the mountains?" he asked the waiter. "Is it safe to cross?"

"Heavens, no," the man replied. "It's never safe, but if you need to go, the best time has already passed. You'll start seeing frost up there soon. Once autumn takes full hold, then the storms start. Thunderstorms, first, then ice storms."

"Best to go in the spring and summer," Owain mused.

"The summer, anyway. Spring brings more storms. It'll wash out the roads, cause rockslides. It's not as bad as in the fall, but still a real force to be reckoned with."

Owain sighed and picked a bit at his food, starving but unable to taste. "What would you suggest for a weary traveler who either needs to cross the mountains or find somewhere to winter?"

"Keep going south. We'll get plenty of cold storms here. Safest place to winter is going to be farther south. Even if you can't find work, at least you won't freeze to death."

It was small comfort, but Owain took the advice and saw the coming of 1854 in Georgia, taking work wherever he could. It was also his first immersive experience in Confederate America, fledgling though it was. He experienced it from a number of angles, depending on where he went and who he wanted to be.

If he played the Virginian, he was treated generally well. Virginia was considered a border state and a little more reluctant to talk secession than the rest of the states. Other than being a border state, Virginia was one of the original colonies, if not the original colony, Plymouth Rock notwithstanding. Jamestown was their historical pride. And now they wanted to throw that away to throw in with the Confederates? At the same time, Virginia was almost exclusively agricultural and depended on slaves. Slaves were easy, cheap, reliable labor. After all, just look at places like New York City and the problems they were having with all the Irish immigrants. Slave labor was far easier to manage. Let the states tend to their own affairs without the bureaucrats sticking their noses in, even if that meant exploitation of the Negro. Everything just worked smoother. Was not a little rough peace better than the tumult overtaking the North?

Whenever he was asked about it, Owain simply said that he did not speak for Virginia as a whole, and, personally, he just wanted everyone to get along. He wanted to be able to find work when he needed it without facing discrimination for this thing or that thing. Some judged him to be right in line with Confederate thinking, others with Yankee thinking. Owain just found it exhausting.

Now, if he played the "Irishman" during these conversations, things went a little differently. Often he was accused of being a Yankee who sympathized with the Negro because he faced discrimination in the North. But that was exactly why things ought to remain as they were, the reasoning went. Everyone had their place in society. The Lord had willed it so, and the government of man ought not interfere. By ending slavery, it would only add hundreds of thousands of Negros to the slums already inhabited by poor immigrants, and then it would be even harder to find any meaningful work. Part of it came from the influx of workers, and part of it because the entire Southern industry would collapse with the mass exodus of the slaves. Prices would go sky high for tobacco, cotton, all the goods that even life in the North depended on. Just think about that next time he went around preaching freedom.

Honestly, Owain hadn't said anything one way or the other.

But there was another angle he played, one he didn't bring out often, and that was the Londoner. When he brought out his London accent, things changed just a little bit more. He was often regarded with suspicion, even a little hostility, like a "foreign Yankee" as someone had called him. The United Kingdom had done away with slavery and was putting pressure on the South to do the same, or else lose a ton of trade with Europe. Who were they to dictate how the South conducted its business? Almost as bad as the politicians in Washington, damn foreign Yankees. Why couldn't they mind their own damn business? They were a whole ocean away!

Owain himself did not often get involved in these political debates, mostly because they could get quite heated and he didn't want to risk his years of progress being a good man on something as petty as political business that really wasn't any of his business. Yes, he'd lived in the country for several years, but he still really just wanted to find his brother.

He wrote to his ma again while living in Georgia. By now, he was better able to predict a response time, assuming she got the letter quickly and replied just as quickly. Being advised to not attempt travel through the mountains until at least spring, which came later in the mountains, he figured he had enough time to write.

He received a reply letter in April, just days before he was set to begin his journey.

"My dear Owain,

"It pleases me to hear from you and know you are doing well. You don't know how long I have waited for this time, when we can exchange letters freely and not hear bad news. I know it sounds cynical and you may feel guilt or discouragement, but please do not. Just know that I am your mother, you are my son, and I love you no matter what.

"Georgia sounds like a fine place, certainly warmer than home! I'm afraid my old bones don't weather the weather half so well as they did when I was younger. I swear it gets colder every year, but that could be just me.

"And don't you worry yourself. Your sisters and their husbands and children are taking good care of us. They make sure the wood is cut and split and stacked, and they take care of the animals. Your pa is trying to decide what he

wants to do with the land when we're gone. He's thinking about giving it to Adith and her husband. He inherited a bit from his father, but certainly not enough if they wish to have more than one child.

"Your pa sends his greetings and says to stay out of trouble. If you've been honest about your exploits, keep up the good work. It sounds like you're making good progress in finding your brother. I never knew he was so good and hide-and-seek!

"Love always,

"Ma"

His mother the optimist, Owain sighed. He hadn't made any real progress in finding his brother except to find the state and keep going south! He had to get moving. April was here and if he started up through the mountains from the north of Georgia, he should be just fine to travel the trails as good weather pressed north.

He set out, fully intent on this being his one big push to search out his brother. His first part of the plan was to stay in the lower foothills until he got to Virginia. As much as he wanted to fly with the crow, it would only cost him time and distance. Going around a mountain was sometimes easier than going over it. Seeing how he was just one man, he had to play it smart.

He didn't have much with him. With his mind still focused on finding Teo, he never allowed himself to accumulate a lot of stuff. Whatever he did acquire, he had to be able to pack up quickly and it generally had to be a necessity for travel. He had three blankets, a pot, a pan, a spoon, an extra change of clothes, a couple small knives, and one large knife that was practically a sword. He kept that on his person for defense, if necessary.

It was June when he set foot in a small town on the border of Virginia and North Carolina, not five miles from the foot of the mountains, nestled in a small valley in the foothills. As soon as he set foot in the one restaurant, he was barraged with questions.

"How is it out there?"

"Where did you come from?"

"Is it safe to go out now?"

"What happened to you?"

"How did you survive?"

"Were there others with you?"

Owain was stunned and confused by all the questions, but he got the story easily enough. Seemed as though the roads through the mountains were simply rife with trouble this year. If it wasn't the Indians, bands of highwaymen were beating and robbing people, leaving them to die if not killing them outright. Certainly it was no place for a single man out wandering. It was hard enough for supply and trading wagons to get to town.

He stayed there a short time, fully intending to set off in a week or two, once he'd rested and gathered his nerve to actually enter the mountains, but as more reports came in detailing the attacks by the highwaymen and the Indians, Owain knew he was looking at yet another delay. He was going to die before he ever got in those mountains.

Rangers and trigger-happy volunteers all ventured into the mountains, looking to put an end to the attacks, but few ever came back. Certainly none of the volunteers, and only about half the army rangers. Of course, the army wasn't too well-liked by the normal folks. Despite needing them to stay safe from the Indians and such, their presence was seen as an act of aggression from the North, encroaching on the South and their rights.

With the town isolated because of the dangerous roads in and out, there was plenty of work for willing hands. Owain initially helped out just to get some food, get cleaned up, and pass the time, but before he knew it, it was September again, and cold winds were starting to come down from the mountain peaks. He cursed his rotten luck, but figured that at least he'd made it this far and he wasn't still idling in New York City.

He ended up boarding with the town blacksmith. Work was fairly steady over the winter, the shop was always warm, and the smith was glad to have another strong arm around; his young apprentice was still small and couldn't do all the chores just yet. Owain's job was primarily just hauling stuff here and there, running errands, keeping the shop clean and other tasks better suited for the apprentice, but as long as he was warm, dry, and had some kind of shelter over his head and food in his stomach, he kept his mouth shut.

More than once over the summer, his beast had told him to begin his trek anyway. He was still strong; he could defend himself against any Indians or highwaymen. What was he afraid of? He was only as old as he allowed himself to be. Why was he hiding in this town full of weak women?

It was a constant battle, one Owain tried to push to the back of his mind. He kept his mother's letters close and her kerchief closer. He rarely took it out because he didn't want to lose it, but he made sure to touch it every night to ensure it was still where he stashed it. Those things were perhaps the only things that kept him sane, kept him focused on the task at hand, however slowly it seemed to be progressing.

His break finally came around Christmas. A small wagon train limped into town, coming down from the mountains. They'd clearly been through a few scraps with someone—Indians, highwaymen, it was impossible to tell. It was amazing they'd even made it through some of the passes as the countryside was routinely dusted with snow, sometimes more than dusted. There were seven men, and reportedly they'd started out with twelve. One deserted, four gone to sickness. Come spring, they needed to take on at least another hand to go back through the mountains.

Owain expected that the people would be hesitant because of the bad year of attacks. He didn't expect the people to outright refuse because of the group itself.

The men fancied themselves Confederates, but apparently no one else did, even the larger Confederate community. "Immature" was a popular word to describe them, as they apparently thought they were going to construct some elaborate network of spies to relay Union information to the South, stop dissenters, catch runaway slaves, and build and stock major strongholds for the Confederates to use as they carried victory after victory into the North. It was all a bit fanciful.

Nevertheless, it was just the ticket Owain needed to get into the mountains without being a single man on a foolish journey. He needed some measure of protection, and these Confederates might be able to provide it. He approached them one morning in the restaurant. It was just after New Year's and the year was now 1855.

"Do you know of any Welsh settlements up in the mountains?" Owain inquired politely. He was still using his Virginian accent in this town.

"Welsh?" one man asked. "Aye, there's Welsh up there. Welsh, Irish, Dutch, German." He shook his head. "Damn Pacifists."

The others muttered agreement, except one who said, "Maybe some, but the Germans are good for a scrap any day."

"If they're not for us, they're against us, and what good are they, then? Even those who just want to 'keep to themselves' are liable to snitch on us."

"I need to get to one of those settlements," Owain cut in. "Can you take me there?"

Now they studied him. The first man asked, "What's it to you?"

"I'm looking for my brother, but I can't go up there alone."

The Confederates traded glances. Then, "Can you drive a wagon?"

"No problem." It wasn't much different than a carriage, right? At least he had plenty of experience with horses, so that had to count for something. Plus the blacksmith was busy fixing up all the metal on their wagons, the woodsmith fixing the wood, so Owain was learning a thing or two there.

"All right," the first man said. He was a tall man but easily half Owain's size as far as muscle. "We're heading north. You help us drive our wagons up there. Shouldn't take more than a few months. Once we're unloaded there, we'll head back south. We're trying to make it back before autumn. On our way back south, we pass by a couple settlements. Whichever one is yours, you can stop there. Fair?"

"Sounds like a good deal to me."

They shook on it.

"Great. I'm Henry." He went around and introduced all the men, though Owain knew he wouldn't remember them all right away. "And your name?"

"Walter."

"Welcome, Walter."

"When do you plan on leaving?"

"Just as soon as the weather clears. Don't worry, we won't leave you behind."

Owain wasn't about to let himself get left behind, and suddenly the winter seemed to drag on even longer, even slower. He tried to keep himself entertained, busy with chores, but it only lasted as long as the blacksmith was busy. Even so, his apprentice had hit puberty at some point in the fall and seemed to shoot up two feet and fifty pounds overnight. Owain still helped, still got room and board, but he knew that in just the course of a year, he would no longer be necessary. He had to go with the Confederates.

"I wouldn't trust them if I were you," the blacksmith told him as the weather made a shift toward spring. "I'm no Yankee, but I wouldn't trust them to have my back in a fight. I expect they're all cowards at heart. Grand plans in their minds, but stupid. Their mas obviously didn't switch 'em enough."

"Might be they just have to grow out of it," Owain suggested, even though the men ranged in age from sixteen to thirty; one of them had to know better.

The blacksmith just shook his head. "Nothing brings out the foolish and the cowardly in a man like war. I don't like it, but mark my words, war is coming. North and South, just you watch."

"It also brings out the best in some men."

"Aye, we all have our heroes. The problem, though, is that heroes are few and far between. That's why they're heroes, and not ordinary. The rest are all stupid."

Owain merely nodded. "Well, with any luck, I'll find my brother and we'll be able to simply sit this one out."

"I wish you all the best in that endeavor, I really do. No man ever regretted not fighting, and civil war is nothing to be excited about."

"Speaking from experience?"

"My great-grandfather fought in the Revolution. My pa told us boys that while great-grandpa was proud of America winning independence, he never felt any pride for some of the things he did. He was friends with some of them Englishmen, had a drink, played cards. They were not the face of their homeland; they were simple blokes who just wanted to live how they wanted, nothing more. They harbored no real ill will for the revolutionaries. My pa fought in the War of 1812, and he never considered himself anything but a man following orders." He sighed. "Ah, but it was a long time ago. Perhaps that's the problem. You just can't go too long without a good war. The young men crave it, I think."

Owain did not reply.

Chapter Twenty-Two

The Confederates

Being farther south, the weather got nicer sooner than it did in New York, and the Confederates were ready to go by mid-March. There was no cheering, no standing ovation, no young women tossing their handkerchiefs to the men to remember them by. Actually, the whole thing passed very innocuously. Any reaction they did get was disbelief, resignation, and not a little scorn. Owain was just glad to finally be getting underway and going into the mountains. With any luck, he would be spending Christmas with his brother.

There were eight of them traveling, and they had six wagons plus half a dozen more horses and burros with extra gear and supplies. One of the donkeys carried all the supplies they would need for the trek, and another carried extra provisions, but the majority of their meals would be hunted or foraged. It might make for slower going, but it was hard enough to get up and moving in the morning as it was; adding even more horses or donkeys to the mix—especially donkeys—would only slow them down.

As for the wagons and the other pack animals, they carried supplies to these fabled Confederate strongholds. Owain was no battlefield tactician, but he was fairly certain that all the supplies they were carrying wouldn't be able to sustain more than a dozen men for a couple months, and that was assuming they were getting other supplies in between these trips or otherwise supplementing everything in some other way. The guns and ammunition, fine, but even he knew that war and battle was only five percent fighting, ninety-five percent waiting. It was the waiting part that counted most, especially when it came to food. A Confederate stronghold in the North meant the North would probably have little trouble surrounding it and trying to starve out the occupants. That's when beans mattered more than bullets.

But he said none of this out loud. He wasn't in it for the cause; he just wanted to get a ride into the mountains so he could find his brother. Only the blacksmith wished him well, wished him luck in finding his brother.

Owain sent one last letter to his ma, letting her know that he was going into the mountains now to look for Teo. He asked for prayers and well wishes, both that he would find him and, once they did reconnect, that he would be able to make amends and build some sort of life for himself with his brother. Henry and the others were shouting at him to hurry up as he delivered his letter to the postmaster, then went to join them.

A couple of the larger men, Jack and Jacob, rode up front on horses, rifles in hand. Following them were a couple of the pack animals, then the wagons, then more pack animals, and finally George at the rear, also with guns at the ready. Owain rode with Frederick on the fifth wagon in line, but otherwise the wagons only had one driver, if that. Being short on men meant the middle wagons just had to keep going, follow the leader. Henry rode on a horse, moving from this position to that position, looking for trouble or making merry with his men and trying to keep the mood light, or at least less than dismal.

It didn't take long for the town nestled in the valley to shrink to the size of a child's playhouse. Owain looked across the dazzling greenery of the valley. Some places there was still some snow, other places still brown and not yet revived by rain, but it was still a stunning sight. It really did remind him of home in a way, and he understood why his brother had chosen to settle here, if the rest of the mountains were anything like this.

Then thick pine boughs snapped closed around the rear of the wagon and the valley disappeared. All that was left was the forest and the trail through it.

The main road probably would have been fine if they were merely riding on horses, but with the bulk of the wagons, it was a less than comfortable ride as the wheels bumped over rocks or slid down into ruts and washouts. Not a few times, one of the ruts would be so deep that they actually had to lift the wagon to get it out. In addition to protection, Jack and Jacob had to warn the wagons of upcoming hazards. Sometimes it worked, sometimes it didn't. Owain did his best to heed instructions, but the horses did not always agree with or listen to him.

"So, where are you from?" Frederick asked amiably. It was their third day out. "Sounds like you got a Virginia accent, but what's your interest in all these Pacifist settlements up here?"

Owain dropped his American accent. "No, I'm from Wales."

"No kidding? Hot damn, you had me fooled!" The man got an odd look on his face. "You're not a Yankee spy, are you?"

"No, just a Welshman looking for his brother. He came over years before I did, and I don't know exactly where he went. I've had to learn to talk like an American or else I couldn't find work."

His answer was not as well-received as he might have hoped. Apparently it merely pegged him as a potential spy, a snitch. A liability. All the same, however, they reasoned, he had to have known that his admission would cause them to suspect him. Therefore, either he was a terrible spy, a turncoat, or it could be that he really was telling the truth. Maybe there was nothing malicious about his intentions; he was just picking up a job so he could get into the hills so he could look for his brother, safety in numbers versus trying to go it alone.

While personal opinions were divided over him and his intentions and loyalties, the general consensus was that he could not be immediately trusted. Therefore, until some test was devised to prove his loyalty or lack thereof, banter was approved, but give away no secrets of the Confederates.

Owain highly doubted that this lot even possessed any real secrets of the Confederates, given how they were treated by the rest of them. Even this "secret stronghold" was probably pretty well-known. Still, he kept his mouth shut and meandered along with the group. By the end of the first week, he was driving the wagon by himself. Actually, the wagon could probably drive itself, the way the horses dutifully followed each other.

It was the eleventh day of their voyage when he was invited to go scouting with a few of the men before they officially set out. All of them, to be precise, far more than a mere scouting party. Owain had a pretty good idea what they were about. Somehow or another, they were going to test him, test his story, test his loyalties. Or maybe they were going to skip that part and go straight to the lynching. Whatever the case, he went with them quietly, away from the camp. One against seven wasn't very good, but Owain didn't need to dominate or win, he just had to be able to get away, assuming that would get him anywhere. Jack and Jacob rode on their horses; indeed, they rarely got off. And these men knew the mountains much better than he did. His odds weren't looking too good.

They were just about to set out from camp when they were suddenly assaulted. At first it was the noise, drums and glass bottles and yelling, all around them, echoing indistinctly in the trees.

"Injuns!" Jacob cried, half a second before a lead ball thumped him in the chest. He fell off his horse and did not move.

Owain was near the outer ring of the camp by a bush. Simple reflex caused him to reach in and lift a full-grown man off the ground and toss him in the center of the camp clearing. The attacker wasn't an Indian, but a highwayman wasn't much better.

Before Owain could do anything about the first man, a second ran up to him on his right side, gun in one hand, knife in the other. Owain knocked the man's hand away, sending the gunshot wild. Instinctively, he clamped down on the man's wrist and pulled him close, in for the kill as he bashed his face into the smaller man's and threw him on top of his friend.

In a moment of clarity, Owain saw that there were only four attackers total. The two Owain had just put down were now scrambling to escape while the other two were limping off into the bushes. As quickly as the attack had started, it was over. Owain was fully prepared for Henry to give the order to pursue and eliminate, but he did not. Instead, he called everyone in for a damage assessment.

Jacob was dead. All other wounds were comparatively minor. Owain could see the others did not like the thought of leaving him in a shallow grave, but they had to keep moving. They had to get the wagons ready and get back on the trail.

Wounds were not treated until they were well underway.

"Infection will get those highwaymen bastards," Henry mused angrily, pulling a bandage tight around his arm where one of the attackers had cut him with a knife. "I hope it takes them slowly."

Owain could not find it in himself to agree. Mostly he was just tired. He was getting older, and some of the things that used to matter so much to his hotheaded younger self just came across as unimportant anymore.

His beast agreed with Henry wholeheartedly, however, and it screamed at him. Fighting with those men had awoken the beast, rekindled the fire. He needed more! Or so his beast said. Owain had learned how to separate the beast's will from his own. It had come about one night, lying awake after another nightmare, pondering the many conversations he'd had with Father Forthill. He'd shaped his beast to be a third party, a thing in its own right. If that was so, then they were separate entities, and he was not obligated to heed its every demand. True to Forthill's word, the beast did not like being found out and countered. Owain fully expected the beast to change its tune, like it had in London, but for the moment, the beast was not in control of him; he was in control of the beast.

"And you, Walter," Henry was saying. "You don't say a lot, but you are certainly a force to be reckoned with in a fight. You threw two men!"

Ah, so the grieving over Jacob's death was complete and now they were moving on to the war stories. Owain simply looked at the reins in his hands and said, "My name isn't Walter. It's Owain."

"Walter, Owain, whatever your name is, we're glad to have you with us. Glad to see you know where your loyalties lie."

My loyalties lie in staying alive, he thought. *It has nothing to do with who you people are or whatever cause you're fighting for.*

He did not say this out loud.

They had no further trouble that day, but they continued trekking long after they normally would have stopped to camp, and they were on their way fairly quickly the following morning. Conversation on the road was stunted, and everyone was on high alert. This went on for several days, but eventually, things settled back down into the same carefree comradery they'd had when they started off. The difference was, this time, Owain was a part of it. He was included around the campfire in the nightly banter.

"So, I have to ask," Wallace said one night. He was sixteen but could drink almost as much as Owain when he wanted to. "How is it that you can have England, Scotland, and Ireland, and then you somehow get Wales? Are there actually whales in Wales?"

"Um, I don't know," Owain answered. "I don't think so."

"Then why is it called Wales?"

"Because the English hate us, that's why."

"Then what do you call Wales?"

"*Cymru.*"

Wallace leaned back and drunkenly slapped his knee. "Now, how do you get Wales out of that? It doesn't even sound like it. At all."

Owain shrugged. "I don't know. Like I said, the English hate us."

"Well, they don't like us too much either," Henry mused. "See, here's what I don't understand. The North, the Brits, most of Europe, they can't stand us. They lecture us constantly about slavery and how unethical it is. But the thing is, they love our cotton. Half the economy in the North is cotton and textiles. Where do they think that cotton comes from?" He shifted position on the log he was sitting on. "You can't have it both ways. You can't rally for abolition in the morning, then go buy several yards of cotton fabric in the afternoon. It just makes no sense. Either you have cheap goods from cheap labor, or you have chaos. And that's what we do for the Negros, too. We take chaos and bring it in to order. I don't know that too many of them would survive if they were freed, anyway. They would simply devolve back into apes, killing each other and causing havoc for the white folk."

Owain had met several Negros in the North who, sure, weren't rich, but they were doing well for themselves and their families. He did not say this out loud, either, and instead settled for, "So how would you settle things? If the North doesn't want things to stay the same, but the South doesn't want to give up its cheap labor, and no one wants war, what would you do?"

The looks on their faces told Owain that they probably hadn't considered any alternative but war. They'd been told war was coming, their blood was hot, and they were preparing for war. It was odd to think that he'd been just like them once, albeit a bit more extreme. Time was, he could think of no other way to settle a dispute besides fisticuffs. Landing in jail was a point of pride. Drink was a bonus, not a necessary catalyst.

Was it hypocritical of him to ask him these questions, lecture them so? After all, he still hadn't conquered his own demons, be they the beast that still lurked in the back of his mind, or the night terrors of Beaumaris that still plagued his dreams. Should he wait until he'd dealt with them before telling others not to give in to their own demons?

He tried to think of what Forthill might have advised, but found himself unable to really bring anything to mind. He was momentarily stunned into his own mental silence when he considered that he'd escaped from Beaumaris seven years ago. Seven! Had it really been so long? There were plenty of nights when he woke up still expecting to find straw and rats and angry gaolers. But no one had apprehended him. He hadn't heard of anyone hunting for him. His ma hadn't said a word about anyone approaching them demanding to know where he was. Could he really be free and clear?

It was a bizarre feeling. Seven years escaped from prison, and he was, well, he was doing all right. He hadn't gotten drunk, hadn't gotten in any major fights, certainly nothing more than heated words. He hadn't been in a jail of any form since coming to America, unless he counted the boardinghouse in New York City. Could he count himself a good man now? He definitely didn't feel like one.

He looked around at the young men with him around the fire. Experience was the best and worst teacher. Did he not owe it to himself and to them to try and teach them before experience came knocking?

Well, his inquiry as to an alternative to war was not well-received. The other guys tried to laugh it off at first, but once they realized he was at least semi-serious, they didn't take it too kindly. They asked if he was a damn Pacifist like the rest of the Welsh and Irish hiding up in the mountains. They asked if he was planning on selling them out. They asked whether he was truly committed to the cause. When he politely reminded them that he had only signed up to be a wagon driver for this one endeavor and then he was leaving for one of the Welsh settlements, as per their agreement, they disliked that even more.

By the time they set off the next morning, Owain was wondering whether they were again considering inviting him to "scout" with them sometime soon so they could kill him. At the same time, his demonstration of strength against the marauders might help to put a damper on that plan and so buy him some time. He really didn't harbor any ill will toward them. He was just fine to help them drive their wagons to their secret Confederate stronghold, and he had no plans of selling them out to the Northerners. Apparently, they just didn't believe that anyone could be a neutral party in a war that hadn't even started yet.

Had he really been so blind once? Had he been just like them, where fighting was always the answer even when it wasn't, and anyone who thought otherwise was weak? He might have wept aloud if not for present company. He was glad to not be that way anymore, regardless of what his beast tried to make him think and do. It was also not lost on him that maybe he'd been placed with these men for a reason. Maybe he'd finally reached a point where God could speak to him and show him something that he would finally understand. Maybe it was one reason he'd been allowed to escape from prison.

Of course, he could not presume to be so arrogant. He desperately wanted to believe Forthill, that there was some kind of plan or purpose in store for him, something only he could accomplish because of his...unique life. If that was true, then he had little room to argue about it or try to fight God's plan. At the same time, he still had a lot of work to do on himself before he could begin preaching to the masses. Six wayward Confederates, though...

Their first major delay in their trek came when a storm had triggered a major rockslide and buried the road. The group spent several days looking for the easiest route, only to discover there really wasn't one. They ended up taking the supplies out of the wagons and ferrying them around the debris before attempting to maneuver the wagons around. They lost the first wagon and both horses. That caused them to lose another day while they planned how to not lose the rest of the wagons. They ended up not losing any more wagons, at least not the complete loss that the first one had gone. But by the time they were completely on the far side of the rockslide debris, three different wheels had been smashed, and something had gone wrong with the clips on another wagon. They ended up stripping that wagon of everything it was worth, taking those wheels off to fix the others that had broken, and carrying on, going from six wagons to four. Some of the load was distributed to the horses, some to the rest of the wagons.

And onward they went.

The good news, though, was that because of the team they ended up losing, they had enough horse meat to last them a while. Wallace had been able to scramble down the ravine and cut them up something decent.

Owain was in fact nibbling on some horse jerky when they came across their second major delay. They were just nearing the road leading to some of the Welsh and Irish settlements when an "informant" approached their party and warned them that Unioners were about. He never really elaborated on this statement, and Owain suspected the young man just wanted to feel as though he'd done something important to help the cause, of which he was little more than a spectator, sitting way up here in the mountains. Nevertheless, Henry made the call to pack up and take a detour.

Owain wanted to protest, citing the settlements and their agreement. He did not for the simple fact that he agreed to help them deliver the wagons to this secret stronghold before returning to the settlements. He hadn't fulfilled his end of the bargain yet.

All the same...so close, and yet so far. Owain ground on his horse jerky unhappily. His beast lurked in his mind like a stalking cat, but he kept it at bay. He had to fulfill his promise and deliver the wagons.

But what if the Unioners caught them? What if he was arrested? Could you be arrested for being a Confederate? Maybe not, but conspiring against the as yet lawful government of the land, maybe. He wasn't even really conspiring, he was just helping. Was that still conspiracy? He was really just trying to find his brother. Would the Union understand? He was Welsh. He was a Pacifist. The Confederates were all complaining about how he was a Pacifist! Surely they couldn't blame him for that?

By the time his thoughts came back around, they were well away from the settlements. And they kept moving away. Off the main road onto side roads, trails, places Owain could not believe the wagons could traverse except that he watched them do it. Multiple times he thought they were hopelessly lost, and then they would pop back out onto a road. They would follow it for a little while, then dump off the road and onto another side trail.

Owain did not ask about the roads or where they were going. Bypassing the settlements, while he was able to keep his irritated beast at bay, had still caused a shift in his thinking. Before, he'd been glad for the company and the adventure, and he'd been eagerly anticipating finding the settlements and his brother. Now, though, he'd left his anticipation back there at the point in the road where they had been diverted. That was where he wanted to be. That was where he wanted to go. He no longer really cared for the banter around the campfire at night, no longer really cared about delivering the wagons except that was what it was going to take to be released from this bargain and let him return to the settlements.

Between the time spent at the rockslide, plus the time spent detouring this way and that to avoid the Unioners, plus considering how far north they had gone, it was late August before they reached the so-called secret Confederate stronghold.

In reality, it was an abandoned outpost from the numerous wars against the Indians, now occupied by men who fancied themselves the Confederates' northern line of defense. These men were all over the age of forty and evidently had little else to do with their lives considering none of them appeared to be married. Or if they were, they'd left their women safely back home in the South where there wouldn't be any fighting.

Their little band of young Confederate heroes was greeted by a man easily fifty years of age, maybe closer to sixty, with bad teeth, putrid breath, a festering sore on his chest, old clothes that could certainly use mending, and an attitude about as cheery as his appearance. He chastised the young'uns for being late. What if war had broken out?

What if they'd been attacked or compromised? What if this, what if that? What if the Lord had come back again to collect all His children?

Owain wanted to ask, well, if any of those things did happen, what did he expect anyone present to do about it? But he was learning, and he kept his mouth shut.

This was not the pride of the Confederate army, Owain saw. This was a band of misfits and rejects. Might be that Jefferson Davis and Bobby Lee had sent them to this outpost themselves, knowing it was abandoned and far out of their way. If the Indians didn't scalp them, hopefully sickness would take them. Anything but allowing them into the army proper. Considering how small the Southern army sounded and how green most of the men were, Owain figured it took a special person to be rejected even from that.

But he kept his mouth shut.

And he was scrutinized. Heavily. Who was he? Where did he come from? Was he a Pacifist like the rest of the damn Welshmen in the mountains? Was he liable to snitch? Who were his friends?

Despite their apparent misgivings on the road about his Pacifism, Henry and the rest of the men came to his defense, declaring him a real hero, a real trooper. He'd taken on four Injuns in hand-to-hand combat, defending the wagons and avenging Jacob's death. Owain had a hard time judging how seriously the outpost guards were taking them, but they didn't order him locked in some abandoned jail cell, so he figured that was a good start. At any rate, they put him to work, unloading the wagons.

The outpost was sorely rundown and in need of repair. The only thing that looked maintained was the outer wall and the watchtowers, but most everything interior was suffering from neglect. The Confederates were not blind to this fact, and now that the strong backs had returned, once the wagons were unloaded, they were given more tasks. Logging, carpentry, fixing up the stronghold a bit while they were here and resting.

So much for rest, Owain thought, but he was glad for the work. It seemed a futile endeavor, but hard work felt good.

He quickly learned that the carpenter who had been with them for several months had perished of illness the winter before, and that was why nothing got done, aside from the fact that all the other full-time residents were either too old or too weak themselves. Of the thirty or more men, Owain counted maybe five who looked well enough to do anything. Maintaining an old outpost was tough. He hoped they wouldn't be staying here for long.

"Where are we, anyway?" Owain asked as they continued to grab supplies from the wagons.

"Pennsylvania," George told him. "Go a little farther north and you'll reach Lake Ontario. A little farther west, Lake Erie. Head straight east and you'll end up back in New York."

"Really?"

"Absolutely. America is a big place, but eventually it all comes back around."

"I didn't think we were that far north."

"Oh, absolutely. Where did you think we were?"

"I don't know anymore."

With his apparent lack of confidence in the geography department, all the men in the fort took it upon themselves to not only give him a geography lesson, but a history lesson, too, as they sat in a proper mess hall for supper that evening. Owain decided that both the geography and history lessons became less and less reliable the more the men consumed great quantities of alcohol.

Maybe the men knew they were the rejects of the Confederates. Maybe they were perfectly aware of their situation, how everyone else wanted them out of their hair. Maybe they volunteered to sit in this outpost for the simple fact that the chain of command could not easily reach them here. No one was going to discipline them for anything, obviously, so why bother with half the stuff the army went through? The only thing they really lacked, which they were more than grumpy about, was women. Every so often, a pimp and his wagon full of women would come rolling through, on their way between New York City and Detroit, but those visits were few and far between. The last wagon had come through in April.

Owain thought about telling them he had been celibate for nearly a decade. Then he gauged their disposition and decided it best to keep his mouth shut. He had learned that when all else fails, just stay silent.

They stayed the night. Owain was glad for a bed again, even if it was an old army cot. At the very least, it wasn't a thin blanket on the hard ground. It was also pretty nice not to have to take watch and keep an eye and ear out for various threats. To be able to lie down and sleep through the night was a welcome thing. And to wake up to breakfast already prepared, with a pot of black coffee—not something he normally drank, but it was something other than the usual—was also a wonderful thing.

Being one of the young'uns, Owain spent the day helping out, mostly just using his strength to hold or haul or what-have-you. He was glad to be needed, though he knew his strength was beginning to wane. It was just a fact of life that he was getting older. 1855, shoot, if he remembered his birthday correctly, he was turning forty years old. Damn, where had the time gone?

By the end of the week, Owain figured he was pretty well-rested and recovered from the trek. He had even gone beyond his end of the bargain by staying and helping them fix up the old fort. He approached Henry and mentioned the deal and his desire to leave.

"Aye, you've done right by us," Henry agreed. "But listen. You said it yourself that it's not safe for one man to travel alone. That's why you hitched up with us in the first place. Wait a little longer. We're just fixing to leave and head back south again here right quick. You can tag along with us until we get to your settlements. Safer that way, right?"

Owain agreed to wait.

Finally, the prospect of seeing his brother again was within reach.

Chapter Twenty-Three

The Highwayman

It was nearly October before they left. Every time Owain threatened to leave, Henry would say they were just about to leave, just had a few last things to do. Then old Pete, who fancied himself the Commander of the outpost, would say something, guilt the men, shame them into staying and helping them with one more thing. And Henry and the others would bow their heads and meekly obey. Finally when Owain made the ultimatum that he was leaving on the morning of the first frost, the others got their things packed up and actually made ready to leave. Even so, only four of them were allowed to leave; the rest had to stay and help keep things maintained through the winter.

The outpost Confederates were not thrilled to see them leave, but made sure to send them off with a list of supplies and demands, things to remember to bring back with them next year. Henry promised them they would remember, and the whole lot of them departed like a pack of whipped puppies. This attitude carried on all that afternoon, leading into a rather disgruntled campfire that evening. Henry and the rest didn't much like Pete and the other old men at the outpost, but they had their orders. They had to keep the outpost supplied.

By the following morning, the group was back to their normal selves. It was just Owain, Henry, George, and Jack. With the wagons empty save for what they would need for the voyage itself, the going was much quicker, or maybe it only felt that way to Owain who was thrilled to be heading toward his brother. Five years it had taken him to get here. As far as he knew, his ma still hadn't told Teo he was coming, or that he was even in the same country. What a surprise it would be—for both of them, no doubt.

338

The good news, Owain figured, was that with at least five years of good behavior under his belt, Teo had to believe that his wild older brother had changed somewhat, right? That would at least get him talking, right?

It quickly became evident that the Confederates hadn't changed a bit, once they were well away from the outpost. They still talked about the impending war and their glorious place in it. They often made jabs at Owain and his Pacifism, tried to get him to join up with them. Sure, maybe he could visit his brother, but then he could keep riding with them, right? No, he just wanted to find his brother and settle down.

That led into more jokes about him having to settle down quick because he was no spring chicken. He was the oldest out of all of them. He could be Wallace's father for gosh sake.

While Owain laughed along with them, inside, the joke really hurt. It only served to remind him what a waste his life had been. He might have a slim chance of starting over, but he greatly feared it would be too late. He would die with no heirs and none to really mourn him. Maybe his own brother wouldn't mourn him, just bury him and go about his day.

He knew it was his beast, changing its tactics, as it was wont to do. Anger wasn't working right now; might as well try depression. He was aware of it. He knew what was happening. But still it wore him down. He remained fairly docile on the road, lost in his own thoughts. For years, he'd wanted nothing more than to find his brother, make amends, start over. Now that he was this close, he began to question whether it was even a good idea to try.

At night, he lay awake, hand over his mother's kerchief. Why did she have such faith in him? Did she really believe that he and Teo could become the brothers they should have been from birth? What if Teo rejected him? Was that his fault? Maybe, but what would he do then? He had no other plans. He was relying on this.

The others noticed his rather demure attitude as well, and they asked him about it around the campfire.

"How long has it been since you seen your brother?" Henry wondered.

Owain shook his head. "Fifteen years? Twenty?"

The other two men whistled. Henry nodded. "That's a long time. You look nervous, though, Owain. Don't your brother like you?"

"Not one bit. The only good thing I can say is that we didn't get into a fight the last time we saw each other."

"Your brother as big as you?" George asked.

"Hardly. I always beat him in a fight."

"But it's a good thing you're looking for him, right?" Jack inquired. "Why are you looking for him?"

Owain shrugged. "Got nowhere else to go. I can't go home to Wales. I don't know what I'm going to do if Teo rejects me. I'm old, have no family, nothing to my name."

"You can always come with us," Henry told him. "You've been a good man to us, done right, done lots of good for the South. You fight with us, we win, you can claim any piece of land you please. Do whatever you want with it and don't have to answer to nobody. Understand what I'm saying?"

"I understand, but I still have no plans to go with you. But I do thank you for the work and the friendship. It has been an enjoyable journey at least."

"Listen to him, sounding all uppity," George said, jabbing Owain in the ribs a little harder than necessary. "If you like us, Owain, all you got to do is say so. You don't need to pull out all the fancy words. We're a simple bunch of guys here, isn't that right? See, that's right."

It was the first time in a long time that Owain felt anything even remotely like belonging, but he was careful not to entertain it too much. As much as he wanted to belong, he wanted to belong with his family more. First he had to find his family and hope they still accepted him.

The closer they got to the settlements, the worse he slept. He often volunteered for watch duty just so he could avoid sleep as much as possible. Aside from the nightmares about Beaumaris, now he had awful anxiety over his family and how terribly he'd treated them in the past. He wasn't even sure half the fights he dreamed about even happened, but they were so realistic he couldn't say they hadn't happened either. It was a terrifying thing to consider, that he couldn't remember parts of his life.

Because of their delay and detouring around the road on their trip north, Owain had little to go on now that they were mostly navigating the road on their way south. He couldn't say just how close to the settlements they were. He guessed that because of the detour, they added probably a couple weeks onto their journey. Subtracting back from the time they left the outpost, factor in fewer people and a lighter load, considering the time from when they'd been informed about Unioners...

Well, he couldn't say for sure, but they had to be pretty darn close.

"How far is it from the road to the settlements?" he asked Henry politely.

"Oh, not too far, if you're on horseback," the man said, slightly evasive. "Take longer if you're walking."

Owain could have figured that. He also hadn't been expecting them to just give him a horse and let him ride off. Most likely, they would see him to the settlement, water their horses and such, maybe stay a night just to rest and take a break, then carry on in the morning.

"How far is not far?" Owain inquired. "Should I plan to have to camp?" He looked down the road to another road branching off to the west. It looked like a fairly well-used road. "Is that it there?"

"Yeah," Henry replied. "Yeah, that's it. Come on. We won't let you go off alone in Indian country."

The caravan slowly lumbered to the right and dipped down onto the secondary road. Down one hill, back up another, and repeat at least three times. On the fifth dip, Jack went up front while Henry and George dropped back a bit. Owain thought they were going to ride beside him, crack jokes, ask questions, make one last push to recruit him for the Confederates. What he got was far worse.

The whole line came to a halt, Jack stopping the lead horse, then working his way back to ensure everything and everyone stopped. Henry and George dropped back on either side of him where he sat on his wagon, looking at him but not saying a word. Jack continued down the line. The lead horse was near the top of the next hill, the rear-most horse just coming down the previous one. Owain sat on his wagon right in the middle of the valley, the lowest part of the dip. Then Jack returned and rested his horse beside Henry's.

"So, you think you're leaving us," Henry stated.

"I fulfilled my end of the bargain," Owain reminded him. "I helped you drive your wagons north. I even stayed in your outpost and helped you with construction and maintenance. I've done more than we agreed. Now, I need to go find my brother."

"And tell your Union-sympathizing Pacifist brother who we are, where we are, how our supply lines run? Are you mad?" Henry gasped a laugh. "Did you really think we were going to buy that? Going to visit your brother...we know the Union has their eyes set on Charleston in the war. It's a perfect place to hunker down while crossing the mountains, gives them a place to rest and resupply. Why do you think we have that stronghold up there? So our guys have a place to do the same that isn't hundreds of miles away in the damn South! Virginia is going to be a Confederate state in the end. How insulting would it be to have a Union stronghold in a Southern state? That's why we got a Confederate stronghold in a Northern state, you understand?"

Owain sighed and willed himself not to lose his temper too early. His biggest weakness had always been that his rage never lasted, and he didn't want it to fizzle out in case he really needed it in a fight. "Your 'stronghold' as you call it is old and decrepit. It could barely survive a winter, never mind an attack. You get sent up and down these mountains on a wild goose chase, keeping you busy so real Southerners, real Confederates, can plan and devise without you getting in the way and mucking things up."

George drew his pistol and pointed it at him from behind. "Say it again, Pacifist." He spat at the last word. "Then we'll see who's the better soldier."

Now Owain shifted position, ready to spring in any direction. He could see the men trading uneasy glances. "I took out two bandits by myself while you and half a dozen others couldn't hardly manage two more on your own. Now what does that say about who's the better soldier?"

He leapt off the wagon a split second before George's pistol went off. Owain's ears were ringing and his ribs were stinging as he bowled into Henry, dragging the man off his horse. He landed on the younger man.

Henry's head snapped back and it dazed him long enough for Owain to scramble to his feet, grab hold of Jack's leg and pulled him down off his mount as well. Jack was in the middle of trying to draw his own pistol, and it clattered to the ground as he went down.

Owain made for the gun, scooping it up but having little time to do anything with it before George was ready and got off another shot at him. One of the horses on the wagon whinnied and reared, prompting the other to do the same. Up and down the line, horses and donkeys knickered and brayed and nervously shuffled their hooves. Wagons creaked and moved. Owain took advantage of the chaos to try and move farther up the line, hiding behind all the moving animals and wagons.

This only worked when it came to George who was on the opposite side of the line. Jack and Henry, however, still had a clear line of sight on the same side. Henry was drunkenly trying to stand, grasping at Jack who tried to both haul him along as well as charge toward Owain.

Jack was arguably the greatest threat. He wasn't the biggest, but he was the strongest and the most well-built. He knew how to use the strength God gave him, and he was just as terrifying if he got on horseback. George was the biggest of the three, but he was not so coordinated with his strength and size. He could lift or he could move, but he had a terrible time trying to do both at once. His skill came with the sword and pistol. Henry was the smallest by way of muscle, but he was the tallest and an impressive sprinter. He'd been neutralized for the moment, a dizzy head impeding his ability to run, or do much walking at all.

Owain was quickly forming a bit of a disjointed idea why they'd been chosen to return south. Able to handle themselves well enough, but if he couldn't be swayed to join them, then the three of them ought to be able to take him on. Right?

George got off another wayward shot, causing the horses and donkeys to fidget more. Jack yelled at him to stop being a moron and get around Owain, cut off any escape. George did so, moving just a bit farther up the line on the side opposite Owain.

Owain found himself trapped with very little advantage except for the twitchy animals keeping George from showing off his pistol skills.

Jack had dropped Henry and was now charging at him full bore, sword raised. At the last second, Owain tucked and rolled forward, just under the blade. He did not have time to stop and aim as he came up on his knees, twisted, and fired his pistol, the one he'd stolen from Jack, and the only shot he would likely have. Jack snarled in pain but did not go down.

Moving forward had put Owain directly in Henry's way. The fast man was still a bit dazed, but he was lucid enough to have his sword out and already moving through the air while Owain fired the pistol. Owain narrowly avoided Henry's blade and sat back heavily on his seat. He took a risk, then, diving through the line of agitated animals.

He emerged safely on the other side, but he soon had George barreling down on him on his mount. Thinking fast, Owain ducked back into the stomping animals, slid between the team still attached between one of the wagons, and unlatched them from each other. At just the right moment, he gave the horse a cut from the knife. It wasn't fatal, but it was more than a spur. The horse panicked and reared. George's horse did the same, throwing its rider.

Owain scrambled under the wagon for safety. It rocked and moved a short distance, and he heard more panicking horses out in the open. When he finally managed to crawl out from under the wagon, standing on George's side of the line, he found the big man on the ground, a bloody mess, trampled by multiple steeds.

He had only a moment to process this before a shot clipped the wagon beside him. Dust and splinters irritated his eyes and he was momentarily blind. Still, he went to the ground and crawled over to George, or what remained of him. Owain took the dead man's last pistol and ran for the next forward wagon in line, keeping Jack and Henry in his peripheral vision as they tried to match him on the other side.

In a great feat of strength and flexibility, Owain heaved himself onto the wagon's driver seat, stretched out on his belly, and didn't even really look before he put his hand around the corner and fired. He didn't stop to look and see if he'd actually hit anything before he rolled off the seat, dodged more nervous hooves, and continued up the line.

As he got past the wagons, he noticed that only Jack followed him now, speeding along like a fast moving iron horse. Owain had no real clue how to take on the big man. He was still strong, but his rage had gone, now replaced by fear and panic. Combined with his age, he honestly wasn't sure if he was all that invincible in a fight anymore.

But he hadn't always been this strong. There was a time when he was but a child and had to cause mischief in other ways. It often involved farm animals in some fashion. And once, it involved a donkey.

The first donkey Owain came to, he started beating on. Fists, kicks, the burro snorted and stared at him, ears flat. With Jack but steps behind him, he increased his assault, narrowly avoiding having his hand taken off in a vicious bite, but his timing could not have been better. The donkey snorted, gave a short bray, and kicked, catching Jack square in the chest. The big man went flying. Owain jumped back as the donkey snapped again, pawed the ground, and made as if to seriously hurt him, too. He went back to the wagon and went around back.

Behind him, Henry lay on the ground, not moving, the ground around him soaked with blood. Ahead of him, Jack also lay on the ground, but he was moving, and Owain could hear wheezing breaths. Cautiously, he approached.

As soon as he saw Jack, Owain knew he was a dead man one way or another. He had not sustained a glancing blow in any form; it had been a direct strike. His ribcage had been crushed and the man could not breathe. The donkey glared at Owain and made a grunting sound but did not move. Owain knelt beside Jack. The big man was struggling to stay conscious, though his eyes rolled back in his head several times.

"You bastard," Jack said, blood bubbling from his mouth and nose. "Damn Unioner."

Owain shook his head. "I'm not a Unioner. If I must be anything, I suppose I'll be a Pacifist. It sure beats everything else I've done with my life."

He wasn't sure how much Jack understood, but he figured it didn't matter as he took a knife and cut the dying man's throat. It was probably one of the hardest things he'd ever done in his life, and yet it was probably the only death that was necessary in that the man was suffering greatly. Still, once the deed was done, Owain dropped the knife, wandered off into the woods a short distance, sat down, and wept.

He wept for himself, that he seemed incapable of outrunning his past or his heinous abilities. He tried to be a good man. He wanted to be a good man. Had this somehow been orchestrated so that he would have no choice but to kill his comrades and not be a good man? Was he just predestined to be an awful human being? Had God delivered him from Beaumaris only to abandon him in the wilds of America? Jut what was he supposed to do?

And what would happen to him if someone found out? All he wanted to do was find his brother. Was he not meant to find Teo? Was God trying to stop him in any way possible? He didn't understand.

Owain figured he must have taken a short nap because the next thing he knew, the shadows had moved. Not far, but they had moved. Grunting, he got to his feet and retraced his steps back to the road.

The freed horses and donkeys had wandered off a bit to look for food, and the hitched horses looked like they desperately wanted to follow suit but were presently unable. Jack, Henry, and George remained where they were, flies looking for a late-season snack before winter.

There was no way Owain could keep this whole wagon train going by himself, but he didn't know how he was going to explain himself, either. Should he keep going to the settlement and ask for help? What would he say? How could he hide the bodies? He could say it was an attack by Indians; that was believable enough. Except for the part where nothing was taken or destroyed, and the bodies still had their scalps.

Not Indians, then, he decided, but bandits. Bandits had attacked them, killed three of them, and Owain was glad to escape with his life. That would be his story, assuming anyone asked.

He felt deplorable for the lie, but he truly felt helpless. He couldn't drive the train, didn't want to take it south anyway, didn't want to have to explain it to the settlers, certainly couldn't tell them that the three men had tried to kill him. No one would ever believe him. And if Teo heard about it or got involved, he could point out all the wrong Owain had ever done, and then they would never be able to reconnect.

So Owain went around to all of the wagons, unhitched the teams, and let them run off. Well, they went a bit off the road and started nuzzling around for grasses, but they were away from the wagons. He kept only one horse, tying it off to a tree so it couldn't run, but with enough rope to let it nose around a bit. He unloaded the rest of the pack horses and donkeys, all except the one he'd antagonized. He couldn't get within five feet of that donkey before it threatened to kick, bite or just straight out charge and trample. Well, he could keep his pack, Owain figured. Might be he would wander into a settlement before long and someone would take him in.

With the sun going down, he gathered up what strength he had left, then went about tipping over the wagons. The first two he did with his bare hands. After that, he had to get creative, using levers and rigging and so on. The noise and the chaos got a few of the horses to scatter, but he didn't pay much attention except to the one he'd tied off.

By the time he got all the wagons tipped over and the contents scattered somewhat, it was well dark and he was exhausted. He looked around the scene, everything quickly turning into mounds of shadow. Well, as much as he wanted to respect the dead, he didn't think it likely that a troupe of bandits would stick around to bury bodies. He'd think about it overnight and bury them in the morning if it bothered him too much.

With that thought hanging over his head, he gathered up some wood and started a small fire, just enough to stave off the worst of the autumn chill. With plenty of provisions from the wagons, he did not go to sleep hungry. He wasn't sure how he should feel about being able to eat a full meal after killing three men. Did that mean that nothing had changed from the time he'd sat down to drink in a room with six dead men? Was he really the same man? Was it even possible for him to change? Should he even bother?

He lay there in the dark and felt his ma's kerchief. How hadn't he lost it in all of his adventures? He was grateful he still had it, but he still couldn't figure out what his ma had seen in him. What hope did she have for him? Was her one greatest trait also her greatest flaw?

Maybe it was up to him to fulfill what she thought she saw in him. He was taking responsibility for himself.

By lying about what happened here.

If it had been lighter and warmer, he probably would have taken off, disgusted with himself, as if he could outrun the one person he hated most sitting at the campfire: himself. But as it was, it was cold, dark, and he was in unfamiliar territory. It would have to wait.

He did not sleep well, but it had little to do with his actions of the day. He found himself more worried about anything that might come sniffing around, attracted to the smell of blood. Wolves, bears, the men told him about mountain lions that prowled these hills. Wolves and bears were bad enough, but the mountain lions were by far the most dangerous creature out here, they said. There could be one ten feet away in the bushes but you wouldn't know it until you got up and went over there to take a piss.

Owain could only hope that the mountain lions were more interested in prey that was already caught and cured versus one that was still moving. All the same, he slept lightly and woke up for just about every little sound. At one point, he heard the distinct screaming of a horse in distress, and by morning, the rest of the horses and donkeys, including the bad-tempered one, had cozied up to his fire with him.

Returning to the road, there was certainly evidence of predator activity in the night. Something had begun gnawing on Jack and pulled him partway off the road, and something else had taken heavy interest in George. Henry appeared unmolested, but that wouldn't take long to fix.

In the end, Owain elected to leave the bodies as they were. The scavengers would have them finished off in just a couple days, if that. He couldn't take the horses, but he wouldn't be surprised if some began following him when he left. He packed up a few bags and attached them to the one horse he'd chosen to keep and ride. At the last minute, he also elected to bring a donkey with him, too, repacking a few bags with more provisions and supplies in the event he didn't find the settlements right away.

In addition to the food and precious few medical supplies, Owain also helped himself to several pistols, a second sword, some extra knives, and a little cash the men had on hand. Half of it was Union money, but the other half were freshly printed Confederate bills, just starting to circulate around the South as another act of defiance.

He tied the donkey's reins to the horse's saddle and mounted. He looked around the scene for a minute, wondering if he'd forgotten anything, wondering if anyone would even notice if he had. No one else had been through here, and he hadn't seen or heard evidence of anyone else in the area.

But the longer he lingered, the more likely it was that someone would find him. If he put some distance between him and the scene, at least a few days, he might be able to avoid suspicion. Forcing himself to look away, he turned the horse back the way they had come and started back up the road.

A few miles back, they'd crossed a small stream. It wasn't much, but it was the only one he really knew of, and he could water the horse and the donkey and think without three dead men staring at him and interrupting his thoughts.

He wasn't even sure if this really was the road to the settlements or if it had been a convenient excuse to get off the main road and kill him in the shadows with no witnesses. He had to think on it a little. Maybe he'd run into the little Confederate spy again, warning him of Unioners about. Owain would thank him and ask which way to the Welsh settlement.

He arrived at the stream no worse for wear, but short days made him anxious. He didn't want to double-back at all, but the animals needed water, and he needed to think. His mind was muddled and confused and his thinking did not progress very well. He ended up camping a short distance from the stream that night, again sleeping lightly in case a mountain lion decided to take advantage of him separating from the herd as it were.

As expected, a few horses continued to follow him, having little better to do and not knowing what else to do anyway. Owain decided not to dissuade them. If nothing else, they would provide meat through the winter if it came to that.

Owain finished up his breakfast, drained his canteen and filled it again, got his mount and his pack animal across the stream, then paused once more. Should he go back down the same road? Should he continue on and see if there wasn't another road that might take him to the settlements? He had no map; the Confederates worked by memory alone. These hills were vast and unforgiving, and winter wasn't much of a friend herself.

Well, he couldn't just stand there like a startled rabbit. At some point, he had to move. Taking a breath, he heaved himself into the saddle. Behind him, the donkey snorted and shook its head. With a sinking feeling in his gut that all of this was going to go horribly, horribly wrong, he nudged his horse and began moving. All around him, he felt as though something was watching him, and more than once he could have sworn that Jack, Henry, and George walked beside him on the road.

CHAPTER TWENTY-FOUR

THE VISITOR

Owain must have spent a week or more wandering the roads. He initially bypassed the first road—the one where he'd killed the three men—and continued on until he found another road. That proved a fruitless endeavor. So he returned to the main road and returned to the first road—the one where he'd killed the three men, but by now, wild scavengers had dragged the bodies away and scattered any remaining supplies and provisions—and ended up wandering into a valley with a German settlement on one side and a Dutch settlement on the other. Neither one knew what to make of him, but they were happy to take his extra horses off his hands, the four that had survived the trip, anyway. The Germans and the Dutch were pretty useless when it came to information—and they could barely speak English anyway—but they basically knew the Welsh and Irish settlements; they were farther south. He got a hot meal and a warm bed that night and started off south once more the following morning.

He got off the first road—the one where he'd killed the three men—bypassed the second road that had proven futile, and traveled a few more days before coming across a third west-bound road. Hoping and praying because he didn't want to get caught out in these mountains in the winter and he had little desire to go south again, he turned off onto the road.

It didn't take two hills before he saw the valley he was certain had attracted the immigrants. Long and beautiful, it wasn't difficult to imagine it in its full summer cloak of green. Just the sight of it told Owain that he was on the right track. He had to be. There was no way any self-respecting Irish or Welsh immigrant could pass this up and think that there would be something even better on the other side of the hills.

He ended up camping that night, but the following day he came across a small town. Actually, to call it a town was to overestimate what it was.

It turned out to be the wrong settlement. This was the Irish settlement. They were happy to talk to him and get water for his animals, but the Welsh were just a little farther north. No, he didn't have to go all the way back to the main road. Just keep following this road along and it would eventually branch off west and north. Take the north road and it would see him to his own people.

Partway up the north road, his donkey stumbled off the road, a rock sliding out from under its sure hooves. Owain had just enough time to cut the rope tying it to his horse. The donkey didn't slide far, and it didn't die, but it did break a leg. Owain was forced to butcher the animal, and then he had the dilemma of what to do with all the supplies the donkey had been carrying. It hadn't been a whole lot, but he couldn't ride the horse and load it down with even more weight.

He camped where he was that night, cooking up the donkey meat, turning it into jerky. He also ended up fleshing the donkey's hide and laying it over his horse's saddle the following day so it could dry and cure in the hopes that he might be able to use it for winter furs. The donkey's bags he attached the horse's saddle as well, and he just took the reins and walked.

The Welsh settlement was about the same size as the Irish settlement, at least as far as "town" went. The chapel stood silent, evidently a weekday. A Pony Express station was also quiet for the time being. In the early morning, not too many people were out and about. Mostly it appeared to be children shirking chores and some older men and women getting together to trade gossip. There were only a few younger adults in the mix, and they were the ones to meet Owain as he walked into town.

"You know horses are for riding, don't you?" one young man joked. Owain judged him to be maybe twenty-five to thirty years old.

He nodded. *"Dw i'n gwybod."* (I know.)

The man grinned. *"Dyn Cymru."* (A man of Wales.)

"Ie." (Yes.)

"Beth ydy dy enw?" (What's your name?)

"Owain."

They grasped wrists.

"Croeso, Owain," the man said. "My name is William. Have you been traveling long?"

"At least five years. One year up and down these blasted mountains, looking for this place."

The man, William, was still smiling. "Well, as you know, if a Welshman doesn't want to be found, he'll find a way to make it happen." He laughed. "Come over here, let's get some water for your horse. Maybe you need the trough, too, eh?"

"I would be grateful," Owain told him. "Food I have plenty of, but water I do not have in abundance."

He followed William to a trough and a couple more young men brought water to fill it. Owain brought out his canteen and took a modest drink. If there was any good news from the last day or so having to walk, it was that his seat didn't hurt so bad from the saddle. He allowed himself to relax for a minute. So close. He was so close to finding his brother. At the very least, he'd found the settlement. It was only a matter of time now.

He was pleasantly surprised when someone brought him some bread and a bit of cheese to eat. He hadn't had fresh cheese in ages, and even the smoked stuff had run out a while back. And the fresh bread was almost more than he could stand.

"You have been traveling a while, haven't you?" William observed.

"Far too long, I think," Owain said around a mouthful of food. He swallowed hard. "Far too long. I hope I'm at my journey's end."

"Oh? What brings you this way? Trying to escape this impending war everyone seems to think is right around the corner?"

"Well, there is that. No, the whole reason I even came to America—" *Besides escaping prison and an entire island of four nations who knew my name far too well. "*—is to find my brother." He took another bite of bread and cheese. "Does the name Teo Forbes sound familiar?"

"Oh, Teo Fforidd?"

Owain's expression and sudden jump in posture must have been confirmation enough. William grinned again. "Bastards in U.S. Customs changed his name to make it more 'American.' Almost as bad as the English he says. Yeah, I know Teo. Everyone knows him. Teo and Maisy, nicest people in the whole valley, I swear. Well, besides my wife and mother, but that's all formality, you know? Shoot, he's your brother? I don't remember that he ever said anything about having a brother. I know he said his parents and sisters were still back in Wales."

Owain cleared his throat and scuffed the dirt with his foot. "Well, we weren't on the best terms the last time we saw each other. That's my fault, though. But I'm here to find him, see if there's a chance we can reconnect."

"Oh, absolutely." William nodded. "So you probably need to know where he lives, right?"

"It might make things easier."

"All right, listen. You see this road here, right? This will keep taking you west and eventually it will branch off to Charleston. Don't go that way. Instead, you take this road here. Well, it's not much of a road, more of a well-used trail. You keep following that north. There will be another trail branches off down farther into the valley. Ignore that and keep going north, keep going up. Eventually, you'll find another trail going off to the left and it kind of switches back south. Take that one. It'll bring you right past his farm."

Sounded complicated, but then, if a Welshman didn't want to be found, he would find a way to make it happen. Owain thanked William and said he would be on his way posthaste.

"No need to rush out of here," William told him. "What news of Wales?"

"Sadly, my news will be rather outdated. I've been in America for five years."

"And it's taken you this long to get here?"

Owain shrugged. "I didn't know where my brother lived. Like I said, we weren't on good terms when we separated. It's probably been fifteen, twenty years."

William whistled and shook his head. "I don't know, I just can't imagine Teo being angry with anyone. I mean, I've seen him angry and frustrated, but the man couldn't carry a grudge if you put it in a bucket for him. I'm sure that whatever past grievances you two have, he'll be more than willing to forgive. And you've certainly come a long ways to find him. That's got to count for something, don't it?" He did not wait for an answer. "Well, I suppose it's really not my place. At any rate, you are welcome here. Good luck with your brother."

"*Diolch yn dda.*" (Thank you very much.)

With that, the young man wandered off to resume whatever errands he'd been in town for in the first place. Owain finished off the bread and cheese, took a drink of water, but did not move right away. Now he knew. He knew where his brother lived, and he knew how to get there. Well, he had directions on how to get there. All he needed now was to actually get moving.

Before he could grab his horse's reins, he was approached by an older woman, easily his ma's age.

"You're looking for Teo and Maisy, aren't you?" she inquired.

"That's right," Owain said.

"Yes, I heard William talking about it. Whatever you're going up there to do, please do it gently."

"I don't understand."

"Oh, they just suffered a terrible loss of one of their children. Do be gentle when speaking to them."

Owain nodded. "I will."

The old woman managed a small smile. "Yes. I know you will."

Then he grabbed the reins and turned toward the trail William had pointed out.

Follow this trail up. Ignore the one going down into the valley. Continue to the branch and take the left. Right? Or was it take the right? He said it would switchback, so it must be the left, unless the whole geography of the valley changed between one trail and the other.

Owain had assumed, perhaps foolishly, that the trail was going to be easier to follow and maybe not so long. Maybe Teo lived within half a day's walk of the little town, if everyone knew him so well. He was the more sociable one, the friendly one, and Owain had little doubt that he was part of the chapel choir. When God gave a man a voice like that, it wasn't unreasonable that He would expect something in return.

But the trail stretched out before him almost endlessly. It wasn't an easy trail to navigate, either. It was generally fine for a man and his horse, but a wagon, even a small one, would have a terrible time and very little margin of error. With the heavy frost still lingering, Owain's crunching steps were only amplified. A few streams of water from late season rains and maybe some snowmelt from snow that hadn't quite stuck were now frozen and proved treacherous when unexpected. More than once, Owain had a foot shoot out from under him and almost throw him down the hill. He could only hope that his horse didn't stumble and break a leg, too. In the event that Teo did run him off, he needed to be able to leave and survive the winter.

It was late afternoon before Owain found the first trail leading down into the valley. Well, he thought it was the trail, but it could have just been a regular washout. Whatever the case, he made careful steps around it so he didn't fall and break an ankle. The horse took the safe way and jumped over the washout. And upward they continued.

They found the fork in the trail before it got completely dark, and Owain judged the grove of pine trees to be an excellent spot to camp for the night, if only to block out the wind. He gathered some of the dead sticks and needles under the pines to start a small fire, and pulled out some of the provisions to gnaw on. He was hungry, certainly, but mostly he was anxious. He had little doubt that he was going to find his brother tomorrow. What would he do? What would he say? What could he say?

He brought out his mother's kerchief. The cloth itself was dirty, but the stitching remained in tact. He still had a few of her letters as well. After he made contact with Teo, he would have to write to her. He hadn't written since he started out with the Confederates, way back in the spring. She deserved to know what was going on. Truth be told, he wanted to hear from her as well, get news of home. Maybe finding his brother and making amends would get his pa to open up a little, too.

All of it fantasy until he was able to find his brother, he mused. He wondered whether he should have a plan in case Teo rejected him. It would probably be a smart idea. If Teo threw him out, drove him off, or simply asked him to leave, Owain had little doubt that his beast would try to seize on the opportunity, and nothing good could come from that. He needed a plan, a way out without anyone getting hurt.

It would be far too awkward for him to try and settle elsewhere in the community. No doubt everyone would know of his shame within the month, and he didn't want to cause trouble for Teo who was already established and in good standing. He really didn't want to return to New York City. As much as he preferred the weather in the South, the politics and the impending war didn't strike him as a particularly desirable part of the real estate.

Wasn't there supposed to be a city somewhere in these mountains? It was hard to imagine, for as few people as he'd seen on the road. All the same, that might be an option. These mountains were beautiful, delightfully reminisce of home. He would be near his brother, in the event they ever did make up in the future, and it was out of the way of the war. Yes, that sounded like a decent prospect he could live with, at least for a while. But only if Teo rejected him. If there was even the slightest chance that he and his brother could be friends, he would take it.

Owain didn't realize he'd fallen asleep until he woke up, and he woke up primarily because he was cold. He stoked the fire a bit, enough to shake the chill and warm his food, but he roused his horse and they were underway soon enough.

Up the left trail, farther up the hill, he told himself, easily finding the switchback and continuing ever upwards. Snow had fallen in the night, and Owain had a sneaking suspicion that this time it was here to stay. He shivered once but pressed on, determined not to stop until he found his brother's home.

He circled around a small hill, then another. Owain began to despair. What if Teo actually had told the other townsfolk about his wayward brother and gave them instructions that if, for some ungodly reason, he ever came calling, to give him false directions and get him as far away from the town, and him, as possible? Owain might have been hurt if he didn't understand why his brother might do something like that.

Might be that he just continued on for a bit, looking for this fabled city in the mountains, Charleston. Maybe he would just bypass this whole endeavor. He would get to Charleston and write his ma. *Sorry, Teo rejected me, threw me out. He wanted nothing to do with me. Thanks for believing in me and for encouraging me all these years. I'll still write, and hopefully I can make some small life for myself, but it won't be with Teo. Or you. Or anyone else in the family. I'm sorry.*

Owain was deep in his depressed musings and didn't stand a chance against a flurry of feathers and squawking that suddenly burst from the trees. He let out a startled cry, flailing his arms about wildly, and even the horse did a little dance. Jumping back a step, Owain found himself facing a chicken, a very angry rooster to be precise.

The rooster had all its feathers fluffed out, wings out, tail feathers spread threateningly. It clucked and made a few other noises at him before racing forward to deliver another series of scratches and blows. Owain tried to swat it out of the way, but the little bugger was fast. It bounced away several feet, turned, and assumed the posture that said it wasn't done with him yet.

Slightly confused and a little embarrassed that he'd been ambushed by a damn chicken, Owain continued down the trail, hoping to get clear of the little fury. To his dismay, he found the rooster start to run after him and his horse. Then the chicken took flight, touched off the horse's head—causing the horse to rear and rip the reins from Owain's hand—and went for a full facial attack on Owain.

Owain put his hands up to shield his face, but the chicken's claws still managed to rip through his sleeves and bloody his arms. He lashed out and tried to catch the rooster, but it was already falling, pecking and squawking and continuing to tear at him on its way to the ground. Once there, it jumped up to scratch at his knees one more time before finally running off, disappearing as fast as it had appeared, but still cackling as if laughing at him.

After a second or two, Owain lowered his arms. He was scratched and dirty and bloody and his clothes were torn in multiple places. As he grumbled to himself and tried to brush off the worst of it, he heard a female voice.

"Welly! Welly, what trouble are you getting into now?"

Just down the trail, around a pine tree, came a woman a little younger than him. Her most prominent feature was her pregnant belly, and she huffed and puffed, shooing the rooster back to wherever it had come from. Then Owain saw the long brown hair and eyes that were the purest brown, the most hypnotizing eyes anyone had ever seen. And they could only belong to one person.

"Oh!" Maisy said, taking notice of Owain. "Oh, my goodness, I'm so sorry! He's such an awful little rooster." She approached and fussed over his torn clothes. "Oh, and now look what he's done to you." She sighed and looked at him. Owain was sure she would recognize him and stunned when she didn't. "Listen, why don't you come up to the house? I'll get these patched up, you can get a hot meal, and then be on your way."

"That sounds right pleasant," Owain said, unsure what else to say. He'd been so focused on meeting his brother, he hadn't even considered what would happen if he met Maisy first. He wasn't even sure if her not recognizing him was a good thing or a bad thing.

His heart thudded loudly in his chest as he followed her down the trail, through a row of pines. Once on the other side, the hillside opened up to reveal wide pasture dotted with sheep, goats, a cow, and numerous chickens, all foraging for anything good under the snow. A barn was situated in the hillside itself, allowing for two floors and easy access to both. Not far from that was a cozy little cottage, smoke coming out of the chimney.

"Teo!" Maisy called. "Teo, come out and meet our visitor!"

Owain was surprised she couldn't hear his pounding heart. He might have said the temperature dropped as well, but he knew it was just his sweat freezing to his body. He wanted to run away, be anywhere but right here, but he couldn't. He hadn't spent five years wandering around America, at least one of those years in the mountains, just to run away at the last minute. He was a coward, he knew, but this was something he had to do. He had to face his brother.

A minute later, there were some crunching footsteps, and Teo walked around the side of the cottage.

The last time Owain had seen his brother, he'd been newly married, strong but still slight of build, and as tidy as he could manage to impress his new wife.

The Teo he saw now was much older, much wiser, and much tougher. He still wasn't as big as Owain, but he'd certainly filled out to be a formidable opponent, make bandits think twice about trying anything. His hair was tinged with gray and unkempt, and the rest of him was dirty with the day's work, not filthy, but he'd clearly been working.

Teo set eyes on Owain, and immediately, Owain knew this was not going to go well.

"Maisy, get the kids and get in the house," he ordered, with all the authority of Captain Martin commanding his crew. In three long strides, he was at the door to the cottage where he grabbed a rifle.

"What?" Maisy wondered, slowly moving away from Owain nonetheless. "Teo, this isn't how we treat guests."

Teo had his rifle at his shoulder, pointed straight at Owain. "A guest implies you want him around. My brother is not a guest here."

Now Maisy looked at her "guest," studying him. She never said anything, but her expression said that the recognition was starting to kick in. Time and circumstance had aged Owain, and not gracefully, but he was still the same man he had been years ago. Gingerly, she ducked out of the area, calling for her children.

Owain made a small motion. "Teo, I—"

"Shut up," Teo spat. "Turn around, and go back to whatever hole you crawled out of."

"Please, Teo, I just want to talk."

"Well you just did. Now leave."

"Don't you even want to know why I'm here?"

"Whatever it is, it can't be good."

Owain sighed. "Teo, if you had wanted to kill me, you would have done it by now."

Teo just glared at him. "Unlike you, I don't enjoy killing. Yes, it's difficult. But I will do it."

"No, you won't." Owain shook his head. "Please, Teo, I just want to talk. Can I show you something to prove my intentions? I know it's hard to believe, but I have changed. Or I'm trying to."

"You could have nothing of interest. You can't change."

"Then neither can you. Which is why you won't shoot me. You're a lover, not a fighter, the nicest man in the valley according to the folks in town."

He could see his words were slowly making their way into Teo's mind.

"And what if I have changed?" Teo asked, adjusting his grip on the rifle.

"Then all you've done is turn into me," Owain replied.

They stood there in an ominous standoff for what felt like an eternity. Neither of them moved. Teo watched Owain like a hawk, and Owain focused on his breath, puffing in the cold. He tried not to move, tried not to spook his brother, but he could only suppress a shiver for so long. Finally, Teo spoke.

"What do you have to show me?"

Owain made his movements slow and deliberate as he reached in his shirt and removed the stitched cloth. He showed it to Teo and tossed it as far as he could. He didn't like to, but if Teo was nervous about getting close to him, then this might be seen as a show of trust. Teo eyed him for a moment, then lowered the barrel of the rifle and stooped to retrieve the cloth. Owain did not move. His feet were starting to get viciously cold.

"This is ma's stitching," Teo said finally.

"It is," Owain said. "I have some of her letters, too. I've been writing to her, when I could. I've been in America for five years now."

Teo tucked the cloth in his own shirt and readied his gun, though he did not point it directly at Owain. "The last time I heard anything about you, Ma said you'd gone to prison for murder and were sentenced to hang. I have a hard time believing you were granted clemency, which can only mean one thing: escape."

Owain let out a breath and studied the spot on the ground where the cloth had fallen. "Yes. I did escape. I know you won't believe me when I say the priest helped me, but he did. In a way. I hid out in Scotland over the winter and returned home after that. Ma helped me get passage on a smuggler's vessel to get me to New York. I worked there for a while, and then I started kind of moving this way, trying to find you. It's taken a long time. But I haven't been in jail. I haven't touched a drink in almost three years. No trouble at all."

He could see his brother was struggling to put all the different concepts together. On the one hand, Teo liked to generally believe the best about anybody. He was a lover, not a fighter, much like their ma. On the other hand, he was having to consider that his older brother might have changed. Maybe not in the best way, as escaping from prison was not a way to bolster confidence in one's ability to change, but it was a work in progress, anyway. And three years without a drink was utterly unheard of with Owain Fforidd.

"What do you want?" Teo asked finally, his stance still telling Owain to stay right where he was.

He sighed. "I have nowhere left to go. I made my peace too late. I'm too old to start a family and build a homestead, and I think we both know that city life would never suit me for very long. I've been living on the Lord's mercy for the last six, seven years. I don't know where to go or what to do. I need your help. I'm only asking."

"And if I told you to get off my land and never come back?"

"Then I suppose I shall have to find someplace else to live out the remainder of my days. I don't expect there to be too many."

"You're a survivor," Teo stated. "You always have been."

Owain frowned and nodded. "All right. For what it's worth, then, I'm glad to see you've done well for yourself. At least our parents have one son they can be proud of."

He took the horse's reins, turned, and started back up the trail. He didn't get ten steps before Teo said, "Parent."

Owain paused and looked back. "What?"

Teo's expression was grudging as he put the rifle up and repeated. "Parent. Pa died last winter. Pneumonia."

It was like being punched in the gut, and Owain found he could not speak for a long minute. Then, "The last letter I sent to ma was this spring, before I started into the mountains."

Teo huffed and nodded. "Sounds about the time I heard of it." He ran his tongue over his teeth, still nodding. "Pa's gone. Adith and her family have taken over the land, moved in to take care of Ma."

Owain nodded absently. "That's good."

He made as if to continue up the trail, but Teo called him back. "Owain, stop." He turned again. "Turn your horse out to pasture for a bit. I'll find you one of my coats to wear. Maisy can mend yours. Let's you and I take a walk and talk a bit."

Owain's hope, which had started out as a small fire in New York, roared to life in the mountains, had quickly cooled since the beginning of their conversation. He thought it had died all the way down to ash, but there remained a few coals which he hesitantly nursed as he handed Teo his ripped coat. He unloaded the packs from the horse's saddle. Unsure what else to do with them, he set the saddle and reins in the snow beside the packs as well. Then he got the horse pointed in the right direction and let it wander off to join the sheep and goats and everything else nosing around in the snowy pasture.

He did not presume to approach the cottage, but remained where he was, feet ice cold in the snow, his upper body quickly chilling as well. It was a minute before Teo emerged from the cottage, heavy coat in one hand, rifle in the other. He approached Owain cautiously, as if approaching a wild animal. Again, Owain made his movements slow and deliberate as he took the coat that was offered to him. A better pair of gloves was also handed to him.

"That should keep you from freezing for a while," Teo said.

"It is much appreciated, thank you," Owain told him, hoping he sounded as sincere as he felt.

"I still don't know that I believe you've changed, but I know our ma's stitching, and it took a lot to find me up here in the mountains, a dedication that I don't remember you ever having before. We're going to take a walk. Maybe by the time the sun goes down and we get back, you'll have earned at least a place in the barn."

"That would be more than I have a right to ask for."

They started out across the field.

CHAPTER TWENTY-FIVE

THE CAVE

There was a drought that year, and even with all of us working all the fields, there just wasn't enough, not to last all of us the winter. Farming was a tough life, I could understand, but I had to provide for Maisy and Teo. I heard there was work in the south. Blacksmithing, iron works, glass blowing, a whole bunch of factories opening up in the south, bringing industry to Wales. Maisy resisted the idea at first. Neither of us wanted to leave everything we'd ever known, but I couldn't stand the thought of them going hungry. Finally, before the snows got too bad, we headed south."

Owain and Teo were out in the pasture, walking the tree line and talking. Teo elected to tell his story first, all that had happened after Owain had stopped by to say goodbye before heading to England.

"It wasn't hard to get a job in the glass works, but it was hot, dangerous, and if you looked at the fire and the glass for any length of time, you could easily go blind. Hours were long and wages were low. Often I would leave before sunrise and return home after dark. Maisy didn't like where we were living, and the neighbors were less than desirable even for a man like me, never mind a woman and babe alone. Even when I was home, I was usually ill, too exhausted to really do anything, even make small repairs to our rented room. It was no life I wanted. In that moment, I would have rathered died a proud farmer than a wretched factory worker.

"We returned home to the farm. I was still very ill and I ended up staying abed for several weeks while Ma and Maisy took care of me. When I finally started recovering, she suggested we go to America. Things in Wales weren't improving, but there was plenty of fine land in

America. Again, neither Maisy nor I wanted to leave, but we felt we had little choice. Just as soon as we could get up the funds and the papers, we left, arriving in New York, same as you.

"I worked in New York City for a short time, just long enough to save up a little and learn more about this country. It was by chance that I heard of settlements in the mountains. Dutch, Irish, Welsh, little pocket communities here and there. It would be a long and dangerous trek, I knew. Maisy was not thrilled at the prospect. Moving had been hard enough on its own, but she was pregnant with our second child at the time and didn't want to travel much while expecting. I told her that would be the best time to travel, before the baby arrived. She reluctantly agreed.

"We made it to Richmond before she gave birth, and we stayed there for several months so she could recover and they would both grow stronger, well enough to travel. In the springtime, we set off again. In fact, we met a couple other Welsh and Irish families all going the same way. We banded together for safety and started up into the mountains. We separated once, as the Irish departed to find their own community, but we continued on until we found the small town you likely came through. I agree, it's not much of a town, but it's the hub of the community.

"The people helped us get settled, showed us the land and helped in building houses and barns. It was mid-summer when we arrived, so the growing season was greatly shortened, but everyone was glad to come together and help us out, both to maximize our crops and to share their own if needed.

"It took a few years before my anxiety was somewhat quelled. That was how long it took us to get our fields just right, prepare the pastures and fill them with animals, and keep the animals alive and healthy through the winter in addition to ourselves. We've had a few bad years, true, but our bad years here are still better than our best years in Wales. Ever since, we've just been working the land. You obviously saw that Maisy is pregnant again, but she swears this is going to be the last. I don't blame her; it's becoming hard on her, much harder than it was twenty years ago."

Owain felt much better with the heavy wool coat and thick woolen gloves, but his feet were still quite chilly and it was rather uncomfortable. Still, he did not complain.

They walked in silence for a few minutes before Owain asked, "The Pony Express stable looks abandoned. How have you been writing to Ma?"

Teo nodded. "It's been abandoned for some years, but sometimes the riders will still stop, if only to water their horses and get out of the saddle. But the closest post office is in Charleston. I go down about once a month to buy, sell, trade, and so on, and I also check for any mail they might have for me. In five years, Ma never said a word about you coming here. I knew you went to England because you said goodbye. Then Ma told me about you going to prison. After that, I had just as soon assumed you were hanged."

His gaze was scrutinizing and questioning. Owain hated telling the priest about his miserable life, and he was less eager to tell Teo of his exploits since he left for England. At the very least, Teo was already aware of his awful nature up to that point, and there was little to tell about his time in America. He was just going to omit the part about the Confederates. Bad blood between brothers was bad enough without dragging war and politics into the mix.

Nevertheless, it was a long minute before Owain began speaking. At first, his voice broke and he tripped over his words so that they made no sense. Only when he stopped, calmed himself down, and told himself to just tell a story, was he able to get it all out there.

He spoke of his aimless wanderings in England, looking for work, trying to be good. It hadn't always worked out, but he really did try. Sometimes it was his own stupid fault he couldn't find work. Sometimes it really was the underlying—and sometimes obvious—prejudices of the English against the influx of Irish immigrants. Nope, it didn't really matter that he was technically Welsh. The point wasn't whether he was or was not Irish, but that he wasn't English.

He spoke of his arrival and early days in London. He'd been surrounded by people who were just as bad as him; he'd thought he was the only one. He worked hard to stay clean, but it wasn't easy, and he'd failed miserably, at least initially. He usually had work of one form or another, yes, but it was primarily just a means to get money so he could drink. Barring that, he enjoyed being the strongest one on the various work crews, and he devised awful ways to gain...something. It really wasn't respect, now that he thought about it. Attention, maybe, but it certainly wasn't respect.

Then he talked about his coming around and getting himself cleaned up. He talked about educating himself, learning to read and write and do math. More than that, he learned banking and investing. He earned money, learned how to walk and talk like a wealthy man. He had fine clothes and, after a time, a nice place to live. He'd managed to pull himself up out of the gutters in an economic sense, but in his soul, he had never left, though that would not become apparent just yet.

Owain paused here for just a moment. It was probably ten years now since he'd first met Paige, just under ten years that she'd been dead. Sometimes, if he lay awake at night and his demons came calling, he would find himself wondering if there would have been any way to save his marriage, maybe stop it from happening and save Paige years of abuse and heartache.

Nevertheless, he spoke of Paige to his brother. He spoke of her beauty and charm, her quick wit and intelligent mind. He spoke of her intimate knowledge of the bank and how she knew a thing or two about banking and investing. He spoke of their courtship, how her father hated him but saw him as a way to plant his bank through the Isles, maybe take root in America as well. He talked about their marriage, their week at her father's villa, and their business honeymoon to Wales. He talked about their detour back to see the farm, and he spoke of how Paige and his ma really hadn't gotten along, though they definitely tried to keep things civil for his sake. He recounted his ma telling him that she was glad he'd made something of himself but he really could have done better with his choice of wife.

That got a laugh from Teo, though he badly tried to rein it in. It made Owain feel good to see his brother laugh, when hardly an hour ago he'd had his rifle pointed at him. Maybe there was some hope for reconciliation.

He continued on, first telling of the good times he and Paige experienced, few though they were. There was a time when his marriage was happy, and Owain mentally kicked himself anew as he recalled those days. Eventually, he had to admit to the bad days, when he returned to drinking. It didn't matter the reasoning now, because he was responsible for his own actions. Drink no longer covered it as no one had forced him to get drunk. He told of the mild reprieve, when Paige announced her pregnancy and all was right with the world again. Then things became irreparably terrible between them—again, mostly his fault, though she was not without her share of blame (not that it mattered since she was dead now and it was largely his fault)—and he turned back to drinking.

Then Victoria was born and all was well with the world. He was happy. He had a family. He loved them. He just...loved his drinking more, especially the nights when the baby woke up crying and he already had a hangover. Paige hated him; that was no longer a secret between them. He again turned back to drinking, this time with no end in sight, and nothing could cure him of it, even for a short time. He hit Paige. He beat her terribly, though he was careful never to touch her face or anywhere someone might see.

He shamefully told of the day he turned his hand on Victoria, how Paige had grabbed her and run out the door. She broke her silence and he went drinking. He drank so heavily that night he didn't even know what happened except he woke up in jail. No one came for him. He learned that Paige had not only divorced him but had already remarried. Her father had stripped him of all assets and possessions, all titles, and accounts, everything but the clothes on his back, leaving him to beg on the streets of London. Not only that, but if he even got near Paige or any of her father's associates, he was to be arrested again.

He recounted the tale of Paige's demise, how her new husband killed her and Victoria. In some sick way, he still loved her, and it only enraged him to know that her killer was going to get off scot-free.

He again told of the night he killed that man, plus his ex-father-in-law, plus four more men who didn't need to die except they were just unfortunately in the room at the time. He told about how afterwards he'd taken the brandy and sat and drank all night until his ex-mother-in-law found him in the morning.

Owain told his brother about the trial and the unusual move to have him sent back to Wales, to Beaumaris. He did not speak much of Beaumaris itself, the black cells and the awful treatment by the gaolers. Instead, he elected to talk about the priest, Father Forthill. What started out as a simple confession turned into a huge movement across Wales, maybe even the whole British Isles to tell his story of tragedy and redemption. He only mentioned that he tried to kill himself twice while imprisoned, one of those times being after the gallows was destroyed in a freak storm.

Then he told of his escape, from its inception to its execution, how he'd trained himself to play dead and gotten out by stealing the undertaker's boat. He talked about finding the little abandoned cabin and how simply starting a fire meant the world to him. He talked about being found by the warden and several gaolers and how he'd convinced them to simply stay the night, return to the gaol in the morning. He detailed his escape from the shackles and recounted his conversation with Forthill the best he could remember.

He spoke of his second escape, how he made it all the way to Scotland and stayed there through the winter with a community of pagans. Come spring, he was given a horse that he could travel. Owain spoke of his journey south, unsure where he was going but hoping that home was still an option. He told his brother how their pa had met him at the door with a rifle—"right similar to you," he added, much to Teo's amusement—and how it had taken intervention from their ma before he was heeded.

He spoke of his last time back home, helping their ma, trying to learn from their pa. Their pa had had no faith in him but was glad to get him as far away from him and from Wales as possible. Their ma believed in him, though, fixed his clothes, made him a cloth that he might be able to talk to his brother. She did everything she could, even talked to some of his more questionable acquaintances from years past, to help him get passage to America. He recounted the last time he looked upon their parents, their childhood home, before turning his horse down the road.

Then came the tale of his trip to America, though it was rather boring, comparatively speaking. He worked on the ship for part of his fees and got into the country with little trouble. He spent several months in a boardinghouse, fighting off sickness before being released into New York City. After that, it was dull work for little pay, exchanging letters with their ma to try and get a better idea of where his brother was hiding. Then it was a slow trek south for the winter, and back north, and a year wandering the mountains before finally finding the Welsh community who happily pointed him in the right direction.

By the time Owain considered himself finished, they'd walked all the way around the pasture and the fields at least once and were making their way around again. Owain had even given a fairly condensed version of events. To think that speaking to the priest had taken months.

For a long time, Teo did not speak, and Owain was afraid that as soon as they reached the cottage he would have the rifle out again telling him to leave. They had just turned the last corner, heading back that way, when Teo finally spoke.

"It takes a lot for a man to admit his faults and confess to crimes for which he's already escaped the noose. It takes even more for a man to admit it to his own brother." In that moment, Teo had never looked or sounded more like their pa. "I expect that there are things you're not telling me, but that which you have told, I do believe you. Not only because a majority of it fits your character and the man I once knew, but because you were never much of a liar. You weren't smart enough to be able to lie, and you gain nothing for telling the truth now."

"I'm not sure if that's a compliment," Owain said, half to himself.

Teo ignored him. "You know you would never be able to gain sympathy, and telling the truth is only more likely to drive people away." He nodded. "I believe you, Owain. To a small degree, I respect you for it. That you had the courage to seek me out, knowing I could have turned you away or killed you outright, and that you spoke the truth even so."

"It means a lot to hear you say that."

They drew nearer to the cottage.

"Come inside," Teo said. "Get something to eat. We have a bit more to discuss, I think, but if I'm cold, then you must be freezing after being out in this all day."

Owain mutedly expressed his gratitude even as his whole body relaxed and rejoiced at the prospect of warmth and a hot meal. He was fairly certain that they both quickened their step just a bit. Maisy was inside, watching them through a window. Teo made some kind of motion or gesture, and a second before they arrived, the back door swung open. Teo moved with all the comfort and familiarity of a man entering his own castle, while Owain treated it as a mouse entering a mousetrap, trying to figure out how to get the cheese without setting off the trap.

"Things are all right now?" Maisy wondered, keeping one eye on Owain at all times and her husband between them.

"Not perfect," Teo told her, "but he can have a hot meal, anyway. We still have a few things to discuss."

"Your ma said he'd killed some men and was bound for the gallows. What happened?"

"I'll tell you later."

His tone was a dismissal. Maisy was clearly displeased, but she fetched bowls of soup for the two of them, excusing herself from the room and heading out to the barn, children in tow.

Teo took their cold, snowy coats and hung them up by the fireplace to dry. Then he and Owain sat and ate their soup in a tense silence. Teo was still the king of his castle, and Owain the mouse in the mousetrap.

"Where's your oldest boy?" Owain ventured cautiously. "Is he grown and married already?"

Teo managed a small smile and shook his head. "No. Poor boy doesn't see too many girls, and he wouldn't know how to talk to one if he did. Shy lad. No, he works in the mines. Maisy wants him to leave the mines. She's never liked him working there, but it's gotten even worse since..."

"Since...?" When Teo did not answer, Owain decided to push just a touch. "The people in town said you just lost a child."

For several long minutes, Owain was sure his brother was going to shoot him. He did not say anything, did not make any obviously threatening gestures, but there was a certain shift in his posture and the way he continued to eat that said that fratricide was not out of the realm of possibility right now.

Then it passed and Teo said, "Yes. Our youngest boy. Well, I say that as if we've had plenty. No, like our pa, we've had only two boys and a myriad of girls. We're waiting to find out what this next is going to be, but I have a suspicion that it's going to be another girl. Teo was our first. He's eighteen years old or something close to that? I can't even remember, honestly. Then we had Tommen." He shook his head slowly. "Would that God had taken me instead."

"Don't let Maisy hear you say that."

"Last time she did, she hit me with a stick. But she's even more tore up."

"Can I ask what happened?"

For a second, Owain wasn't sure Teo would say anything. Then his brother shifted position and sighed. "He was only eight years old. The kindest, most thoughtful boy you'd ever know. But he had a mischievous streak, liked to pick on his sisters. He loved to play with Teo when he could. He was adventurous, too. When he could get away with it and dodge his chores, he would run off into the forest and have his own little adventures as all boys do. He would come back with rocks or sticks or pinecones or whatever interesting things he could find. He had a collection of rocks that he liked, seashells from no one knows where.

"Last year, he found a hollow log, and whenever Teo was around, they would work on hollowing it out more and making it smooth. Over the winter, Teo cut it in half and made some other modifications, then they climbed up one of the nearby hills and slid down on the logs. Tommen got stuck in some undergrowth, though, and I had to bring an ax and a saw and everything else to cut him out, but they looked like they had fun, anyway."

Teo took a breath and shook his head. Then, "But his favorite thing, more than bringing pretty things to his ma or running off on adventures, he liked to climb. He would climb fences, the side of the house, the barn, trees. If he could get a purchase, stand back because up he would go. He liked to climb rocks, too. Nothing was off-limits."

He made a general gesture to one side. "There's a cave not too far from here, a mile or so, that Tommen always talked about exploring. He wanted to explore it. With Teo working in the mines, Tommen wanted him to show him how to properly explore a cave. Teo told him no. The cave is sealed off—not completely, but enough to make the point—which meant that something bad was in the cave and they shouldn't go in there. Tommen still wanted to go. He just wanted to step inside, just to see. He was curious and he wanted to look.

"But Teo kept telling him no and telling him no, so...he decided he wasn't going to wait for his brother anymore; he was going to go explore the cave on his own."

Teo shifted position again to look at Owain. "No one understands this cave, but many people have disappeared in it over the years. Dozens, hundreds, no one knows. They just vanish, never to be heard from again, or so people think. Every so often, someone will come wandering out. They will swear to Almighty God that they've only been gone a few minutes, an hour at most, when it's really been weeks, months, years have passed before missing people come out again. The pastor at the church has declared the cave cursed by ancient demonic gods that the Native Americans in the area used to worship, but that hasn't stopped an occasional adventurer from wandering in."

"Including Tommen," Owain stated.

He nodded. "Yeah. Including Tommen. Weeks went by. Months. He still hasn't come out, and I don't know how long we can wait. Actually, we can't wait any longer for something that may never happen. Maisy doesn't want me going in and falling prey to whatever took him." He rubbed his face. "I don't know. Maybe I'm a fool for hoping that the cursed cave will give me back my boy. The harvest is in and the snow is sticking. It's time to hunker down and wait out the winter."

It was then that Owain considered that he wasn't the only one getting older. So was everyone else. His brother was only a few years younger than him, and he'd experienced his own life of hardships. A morbid sense of foreboding draped itself over Owain as he considered that his life, his brother's life, they were coming to a close. They were. It was a fact of life. Everybody died. Teo had made a good life for himself, been the good son that their pa had been proud of. Now their pa was gone. Their ma wouldn't be far behind him. But Owain...he was a shame to his family. His desire to change might be pure, and it might even be doable, but to what end? What could he possibly accomplish in his life now?

"I'll do it."

Teo looked up from studying his fingertips. "What?"

"I'll go. I'll look for your son. If people have emerged from that cave after months or years, maybe there's a chance that he's alive. If not, at least you'll know for sure."

To his dismay, Teo did not immediately jump on the idea. After a moment of silent contemplation, he stood and motioned for Owain to do the same. He grabbed his coat, grabbed Owain's coat which had been mended, and the two of them went outside. After a moment of consideration, Teo went back in and grabbed a couple lanterns. He handed one to Owain.

"Follow me."

Owain did so, and they got on a narrow game trail that first led down a gentle slop, then back up. Looking up, Owain could see the trees were thick straight ahead, and then they abruptly ended. To Owain's eyes, it appeared that a rockslide had caused the initial landscape, uncovering the cave, and then eager miners or curious adventurers had carved it out a little more for easier access.

The trail suddenly sloped upward. Owain wasn't prepared and tripped over himself trying to compensate. He paused for half a second as Teo held out a hand to him, then took it. That simple gesture both shamed and heartened Owain, and the coals of his hope began to fan back into a flame.

The ground leveled off and they stood above the tree line at the mercy of the wind. Before them loomed a large cave. A great stone had been rolled in front of it, but not quite all the way, as if the people who had done it got it most of the way before growing weary and figuring that it spoke for itself. Later on, someone else had moved logs and other debris to try and block the rest of the opening. Nevertheless, an opening remained, an enticing thing for an adventurous child.

"This is the cursed cave," Teo stated. "As you can see, even those who were here before us knew something wasn't right about this place. If I had known it was here, I would have built my house somewhere else. Anywhere else. Even after I learned of it, I thought that surely it was too far away for anyone to want to make the trip. Even if someone did, the warnings ought to be enough, especially for a child. I don't know, maybe I just didn't teach him right."

"I'm sure you taught him fine," Owain said. "But while we're talking about me being a despicable person, let's not forget that you got into trouble sometimes, too."

That got a small smile from Teo. "Yes, I suppose you're right. I just...I wish innocence wasn't punished so forcefully, so...absolutely." He looked at Owain. "You really think you'll be able to find him?"

"I don't know. I've never done anything like this before. But I want to at least try. I want to do something right."

Teo sighed. "I hope you're right. For your sake. Which is why I'm going to tell you this one thing: if you're serious, if you really intend on going in there and looking for Tommen, either you bring him back alive, or don't come back at all."

Owain felt his heart sink and his hopes die. "What?"

"I believe you want to change. I really do. I just don't know how far I can trust you, and I have a wife and children to look after. If you can find my boy, then we'll talk. But if not, then don't bother. I don't mind if you want to stay in the community and try to build a life for yourself, make a good life for yourself as a good man. You're just not going to do it with or near me."

"What if I find Tommen...not alive?"

"Maisy and I are still trying to get over it. I thought I was, or near enough. Maybe I never was, clinging to this superstitious hope, whatever you want to call it. The fact of the matter is, our boy is gone. Short of him walking in door alive, nothing is going to change that fact. And again, I don't know how far I can trust you. Stay in the community, fine. But stay away from me."

Owain wanted nothing more than to shout his frustration at the sky, but he refrained.

"If you want," Teo said, "you can sleep in the barn tonight and come out to start searching at first light."

After a second of hesitation, Owain shook his head. "No. If you don't want me here, then you don't want me. No time like the present to begin my search."

"I want to believe the best in you, Owain. I do. I wish I had the kind of open trust that ma has. But I don't."

"I'm not saying I blame you," Owain said, preparing his lantern. "I probably wouldn't have been so nice if our positions were reversed. I'm grateful for the chance, and I'm going to do my damnedest to bring your boy back to you alive. I guess I just never quite get over how much the stupidity of my youth has really cost me."

Teo's expression was unreadable, but sorrow was definitely in there. "Be safe, brother. Know that no matter what, I wish you the best."

Owain did not reply as he handed Teo the lantern before climbing over the logs and debris to get in the cave. Once his feet were safely on the ground, Teo handed the lantern back over. It took a minute, but then the wick sputtered to life.

"I would wish you all the best, too, Teo," he said. "But it looks like you've already got it."

Then he turned and let the lantern take him deeper into the cave.

TIME

Chapter Twenty-Six

The Trap

The flame danced in the cave, sometimes illuminating everything enough to get a vague idea of the shape and size of the cave, and sometimes doing little to show even the lantern itself.

Owain had never gone caving before, not really. He might hide in one for a short time, but overall, he tended to avoid them. As good as they were for hiding, they were also equally useful for trapping someone.

His determination to do right by his brother had brought him in, but his inexperience was going to cut this particular exploration short. Caves were cold and damp, two very bad things when you're already cold and wet. Despite his newly mended coat, Owain was still shivering. His feet hadn't fully dried and warmed over dinner, and the walk up to the cave in the snow had frozen his feet again. The chill of the cave was doing little to help him.

Another thing that was going to cut his trek short this night was sheer terror. His fears of Beaumaris and the black cells, dormant for years, now came roaring back to life as he stood in the darkness of the cave. Not a few times he could have sworn he heard something. A scream. A laugh. An echo of any number of sounds. His heart began pounding and he jumped at a noise that he came to realize was him, adding his own screams to the darkness that quickly devolved into the sobs and wails of a frightened child.

Terror gripped him, freezing his heart even as his legs and feet tried to sort themselves out so he could flee. Had to get out. Had to run. Had to get out. Had to escape. Had to flee. Run, run, run, run away, get out, flee, escape, get out, run!

He was able to slow down just a touch when he saw the cave entrance ahead of him, and he found himself thanking God that he hadn't gotten lost. What if he had? What if he'd taken a wrong turn and been stuck down there in the darkness forever? No, couldn't think about that. There was the entrance. He was going to escape, he was going to be all right. Perfectly all right.

From his time in the black cells, Owain knew well that the darkness wreaked havoc on a man in more ways than one, including his sense of time. He also knew that no matter the tricks that the darkness tried to play, there was no arguing with a lantern that was still well-lit. Sure, it hadn't been completely full when he entered the cave, but there was no way the lantern should have been able to see him through the night and into the next morning, if the light at the entrance was any indication. The nights were just too long this time of year to allow for that.

There was no way that there should have been more light when he exited than when he entered, say it that way. Still, he wasn't arguing, as he scrambled over the brush and other debris, desperate to get back into the light, into the real world.

He tumbled out and landed on his side, but he did not let go of the lantern. It wasn't until he got himself upright and standing that he again froze.

There had been snow when he went in. It had covered everything, blanketed the land, the ground, and frozen his feet. It had been growing steadily darker, and the temperature had been dropping. The air right now wasn't even very warm, so there was no way all that snow could have melted. At the same time, the air was still warmer than it should be for the time of year.

Furthermore, there was no way a leaf, once turned color and fallen, could be put back on its branch. The trees had distinctly more leaves on them now than they had when he went in. Looking off to the side, just down the trail, he spotted a tree that he could have sworn was only a sapling. Maybe he was mistaken as he hadn't been paying especially close attention, but a single maple sapling fighting for life among a cluster of pines was fairly memorable. Now a couple of the pines were fallen over, dead, and the maple appeared to be thriving.

The trail down was different, too, he noticed. Instead of going straight down, it was almost as if it had a curve to it now, the straight trail grown over and the rest of it more or less just haphazard fallen trees that happened to make a path.

Something wasn't right. He'd gone insane in that cave. Somehow, someway, something had gone screwy in his head. He wasn't right.

His first thought was that he had to get back to Teo, had to find his brother and ask what was going on, if anything was going on. Even if his brother drove him away in the end, he still needed to know that some things were still the same. Had to get back. Had to find his brother.

Was this the sickness that Teo had spoken of, when men vanished into the cave and came out again? Could he have been gone for weeks or years and not realized it? He'd dismissed it as fantasy, but Teo had put at least a little stock in it. Now he, Owain, was afflicted with madness. He couldn't have been gone long. He hadn't been in the cave for very long.

He shook his head, gripped his lantern, extinguished the flame, and stumbled toward the trail on numb legs. Something wasn't right. Maybe he was mad. Maybe the cave really was cursed by demonic forces. He had to get back to Teo and figure things out, set a starting point for himself. He had to establish something concrete.

His first problem came when he considered that without the same trail to follow—and that trail was most certainly gone, he discovered—he had no idea where he was, and no real idea of how to get back to where he needed to go. He knew a few tricks about not being found himself, but he knew very little about tracking someone else. It had taken him years to find his brother, after all. Still, he wasn't about to stop and freeze. He tightened his grip on his lantern even more as he navigated his way down the slope and through the woods.

Maybe that rooster will find me again, he thought ruefully.

But there was no sign of the rooster or any livestock at all. He didn't hear anything, didn't see anything, didn't smell anything. He could not detect any smoke as from a chimney. He heard no voices or other sounds that he might expect from a farm or any human establishment. It was almost as if he were completely alone. He didn't even have his horse.

Unbidden, he barked a laugh and shook his head. It had been a test, then, to see if he would really risk himself and his sanity for someone else. Under threat of total excommunication, would he still try to help his brother? Of course Teo would allow him back. He had to, to reclaim his horse. He would never survive the winter otherwise. Horses were transportation, companionship, pack animals, and, in dire straits, food and fur.

Yes, he could approach his brother. Maybe there would be words because he hadn't found Tommen and brought him back alive, but all would be well. And the more Owain thought about it, the more he realized how ridiculous the challenge had been. A cursed cave, ha! And finding anyone alive in a dark cave after many months of being gone? Impossible! It had all been a test, an elaborate ruse to see just how desperate he was, how committed he was to changing. He would never find Tommen alive, which meant he would have to go back to Teo, tail between his legs, and beg. Something that Owain Fforidd, mass murderer, just did not do. It was not in his character. But Owain Fforidd, mass murderer turned good man, might do it in order to prove that he'd changed and wanted to have a relationship with his brother, a real relationship. Relationships were as much about failure and forgiveness as fun and folly.

Owain let out a breath and slowed his anxious pace. All was well. It really was. He didn't need to stumble upon his brother looking like a miner gone mad from too many nights in the dark, although the thought of it was still heart-pounding. He understood now. It had been a test. Teo wanted to see that he would be willing to risk everything, accomplish nothing, and have to ask for forgiveness from those he'd wronged the most. Oh, he was a clever one. Owain admired him for it.

All the same, he really couldn't get over how the temperature was so much warmer, the snow had gone, the trees had more leaves now than when he went in, and the trail back to his brother's home had disappeared overnight.

Up ahead, he spotted a break in the trees, and the ground there looked well-packed. A road, then. Maybe he could start there and get himself oriented to his surroundings. Then he could make his way back to his brother's cottage, or maybe just back to town first. He needed to find something that he remembered, something familiar.

He slid down a small embankment to the road. It wasn't any road he recalled; it was huge. Wide and packed down, it bore the marks of horse hooves, wagon wheels, footprints, and other marks he did not recognize. It also provided a clear view down to what appeared to be a city on a large, winding river.

"That must be Charleston," he said aloud.

With something concrete in his mind, he looked around at the landscape. Charleston wasn't too far from his brother's cottage, just over a couple hills. He needed to go back the way he came, up and over, and then—

A strange noise caught his attention. It was a rumbling sound. With the trees and the mountains, it was difficult to pinpoint a source until it was almost on him. Something was coming down the road. He only had a couple knives on him, and he'd never fought a bear or a mountain lion before. At the same time, this rumbling was constant, and didn't sound like any animal noise he'd ever heard. So what...?

Owain was sure his eyes got as big as the moon when the contraption finally came around the corner in full view. It looked like a carriage, but not only was it made of metal, it needed no horses to make it move. It moved of its own accord, and the rumbling sound came from the small box attached to the front of the thing. There was a glass window in front, where he could see four men inside the horseless carriage. One of them had something in his hands, a wheel of some kind. Owain saw that as the man moved the wheel, turned it right or left, so the large carriage moved as well. The ground wheels also were not made of wood, but looked like metal covered in some kind of tar. Rubber, he decided. Another rubber wheel sat on the side of the contraption for unknown reasons. More glass windows were on each side so all the men could look out and around.

The whole thing was almost a carriage, but lacking several important elements, namely, the horses. It wasn't until the last second that he considered that regardless of what the thing was or how it moved, it was still heading straight for him, and he got out of the way at the last second. The carriage lumbered past him and came to a stop some ten paces away. One of the men poked his head out his window.

"Need a lift, old timer?"

Owain opened his mouth to ask what this contraption was and how it worked, but finally settled for, "Where you headed?"

"Charleston, where else?"

He wanted to tell them no, thank you, he was just looking for his brother, then stopped, reconsidered, and finally agreed. Teo came into Charleston once a month, to the post office to send letters back and forth to their ma. Maybe he could get directions from the post office to his brother's cottage, or at least the town.

The carriage door was opened for him and he climbed inside the back seat.

He felt utterly conspicuous, in more ways than one. The most obvious difference was their clothing. Owain wore simple cotton clothes with a heavy wool coat and gloves. These men dressed in something that vaguely resembled English finery. Their coats had wide shoulders, straight sleeves, and just a few buttons in front. Their pants weren't much different. They had cloth tied around their necks, too, almost like fine nooses. Owain didn't want to think about that and deliberately looked away.

"You don't get down to the city much, do you, old man?" the man beside him said, grinning. "Probably never seen an automobile before, have you?"

"Automobile?" Owain wondered.

"That's what they're calling them now. Used to be horseless carriages, but now they're automobiles. Fine piece of machinery right here. Henry Ford is really on to something, I think."

Owain elected not to say anything.

"You a miner?" the man on the far side asked.

"Um, no. No, I'm not."

"One of them mountain men, then. You ain't crazy, are you?"

"Honestly, I don't know. I got separated from my brother and was out looking for him, or at least his farm."

The men grumbled and murmured among themselves for a second. Probably they thought he was crazy, one of those old people who began to lose their memories until they were little better than newborn infants.

Owain had met a few of those in London, watched once proud bankers and investors become dithering idiots. He held no ill will for them, just thought it may have been more of a mercy to kill them rather than force them to live, knowing that each day was going to be worse than the last. Sometimes it had frustrated Owain to have to deal with them. Considering it now, he couldn't imagine how frustrating it must have been for them, to know that they once knew things but now they didn't.

He felt like one of those people now, in a way. But like many situations, he'd learned that the best way to handle it was to shut up and say nothing. Eventually, the other men in the car—all young, maybe in their twenties or early thirties—turned their attention and conversation back to whatever it had been before they picked up a hitchhiker. Owain didn't pay close attention, but it sounded like they were talking about girls. At least that hadn't changed, he thought.

The main thing about this horseless carriage, this automobile, was that it could really go when it wanted to, at least as fast as a galloping horse. Maybe it was the automobile or maybe it was the road, but Owain felt, numerous times, that it was more like a bucking bronco going full gallop. This thing wasn't safe! No wonder it was enclosed, else they'd all be tossed outside, like being thrown from a horse. At full speed. If there was any real advantage, it was that they weren't going to get saddle sores from the trip.

The automobile kept up the speed, too. It didn't slow down except around some corners, didn't require a rest, didn't require water. It just kept going along. Owain watched through the front glass as they sped along. The city grew larger and larger, though it was by no means as big as London or New York City. The river wound this way and that, disappearing down the valley. Pretty soon, they were coming upon a bridge. The automobile slowed a bit but was otherwise undeterred.

Now how did the automobile slow down and speed up? Owain watched as the man up front worked the peddles and moved a large center stick this way and that, but the intricacies of the machine were lost on him. He might have said this was something the Army had developed, except he had a hard time believing these young men were soldiers.

"How is talk of the war?" he asked suddenly.

"War?" one of the man questioned. "What war? The Great War is over. We won! Drove those Prussian bastards right back to the hell they crawled out of!"

Prussians? The only Prussians he knew who were involved were the ones the Confederates called Pacifists. Did that mean the Confederates really had won?

At the same time, how could a war have been won without it ever even starting? Owain knew he'd taken a little time getting from the stronghold to his brother's cottage, but certainly not long enough for a war to be begun and finished, not unless it was a very, very short war. If it had been a short war, he would have expected the North to win; they had the industry and the army. The South just...didn't. They may have had the fighting spirit, but it wasn't always enough when your enemy was just plain better than you.

Maybe it had been all politics, then. Maybe there had been a couple battles and, when everyone realized they didn't want a war, certainly not a civil war, some sort of agreement had been reached. Problem was, the way these young men made it sound, it hadn't been political; there had been fighting. And a lot of it. Or maybe it was just them. A group of young men, their blood hot, excited for victory, they were prone to embellishment.

Owain let it go. He had to, once he saw the state of the city.

The architecture was different, fine. He could accept that. The layout and the amenities were a bit different, fine. He could deal with that, too. There were more automobiles on the roads, intermixed with horses and traditional horse-drawn carriages and wagons, as well as innumerable pedestrians.

It was the people that really caught his attention. Not even the men, really, though their clothes be outlandish. It was the women. God Almighty, the women.

Except for his wife and any number of women whom he'd paid for sex, never had he seen a woman's skin bared in broad daylight. Even the prostitutes in the brothels had worn skirts down to their ankles—a few inches above their ankles if they really wanted to be scandalous. Here, the skirts were mid-calf, even up to the knee. Shirts had short sleeves, even no sleeves, and the neck was cut low. Some just showed the bare chest, but a few teased cleavage. Jewelry was big and gaudy, almost to the point of being tawdry. Hair adornments were all over the place, most of them sporting short lace veils and feathers of some form. Some women wore evening gown gloves to their elbows for reasons Owain could not begin to understand, given the short skirts. And there! A group of women wore pants. Pants, of all things!

One of the young men laughed and slapped him on the back. "You don't get into town much, do you?"

"Um, no. No, I don't. It's been a while." Owain swallowed nervously.

Teo had only talked about the post office. He failed to mention that Charleston was apparently a city of prostitutes. What else did he do on his monthly excursions to town? Was he faithful? Did Maisy know about all of this?

"Wait, wait, what's that?" Owain asked, pointing. " 'Whites only. No Colored.' " Another sign. " 'Colored waiting room.' "

"Why?" one of the men asked, his tone decidedly less friendly. "You got a problem with it? You a sore loser, Confederate?"

"I'm not a Confederate at all. I've just...never seen one before." Sore loser? So the North had won, then. And defeated the Prussians? What?

"Well, there ain't too many of them around here, that's true," another man said, tone neutral. West Virginia is pretty white. There's more automobiles than colored folks around here, and if you ain't never seen an automobile, it don't surprise you never seen a colored folk neither."

Owain wanted to inform him that he had seen colored folk and plenty of them during his time in the South, but given their general attitude toward Confederates, he elected to remain silent on that matter.

"What year is it?" he ventured cautiously.

"The year? Boy, you really don't get out much. Or maybe you are crazy. It's 1923."

1923? Nineteen...twenty-three? Nineteen...twenty-three. Nineteen twenty-three. 1923. Owain could feel the blood leave his face as he looked outside again.

Nineteen twenty-three. 1923. No, no, no, no, no, no, no, that wasn't right. It was 1855. Somewhere around November, he wasn't quite sure, but he knew it was 1855. Eighteen fifty-five.

1923, that was seventy years. Seventy years he'd been in that cave. But how? That...it just wasn't possible.

His brother would be dead. He'd died waiting for him to come back with his son. Owain hadn't returned. Teo probably thought he hadn't found Tommen and wandered off, just like he'd told him to. Come back with Tommen alive, or don't come back at all. And he'd done just that. Or not done, as the case may be.

No, this had to be someone's idea of a joke. A cruel joke. But why? And how would they even know to play it on him? Had Teo orchestrated this? No, it was far too elaborate and precise; Teo couldn't have known when he was going to come out of the cave. Only God could do something like this to him.

All right, God, you got me. You've frightened me. Because a noose apparently wasn't frightening enough, now you've got me thinking that seventy years have passed. What's the joke?

Owain had seen some strange things in his time. During his time as an investor, even if he hadn't dealt directly with foreign traders and investors, he'd at least seen them. People from all around the world. All across Europe, China and Asia. He'd seen a number of Negros in the South, carrying on their own traditions even as they toiled in the fields. He'd seen America from North to South, traveled through countless cities and towns, a dozen states. Each one was different, but they were also very similar.

None of it was like what he saw before him now. He couldn't even be sure he was still in America except he wasn't sure how he could have left. Of course, he couldn't explain how he'd jumped seventy years into the future, either. A pit opened up in his stomach even as his whole body twisted with fear.

"All right, old timer, this is where we're stopping," the man with the wheel said, bringing the automobile to a halt and turning it off. The rumbling ceased and the quiet was almost foreign. "You know where you need to go?"

"Um, the post office," Owain told him, hoping that still existed at least.

They clambered out of the car, Owain still holding his lantern.

"Yeah, sure." One of the men pointed south. "Two blocks that way, take a left. And be safe when crossing the streets; people are absolutely scrambled."

"Thank you. I'm afraid I don't have very much money..." He dug in his pockets, but the men waved their hands dismissively.

"No problem," one said. "Listen, we're young and dumb, but our mamas still taught us to respect our elders. Consider it a favor."

"Oh. Thank you."

Actually, Owain's first thought was, *Do I really look and sound that old? Confused, sure, but old?* He felt rather insulted, honestly. But the young men were already going about their business, ducking into a store. Taking a breath, Owain turned south and started walking. He crossed the first street with little incident and kept going. His attention was divided between wanting nothing more than to find the post office and looking at all the scantily-clad women. Hey, he was changed, but it was like trying to ignore the water while on the ocean. And besides, he was still a man.

He found the post office easily enough. On one wall were posters of wanted men. Thankfully, he did not see his name or picture up there.

"Can I help you, sir?"

He turned to see a man standing behind the counter, watching him intently. Owain cautiously stepped up to speak.

"Yes, um, I'm looking for my brother's house. I haven't seen him in a long time. He lives in the mountains. But I know that you deliver mail to him. I was really just hoping you could give me directions."

The man considered it for a moment and nodded. "That might be something I can do. What's the name?"

"Teo Fforidd." He spelled it out while the man flipped through a large ledger.

"Sorry, sir, no one by that name in my book," the man said.

"What about Forbes? His name got changed when he came over."

The man looked here and there and finally nodded. "All right, I have a Tommen Forbes listed —"

"Tommen? Tommen Forbes?"

The man nodded. "That's what I said. Anyway, I'll write down the official address. If you want to follow it, go ahead. But my guy who runs that route is still out. You can come back tonight around seven o'clock, or tomorrow morning before five and you can talk to him. Hell, he might even let you ride with him."

"That would be perfect."

The postman gave Owain the address and wished him a good day.

Owain left the post office feeling elated. So Tommen had wandered back on his own. Owain was in the clear and Teo would accept him back regardless if it had been a test. All was right with the world once more!

But what to do for the next few hours? He was still stuck in a strange town, and he still hadn't been able to prove one way or the other whether it was 1855 or 1923. It seemed a ridiculous notion that he should have to prove whether today was today, but something just wasn't right here, and he had to know. He had to assure himself that he hadn't gone mad in that cave.

At the end of the block, he spotted a newspaper stand. Must have been slow news today since the man or his young helper weren't jumping out at everyone, desperate to sell a newspaper. Trying not to look like a madman, Owain strode up to the stand, fished out a little money, and turned over a penny to the boy.

October 3, 1923. There it was in black and white, the year 1923. There were just too many large, disconnected factors when it came to saying this was a joke. But he still couldn't make it all fit together in his mind. This just wasn't possible! There was no explanation for how all this happened, how it came to be. It was impossible!

Had God done this to him on purpose? For what reason? Was he just not meant to find his brother? Was his quest so errant and his will so bold that the only way to deter him was by literally taking him out of the time where he was and throwing him into the future? His brother was dead. His sisters would all be dead. His pa had already died, but his ma was surely gone now, too.

Owain's heart was racing and he vaguely realized that he was practically running down the sidewalk. He deliberately slowed his pace to something like a fast walk, though he was sure he still appeared as a madman to outsiders. A wild noise echoed in his mind and he realized that an automobile had come to a stop, almost running him over. The driver was yelling at him. Owain put up a hand and may have yelled a pardon, but he got across the road to the other side with no further incident.

Still panicking, he ducked into the first shop he came across. To his horror and relief, it was a pub.

Horror, because he wanted to be a good man, a changed man. This was a scene he knew all too well, knew exactly where it led.

Relief, because this was a scene he knew all too well. This was something familiar. This was something that hadn't changed in seventy years. This was a place where he could get his bearings.

And what the hell, he might as well have a beer, too. Changed man or not, he needed to figure things out, figure out what had just happened to him, and he knew he couldn't do it completely sober.

He ambled up to the bar and sat down. Familiar. Friendly.

"What can I get for you, old timer?" the barman asked from the other end.

"A beer. Any kind," Owain told him, heart still hammering in his chest.

"Ha! You and me both! What else do you want?"

"This is a pub, isn't it? You don't serve alcohol?"

The man walked over and leaned on the bar. "Listen, I'd love to. But Prohibition has forced my hand."

"Prohibition? You mean there's no alcohol?"

"Nowhere in these great United States." He lowered his voice. "Now then, if you make it yourself, well, who's going to know? And sometimes, those people who do make it themselves might be convinced to, ah, part with it. For a nominal fee."

"How much?"

"Thirty-five cents."

It was far more than he wanted to pay, but Owain obliged. If the United States really had outlawed alcohol, well, it was a good way to keep a drunk man clean, but with everything that was happening to him lately, he would take it where he could get it.

He didn't remember a whole lot about what followed. He got a second beer, got talking. Someone else bought him a third, and he talked some more. He may have started saying something about it being 1855 and jumping seventy years; he was fairly certain he mentioned it at least. Then there were more people, and yelling. Then he was yelling. He took his lantern and swung it at someone or something. It connected.

Then something connected with the back of his head and he was out.

Chapter Twenty-Seven

The Jailer

He ended up in jail with a vicious hangover. But that, too, was familiar, almost a comfort. Not much of one, but he needed the familiarity of anything at this point, good or bad. At some point, he was given food and water.

He found himself in a cell with maybe a dozen or more other men, all of them looking like they'd had a rough night. He didn't recognize any of them from the pub, but he hadn't exactly been in there to meet people and be friendly. None of them were glaring at him or sizing him up, though, so that was a good start.

There were footsteps outside the cell, getting closer. Owain gave a cursory glance in that direction but did not move like the rest of them. Two jailers came to the door.

"Everyone back!" one barked, far too loud for Owain's taste. "James Campbell?"

"That's me," one man said.

"Your wife said to leave you here, but your brother came to the rescue." The jailer unlocked the door. "Get out."

The man was too happy to leave the cell, slipping outside and vanishing down the hall with the jailers.

A few more men were retrieved by various family members throughout the day. By about noontime, or what Owain approximated as noontime, there were ten of them left. By now, no one moved except to look up when the jailers came around, and Owain didn't even bother to do that much.

"That the one?" one of the jailers asked.

"That's him," the second replied. "Came in stark raving mad, claiming it was 1850 or something. I think Ralph's moonshine may have been a little strong this batch myself."

"Well, I can't speak to that, and I'll pretend I didn't hear it, either. You! Forbes!"

Now Owain looked up, even managed to sit up.

"That is your name, isn't it?" the one jailer said.

"Actually it's Fforidd, but that got changed, too, it seems," Owain said, rubbing his face.

"Come with me."

He doddered to his feet and meekly followed the jailer down the hall. He was shorter than Owain, maybe five-ten, well-built. He had a full head of thick brown hair that almost looked red in a certain light. He also sported a thick, full beard, and he walked with a quiet confidence, not strutting, but not uncertain.

Owain was taken to a small room with a few chairs and an empty table and told to wait, which he did. He did not even presume to help himself to a chair. The jailer returned a few minutes later, hat and coat gone, all weapons relinquished except for a revolver on his hip.

"Come with me," the man repeated. "Let's you and I have a chat." They went out the door to the outside. "I'm Mark. Mark Walker."

"Owain Fforidd, but sometimes I'm called Walter Forbes."

"Do you know what an automobile is? Have you ever ridden in one?"

"Earlier today. I was up on the mountain and some young men gave me a ride down."

Owain followed Mark out to the street where an automobile was parked. Mark motioned for Owain to get in, which he did. Mark got in, started it up, and soon they were rumbling along.

"Are you taking me to the asylum?" Owain wondered.

Mark grinned and shook his head. "No. Actually, I'm taking you to my house. Get you cleaned up, get some food in your belly, and then we'll talk about what happened."

"How do you know what's happened? How much did I say when I was drunk?"

"Enough to catch my attention. Don't worry, we'll talk about it. How does a bath and a hot meal sound?"

Owain sighed. "Sounds mighty fine, honestly."

"Excellent. I'm a bit peckish myself. Let's see if we can't make your day just a little better, hm?"

It sounded too good to be true, but Owain found he had no other options. So he just kept his mouth shut and went along with it.

Mark lived in a house unlike anything Owain had seen before except in rich London, and even then, it was still unlike anything he'd really seen before. When asked, Mark lived alone, no wife, no children, and no hired staff. No slaves either (apparently that was also outlawed now). Just him. So much room for just one man.

And indoor plumbing? Water at a whim? Unthinkable! Owain simply stared at the water coming out of the faucet, turned it on and off several times himself just to be sure he was seeing straight and the alcohol, the moonshine, wasn't still messing with him. But no, there it was. Fresh water at a whim. There was even hot water, too. No need to build a fire or anything, just turn on the other faucet and there it was.

There was also this thing about indoor electricity, just flipping a switch and instant light! Mark explained that these were both very new inventions and hardly common except for those who had the means. For Owain, though, it may as well have been a bona fide miracle from God Himself.

Owain felt his anxiety ramp up again, but it was quickly dissipated as he got in the bathtub full of warm water, an electric light hanging over him from the ceiling. Elsewhere in the house, he could hear Mark in the kitchen. A few minutes later, the wonderful smell of food. Pot roast, if his nose did not deceive him.

Mark had gotten out some of his own clean clothes for Owain to wear, but no matter how great the intentions, the clothes just wouldn't fit, and Owain was forced back into his old clothes. Gingerly, he left the bathroom and headed out to the kitchen.

"How does a big man like you try to sneak around like a church mouse?" Mark asked, not looking up from his work. "Never mind, don't answer that. I understand. I hope you're still hungry because I can't eat all of this by myself."

It was indeed pot roast, complete with mashed potatoes, green beans, and rolls. Owain tried to be a little dignified about it, but his appetite won out and he devoured his plate plus a second helping. Meanwhile, Mark ate but a child's portion, his attention more on Owain than his food.

"Feel better?" Mark asked as Owain sopped up the last of the gravy with his roll.

Owain just nodded.

The man shifted position in his chair. "That's good. Now then, why don't we talk a little bit about what's happened?"

It ruined Owain's last bite, but he agreed.

"The year is 1923. If you really are from 1855, then that's a seventy year jump that you've made. A lot of things have changed, and everyone you ever knew is quite likely dead."

Owain felt his heart stop, but he did not respond.

"Just judging from what you've already said, my guess is that you went into an old salt cave. Maybe you heard legends that it was cursed, that men went in and didn't come out for months or years later."

"You know it?"

Mark nodded. "I know it. I've never been in it, but I've been to it. And I've met others who have gone in it."

"Any children?"

"Mercifully, no. Of course, adults aren't much better. To date, of the ones I have met, only one of them has survived."

Owain looked at him warily. "What do you mean, 'survived'?"

Mark shifted position again. "I mean that the mind is a fragile thing. Jumping weeks or months into the future, a man can recover from that. He may be confused and afraid, but little has changed. A few years into the future, maybe he can get himself back together. But when you start talking in decades...people have a hard time letting go and accepting what's happened. Most often, it really has to do with losing everyone you once knew and loved. People can adapt to new technology easier than they can adapt to such sudden loss and the feeling of lonesomeness."

"What happened to the rest of them that didn't survive?"

"I was given only two choices: take them to an asylum and hope they eventually came around, or kill them. I believe death is a mercy for such a person. Just a bad nightmare before they meet their Maker."

"Is that what you intend to do to me?" Owain indicated the revolver at Mark's hip.

"Do you want me to?" Mark countered. "I'm asking seriously. I have done it. I don't like to, but many times, it is necessary. I don't know what kind of life you had before, but it's gone now. Wife, children, they're all gone. Might be that grandchildren would still be alive—"

"How old do you think I am?" Owain cut in.

Mark put his hands up defensively. "All right, I'm sorry. The point is, I don't know. But whatever you did have, it's gone now. Completely. You will never get it back. You will never speak to your parents again, your siblings, your wife and children. It's all gone. On the one hand, it's all gone. On the other hand, it's a chance to start over, if you want."

Owain sighed and rubbed his face, ran his fingers through his hair which had gotten quite long, actually. Finally he said, "I'm a murderer. I escaped from prison ten y—well, I suppose it would be eighty years ago now. 1847, anyway. I came over to America looking for my brother and for a chance to change my ways."

"Where are you from?"

"Wales."

"Really? I didn't even notice an accent."

Owain shook his head and put a fist to his mouth as tears sprang to his eyes. "Nope. You wouldn't. Because...my wife—well, my ex-wife, she taught me how to speak with a London accent and an American accent."

Mark frowned. "Did she come with you to America?"

"No. She's the reason I ended up in prison. I beat her and she divorced me. She remarried, and then her new husband killed her. And our daughter. So I killed her new husband. And my ex-father-in-law. And four of his associates." Owain sniffed hard. "I was supposed to hang, but I escaped." He wiped his eyes. "Is this God's punishment for me? That I should lose everything so completely?"

"I should say that maybe it is God's provision. You have a chance to start over. Completely. No sane person would arrest you for a murder committed eighty years ago. They could never prove it."

"But my ma...and my brother...they never knew what happened to me, not really."

Mark was silent for a long moment. Then, "No. They wouldn't."

"They would think something terrible had happened to me. Maybe I was killed or just got lost in the cave and never came out." Owain wiped his eyes again, though the tears had stopped. "My brother lived not far from the cave. He's the one who showed it to me."

"Who was your brother?"

"Teo Fforidd. Well, Teo Forbes. His son, Tommen, he went in the cave, too. Teo told me that if I wanted to stay with him—we weren't on good terms, me being a murderer and all—I would go in and find his son." He sniffed. "But, I asked the postman and he said that Tommen is living up there. So he must have come out."

Mark shook his head. "Not the same. Everyone around here knows the story of Tommen Forbes, the little boy who disappeared in the old salt cave. Teo Sr. had a son, Teo Jr., right?"

"That's right."

"He named one of his sons Tommen, for his lost little brother. That's the Tommen living up there now."

Owain sighed. "Oh."

"I'm sorry. That doesn't mean that little Tommen didn't come out, or that he won't ever. It might just be a little while."

"Yeah, another seventy years after I'm gone and he has no family left whatsoever."

Mark's expression turned unreadable, but it was somewhere between amused and excited. "See, that's where you're wrong."

Owain shook his head. "I don't understand. I'm forty years old. There's no way I'm going to live another seventy years, not after the life I've lived."

"Maybe not, but how about a new life?"

"I still don't understand."

"Follow me. It's easier to show you if there's activity going on."

It didn't have to be a lot of activity, Mark explained, just enough to notice that stuff was happening, or not happening. They went outside. Mark lived on the outskirts of town, close enough that he could go to work every day, but still with some privacy. He had a few neighbors, but they were spread out at a respectable distance. There was a little activity going on out here in the middle of the afternoon, people outside in their own yards, birds singing and flitting from branch to branch in the trees, squirrels busy storing nuts for the winter. A wind came through and shook the trees, sending a flurry of leaves spiraling to the ground.

Suddenly, everything stopped. The leaves froze in mid-air, the birds as well. The squirrels stopped chittering, one as still as a statue upon a small branch, gnawing on an acorn. People stopped moving and speaking, and an automobile coming up the road came to a dead stop. And all of this was awash with a faint golden hue, as if a beautiful sunset had settled over the land.

"What happened?" Owain asked, heart leaping into his throat.

"Put simply, I stopped Time," Mark answered.

"You stopped Time? Time? Seriously?" Owain took a few steps away from the man. "What magic is this?"

Mark shook his head. "Not magic. Time is one of the basic elements of the universe. We can mark it out however we wish, but the truth of it is, Time is an element. It can't be broken down any more. It is one of the purest things to spring forth from the imagination of God Himself. Some of us are trained in its manipulation, to make it go faster or slower at will, and there are other things to learn. In time, it slows your aging until it simply stops, or appears to."

Owain was paralyzed with fear and could only force himself to swallow.

"I know it's a lot to take in," Mark said, remaining calm. "I know it's unlike anything you've ever seen, and if you've heard anything about it, likely it came across just as you described, magic and sorcery."

"Why would any man want to control Time and do such a thing? Even if it's not magic, God must be angry about it."

"I don't know," Mark admitted. "But consider this, why would anyone want to do such a thing? There are people out there who want to twist and bend Time for ill gain. Maybe monetary gain, maybe political gain, maybe something else entirely. If you could stop Time like I am now, as a criminal, what could you accomplish?"

Owain looked around at everything, frozen in place. "Could you kill a man?"

Mark nodded. "I could walk or drive into Charleston, kill a man, and return home. No one would know until I released the Band. That's what it's called, when you stop Time. You encase yourself in a Band."

"Has anyone ever done that? Killed someone and that person, the victim, never knew until they were dead?"

"Yes. Which is where I come in. And others like me. We're called Timekeepers. We're like the police of the Time industry. Our governing body is the Hands of Time. We apprehend and prosecute criminals unrecognized by the common judicial system." He continued before Owain could speak. "This is the offer I make to you, Owain. Accept Time, learn to use it as I have, become a Timekeeper. Do something good with your life, a new life that you build however you want. A fresh start. Or, I can send you to meet your brother."

Owain looked around again at the frozen elements and ran a hand through his hair. "Back in Wales, when I was in prison, the priest told me that I was not destined to die there. I would not hang. My path involved a cave, far away across the ocean."

"Sounds like he knew what he was talking about."

"I just don't know that I can. How can I lecture others about murder when I myself have murdered? How can a thief condemn others for theft?"

Mark shrugged calmly. "Perhaps by experience. Believe me when I say I do not enjoy the trials and punishments that the Hands of Time bestow upon criminal Runners. If repentance is genuine, I am more than happy to accept it. If rehabilitation is possible, then it ought to come from those who have been rehabilitated. It sounds like you have been to some dark places, both literally and figuratively. Some men will only listen to those who have gone before them, down those dark paths."

"I've been right up to death's door," Owain murmured. "I escaped less than a week before I was supposed to hang. I thought, a bad man who has changed can do more good than a good man who is dead."

"That may be true. I would certainly believe it."

He shook his head. "But I can't. Not yet. I...I have to get clean first. I can't help others get clean if I'm still in the mud pit with them." He looked at Mark. "I need to go to chapel."

Mark nodded calmly. "Today is Saturday. I'll take you to church in the morning, if that's what you want."

Owain nodded vigorously. "It is. I do. I need to get myself right with God before I can have any authority over anyone else, least of all myself."

Mark did not disagree, but he stopped Owain from going back inside. They had to return to their original positions when the Band was first created, otherwise, it would appear as though they'd simply appeared out of thin air, he explained. It wasn't about slowing down Time for everyone else, but speeding it up for themselves. They had been moving faster than anyone else, faster than anyone would be able to normally perceive. They had to keep this a secret.

Mark dropped the Band and life went on as though nothing had happened. Birds flew, squirrels chittered, and leaves fell. The two of them went back inside.

"At any rate," Mark went on, sitting to relax in a plush chair in his living room, "we need to figure out a few things for you, about your life."

"What do you want to know?" Owain inquired, gingerly taking a seat in another chair.

"Everything. And I don't mean your past life. That's all it is at this point. A past life. It really happened, and it's really you, but now things need to be adjusted a little. If you're forty now, that means you were born in 1883."

"Oh. That might be a little difficult to say I was born in 1815."

"Indeed it would. What year were you born?"

"I said 1815."

"Wrong. What year were you born?"

"Oh. Um, 1883."

"What year?"

"1883."

His name was Owain Fforidd. He was born in 1883 in Wales. His younger brother came over to America before him while he stayed home to help his ma and pa on their farm. He never married and had no children because he'd always intended on going into the clergy but was never able to leave home on account of helping his parents, for they were often ill. After they passed, he came over to seek out his brother. He arrived on Ellis Island in 1921 and spent two years searching for his brother. Unbeknownst to him, his brother had died. The rest of the family had taken over his land and farm. Now Owain was trying to figure out what to do with himself.

In a way, it was kind of everything he'd ever wanted, even if he never realized it. A chance to build whatever life he wanted, construct the world into which he was born. And yet, spending the better part of an afternoon with Mark doing just that...it made him feel nauseous.

Was this right? Should he be doing this? Was it dishonoring his family? Was it angering the Almighty? How far could he trust Mark, this man who had offered to kill him? He had no clue what to think, what to make of all of this. At times, thinking about it, it all seemed so overwhelming he thought about telling Mark just to kill him. Other times, he told himself just to keep his mouth shut and go along with it. Less trouble had come from his silence than his words.

Finally, just as the sun was going down, Mark stood and stretched and announced that their "life-building" session was finished for the evening. He had to get some sleep. He worked odd hours and sleep did not always come easy, so he took it when he could.

"We'll go to church in the morning," he promised, yawning. "I know just the one. For tonight, you can sleep on the couch."

Owain nodded. "Thank you."

"It's not the most comfortable, but—"

"No. I mean. Thank you. For helping me."

The man shrugged. "I try. It's all I can do, just try, and see what happens."

Mark wished him a good night and wandered off to bed. Owain was still quite awake, but he obediently lay down on the couch. It wasn't a plush feather bed, but it was nicer than a jail cell or the cold, hard ground. It was funny to think that at some point, he ought to at least go back up and retrieve his horse. But the horse would have died long before Teo.

Everything was gone. The whole world that he had known, completely gone. All the people in it. The priest, Father Forthill. The warden and his gaolers, especially that one gaoler who particularly enjoyed beating him.

His ma.

His brother.

His brother's family.

His sisters and their families.

All gone.

Owain quietly cried himself to sleep, all the while debating whether he shouldn't ask Mark to kill him. But then he was waking up. Day three in the year 1923. He was still alive, and the world kept turning. His hangover had gone, thankfully. His stomach was hungry, and, despite his fear and anxiety, part of his mind also wondered what he planned on doing today, what his goals were, what he hoped to accomplish.

He was going to church, for one. That was one thing he had to do before doing anything else. He had to get right with God and step into his new life a changed man, free and clear of all condemnation both on Earth and in Heaven above.

Then it would probably be lunch time. Eating and food hadn't changed, and it was one thing he found he could look forward to with no shame or guilt. Food was food, and he enjoyed it. Probably his years of being on the road or in prison, and constantly starving both times, had instilled in him a greater appreciation for food in general, to say nothing of how he already enjoyed cooking.

Strange how old instincts kicked in when his mind wasn't working. Survival of self, first and foremost. Where is food going to come from, how is he going to stay safe, and where is he going to sleep? Sleep, well, Mark seemed to have opened up his home for the time being, so that was tentatively taken care of. Safety, well, he wasn't in any immediate danger that he could perceive, so that had to count for something. Food...Mark was kind enough for the time being, but, like shelter, it was only a temporary arrangement, and he had little desire to go rooting around in the man's kitchen. Shelter could be made anywhere out of almost anything. Food could be a little harder to come by, especially in the fall and winter.

He lay on the couch for a short time, wondering what time it was, wondering if this was all really happening, wondering how long Mark planned on sleeping in before going to church. True, Sunday was a day of rest and even farmers might ignore the cockcrow for a few minutes, but eventually...time to get up.

Owain pulled himself upright and looked around. The house was quiet. Moving carefully, he got up and walked around, tried to take it all in. So this was what houses looked like now. This was how people lived. It was almost like city living, but kind of in the country, too. It was bizarre.

He went back to the couch as an unfamiliar rumble approached the house. It took him a minute to realize that the rumble was an automobile. A few seconds later, Mark walked in, carrying several bags.

"Have you been awake long?" the man inquired politely.

"No," Owain replied simply, unsure if it was even true.

"Well, you were asleep when I got up, and I figured you could use all the rest you could get. I went into town and got some clothes for you. I'm pretty confident they'll fit, but go ahead and try them on." Mark crossed the room and handed Owain all but one bag. "They're pretty generic, compared to the rest of the Roaring Twenties, but you won't look like a hermit just come off the mountain. Anyway, get cleaned up a bit and then we'll go to service."

Owain nodded as he briefly glanced through the clothes, three shirts and three pairs of pants, along with a few other necessities and accessories. A hairbrush, for one. It took him longer than he normally would have preferred to get ready, but even such a simple task felt so difficult when everything looked and felt so foreign. The clothes were wildly different, though it was nice to have clothes that were new, clean, and they even fit well. He brushed his hair back, then asked Mark to cut it short. Once that was done, he took the razor and got himself cleaned up.

By the time he was done, he didn't even recognize himself. In a way, it was terrifying, because it also reminded him of his time in London, when he ended up becoming something he wasn't, and it had nothing to do with the murders. But it was also a chance to start fresh, be the man he wanted to be. That meant changing a few things and getting rid of pieces of himself. It was making a physical change in order to signify and metaphorical or spiritual one.

"So, which one is the real you?" Mark wondered.

"Doesn't matter," Owain found himself saying. "Because it's not the shell that matters. It's the man inside."

Half an hour later, they were sitting in Sunday service at a small church elsewhere in the outskirts of Charleston. It wasn't the exact same as what he remembered from home, but it was wonderful all the same. Not much had changed in the spiritual department it seemed, except for the part where plenty of people had departed from the church—both Catholic and Protestant—on account of The Great War. Owain was dealing with the aftermath of his own great war. Maybe he was still fighting.

He went up to the altar afterwards to pray, Mark keeping the preacher at a respectful distance for a time.

"God, I don't know what this is," Owain said, speaking in Welsh to hopefully avoid any eavesdroppers. "And I still don't know how to pray, so you'll have to forgive me for that, too. I choose to believe that this is the second chance I've been waiting for. It's not the one I would have chosen. It's not the way I thought any of this would turn out, but it's what You have deemed best for me. It's going to take some getting used to, and I'm sure I'll mess up. A lot.

"All I want is to make this second chance count, to do things right. Not my way. My way has brought me nothing but trouble and it's taken me to the brink of death. Maybe this time I'll try it Your way. If You'll have me. If You can forgive my past sins and let me start this new life as a new man, a new creation. Show me Your Way. I have no parents anymore, but I hear that You're the same God in 1923 as you were in 1855 and can be a Father to anyone.

"I don't know how much I trust Mark, honestly, and I'm terribly skeptical of this Time business, but man has no power except what You have given him. If You say man can manipulate Time, then it must be that man can manipulate Time. Maybe there's a story behind it, maybe there's a reason to it, but I don't know. Maybe I don't need to know. Like I said, my way has brought nothing but trouble, and I'm sorry for it. I guess this is a step out in faith for Your way. I don't know how this works. Guess I'll just keep going in one direction until you direct me otherwise. How does that sound? Probably sounds like a stupid human, but I'm trying. I really am.

"I want to believe Father Forthill when he said that You don't forsake anyone, no matter how evil. As long as I draw breath, he always told me. Well, if he's up there with You, tell him..." Owain let out a slow breath. "Tell him I said thank you. For not giving up on me. And if one mortal can care so deeply about a person for their soul and not give up on them, I guess You can do it a thousand times better.

"I want to get it right this time. Show me how."

He paused. There was a lot more he wanted to say, but it was all just variations of everything he'd just said. Finally he tacked on an "Amen" and stood.

Gingerly, the priest approached. Owain wiped his eyes and nodded. The priest embraced him and welcomed him into the family. Owain simply said he was glad for the second chance. Even Mark, who proclaimed to understand what had happened in that cave, could never understand how he felt now. The relief, the peace, the hope, even. For the first time in his life, the mat where the beast had always lain or prowled around or raged...was empty. It was gone. And his mind was now flooded with thoughts and emotions he didn't even know he was capable of experiencing.

Owain Fforidd walked out of that church a changed man.

Chapter Twenty-Eight

The Test

My name is Owain Fforidd. I was born in Wales in 1883. I wanted to become a priest, but I had to stay home and help my ailing parents on their farm. My brother came over to America in 1908 with his wife and children. In 1921, after my parents died, I also came over to America in search of my brother. I did not know that he had passed away. I now live in the state of West Virginia with a friend until I can figure out what to do with my life."

Owain signed the paper, rolled it up and stuffed it in a bottle, put the cork in the bottle snugly, and tossed it into the ocean.

It was six months since Owain walked out of the salt cave into 1923, and it had been quite a tumultuous time. He still didn't understand a lot. A lot of things confused or frightened him. And despite his promise to God to change, he had returned to alcohol on a few occasions, quickly learning the whereabouts of a few illicit moonshine brewers. After his last stint landed him in jail again, Mark thought it would be a good idea to take him on a short tour of America, show him how things worked now, show him a few things he would need to know, places he ought to be familiar with.

One of these places was Ellis Island, the immigrant processing center in New York City. This was where he supposedly came to get into America.

It was a lot different than the boardinghouse, say it that way.

Mark had drilled his new life into his head so vehemently, sometimes even Owain wondered whether everything else really happened. Real memories mixed with a falsified story to conjure up something totally new in his mind. Honestly, he didn't like it. He didn't like not remembering things, but this distortion was far more abominable in his opinion, and several times he considered asking Mark to off him. But he did not and simply carried on as he always had. He kept his mouth shut and trudged along because he had no other choice.

As far as this whole "Time" thing went, Mark had demonstrated more of it, explained what it was and basically how it worked. He explained more about the Timekeeping system, that there were ranks and officers, much like a standard police force.

There were other aspects of Time as well, he said. There were Harvesters, who extracted Time from dying people and sold it to Merchants who then sold it to others in the form of Time Capsules. These Capsules were used to lengthen one's lifespan. Mark demonstrated this a bit by "anointing" Owain with a One Base Year Time Capsule.

"Voila!" Mark said. "You will now live one more year than you would have normally."

"I don't feel any different," Owain told him, immensely skeptical. "And I don't know how I would feel about that, lying on my deathbed, thinking that I could have died a year previous. And what happens if I'm run over by an automobile, or get killed in a fight? Will it help me then?"

"No," Mark explained. "It only affects your natural lifespan. Time is a tool, not medicine. You can heal your wounds, but that's only because you are condensing the Base Time needed to heal into only a few seconds or minutes or what-have-you. If you don't set a bone correctly, Time will still heal the wound, but it will be crooked and painful."

But perhaps the most wild part of Mark's explanation of Time was when he talked about the Scouts. They were tasked with bringing new peoples into Time. And by new peoples, he meant other races. And by other races, he meant aliens.

Yes. Extraterrestrial beings.

Yes. From outer space.

Yes. Living on other worlds and, sometimes, traveling through space in flying saucers.

Owain had told Mark to stop at that point just so he could process it.

Manipulation of Time? Fine. He could wrap his head around that after a while, giving it little bits of his attention at a time and gradually coming to terms with Mark's demonstrations, as well as his own experience. All right, fine, that was acceptable. It was a tough piece of meat to swallow, but he could do it.

Extraterrestrial beings from outer space? That was a little tougher.

Man was created in the image of God, and all the beasts were beneath him. Where did aliens fit into all of this?

Had his prayers been in vain, simply talking to the air? Was God not the way the Bible proclaimed? Was the Bible perhaps incomplete? Had Mark simply been humoring him when he said he wanted to go to church and get right with God? And what of his beast? Had it only ever been a figment of his imagination, something to simply point to as a cause for his misbehavior? Would he never truly be rid of it?

When he posed these questions to Mark, the man simply stated that just because man could not perceive the whole picture of something did not mean that the part he could see was untrue. It was merely incomplete. He didn't know where aliens fit into God's design and Creation, but he simply worked with what he saw.

It was that conversation which led to Owain drinking again which landed him in jail and so sparked this tour of America. He needed to get himself grounded again, Mark said. Get his mind out of outer space and back on Earth, back in the real world. Humans had very few dealings in the Time industry and most of their time was spent simply living, with a few secrets on the side. That was what he needed to focus on right now.

The idea behind writing down his new life was just to solidify the idea. The idea behind stuffing it in a bottle and throwing it in the harbor was more just because it would be interesting to see where it went and if it would ever come back around.

"So, what do you remember about this place?" Mark asked casually, walking up beside him.

"Not much because it's been a few years," Owain told him smartly. "I know I'm glad I only had to come through once."

"Good answer."

"I know it's necessary, but I feel terrible about lying about myself. Wouldn't it have been better to say that I was a miner who got lost and separated from the rest of the group in that old salt cave?"

"Maybe, but this is the life you've built for yourself. As for feeling bad about lying, that's when you have to drill it in your head even more. You have to really believe what you're saying."

"I'm trying to be a good man, but my whole life is built on lies."

"Maybe so, but for the time being, the world isn't ready for the truth."

Mark continued to drill Owain on his new life. Where he was from, his family, his education, how he got from point A to point B. As Owain learned more about the world and the seventy years of history he missed, Mark drilled him on that, too, at least so he didn't come across as a completely ignorant buffoon, the only moron in the world who didn't know about The Great War. As for the Civil War, well, he could be excused on account that he was Welsh, but just in case, the North won and the South still generally resented it. The same could be said for his lack of knowledge concerning American geography and all the states that had been formed since 1855. Sea to shining sea, that was America.

Their trip took them from New York City, down to Georgia, along similar roads as when Owain moved up and down the map looking for his brother and a way to access the mountains. The mountains were much more accessible now, and they returned to Charleston in only a fraction of the time, thanks to the automobile.

Owain was living on his own now, renting a small apartment in town. Mark had gotten him a job as a cook for the jail, and so there he remained for the time being while he tried to get everything together. He really didn't do much with himself, honestly. He paid his rent and bought food, but he found he could not indulge in the Roaring Twenties like everyone else. Excess and lavish and materialism were almost foreign concepts, and his time as a wealthy banker made him blanch at the thought. He just wasn't that kind of person anymore.

So then, what was he? Who was he?

He was Owain Fforidd, born in Wales in 1883, immigrated to America in 1921 after his parents died. He went looking for his brother, but he'd passed away as well, and now he was trying to figure out what to do with himself.

"I want to be a Timekeeper," Owain told Mark one afternoon. "I don't know what I'm really going to do with myself, but if I'm going to be living two lives, I need a foot in both."

"I was hoping you'd say that."

The first thing that had to happen was he had to be formally introduced to the Hands of Time. This was the also when Owain learned how humans got to see aliens in outer space when humans couldn't get to outer space by any known mechanical means. Big words like "transdimensional" went far over his head, but the shorthand version was that Mark opened a door in the air that let them walk from Earth into a place called the Wheel of Time, which was the hub of the Time industry, where aliens from all corners of the universe gathered to talk Time.

It was the first time Owain had ever seen an alien, and he may have fainted. It was the only thing he could recall that ever caused him to faint, or else feel light-headed. But like many things, a good nap helped him to process everything.

"You're taking this a lot better than I expected you to," Mark commented as they made their way through the Wheel, dodging some large aliens and being mindful of smaller ones. The whole place was a maze, but Mark seemed to know his way around fairly well. He went on, "I've seen younger man than you unable to function after seeing half of what I've shown you."

"I guess you could say I've learned to adapt," Owain said. His voice sounded distant even to himself as he looked around at everything. Completely new. Completely alien. It was like going from Wales to London for the first time all over again, realizing that he was but an insignificant speck in all of Creation.

"At your age, it's a remarkable thing."

"Once again, exactly how old do you think I am?"

"Getting older every day. If you train well and learn quickly, it will take a year or two before your aging slows. Eventually it will seem to stop, and it may even reverse a touch. Now, you will never be a twenty year old again, but your physical health may improve some. All in the future, of course. You'll learn. You seem like a quick study."

Owain took his words as a vote of confidence as they went before the

Hands of Time, fifty-one aliens of all shapes and sizes from places he'd never even considered existed a year ago. Even so, politics was politics, and the general apathy and even disdain for the two meager humans before them was oddly reassuring. Some things really were the same across the universe it seemed.

After his formal introduction, they met with a secretary who registered him in some sort of...database. It was like a Rolodex, but it was all on a bright window, a screen it was called. It was encoded in electricity, Mark explained, different waves and pulses that brought up different things on the screen. Owain asked if he would be here frequently. When Mark told him no, not especially, Owain politely requested that learning all of this...*stuff* be kept to a minimum if it wasn't essential on Earth. Mark agreed.

He could register under any name he wanted. He could be Owain Fforidd, Walter Forbes, or someone else entirely. This was his official record where he would log all of his training, his abilities, and his lives as he was forced to go dark. That was part of that whole, not aging and having to move around thing Mark was talking about.

He elected to register as Owain Fforidd. First of all, it was his name. But he also wanted to always remember his name, where he came from. He was slowly learning to accept where he was, but he never wanted to forget where he'd come from, where he'd been. He never wanted to forget his parents. He never wanted to forget his brother. And as much as he would like to carve out his time in Beaumaris Gaol and make it go away, he never wanted to forget Father Forthill and the kindness the priest had shown him. His kindness was the reason Owain was here, alive and well, and not buried in the ground on a prison island or sunk at the bottom of the sea. He owed everything to Forthill.

The secretary entered as much information as Owain was willing to give about his former life, though because of Mark's constant quizzing and testing and drilling, he found that he had to stop himself from giving his reflexive answers and think a second to give the true ones. He was born in 1815 in Wales. He walked into a cave in 1855, and when he came out, it was 1923. All local time, of course.

When they finally returned to Earth—with absolutely no time having passed since they'd been gone, which was another thing Owain was a little jittery about—Mark again drilled Owain on his story. Born in 1883, came to America via Ellis Island in 1921, et cetera, et cetera.

That was how they began their training sessions, with Owain reciting this story and answering some random questions Mark threw at him. Only once his mentor was satisfied did they actually move on to the Time-bending portion of their Time lives.

Owain still found it a spooky phenomenon, but he got the hang of it fairly quickly. Once he got his mind set right that it was himself he was altering, not the world around him, he was better able to grasp the basics. Mark told him that there were ways to Band things outside himself, but that was all advanced stuff that he didn't need to worry about right now.

But most of his days were fairly normal, making Time feel like a game or an illusion, an insane secret that only he and Mark shared. Around him, life still went on. He quit his job at the jail and went to work selling automobiles. He couldn't explain it, but he just found these self-propelled machines absolutely fascinating. It was his fascination and amazement of these machines that made him a good candidate to be a salesman, or so the company said. Whatever it was, he was good at his job and his employer seemed to like him.

There were some days when Owain wasn't even sure he recognized himself. He had a good job, wasn't drinking except for a few slip-ups, wasn't fighting. He had a home of his own, did not want for food. Everything was good, everything was calm. The only hink in his life came from his Time abilities, the ability to Band and make Time go faster or slower at will. But even that was a rather minor thing in his daily life. As Mark explained, humans just weren't excessively involved in Time, so even Timekeeper services were not constantly required.

That was just as well, Owain figured. He wanted to solidify his new life, his good life, before getting himself too wrapped up in this kind of power. He didn't need his beast to reappear and conjure up a hundred different ways he could abuse this power. He made a promise to himself that he would only Band when he was home alone and practicing as Mark had ordered, or if his or someone else's life was in danger. It sounded like a good deal, and he was able to keep to it fairly well.

His first real experience with Timekeeping duties came when Mark informed him that he'd received notice of a Runner in their area. He ran moonshine as much as Time and might have friends with him. He wasn't quite the gangster he thought he was, but that didn't mean he wasn't dangerous. Mark asked if Owain wanted to tag along on a little operation to try and apprehend this Runner. Owain was anxious but agreed.

He'd never been on this side of the law before. Well, technically he had, when Welsh jailers tried to recruit and employ him, but this was the first time he had real authority and wasn't acting selfishly. He was doing this for a good cause, or so Mark told him. Besides, regardless of the politics of the Wheel and his misgivings in that regard, any Runner or bootlegger running around with both guns and the ability to manipulate Time probably wasn't in the area on a humanitarian mission.

With the help of the local police, they found the Runner, a man by the name of Jesse Link, and five of his friends. There was a standoff, a lot of gunfire. Mark wielded Time in such a way that Owain became a little afraid of him, even though they were on the same side. The way he manipulated Time and broke the physical laws of nature was a spectacle to behold. He saved more than one cop from certain death as bullets rained, and he emerged with not a scratch on him.

The crooks soon realized they were on the defensive and tried to set up so they could escape. This was largely fronted by Link, and the men ran off into the forest. Mark and Owain confronted Link a short distance away, pushing into Link's Band as he tried to make a three-hour escape in only a few seconds. The Runner turned to face them, but his abilities were no match for Mark who not only apprehended the man physically, but used an ability called Suppression to completely inhibit Link's use of Time. The man's Band shattered and they were once again in Base Time, in sync with the rest of the world.

Mark opened a doorway to the Wheel of Time and together they delivered Link to the Judgment Wing. Owain questioned whether it wouldn't be better, since he was Suppressed, to have him go before a judge and do hard time for his crimes on Earth. Mark just shook his head and told him that there was no punishment on Earth that could match the cruelty of the Grandfathers. He was getting the worse punishment, even if Earth-side justice didn't know. As far as anyone else was concerned, Link simply got away and was at large, armed and dangerous.

It was all a bit much for Owain to take in, being on this side of the law, armed with a weapon none of the regular cops had been able to appreciate. All the same, it felt kind of good to uphold the law instead of break it, and to be the one on the outside of the jail cell looking in, even if his participation had been minimal.

But it was enough to impress Mark who asked whether Owain wanted to continue his Timekeeping. If he wanted to, Mark felt he was ready to get off probation and become a full Apprentice.

"It's been less than a year, though," Owain said. "I thought there was a mandatory probation period?"

"For those who may have been exposed at a younger age," Mark told him. "It's as much about physical and mental development as your actual abilities. Physically, you're fine. Mentally, I know you still struggle, but you've made some impressive leaps in your mental fortitude, and you've managed to stay clean. You don't have to be perfect, Owain, and I think you are more than ready."

Owain hesitated, but still agreed. He was getting pretty good at his basic Bands, and he was very knowledgeable about the workings of the Wheel, the Time industry, things one might find in a common textbook. He was anxious about going before the Hands the following month, but he figured it was normal. Mark also told him that there would be a psychological examination, just to make sure he wasn't secretly going to turn into a Runner.

It all sounded so simple, so straightforward. For a while, it was. His first test was a knowledge test. He answered all their questions. He recited the ranks of a Timekeeper and all the other Time Agents, demonstrated basic knowledge of the Wheel, the Time industry, all the while thinking that five years ago he would have called himself absolutely insane and deserving of a small room in an asylum. He'd been almost unable to cope with just the change in year, jumping from 1855 to 1923.

Now here he was, talking to aliens and demonstrating his ability to change physics. He could bend Time, make it go faster or slower at varying rates. He wasn't even sure what to call this except a miracle God intentionally gave to man to perform. Was that even possible? It must be, he thought. He couldn't even begin to think of a passage in the Bible that forbid man to change the physical universe at will.

His biggest stumbling block, and the one thing that damn near sent Owain into a panicked frenzy, running back to Mark and begging to be killed, was the psychological exam. He was no expert in the field, but even knew the basic premise behind Sigmund Freud's work, followed by his faithful apprentice Jung. Barring that, he was also well-versed in Catholic Confession and other pastoral counseling. That was the sort of thing he'd been expecting.

After his second break following his ability demonstration to the Hands, Owain was taken out of the waiting room again. Before, the corridor had been fairly neutral, like walking through an office building of sorts. This time, though, as soon as the door opened, he froze. Now it had changed, and he knew that stone corridor all too well.

He wasn't sure that he took a breath or that his heart pumped a beat at all as he was made to move and walk down the corridor to a large wooden door. When it opened, he put a hand up to shield his eyes from sudden sunlight, and his aching lungs sucked in a breath. His body began to function again, if just barely. Had he not been of a present mind, he may have soiled himself, maybe two or three times, as much as his heart was racing and the rest of him was panicking.

Owain stepped forward through the door into the sunlight. As soon as his foot touched down, even though he couldn't fully see yet, he knew exactly where he was and what he was walking on. Then the light dimmed and he could see.

He found himself looking out over the yard in Beaumaris Gaol. It was a bright, sunny day, and everyone was gathered. As in, everyone. Not just the prisoners, but everyone he'd ever known. He saw his parents. He saw his siblings. Paige was there with their daughter; she stood between her parents. The men he'd killed, the associates of the bank, and dozens, hundreds of faceless men and women he'd merely used and dismissed over the years.

On the scaffolding with him were four men. The warden, looking rather bored. Just another day, another item of business to be conducted. The gaoler, the big one who always hated him, ready and eager to hang him. The priest, Father Forthill, looking kind and solemn and about ready to be ill but holding out just for him.

Then there was someone he didn't expect the see, the pagan priest from the Scottish community.

"What's all this, then?" Owain asked, his throat suddenly dry.

"Your hanging, what does it look like?" the warden asked. "Your sentence has been delayed far too long. An eighty year stay, I think that must be a record of some form."

"I couldn't decide whether to make the rope short so you suffer, or long so your head gets ripped off," the gaoler said, grinning like a demon.

Owain felt his chest tighten and he forced himself to look at the two holy men. "And you two?"

"No action is without consequence," the pagan priest told him. "It is the rule of nature. The world is a cruel place. As you said often enough, you can choose to jump off a cliff, but you cannot choose not to fall. You have been running for far too long. Nature demands its due. You killed eleven men—"

"Nine," Owain interrupted. "Only nine. Balk and his associates, and the Confederates. And the Confederates were self-defense."

"And the undertaker and his apprentice?"

All right, so there was that.

"Do you deny it?" the pagan priest inquired.

"No," Owain conceded.

Now Forthill stepped forward, ahead of the pagan priest. "Is that all you are, Owain? Are you only an animal, merely subject to nature and bestial desire? Are you every awful thing you have done, that your beast told you to do? Or are you more? I've been trying so hard to reach you, Owain, I really have. You are more. You are more than the sum of your parts. You are more than your actions, more than your mistakes, more than your deeds good and bad. You are a child of God, created in His image, loved and pursued. Here you are, Owain, and I don't know that there is anything more that I can say."

Owain shook his head. "There is nothing more that you need to say, Father. I understand. Which is why I will not be hanging today."

The gaoler crossed the platform. "Oh, yes, you will. I've waited too long for this."

The guard reached for him, but Owain knocked his hands away and drove his elbows into the man's chest so he stumbled back a step or two.

"No," he said calmly. "I've been forgiven. I am a new creation in the Lord and He has given me a new life with which to do good. He has given me a power I could never comprehend or appreciate except now I am of a mind to do so and do it wisely." He looked at Forthill. "Even though I know you're not real, I will still say that I owe all of that to you, Father. I owe you everything that I am today."

Forthill managed a small smile. "Don't thank me. Thank the Lord."

Owain nodded and glanced back at the warden and the gaoler. "Maybe I did a bad thing escaping from prison. And you will never hear me justify all the crimes that I have committed. I am deeply regretful of a great many things. But a bad man who has changed can do more good than a good man who is dead. I am beyond your reach now, and I will work now to do good."

The gaoler stalked up to him again until they were eye-to-eye.

"You are never beyond my reach," he hissed, his breath foul.

Faster than Owain could react, the gaoler snatched him and, in one swift motion, swung him around to the rope. Quick as a whip, he had the noose around Owain's neck and was reaching for the lever to open up the door.

"Die alone," the gaoler growled.

The fear of the rope around his neck had frozen Owain's limbs and he could not use his abilities while in this part of the exam. Fear shot through him like an arrow as the ground suddenly fell away from his feet. He may have soiled himself even before he died. He couldn't be absolutely sure as suddenly the rope tightened. He tried to take in a gasp, but could find no air. Then the rope broke and he continued to fall into darkness. All of this happened in less than two seconds.

Then he hit the ground, hard stone, where he crumpled and scraped his knees. Probably he'd broken his knees, but there would be very little external damage. As he thought about it, he knew he would have a twisted ankle, too. He knew these injuries. Knew them well.

Had his whole life been a lie, then? Had he merely hallucinated everything after he stepped off the bench in his cell in an attempt to hang himself? Was he about to die? The darkness remained a constant, but the fear was subsiding into fatigue. He closed his eyes and tried to breathe, tried to get a handle on himself. It wasn't real. It wasn't real. It was a test. It was the most godawful test he'd ever taken, but it had to end eventually.

When he opened his eyes, he was back in the Seat of the Hands as he had known it previously. A simple room with bleacher-like seating, the Hands watching him intently. Mark was standing over him and offered him a hand which he weakly accepted.

"Are you all right?" Mark asked.

"I don't know," Owain admitted. "None of that was real, was it?"

"It was as real as your mind made you believe it was."

Owain just shook his head. "Did I pass the test at least?"

"The Hands will review it and deliver a verdict in a bit. Come on. You look like you need a nap."

Chapter Twenty-Nine

The Reason

He slept for fifteen hours, but the result was the same. He passed. He was officially an Apprentice.

They returned to Earth where he slept for another almost full day before returning to work in the morning and beginning his new training that evening.

Overall, nothing really changed. He went to work, paid his rent and other bills, few though they were, and generally kept to himself when he wasn't training with Mark. He really wasn't sure what to do with himself. What ambition did he have that he would feel confident in pursuing without devolving back into his dastardly feral ways?

A few times he considered actually going into the clergy, just like he pretended he always wanted to. It would be holy work, leading a life of intentional penury and pauperism. He would feel no desire to accumulate material wealth, and while clergy were respected, they hardly wielded what one might consider power, especially after The Great War had scarred the minds of what few men lived to return to the congregation.

A year and a half later, walking out of a Journeyman test that was a hundred times less stressful than the Apprentice review, he still wasn't sure what he wanted to do. The year was 1926, the Roaring Twenties were showing no signs of stopping, but he showed no signs of going. He had saved up an impressive amount of money just from his day job, never mind the bits he was adding from his Timekeeper salary. All that money, and he didn't know what to do with it.

"Have you ever thought about going into business?" Mark asked him. "You seem to be good with money."

Owain sighed and ran a hand through his hair. "I was a banker once. But given my experiences there, I don't know that I would want to go anywhere near that again."

Mark frowned. "Owain, you can't let your past lives dictate how you spend your present. Actually, that's true of just about anything."

"A sharp knife always cuts."

"True, but men have been wielding swords with deft efficiency for thousands of years. You just have to know how to handle it."

"I don't know. I'm not completely against it, but it feels, personally, to me, a little too soon to be going on those kinds of escapades again."

It was just as well, he figured, as October of 1928 rolled around and suddenly the Roaring Twenties came to a screeching halt. The stock market crashed and the Roaring Twenties felt a distant memory, a dream too good to be true and now the masses had to wake up.

Mark's job at the jail was fairly safe as there was always riffraff to control, but Owain was not so lucky. He was able to hold out a little longer than some other automobile salesmen simply because he was good at his job, but if people didn't have money, they didn't have money. Sales slowed down and the dealer was forced to close.

"Lot of poverty in these hills," Mark mused as they had lunch together in his house the week after Owain lost his job. "We usually see only the crumbs of prosperity but the throes of poverty. But that's the way things are."

"I don't know what I'm going to do," Owain confessed. "I can stick it out for a little while, but—what?"

Mark was shaking his head. "I think it's time for your next lesson in Time: how to go dark and build a new life for yourself."

"I've already done that, haven't I?"

"Arbitrarily, but you think I run up to that cave every time I need to skedaddle? You obviously remember what I've told you about Time Agents' aging slowing; you're experiencing it right now, as a Journeyman. How long do you think I can stay in one spot before people start to notice that I'm not getting older? It's an average of ten years, fifteen if I want to push it. I've been here in Charleston for about eight years now. I think this depression is a good excuse to high tail it out of here. I think you should come with me."

"Where?"

Mark shrugged. "Anywhere. Where do you want to go? As a Journeyman, you have to do some traveling anyway to learn from other Timekeepers. Any place special you want to visit?"

Owain sighed and shook his head. "No. Can't say that I've ever really been afflicted with wanderlust. And besides..."

"Besides what?"

"What if Tommen is still in that cave? What if he comes out?" Owain rubbed his face. The words about to come out of his mouth were so foreign he may as well have been speaking Chinese. "Regardless of everything in my life and all the wrongs I've done to people, Tommen is my nephew and I don't want to lose him. He's the only family I've got left. If he comes out of that cave now, after all the time that's passed, I'll be the only family he's got left."

Mark nodded. "I understand. I do. But we can't stay here forever waiting for him."

"Why not? You want to go out and travel, fine. I can go up to my brother's old homestead and live there, wait for him. Tommen won't know what's happened, and home is going to be the first thought on his mind. Someone ought to be waiting there for him."

"And you're just going to camp there? Find your own food, water, keep it going?"

"Don't need to worry about food. The Food Court in the Wheel can keep me supplied there."

Mark grudgingly conceded the point. "All the same, Owain, how long are you willing to wait? Saying you'll wait as long as it takes is fine and dandy for the first decade or so. Would you wait two decades? Five? A century? Owain, God forbid, but what if he dies in that cave? What if something has already happened to him and you'll be waiting an eternity for something that's not going to happen?"

"It's a risk I'm willing to take."

Mark folded his arms and leaned back in his seat. "So you'll just live alone on a mountain for a century, is that it?"

Owain gave him a look. "I've spent most of my life alone. That's why

I'm able to adapt so well to a new era despite being older. You said that yourself."

Mark shrugged. "Great. Fine. You go up there, live like a hermit for a century—a full century, now over a hundred and fifty years removed from your own time—and Tommen finally comes out. What are you going to do with him? You don't know what the world is going to be like then. Maybe you can continue to live like a hermit, but maybe you won't. If you do decide to bring him back to reintegrate into society, it's going to be a culture shock to both of you, and I don't know how many of those you can handle. I'm glad you've got one under your belt, but do you think you can go for two—add another century, plus a child?"

Growling in his chest, Owain leaned back in his chair.

"I'm happy you care for him and want to see him alive and well, take him in as family. You would also be able to explain Time to him, raise him in it instead of a normal family or the courts having him committed at such a young age for some perceived delusion. Believe me, these are all good things. I just don't know how well it's going to go in the time in between, the actual wait."

"I don't want to just leave him. Ten years is a long time to be away."

"Owain, you're talking minimum thirty or forty years. People have to forget you and you have to come back as a new generation."

"You see my point, then. What if he comes out while I'm gone?"

Mark sighed and rubbed his face. "I understand, Owain. I really do." He rested his chin on his fist and sighed again. "Let me talk to the District Captain, explain the situation, tell him your concerns. Maybe we can come to a compromise."

Owain was willing to agree to that. The District Captain and his two Lieutenants were in charge of overseeing all the Timekeepers in their district, District Four as it happened to be, the eastern seaboard of the United States. Maybe there was a way that Owain could stay in the area and keep an eye out for Tommen.

The Great Depression dragged on with no end in sight. Owain gave up his rented room and moved in with Mark again. Mark still insisted on leaving; his thought was California. The economy wasn't so bad, but business was tough as farmers from the Plains tried to escape the Dust

Bowl. Labor was cheap and hope abounded. He knew a few tricks of the trade and they could go out there as a couple venture capitalists. Maybe they could help bring some life back into the economy as well as mitigate the damage caused by the Depression.

It was six months after Mark contacted the District Captain that the man finally responded, and they met in the Food Court in the Wheel of Time. All food in the Food Court was free, so Time Agents never wanted for nutrition, no matter their dietary needs or preferences. It was the largest open-air market Owain had ever seen, and it was impossible to go through the whole line and leave with fewer than four plates, or it would be if he didn't tell himself to be good and watch what he ate. Because of the slowed aging, that also meant slowed metabolism, which meant he could gain a bunch of weight if he wasn't careful.

The three of them met over fine steaks.

James Adams was the District Captain, a head less than six feet with a head less of hair, he was a bit of a miser, but not without a quirky sense of humor that often left Owain wondering if he was the real butt of the jokes.

Adams was from Boston, and Owain had met him on one previous occasion, when he and Mark toured America and visited Ellis Island and all that. The encounter had been civil, but far less than friendly.

"So, Owain, Mark tells me that your nephew is also stuck in that infernal cave," Adams began. "And you want to stay where you are so you can watch and wait for him when he finally comes out, is that it?"

"That's right," Owain confirmed, electing to say as little as possible.

"How old is he?"

"Eight."

The man made a disapproving sound. "Hardly old enough to support himself in any respectable way, hardly able to comprehend the change but better able to adapt. You don't want to see him committed under a court order, and you want to keep him in the family. I expect you would also want to explain Time to him so things make a little more sense."

"That would be the idea."

Owain wasn't sure whether he would really want to teach Tommen about Time, not at such a young age. He was just a little boy; he ought to be doing little boy things like running around and playing with sticks and exploring new things.

"You've been in the area for, what, a little over six years, maybe closer to seven?" Adams went on.

"Sounds right."

"And from what I understand, you have not yet done any of the required Journeyman traveling."

Owain felt his face turn red. "That's right. Part of that does have to do with the Great Depression that's now hit and some limited resources."

Mark coughed noticeably and said, "I've been trying to talk him into taking out a little chunk of change and coming with me out to California."

Adams nodded and took another bite of steak. "So, this is all about your nephew. Looking for a way to keep an eye out for him in the event he does emerge from this blasted cave so you can swoop in and save the day, but not neglect your other duties and keep yourself out of the suspect light. Mark has explained the concept of going dark, hasn't he?"

"He has," Owain confirmed.

"Then you understand why it is necessary."

"I understand."

They sat in silence, eating their steaks, for an uncomfortable length of time. Only when they were all finished did Adams speak again.

"Well, I understand your concerns, and I appreciate the concern you have for your nephew. I would much rather you take him, raise him as family, teach him about Time, than have him go through the courts and end up being committed. Unfortunately, with no way to know when he may come out, I can't just have you sit out on top of a mountain waiting for him."

"Why not? My brother's home is still up there. There is still family in the area. Or I can build my own shelter. The Wheel provides food free of charge, so I don't have to worry about that."

"Yes, Owain, I get it. You have the logistics covered. My bigger concern, however, is you. Your well-being. Are you really prepared to handle God knows how long with minimal or no human contact, all in the hopes of finding this one boy? How long are you prepared to wait? Can you resist the temptation to go in and look for him yourself? What will you do afterwards? Will you be able to reintegrate into society again? It's hard on the mind, Owain, it really is. Mark's told me about your past life. You recovered well this time because you had only tenuous ties to your old life, and it was a life you were hardly proud of. What about this one? How much have you become accustomed to, how much have you gotten involved in since you've been in Charleston? And I'm not talking about book clubs and bowling leagues. Just sheer presence, just being involved in the daily grind of life, if that gets broken in any significant way, it can be tough to recover. You think you can do that this time around?"

Apparently Owain's hesitation was answer enough as Adams nodded slowly. "Here's what I'm willing to do, because I do admire your persistence and the love you hold for your nephew. I'll have my Lieutenants keep an eye on the news and police reports coming out of Charleston, look for anything unusual involving children. If anything pops up, they'll let you know. I will also have Masters and Journeymen sweep through the area from time to time, looking for anything visual, you know? Maybe ask the neighbors if they've seen or heard anything. Again, if anything comes up, they'll let you know.

"It's the best you're going to get. You need to keep up on your training, and you need to get out of the area. Go with Mark to California, do whatever it is you're planning to do. You get your traveling training finished—or started, as the case may be—complete your Master exam, and then you can do whatever it is you want. If you want to come back and be a hermit, fine. Be a hermit."

"What's the difference between now and later?"

"I think you need more time in the real world before you go off chasing a dream."

And that was that. He could take it or leave it, but he didn't have much authority without completing his Journeyman training and advancing to Master. If he had done that before now, as he'd had every opportunity and advantage while the economy was booming, he might have been able to stay in the mountains as a hermit, waiting for Tommen.

All the same, maybe Adams did have a point in that he should spend a little more time amongst people and work to improve himself so he could be a father to this child when he did come out—and he would come out, Owain told himself. And he would be a good father to him.

Memories of Victoria flooded his mind, physical pain right along with it. He strangled a gasp and forced his body to remain rigid so he would not flinch. Where had this come from? He knew where it came from, the depths of his depraved past life trying to haunt him, cause him doubt. The beast no longer dwelt in his mind, but that didn't mean the rest of the demons had given up on torturing him from time to time.

No. He would be a good father. He would raise his nephew as his own. He had no choice. He had to keep Tommen in the family and teach him about life first and Time second.

But in order to do that effectively, he had to improve himself. He had to be able to function as a decent human being all the time. Not just most of the time. He could not subject Tommen to any of his drunkenness, his rage, his confusion. He could not leave Tommen home alone at night while he went to jail. He could not look his nephew in the eye and say they were related if he was not a human being worth being related to.

He could not camp out at the top of a mountain.

That line of thought made it an easier pill to swallow, and he returned home with Mark without complaining. The following day, they were packing for California.

Mark's stash of resources included an exclusive, rather secretive Time Agent bank account. It was full of cash, enough to pay off the entire national debt and start a thousand businesses in every state. Mark took out just enough to get them going to California, explaining that this particular account could be accessed at certain banks in every state, every province in Canada, and a few select countries elsewhere in the world. When Owain asked for the details, Mark simply stated that he would get the details once he became a Master Timekeeper. When Owain asked about funds for his Journeyman traveling, Mark told him that he would be given an allowance and would have to be smart about it. He'd been a banker once, so that shouldn't be too difficult, right?

Owain could have punched him. But he didn't. He had to restrain himself and be good. Do everything as if Tommen were watching, he told himself. Explain everything to him.

With funds secured, Mark went to work on their new identities, their new lives. The thought of it made Owain sick to his stomach. Another life, another lie. This time around, he'd been born in 1890, came through Ellis Island in 1920 after his brother. His brother had fallen to sickness, and he decided to make his fortune in the city. After the Depression initially hit, he packed up and came out to California with his business partner Mark to rebuild a fortune.

He hated himself for it, the lie. His head told him it was necessary, and all the logistics added up, but his conscience still said it was wrong. He looked back on Charleston with a sick stomach.

The trek out west was just as miserable. It was supposed to be a fine road trip, but the Dust Bowl was an awful thing to behold. Whole houses were buried, automobiles abandoned at the side of the road, animal skeletons everywhere, poking up through the dust and sand.

It was on this journey that Owain learned about blind portals, or short-trip portals. Normally, the Wheel acted as a vacuum that demanded all portals be opened to it, but there was a way to bypass this massive force and instead jump directly from one place to another. It required ten times the energy to do, but with Owain lending his strength and practicing his own portals, it took some of the load off of Mark and they could travel much easier.

It happened that as they were driving through Oklahoma, they were accosted by a sandstorm so huge it made them both nauseous ten miles before it hit. With no way to get around it in time and nowhere to shelter, Mark made the decision to abandon the automobile and jump right to California.

They walked into San Francisco looking about as wretched as most of the Dust Bowl refugees, but with their generous funds, they were able to buy new suits, decent haircuts, a hot meal, and rent a hotel room for a week. The money was enough to make most of the Depression-stricken folk not question them.

Owain knew a thing or two about money and investing. With exception of the Great Depression going on, not a lot had changed since

1840's London. Not a few times he corrected Mark on his terms and stopped him from making terrible deals in their initial negotiations. It quickly became that Owain was the one leading the venture, Mark just tagging along for the ride and taking care of the small logistics.

"I'm impressed," Mark told him. "I really am. Seems you do know a little bit about banking and investments."

"Well, my father-in-law taught me quite a bit, whether or not he realized it at the time," Owain said, surprised he would ever find himself saying anything good about the man, or that Jonathon Balk had ever done anything for him.

It was a battle to keep business afloat during the Depression, and not a few investments collapsed, but they themselves were doing fairly well, or as well as could be expected. It helped when they had no want of food.

Owain once asked whether it would be permissible to bring food from the Wheel to the people starving in their community, or even end poverty across the globe. Mark explained that while that was all well and good — and it may or may not have been done on much smaller scales in the past, under the radar in small neighborhoods — it was prohibited by the Hands. The Food Court was reserved for Time Agents and civilizations who contributed openly to the Time industry.

And, on top of that, he reasoned, if everyone was simply given food, what incentive was there to farm? If hard work was taken away, few people had the inherent desire to work hard, and no one wanted to work for free. The system would collapse on itself. Farming would cease to exist on Earth and they would become dependent on the work of others.

There was some reasoning behind that, Owain figured, but couldn't there be a balance? Give a man a fish, teach a man to fish, but what if the man was so hungry he was too weak to be able to fish? Give him a fish to restore his strength before teaching him to fish. Well, philosophy was far above him; he was just a humble investor.

It was under the pretext of expanding their investing empire that he started on his traveling training, very similar to how he'd gone to Wales on behalf of Mr. Balk to seek out good investments. Owain traveled to other states and other Districts, doing a little investing for his and Mark's company, and a lot of training so he could advance to Master

Timekeeper.

He learned more about Banding and the types of Bands, learned how to heal himself with Pinpoint Bands, learned about Internal and External Bands, learned about Double-Banding, learned about portals and practiced those until he could safely and comfortably travel to and from the Wheel on his own. When he asked about what happened if a portal collapsed when he was halfway through, he was told that the person simply vanished, and the running theory was that there was some sort of in-between dimension where no human could possibly survive because of the physical mechanics. Owain stopped listening at that point.

Actually, because portal travel was so dangerous, usually it wasn't learned until after Master rank had already been achieved. Owain had been taught early simply because he had the strength and willpower to make up for it. He chose to take that as a compliment.

He traveled all over North America, visited all eight Districts. He even learned about an unofficial District Nine encompassing all the Native American tribes. They were not an official District because the Regional Manager refused to recognize them, but Owain quickly learned that if he wanted to make friends with Native Time Agents—all three that he knew of—then he would greet them as being from District Nine. He decided it best just to not touch those politics.

The Great Depression was still going on when he finally returned to California, though one would never suspect that he and Mark were even aware that it was going on, as well as their business was doing. It was hardly six weeks into 1933 and they were a couple of the wealthiest men in the nation with a track record of good investments. Wherever they went, the economy improved so that the Depression was more of a waking bad dream than a suicide-inducing waking nightmare. This wasn't to say that they had no bad investments; they had plenty of those. But they were simply doing well.

It was July of 1933 when Owain went to the Wheel for his Master exam. The knowledge portion was more in-depth, the skill test far more rigorous. He nearly got sick when they mentioned that there was a psychological exam with this test as well. The Apprentice exam had been bad enough, and the Journeyman hadn't had one. Seven years or so since his first psychological exam, twenty personal years since he'd been under the threat of the noose in prison, and still he wanted to be sick.

Nevertheless, he squared his shoulders, forced his food to stay in his stomach, and went out to meet his fate.

He was pleasantly surprised to find a forest behind the door this time, instead of a familiar stone corridor. He didn't let his guard down, but this was far less terrifying than the prison. All the same, the Hands were not known for being shoulders to cry on. Something was up.

Less than ten paces into the forest, he knew exactly where he was and where he was going. He pushed through the tree line and faced the salt cave. Standing at the entrance...was Teo. His arms were folded and his posture was of terrified anger.

"Where have you been?" Teo demanded. "Why haven't you found my boy yet?"

"I'm looking," Owain told him. Then he thought better of it and said, "I'm waiting."

"Tommen is in this cave. He could be hurt or sick or worse. If Maisy didn't forbid it, I would go myself. And you." He pointed an accusatory finger. "You promised to help. You promised to find him."

"I know. I will. But it's a trap. It's going to be years before—"

"You said you would find him. I told you to bring him back alive or don't come back at all. Why are you here?"

"I don't know."

Now Teo got angry, dropping his arms to his sides and seeming to get bigger, nearly intimidating. "Find him! Find my son! Go in there now, you useless piece of trash brother! Get in there and find my son and bring him back to me!"

It was all an illusion, Owain knew, but the words still hurt. He closed his eyes and tried to bring up the last conversation he'd had with Teo, how they'd walked around his fields a couple times, how they'd eaten supper. They'd spoken genially on their way to the cave. He had no doubt that Teo was frustrated about Tommen and uncertain about Owain, but he was incapable of hate. He would never say something like that.

When he opened his eyes, Teo was gone. The cave still stood there, the same as the last time he'd seen it.

Taking a breath, Owain went up to the cave and peered inside. Still looked the same. Grunting and groaning, he squeezed himself through the small opening, wondering if maybe the opening had gotten smaller or if he'd just gained some weight. But he got in.

He didn't have a lantern. At the same time, he found he could see. Not much, but he could, just enough to navigate somewhat safely, going deeper into the cave.

He froze as hemp suddenly touched skin. Instinctively, he hands went to his neck where a rope cinched down around his neck. The rope jerked and he was pulled back. His head hit stone and he saw stars. The light grew brighter, then began to change colors. After a minute, the colors focused themselves into shapes, and he found himself back in the Seat of the Hands. He no sooner recognized his surroundings than he was out.

It was seven hours before he was able to drag himself before the Hands again. He couldn't even say why he felt so awful. The hallucination had been hardly traumatic except for the last three seconds. Maybe that was all it took. Maybe he was just exhausted from whatever drugs they had to have given him to induce these illusions. Whatever it was, he could hardly summon the strength to be happy that he passed his exam and was now a Master Timekeeper.

"I'll be happy for you," Mark told him as he offered Owain a shoulder to lean and limp on.

Owain waved him off, barely able to keep his eyes open. He stumbled through the Wheel like a drunk; even his mind felt fuzzy and uncoordinated. He remembered asking about the drugs the Hands used to cause the hallucinations, but he didn't remember the answer. He just remembered feeling grateful when his head finally hit his pillow.

Chapter Thirty

The Time In Between

No word ever came from Charleston about Tommen. No one had seen him or heard anything about anyone coming out of the salt cave, adult or child. All of the cases of missing children were fairly standard, nothing unusual. No known cases of unusual children showing up in orphanages or churches. As the Depression dragged on, Owain grew anxious. Someone had to be missing something, or else something awful had happened to Tommen.

What if something had happened to him? What would Owain do then? He was glad to be a Master Timekeeper, glad to have some sort of purpose in life, but in the end, it was still little more than a day job. Where would he find personal fulfillment if Tommen never showed up? *Could* he find personal fulfillment? He often mentally kicked himself for never valuing family enough until it was too late, until it had all been taken from him. He was still well-aware that it was his own fault, and that only made him kick himself harder.

Then the Second Great War erupted, and everyone was convinced that it was the End Times. While the United States tried to stay out of it initially, the influx of immigrants and refugees was not well-tolerated in all places.

Owain and Mark were just about to head out the door when Pearl Harbor was attacked. They read about it in the newspaper and later heard it on the radio and saw the film on TV.

Owain had seen a great many things in his day, and he had walked in the halls of the Devil's palace, but never had he imagined that destruction that humanity was capable of producing. Between the first Great War and now this, it was a wonder there were any humans left to populate the planet.

"I'm thinking it's time we went dark," Mark suggested one evening. "A full-on war effort is doing wonders for investing; I don't think we'll have any trouble selling the company."

"Agreed," Owain murmured absently.

"Something wrong?"

He shrugged. "How do you do it? How do you keep going? How many wars have you seen?"

Mark frowned. "Only the one, I'm afraid. It would have been my only one, if not for my mentor. I'm grateful to her. After that, I made damn sure that if there was war, then I was going to be as far away from it as possible."

Owain nodded. Mark had fought in the Revolutionary War, had been there when Washington crossed the Delaware and turned the tide in the Americans' favor. He'd been mortally wounded in battle but survived long enough to get help. One of the nurses had been a Timekeeper, and she'd used her skills to save his life.

They'd had a fling for a short period afterwards, while she trained him up to Journeyman status. Then she died of yellow fever.

"I suppose the only thing we can do is wake up in the morning and go to bed at night," Mark was saying, bringing Owain back to the present. He paused. "You're not coming with me this time, are you?"

Owain shook his head, not looking at Mark. "No. Not this time."

"You can't go back to Charleston yet. You understand that, right?" Mark gave him a severe look.

"I understand. Twenty years isn't long enough."

"It hasn't even been twenty years."

"I know."

Mark shifted in his seat. "What's got you bothered, Owain?"

For a long moment, Owain did not speak, simply sat and stared at his hands folded on the table, brooding. Finally, "Do you think I'm waiting in vain? What if Tommen never comes out of that cave?"

Mark opened his mouth a couple times before finding his voice. "I don't know. I really don't. But there are a few things you ought to consider."

"Like what?"

"Tommen is a child. He's an adventurer. You went in that cave late in the evening, looked around a little, and came out when the darkness started closing in. Right? And you jumped seventy years. Tommen went in during the middle of the day, and an eight year old's imagination will keep him occupied for hours, until he either gets hungry or tired. Honestly, I expect that he is still in there, playing whatever imaginary game he's concocted in his head."

"So I could be waiting another seventy years," Owain stated.

Mark hesitated but shrugged and nodded. "Yes."

Owain sighed and shifted in his seat. "Honestly, I would rather he was still in the cave enjoying himself than be out in the world somewhere now, alone and confused and sitting in a small room with electric nodes attached to him."

"That's one way to look at it."

They sat in silence for a few moments more.

"Where will you go?" Mark asked at last.

"Back east, I think," Owain answered, coming back to life just a little. "New York City was a bit much for me, but maybe something along those lines."

"You know, you can go anywhere in the world. If you know the right people, you may even be able to leave entirely," Mark told him. "Earth is kind of tumultuous right now, not a very nice place to be. There are other worlds out there, human worlds. Colony worlds."

"I know. But I still can't leave Tommen. I want to be available at a moment's notice without forcing people to go looking for me."

Mark nodded. "Understandable. All the same, now that we're in this war, I can't imagine it will last long, or turn out well for either the Japanese or the Nazis. You could return home to Wales afterwards, help them rebuild. Do some good in your home country."

"I suppose I could. It's as unrecognizable to them now as it would be to me, I think." Owain ran his tongue over his teeth. "What about you?"

"I don't know. I might settle down into country life for a while. Get out of the city, out of the rat race. Get away from people for a spell."

"Sounds nice."

"You could do it, too, you know."

Owain shifted in his seat. "I know. I just don't have any decent skills for farming or anything like that. Most of the life skills I know came from the city, from London."

"Well, it's your life, and I imagine you'll have plenty more of them," Mark told him. "As long as you don't forget to keep in touch."

They did keep in touch, and it happened that Owain found work in Detroit, manufacturing cars. It was arduous labor, but he did enjoy the work. With the war and the conclusion of the war in the United States' favor, industry was booming and Owain's strength was in high demand.

Since becoming part of Time and ranking up and using his new abilities, he did notice that his aging had slowed and even seemed to have stopped—it would have had to, seeing how in twenty-five years he still looked in his mid-forties, maybe fifties. Sometimes it was hard to tell. His body also seemed to have recovered somewhat from the worst of his aches and pains and injuries. As Mark had told him, he was by no means a youthful twenty year old anymore, but he usually felt pretty good when he woke up in the morning.

Well, he ought to rephrase. He felt good physically. Sometimes he woke up and had no idea who he was. Was he Owain Fforidd, drunkard and brawler, on the run from the law again? Was he Owain Fforidd, wealthy London banker? Was he Owain Fforidd, condemned man on the run in hopes of one last chance at redemption? Or was he Owain Fforidd, wannabe clergy student who followed his brother to America? Or maybe he was Owain Fforidd, car salesman. He could also be Owain Fforidd, wealthy California investor. These days, he was just Owain Fforidd, car manufacturer. But some days, it was hard to tell.

Some days, in addition to confusion over his own identity, there was also significant confusion over which country he was in. He'd seen New York City when it was little more than a large town, comparatively speaking. Suddenly there were roads and street lights and cars and millions upon millions of people, hoards of immigrants and no shortage of opinions. He'd crossed the Appalachians on horseback with no signs of civilization for miles and miles. Now it was a day's drive.

He'd used the Pony Express and had been thrilled to receive a letter from his ma more than once a year. Now the United States Postal Service delivered mail in automobiles and in half the time. If that didn't work, the telephone brought whole continents closer together.

As if industrialization weren't bad enough, there was the new social unrest to contend with. In his youth, back in the 1800's, slavery was still common practice. Yes, it was being phased out, but it wasn't an unusual thing, and everyone believed everyone had a place in society, a hierarchy as it were. Suddenly all of that was being called into question. In the immediate, it was concern over the Japanese, the Koreans, the Chinese and other Asians. Could they become citizens? Were they people enough? And then there was call for civil rights, abolition of the segregation and the divide between whites and blacks. Sure, Negroes were people enough to not be slaves, but were they people enough to be...people? Citizens? Equal to those with less color in their skin?

Owain would be lying to himself, if no one else, if he said he wasn't conflicted about the whole thing. It should have been easy, he thought. He was once a second-class citizen—no, not even that. He had been far worse than a second-class citizen; he'd been a prisoner facing the noose. He had been held in as much contempt as a slave. And here he was, in the land of opportunity, getting a second chance at life. Would he have that same opportunity if his skin were the color of coffee? Shouldn't a Negro who was honest, loyal, hard-working, and intelligent have the same opportunities that a white condemned murderer had?

He did not struggle against the question. He struggled against the change. So many things had changed in his life, economically, politically, socially, that his very perception of existence was almost unrecognizable. A seventy year leap had been difficult to stomach, but there were still pieces of society that were familiar. The social hierarchy of races, men over women, people going to church on Sundays, that sort of thing. Equal rights for all races? Women voting and going to work in factories the same as men, leaving the home? Crowds proclaiming church unnecessary and defunct? In a hundred years, the world had been turned completely on its head.

How was Owain supposed to cope? How could he reconcile this to the way things used to be? If he had to put a word to it, he might say it was all very frightening.

He called Mark one night to ask about it. Mark had indeed moved to the country, somewhere in the Dakotas, and was very happy to farm and provide for himself without having to worry about other people.

"I would be lying if I said I didn't share some of your concerns," Mark said. His tone did little to comfort Owain. "You know, for the longest time, the names changed, but little else did. Society was basically a revolving door. A few tweaks here and there, but people still got around on horseback, got their news from the paper, and gossiped about everything Sunday after church. During the week, the men did the hard labor, the women took care of the young'uns. Everything got done, everyone had a role.

"Communication, that's what it comes down to. Reading the paper, by the time people got to it, some days had passed since terrible things had occurred, and people already knew that life still went on. Now, you see terrible things happening live on the television, and everyone wants to react because they're not sure the sun will come up if they don't."

"How do you deal with it, though?" Owain wondered.

"You want my honest opinion? You're going to have to be a little selfish. Go to bed at night, wake up in the morning. If you can do those two things, you have a good start. The world is going to change. You can't stop it, so you have to decide what you're going to do with yourself to weather it." He went on before Owain could speak. "Men have finite lives. So do we, if we're not careful; we can die from a bullet wound just as easily as the next man. But our lives are extended. Most men only expect to live sixty or seventy years, and only about forty to fifty of those years are going to be productive in society. Somehow, they think it's not enough and they want to change the whole world in their lifetime, to see a disaster when they're twenty, fix it when they're twenty-five, and live in paradise by the time they're thirty years old. That's how they're going to live and work and act. We don't have to. You've already seen that we can reconstruct new lives for ourselves wherever and however we want. We have a gift."

"You think humanity will ever catch on to Time?"

"I don't know. Fifty years ago, I would have said not likely. These days, well, tough to say. It's not out of the realm of possibility. In my lifetime, Earth has moved up a rank from Scientifically Modest to Advancing, though its use is still disputed in some circles."

Owain sighed.

"I think you've come to a critical moment in your life, Owain. If you were about forty when you jumped to 1923, it's been about thirty years now. Your body is young, but your mind says you're at the end of your natural life span, about seventy years. I think that in an age of sin and darkness, God instituted death as a mercy, not a punishment. There's only so much a man can handle in his lifetime."

"Are you offering to kill me?"

"Are you asking?"

Owain hesitated for half a second, then replied, "No. Not until I have a definitive answer about Tommen. Have you heard anything?"

"No."

"Nor have I. It worries me."

"I know. But if he's your reason for living, then live you must. Only you know how you are going to spend that life, or lives."

It was hardly the answer Owain had been looking for, but he supposed he expected nothing less coming from Mark. The man had said often enough that some days he questioned God, even His very existence, given the whole mess of Time and whatnot, but seeing how he himself was not an infinite, omniscient, omnipresent being, he could not exclude the possibility that one could exist. As far as change, well, he could advise, but he would not dictate. He was not Owain's Master anymore and even so, Owain was a grown man and he'd lived long enough in this era to make his own choices.

Owain scoffed at the notion. Every time he had tried to do something his own way, it usually ended in disaster. On the other hand, did he really want to relegate himself to being a useless, indecisive, fearful child? He liked to think he'd become a decent human being, and being almost two decades completely sober made him feel good about himself, but it was time to start really being a man. He knew that at some point, Tommen was going to walk out of that cave. Owain wanted to be ready, not just financially, not simply because they were blood relatives, but he wanted to be ready. He wanted to be a dad. He wanted to do it right this time.

That meant doing more than simply existing and paying his bills. It meant learning how to interact with people, be sociable, and be part of society. He couldn't just hide Tommen away from the world; a boy needed friends and a healthy social life, an education, and Owain had to stay current on these things so he could be prepared, no matter the year.

He stayed in Detroit for a total of twelve years before going dark. He told himself he did it to avoid the draft, though he knew he would always be too old for that. There was no way he could pass as being anything less than forty years old.

Despite his ambition to prepare himself to be more than just a decent human being and instead graduate into "good man ready to be a father" status, Owain kept his head low for a while, trying to wait out all the social unrest. When it wasn't civil rights, it was Vietnam. When it wasn't Vietnam, it was the president. When it wasn't any of those things, it was some strange goal to land on the moon.

That was the one Owain couldn't figure out. Landing on the moon was supposed to be some pinnacle of human achievement representing unity and exploration and the desire to reach beyond oneself, beyond just the human race, beyond just Earth, and travel among the stars. But then this grandiose story would be suddenly eclipsed by breaking news from the front. Did anyone else see the irony in this? Well, Owain wasn't about to start any political discussions. There was one thing that he hadn't bothered to change about himself, and that was his general disinterest in politics. He watched other men get political and wondered exactly what they hoped to accomplish. If there was no call to action behind it, if it remained only grumbling or shouting and lingering bitterness, how was that helping yourself, never mind your community or region? Owain decided to just let it alone and let things play out how they would. He'd lived through too many presidents to really care anymore, not that he'd started out with much ambition.

Even when dark, in transition between lives, there were ways for Time Agents to keep in touch, and it was getting easier and easier with all the new technology coming out, expanding and improving almost every decade. It was 1962 when Mark called Owain.

"They got me, Owain," Mark told him.

"Who did?" Owain wondered, unsure if he wanted to know the answer. There had been plenty of turmoil surrounding the Wheel and the Hands of Time recently with the elections right around the corner.

"The U.S. Government."

"Oh." Owain let out a sigh of relief. "Is that all? What do you mean, they got you?"

"I mean they tracked me down, got past all of my security barriers, and picked me up for the draft. I'm at bootcamp right now, get one call to let someone know I'm here."

"Um, I think that's jail you're thinking of."

"Ha! You would know, wouldn't you? I'm sorry, Owain, that was in poor taste. I'm just a little upset is all."

"Are you going to bail?"

"Oh, I've thought about it. Believe me, my first instinct when those men showed up on my door was to run, Band, and duck out through a portal. You know what made me reconsider?"

"What?"

"You."

"Me?"

Owain could imagine Mark's nod. "Yup. You. You've come a long way since we first met. I've watched you go from a skittish, self-deprecating, depressed alcoholic—"

"You don't mince words, do you?"

"—to a right, upstanding man, a good man to have in society. You've faced a lot of fears and doubts." Mark sighed. "I guess I thought maybe it was time I faced a few of my fears, too."

"Mark, there's a difference between being afraid of—of—of a snarling dog, and being afraid of war and death. You can see it in their eyes, Mark, when they come back. There's something not right going on over there. War isn't what it used to be."

"Well, there is that. But don't worry; if I do get too scared, I can always bail."

"Don't say that too loud."

"What are they going to do, kick me out? They just drafted me! Yeah, yeah, I know what you're saying. Listen, I have to go. You take care of yourself, Owain, you hear me?"

"Suddenly I'm less worried about me and more worried about you."

"Good to know. We'll talk again, I'm sure."

Owain let out a breath. "Godspeed to you, Mark."

"Yeah." Mark's voice broke. "Thanks. Godspeed to you, too."

Owain hung up and stood by the phone for a few minutes, feeling rather numb. He liked Mark, would consider him his best friend, one of the few real friends he'd ever had. Owain did not doubt that Mark could fend for himself or make a break for it through a portal if he had to, but he was still uncertain. Mark had sworn off war, or at least his participation in it, and blanched at violence in general; even as a jailer, he'd been the more level-headed approach, the good cop. Inmates had respected him. For him to suddenly go along with this, Owain had his doubts. Maybe Mark would freeze up, and it didn't take a soldier to know that standing still was a godsend to the enemy, and he would be shot, regardless of his Time abilities.

But what, exactly, could he do about it? Mark was his own person and he was willingly going along with it. The best Owain could do was wish him well and maybe offer up a couple prayers for his safety.

Pretty soon, Owain was praying fervently for his own safety. The 1963 elections had come to the Wheel, and it was turning into a bloodbath. Cries of deception, bribery, favors, scandal, and every other bad thing to befall an election. The votes were recounted multiple times, and came up different every time. Now, everyone who had thrown their hat in the ring was loathe to give it up. The official number of Hands was to always be fifty-one. After the eighth recount, the eighth set of completely different results, there were over a thousand self-proclaimed Hands. Lines were drawn, alliances were forged, and factions began arming themselves.

Owain took advantage of Earth's status as Unengaged in the Time industry—meaning that the general public and the higher governing bodies knew nothing of its existence and its Time Agents were constantly on the down low—and tried to hide. He remained in the dark, not establishing himself anywhere, forging no new lives. He existed as a ghost among society, both societies. On Earth, he roamed, staying nowhere for very long, often boarding with other Time Agents who were trying to do the same thing, lay low either in or out of established lives. In Time, he simply ignored it for as long as he could. Unless he apprehended a Runner who was truly dangerous, he avoided the Wheel as much as possible.

In all the chaos and trying to remain incognito as much as possible, Owain fretted over news of Tommen, whether he would get it if any were to surface. Multiple times, he passed through the area, just to check things out for himself. Multiple times, he pestered the Region Four Captain and Lieutenants, asking for news, ensuring they were still keeping an eye on things. Eventually, it got to the point where they told him if he was so damn worried, maybe he ought to train to be a Lieutenant himself, maybe try to become a District Four Lieutenant and get access to the area in higher places than a Master might go.

It was a tempting offer, one Owain seriously considered. In order to train to be a Timekeeper officer, he had to learn from two ranks above. Therefore, he would have to train under a Captain. A Lieutenant who wanted to be a Captain had to train under a Manager, and so on.

At the same time, the turmoil in the Wheel was not letting up. Even several years after the initial election, there were still hundreds of self-proclaimed Hands, and assassinations were being carried out right and left, some said all by the same person, a human called Calis Cutthroat. Being human, he could target human officers of any Time Agent duty — or any human Time Agent, for that matter. He could also draw out some interstellar bounty hunters who were charged with protecting their designated Hand or faction from his reign of terror, bring some chaos to Earth.

It was not a safe time to be an officer, and Owain had no illusions that trainees would be spared. He elected to wait just a bit longer, see how things played out.

It was just as well, he figured. It was 1967 when he got the letter.

He was staying in Idaho with a couple other Time Agents. The lead agent, the one who actually owned and lived in the house, handed him a letter one day, and a small box. It had been floating around in the mail for a bit since his listed address was no longer valid, and a Time Agent who happened to work for the post office got a hold of it and got it properly delivered.

It was from the U.S. Government, the Army to be precise. They regretted to inform him that Marcus A. Walker had been killed in action in Vietnam. His actions were very heroic, his bravery unparalleled, and his —

Owain stumbled outside for some air.

How could Mark be dead? How did it happen? When? Why? Was it a surprise attack, a shot to the back? It must have been. Time allowed them to perceive smaller increments of Time than just seconds, so he could have avoided anything he saw, or at least make it less than lethal. He would have run if he had the chance. He never would have let himself be captured. Exposure be damned, he would have shown a portal to the entire world if he could escape being captured and marched to a POW camp.

But all the same, Mark had been in longer than Owain thought he would have been. Four years for a man who'd sworn off war and shunned violence? Owain shook his head. Something about that war wasn't right. You could see it in their eyes. Mark had been affected somehow.

Another thought occurred to him, then. Did it matter now? Even if Owain understood everything that had happened, from how Mark physically died, to his state of mind over the last four years, was it going to bring him back? Was it going to change anything?

Taking a breath, he reopened the letter and read it through several more times before realizing there was a second paper. This one was not from the U.S. Government, nor was it typed up on a typewriter. It was a handwritten letter from Mark.

"March 31, 1967

"Owain —

"A lot of the guys here write to their wives and children, or their parents if they're still young. Seeing how I don't have any of those things, I'll write to

you. But I'm not going to tell any of the guys that I am or they'll think I'm homosexual, and that would not end well for me.

"If you're reading this, it means that something has happened to me. Probably I'm mortally wounded, more likely I'm dead. Then they went through, cleaned out my things, put them in a box, and shipped them back stateside to whomever I listed on my papers. They've done that to more guys than I've cared to count since I've got here.

"I'm sending my things to you because I consider you my friend. As strange as it sounds, considering our difference in apparent age, I consider you like the son I never had. Bailing you out of jail, teaching you how to be a good person, the finer points of society, then releasing you into the world. If I'd ever had kids, I imagine that's kind of how it would go. Sort of. Oh, let's face it, I have no clue what I'm talking about.

"If you're expecting any specific instructions on what to do with my stuff, lower your expectations. If I'm dead, I'm not going to care. If I'm wounded or crippled, I'm not going to want to remember anyway. Keep it, hang it up, donate it, or burn it, I don't care.

"You may be wondering how I lasted as long as I did. I wonder the same thing. Maybe I'm depressed. Maybe I've finally gone insane. I don't know. I wish I did. Maybe I would still be alive then. I think, between the two of us, you were the smart one. Don't envy me for anything. But know that I envied you for a lot of the hell you've been through, hell you survived.

"Back to work, then, I suppose. Go to bed in the evening, wake up in the morning. Sometimes, that's the best you can expect.

"Godspeed, brother.

"Mark"

Owain carefully folded the letter and stuffed it in his jacket pocket before returning to the house. He took the box up to the room he was renting and opened it. Not much. A uniform, a couple photographs, dog tags, and a flag. Not much at all. For a man who began his life fighting for the independence of his own country and ended it fighting...at this point only God knew what they were up against, or if they could pull it off.

He did not remove anything, simply placed the letters on top of the stuff and replaced the lid of the box. He contemplated the box for a while. He considered burning it. He considered burying it. But for the moment, it would have to do to just slide it under the bed.

Chapter Thirty-One

The Split

The war in Vietnam ended. Disco, unfortunately, began. Civil rights were won, and the United States put a man on the moon before the Soviet Union.

In Time, the Dispersal of '63, as the 1963 elections had come to be known on Earth, were dwindling down. Fifty-one Hands were installed—seeing how they were the fifty-one survivors of all the attacks and assassinations—and now everyone was getting ready for the upcoming 1980 elections. It wasn't an enthusiastic endeavor, regardless of what the Hands said about new "safety measures" being put in place in order to ensure something like the Dispersal never happened again.

1980 was a big year for Owain. He voted in the elections—compulsory since he was a Master Timekeeper—and was relieved when things went smoothly. He also began training to become a Lieutenant Timekeeper. He wanted to improve himself, and there were some things that officers had to learn that he knew he needed, not only to become an officer, but to be a good human being in general. Conflict resolution, for example.

It was also the year he decided to establish another new life for himself, working in the fishing industry in New England, sometimes going out on the boat, sometimes working in the cannery.

It was his first life where his fabled story did not involve coming through Ellis Island. Over the years, he'd gotten younger and younger in his supposed crossing, but now he'd reached a point where he'd simply aged out. He couldn't be forty-five in 1980 and still have gone through Ellis Island. He almost didn't know what to do, not having that part of his story anymore, and he felt a little empty. He'd been repeating that lie for so many decades, he very nearly believed it himself.

But perhaps the most significant change he made in 1980 was his name. He'd toyed with the idea a little over the years, but after Mark's death, he really considered it. It wouldn't be a huge change; he'd just take his other alias, Walter Forbes. His only hesitation was that it made him feel dishonest. He'd finally reached a point where he was proud to be Owain Fforidd, really happy with himself. Maybe not overjoyed, but content. He couldn't explain exactly when his shift in mindset came, but he was fine with who he was, or rather, who he had become. In a moment of overjoyed confusion, his head in the clouds somewhere, he almost thought about writing a letter to his ma and letting her know how far he'd come.

He wept for fifteen minutes, then took a two-hour nap after that thoughtless consideration.

It was that little incident which tipped the scales and he elected to change his name. It didn't have to be permanent, he figured. Ten years or so, he could pretend to be someone else, someone he almost was. Maybe he could do better at being Walter this time around. He'd improved on Owain greatly, maybe he could build up Walter a little, too. Then he could alternate personae in his many future lives and be confident in both.

Of course, fishing and living the humble life didn't exactly provide a ton of opportunities for external growth. It wasn't until a few years into his new life as Walter that he considered that it wasn't about the external growth, growing his bank account or his other assets or any of that. If he wanted to be confident and happy with his Walter persona, he had to be happy and confident with himself, no matter his name or the life he built for himself. And a humble life was just what the doctor ordered. If he couldn't find joy and gratitude in the mundane aspects of life, he didn't deserve to have an exciting life free of trouble or worry or otherwise having enormous success.

That wasn't to say he enjoyed smelling like raw fish every single day so that it permeated his clothes and his house, but he had a job, he had a house, he had good finances, he had friends. With things settled down in the Time industry and no further coups or bloodbaths or assassinations, he was able to have better contact with other Time Agents, do his job, continue his training, and bring in a little money on the side. It was a good life, a good time in his life.

He completed his Lieutenant training in 1985.

He'd trained under the Captain of District Seven which consisted of the United States' part of the Rockies and some of the land on either side. He could have gone to the Captain of his own District, except they didn't always see eye-to-eye, and he figured it might be good for him to get out of his comfort zone again, similar to what he'd done for his Journeyman training.

Upon completion of his training, his mentor took him to dinner with his own Lieutenants. Captain Dean White had the appearance of being in his late-thirties, early-forties, prematurely gray and bald, and probably not doing too much literal running after Runners. Hard to believe he'd once been an upstanding Army colonel sent to control the "Native Problem" and tame the West for settlers. One of those Natives had almost sent him to an early grave if not for one of his men being a Timekeeper, who healed the wound miraculously and brought the man into Time.

Darren Bielski was one of his Lieutenants. Six-six and all limb, he was fairly new to the Time industry, considering present company. He looked only about twenty, twenty-five at a maximum. He couldn't be bothered to brush his wild mess of black hair, and while he hadn't been a hippie in the sixties when he became a Timekeeper, he was a true eighties rebel with lots of piercings and multiple tattoos. He thought it made him look tough, as if he'd done time in prison, so maybe people would leave him alone.

"Have you ever done time in prison, or even jail?" Owain asked him.

Darren shrugged casually. "No."

"I have. It's not something I would care to relive, and I don't find it to be a very attractive fashion accessory."

The beanpole shrugged again, but flushed bright red and said nothing more.

Patrick Jar was Dean's other Lieutenant, and the only thing remarkable about him was the realization that there was nothing remarkable about him. Average height, average weight, average build, brown hair, brown eyes, about thirty-five years old. Physically, you could replace him with a suitcase in a crowd and nothing would change. To his credit, however, he had a fantastic personality. Outgoing, respectful, polite, a sense of humor that could make the Buckingham Guard laugh, and he could carry on a conversation about just about anything. And if he didn't understand something, he was always eager to learn.

Perhaps the only aspect of Patrick's life that disturbed Owain the most was that he knew him. While they had never met, Patrick had also been in London the same time as Owain. He had also been something of an investor, though not to the degree that would get him noticed by one so prestigious as Jonathon Balk.

"Aye, I heard what happened," Patrick said when Owain asked about it. "I heard that you beat your wife, she divorced you, so you went and killed her, her new husband, her father, and—"

"Not true," Owain told him seriously. "Frederick Travis killed Paige." He would never forget the name of the man who killed his wife and daughter. "And Victoria. I went hunting for him and got him." He sighed. "And Balk, and the others."

"I also heard you became quite a celebrity with the Church."

"I suppose so."

"You obviously escaped the noose."

Owain nodded, feeling his skin burn hot. "Yes, I did." He looked Patrick straight in the eye. "I've done a lot of things I'm not proud of. If I could go back and change it all, I would. But I can't. I've moved on since then, bettered myself."

"We're glad of your conviction, but we're not exactly saints ourselves here," Dean told him. "You think I still feel proud of myself for the role I played in dozens of Indian massacres and hundreds more deaths? Absolutely not. Beanpole here hasn't learned it yet, but one day he'll grow up to resent all the holes and ink he's put in his skin." Darren just rolled his eyes. "You're a century removed from your past, Walter, and I don't think we'd be sitting here if you were the same man you were back then."

In a way, his comments made Owain feel better, a weight lifted that he did not realize he'd been carrying. It was so obvious, and stated plainly in the Bible that he read every morning, yet he had never really considered that everyone was a sinner. Everyone had a past. In the case of Time Agents, everyone had a life "before." Dean had been shot by Natives. Patrick made the mistake of picking a fight with a bunch of lower class ruffians in a sleazy pub, the kind of place that Owain used to frequent and the kind of men he used to fight. Darren had been in a car accident on his way to kill himself, throw himself off a bridge. They had a unique opportunity to restart their lives. Sure, the outside world may never know of their horrendous deeds, but within Time, among the Time Agents, they were a bunch of sinners with the chance to become saints.

"...don't think there are any Lieutenant openings around here," Dean was saying. "North America is pretty well buttoned up, all the positions filled at the moment. If you're dead set on filling a Lieutenant position, try overseas in some of the more unstable regions. I think we'll be seeing a lot of action over in the Middle East, though you don't have quite the complexion for it."

Owain shook his head. "I'm not going to kill myself for it, thanks."

"Good answer." Dean shifted position in his seat. He opened his mouth to say more, but their food arrived just then. The restaurant wasn't terribly busy, not a lot of eavesdropping ears, but it was loud enough that they couldn't be heard all the way in the kitchen. Dean went on, "So then, what do you intend to do with yourself? I mean, we have extended lives, we can put things off a few years if we need to, but what are some things you'd like to do?"

"Quite honestly, at this point, I'm still just hoping I can reconnect with my nephew. I don't know how much longer I'm willing to wait, though."

"Your nephew?" Darren wondered. "Aren't you, you know, a century removed from your time? Your nephew is, like, long gone. Or are you talking about a descendant of a nephew?"

"No, I'm talking about my nephew, my brother's child." Owain paused wondering how much he should say. "In West Virginia, there's a cave. It's a Time trap, or a Time portal, whatever you want to call it. It's encased in a Fast Band of extremely high strength. I was in for only a short time and I jumped ahead seventy years by the time I came out. My nephew went in before me, and to my knowledge, still hasn't emerged. I want to be there when he does, take him, raise him. Maybe I'll teach him Time, too."

Patrick nodded around a bite of brisket. He swallowed. "That would be good. Keep him in the family and out of a mental hospital."

"That's the idea."

"How old is your nephew?" Dean inquired.

"Eight."

That earned sympathetic looks and grunts of agreement, a non-verbal resolution that this was what must be done. Owain appreciated the support, but he didn't know how much good they could do considering they were presently in the wrong mountain range.

"You haven't heard anything?" Dean asked.

"Nothing," Owain sighed.

"Have you gone back yourself to look?" Patrick wondered.

"I don't know what I would be looking for exactly, if you're talking literally. I've been through the area several times, but haven't seen or heard anything, or nothing obvious."

"What about going behind the scenes?" Darren suggested.

Owain looked at him. "What do you mean?"

"Look, man, at this point, there is probably not going to be any family left to contact, right?"

"There are still Forbeses in the area, but the relation is very distant."

"Exactly. And they're probably not going to claim him. But no matter what, he's going to be a lost child. The world has grown up since 1800. Civilization has probably already crept up to where there was once wilderness where he lived, right?"

Owain frowned. "His old home has been destroyed and there are talks of turning it into a park."

"Civilization, as I said. Someone is going to find him. First place they're going to take him is the hospital. Or that's what I would think."

"You're saying I should become a pediatrician?"

Darren shrugged. "I don't know. Maybe. But consider this: if the kid has no family, the hospital isn't going to send out a search party. Who are they going to call? Give you a hint, it's not the Ghostbusters." When Owain did not answer, the man with many piercings sighed dramatically. "The fuzz. The po-po. They're going to call the cops. Get a missing persons report going, or whatever, missing child, and the cops start talking, try to figure out who he is, where he comes from, and if there is any family out there. The hospital might not say much because he's a kid, but that's the same reason the cops will talk. Get what I'm saying?"

Now Owain nodded. "I understand."

"Good." Darren shook his head. "I don't know, man. Is it the tongue and lip piercings? Do they make it so I'm speaking another language?"

"You do that without even opening your mouth," Dean told him.

"And what is that supposed to mean?"

Owain ignored their banter and instead focused on his food. There was a danger in living so long, in that he could become too accustomed to doing things one way and not being receptive to new methods and ideas. He supposed it made sense that a lost child would be taken to the hospital and the police would be called. It made sense that police would talk, even if only to other police stations. The question then became, how did he go about getting in on that conversation?

The most obvious solution would be to become a police officer, but it was also the most ridiculous. At his best, he could pass off as forty, maybe a little younger if he went with a hard life story that caused him to go gray early—even if he really didn't have much gray hair—or an accident as a young man that gave him stiff joints. At the same time, he was in better shape now than he had been before he became a Timekeeper. Time may not have made him twenty years old again, and it may not heal all wounds, but there were certain healing qualities about it.

All he really had to do was work at it, put his mind to it. He was only five years into his current life. In another five years, if could remain self-disciplined, he could probably work out and get into good enough shape that he could become a police officer. He wouldn't be one of the young guns, true, fresh out of high school, eighteen and invincible, but he would be in good shape. And brains and experience had to count for something, right? It wasn't all about brawn.

All the same, it seemed a ridiculous notion. Here he was, a condemned man, running from the noose, thinking about becoming a policeman. It felt hilarious and hypocritical. Who was he to exert the force of the law over someone else?

Well, he may have been a condemned man, but he was also a redeemed man. He had removed the plank from his own eye. Now maybe he had permission to help others remove the dust from their own eyes, even if it meant holding them down with their hands behind their back. And besides, he wasn't interested in power-tripping. He just wanted to get in on the conversation between police stations and listen for news about his nephew.

He returned home, conflicted. What if Tommen had already emerged and had slipped through the net of Time Agents listening for his appearance? What if he'd emerged fifty years ago, was already grown, had a family, and was, by all appearances, older than his own uncle? What if he wouldn't appear for another fifty years? How long could he stand to wait?

Owain returned to work at the cannery the following day. It was a noisy environment with little time for conversation while on the floor. He'd learned to ignore it and instead concentrate on his work and his own thoughts. At lunch, he talked to one of his coworkers about the idea.

"A police officer?" Hank questioned. "Walt, aren't you almost fifty?"

"Humor me," Owain said. "What do you think?"

The man, who was only a few years younger than Owain, faltered for a second as he popped open his lunchbox. "I think if you would have asked me that question fifteen to twenty years ago, I would have said sure. I mean, even for your age, you're strong and in good shape. Just not enough for the police force anymore. Twenty years ago, oh yeah, I wouldn't want to tangle with you in a fight."

Owain tried not to flinch. Instead he merely nodded, tried to look resigned, a little regretful, which wasn't difficult. "Ah, I guess I'm just wondering about things that could have been, things I should have done."

Hank nodded. "I completely understand. Lot of things I wish I had done in my life. Lot of things I wish I hadn't."

And that was that.

Owain spent the next month or so batting the idea around in his head and wearing a path in his living room carpet. On the one hand, he told himself to be patient and be content with his life. He was working on a lot of self-improvement, no need to get all flustered over the first idea that popped into his head. He needed to think things through at the very least, consider his ideas, his options, his abilities, maybe do a little praying and see if the Lord wouldn't tell him to just stay put and stop trying to do things his own way.

On the other hand, being content didn't always mean being passive. For the last sixty years, he'd relied on others to look for his nephew but had done very little looking himself. He was a Lieutenant-trained Master Timekeeper now, not an Apprentice. If he could be called upon to help oversee Timekeeper operations in an entire District spanning multiple states, why shouldn't he have a significant part in searching for his own kin? The Lord may guide one's path, but if he wasn't going anywhere, it didn't mean a whole lot.

He started working out. It wasn't a lot at first, enough to figure out the state of his body and what he could do, see if this was really going to go anywhere, try and establish a routine.

It was hard, and not just the workout. He hadn't anticipated the mental exhaustion that also accompanied his exercises. Between just keeping up the routine and trying to push himself to do more, be more, when his body said it was perfectly happy where and how it was, it wore on him. Then there was the added mental stress of the reason he was doing it, because he was putting some skin in the game to find his nephew. And that stress was compounded in his many moments of doubt, when he wondered what he would do if he got into great shape for his age, but it still wasn't enough for the police force. What if there really wasn't anything he could do to get in? What if that door was permanently closed to him? How was he going to find Tommen then?

Then he would go with Plan B, become a doctor of some form and work in a hospital. A missing child was sure to be taken to a hospital for evaluation.

He continued with his workout routine, always pushing himself harder but never feeling like it was going to be enough. He was going to be competing with young men, eighteen, twenty, twenty-five years old. Literally half his age. He had to be strong like them. He had to be able to keep up with them, run with them. He had to be able to fight them.

In between his exercises, he also started preparing himself for his alternate plan by studying medical textbooks. He learned about anatomy, diseases, all sorts of things that he felt were way out of his league. Modern education was far beyond anything he'd ever studied, and not a few times, he had to go back to concepts that were being taught as early as second grade. It was a little embarrassing, but he never let on as he perused the children's section of the library. If a stranger asked, he might say he was helping his grandkids with their homework. If someone he knew asked, he was studying for himself.

His coworkers thought he was going through a mid-life crisis. Fifty years old, but darn it if he wasn't going to be a police officer. Fifty years old, but he was going to complete a decade of medical school to become a doctor. Some made fun of him, others gave him sympathetic looks. Only a handful gave him any sort of genuine encouragement.

The first year was tough. The second year, he started keeping a log of his run times and his weights, noting his improvements and being discouraged by how slow his progress was.

"You're not a young man anymore," Hank told him. "We all slow down as we get older." He shrugged. "Keeping in shape is one thing, but you're not going to be a teenager again who only has to look at a bench press and he can suddenly lift an additional ten pounds. I don't want you to be discouraged, but you do need a dose of reality now and again, know what I mean?"

"I know," Owain said, rubbing his face. He sighed. "If you knew you had another fifty years to live, just hit the pause button right now and add fifty years, what would you do with it?"

Hank seemed perplexed by the question, and by the time he came up with any semblance of an answer, the bell rang to signal the end of lunch and time to go back to work.

Owain completed his second year of working out. He'd now spent a little over seven years in his life in New England. He could get away with up to fifteen years, depending on his supposed starting age, but he calculated he had only maybe three years left for a total of ten years. It was kind of how it went. He needed to start planning for his next life, but how? Did he start applying to Police Academies around the nation or what?

He put everything off for a year, instead continuing faithfully with his routine, workout, studying, and all. He wanted to be in the best shape he could possibly be before humiliating himself in front of a bunch of young police cadets.

His answer to his predicament came the following year when the Captain of District Six, primarily the Plains and a little bit of the South, called him up.

"Word on the street is, you're a Lieutenant-trained Master," Elton Windsor said.

"That word is true at least," Owain told him.

"Rumors also say that you might be looking at being a policeman."

"Depends on how much I want to embarrass myself. I've been working out and everything, but I'm still not a spry young man anymore."

Elton laughed at that. "Aren't we all? Well, listen to me close, Walter, because I'm only going to make the offer once. One of my Lieutenants is moving up in the world, going to Europe and all that. I've got an opening here for you. With that, Austin has one of the best Police Academies in the nation. I can't guarantee that you'll get in or pass or any of that, but I can make it so you can at least be considered and have a shot at getting in. You'll have to give them so many years on the force, but you can take it anywhere you want to go, at least in the U.S."

"Anywhere in the U.S.?"

"Eventually, yes. What do you say?"

"When is all this taking place? I admit, I haven't really gotten around to going dark and building a life and all of that. I'm almost fifty-five right now, so I would have to lower my age again."

"Misty only just told me about going to Europe, but it's not going to be right away. If you start now, you should have ample time to set up a life before moving out here."

"Sounds good, Captain."

"I'll call you again once she's within six months of leaving, just to give you a heads up and a kick in the pants."

Owain hung up, unsure how he was supposed to feel, though unprepared and inadequate were certainly floating around in there. He forced himself to relax and reminded himself that he had time. He wasn't shipping out tomorrow.

He continued his workout routine, even upped it a little, pushed himself harder. He couldn't remember the last time he had this much resolve, this much drive. He studied his medical textbooks late into the night. He added in some police procedural books as well, though he was fairly certain that things at the southern border were a little different than things on the northeastern coast, so he took all of it with a grain of salt. And he threw in a few Spanish lessons, too, for good measure. He had to give himself every advantage.

Unfortunately, Misty's European adventure got a little delayed, and Owain was forced to go dark in 1990, even before she left. He called Elton a few times just to make sure the offer was still open. The Captain assured him it was and eventually encouraged him to move to Texas anyway to establish himself in the area a little, get a feel for the local flavor.

In 1993, Owain traveled to Texas via blind portal, taking a direct route from the east coast to the southern border. Two things hit him as soon as he walked through the portal. Texas was hot, and it was dirty. The sun was utterly merciless, and dust was caked on everything. The water was brown, too, with more dirt than the ocean had salt. Owain's first thought was wondering why anyone wanted to live in such a place. This was what America had fought Mexico for? Mexico could have it back as far as he was concerned. Give him thick forests and lush greenery any day.

It was 1994 before Misty finally left for Europe and Owain was instated as one of the two Lieutenants for District Six. Once that was made official, he officially sent in his application for the Austin Police

Academy. While he had been told that all candidates had to go through a formal interview process, Owain couldn't help but feel singled out because of his age. Indeed, even the interviewers—consisting of two Academy instructors and the Austin Chief of Police himself—looked a little surprised when he walked in the door.

"According to your application, you're forty years old," one of the instructors, Dan Willett, commented. "Most applicants we get are in their teens and twenties, maybe hovering around thirty. What brings you here?"

"I don't want to lose the chance if I have it," Owain told them, "and even if I am rejected, I don't want to say that I didn't try. I also figure that a little experience has to count for something, more than physical ability alone."

"You're not wrong there. And while we cannot exclude you based solely on your age, you do understand that you will have to keep up with men and women half your age?"

"I understand."

The rest of the interview was just as strange, and Owain left the room feeling like a complete failure. Maybe it had really been a midlife crisis. Maybe he really was trying to prove to himself that he was young again. Maybe this whole Timekeeper business and the extended lifespan was finally starting to get to him. Maybe he should call up the interviewers and tell them not to waste their time with him. Maybe he should have skipped the Police Academy and gone to med school instead.

He ended up talking to another Timekeeper on the phone about it. His name was Kevin Tanner, a Master Timekeeper who happened to be a nurse in Omaha. He looked about twenty-five years old, was physically fit, everything Owain knew he needed to be in order to get into the Academy. To his surprise, Kevin had a lot of faith in him.

"Actually, I envy you."

"Envy me?" Owain asked.

"Absolutely. Listen, you're all worried that you're not going to get in. And I won't say that you might not have a harder time of it. But you know what happens when you do get in? Twenty years instant experience. You go through the Academy once, and you can tack on a ton of years of experience in your future lives. You have the experience to back you up. Young guys like me? Yeah, the world is my oyster, I can get into just about any school because I am assumed to be fresh out of high school or early college, and I'm physically fit. But that is all I will ever be. I will never be able to list thirty, forty, fifty years of nursing experience on a resume. I will never get a nice pension. I will never get more than a starting wage plus maybe a few raises. I will always only ever be the new guy, the fresh graduate, the greenhorn. I seriously envy you, Walt. If you get in, stay in. Work hard and get that experience. Use it to your advantage."

Owain had never really thought about it that way. He thanked Kevin, wished him well, and hung up.

He got his acceptance letter the next week.

Chapter Thirty-Two

The Officer

Owain had no trouble keeping up with the young guns in the classroom. In fact, he outdid most of them. It didn't help his standing much, however, since he was usually the butt of a number of jokes, all of them age-related. It was all in good fun, since he put a stop to anything malicious the first time they went out on the mat. The young boys expected him to be slow and weak. They did not expect to be laid out flat within four or five seconds. Owain quickly figured out their problem, but he didn't tell them. A lot of them boasted a black belt in this, or state titles in that. The problem was, those were art forms with specific methods and motions and patterns. Owain was the king of street-fighting, where there were no rules, nothing was off-limits, and participants couldn't be afraid of going down in the mud.

Even once the boys wised up and got a little experience under their belts, there was only one cadet who was a real threat to Owain. His name was Richard, and he'd done two tours in Afghanistan. He knew fear, he knew combat, he knew the concept of survival. Richard was the only one who could lay down Owain. Similarly, Owain was the only one who could lay him down. They were a fairly even match and always a spectacle, if the way the others quit fighting to come and watch them was any indication.

"You're good," Richard said, giving Owain a hand off the floor at the end of their last match. "I would've hated to have met you twenty years ago."

"Aye, that's what they tell me," Owain sighed. "Not too bad yourself."

The two of them ended up graduating at the top of their Academy class, Richard edging out Owain for valedictorian by a mere two-tenths of a point.

"Guess I should have studied harder for the final exam," Owain said, shaking Richard's hand at the reception after the awards ceremony.

"You old guys," Richard teased. "Think you already know everything."

Owain ended up getting hired into Austin PD while Richard went to Houston. The rest of them dispersed throughout the area, various city or county departments. One, who was already a certified firefighter, went straight into med school to be a paramedic, thereby solidifying his status as a first responder rockstar.

Once graduated from the Police Academy, Owain also took up training to advance to Captain Timekeeper, training under the Regional Manager. Elton joked that he had created a monster, promoting Owain to Lieutenant and getting him through Police Academy; he was going to start coming after all their jobs now.

Despite remaining in Texas, Owain never really grasped Spanish. He could read it well enough, but he always had a hard time listening and speaking. It was probably why he was usually assigned as a desk jockey. When he did go out in the field, most often he was the backup, the muscle. His job was not to communicate with suspects; his job was to make sure they stuck around long enough to speak and not be a danger to other officers.

Being a desk jockey did afford him a few advantages, like being one of the first ones in the office to learn about and use the Internet. Sure, it had been around for some time in a limited sense, but now it was becoming a real global phenomenon. The ability to look up endless swaths of information, to "email" people and send text without having to pick up a phone. Condensing, combining, and cross-referencing information in a database, tracking criminals electronically, it was astounding.

Owain found himself wondering if life would have been terribly different for him if Beaumaris Gaol had had this technology, the ability to track and collaborate across whole states.

He didn't think about Beaumaris much during his waking hours, and the differences in the prison system then and now meant that he was not all that affected by it when he delivered a suspect to the holding cells. All the same, he still had dreadful nightmares and slept with a nightlight so that if he woke in the middle of the night, he could see that he was home and not suffocating in a black cell. The worst of the fear came just when he was on the cusp of sleep, when his higher brain functions shut down and he could no longer consciously discern his surroundings. Then, suddenly, it was like falling off a cliff as the darkness clamped down on him. The beast could no longer control him, but that did not mean the demons could not torture him.

But during the day, all was well. He went to work, he went home, he worked on his Captain training. His Captain training did not take as long as he expected; it was more politics and classroom learning where Lieutenant had been primarily physical training with only a little classroom work. He remained as the District Six Lieutenant, however, even after he made Captain, the same month that he was promoted to Sergeant at the precinct.

"Year 2000 is coming up fast," his partner, Lorenzo Valdez, commented one evening as they sat on the side of a deserted road. "Think the world is going to end?"

"If it does, my only wish is that it's painless," Owain answered, not looking at him. "I don't think it will."

"I don't think so either. My grandmother would like that, though, if it did."

"Why?"

"For some reason, she's always had it in her head that she is going to live long enough for the Lord to come back. Ever since she was a little girl, my grandfather says, she has always known that she is going to see the Lord riding back on His white horse. Granted, I have no reason not to believe her, but I don't think it's going to be because of this Y2K bullshit."

Owain grinned. "I think people put a little too much faith in math and numbers. By themselves, they're always patterns. The world should have ended a dozen times by now. And if not, just wait for the next cycle, the next iteration of a mathematical formula. Why didn't the world end at year 1000? If not, we'll go for year 2000."

"Exactly. And it's not even like the world is going to end, like, explode. They think the computers won't be able to handle going from 1999 to 2000. But once again, like you said, it's a pattern. Why wouldn't the computers be able to handle it? They go from 199 to 200 just fine. Even my little calculator can calculate up to 99999999."

Owain waved a hand, still grinning. "The world existed before technology."

Valdez shifted in his seat. "Yeah, you lived about that time, didn't you? What was it like, the first time you saw fire? Your grandfather invented the wheel, didn't he?"

"Ha ha, very funny. I'm not that old."

The radio squawked and soon they were on their way to some disturbance.

Time came in handy when on the job, Owain quickly learned. He often recalled the night that he and Mark took on Jesse Link, the gunfire and the chaos, how Mark had wielded Time so as to save his fellows and emerged completely unharmed. Now Owain was the one making the physical world dance to his fife. In the heat of the moment, he thought nothing of it: slowing down Time so he could get a brother out of the way or divert a bullet's path, or speeding it up so as to confuse suspects with how many rounds they had left, or how quickly they could reload.

But when it was all over, Owain sometimes scared himself, the things he could do. It wasn't real fear, more of a spectacle, awe and wonder. Once he was congratulated again as being the invincible man, the one bullets ran away from, he simply went about his day, usually at a desk.

He returned home that night to a quiet house, as he always did. He knew of Time Agents who lived together to split costs and give an appearance of family — as well as, ahem, relieve tension — but the thought never appealed to him. Occasionally he offered up a room to rent for Time Agents passing through, needing a place to stay for a bit during their dark times, but no one really lived with him. He didn't shack up with a woman in order to give the appearance of having a wife.

It was a difficult thing to do, for one. As far as Time Agents went, he was on the older end of the spectrum. Most were surprised he hadn't had a psychotic break when he'd been exposed, especially considering the circumstances. He went with the simplest explanation, that his whole life had been spent just being grateful for being alive, and learning to roll with the tide, take whatever came and learn to live with it.

So if he ever did shack up with a woman, she would need to be about his apparent age in order to make it convincing. There weren't too many female Time Agents of any discipline who looked older than, say, thirty-five. True, he might be able to live with a younger woman and claim she was his daughter, but even now, a century later, he didn't think he was quite ready to take that leap.

This then begged the question of what he thought he was going to do with an eight year old boy, if and when Tommen did appear.

He sighed and made for the living room to relax in his recliner for a bit before going to bed. He'd no sooner sat down than his phone rang. Groaning, he got up and went to pick up the receiver.

"Walter Forbes speaking," he said, hoping his tone adequately indicated that he was not in a mood to talk.

"Walter, it's Paul Hermel." The Captain of District Four.

"What can I do for you? Runner coming my way?"

"No, no, nothing like that. Better. Listen, Lonnie, the Regional Manager, he's looking to retire from his position. He's got cancer and he wants to live out his days not working."

"I can understand that."

"Rumor has it that I'm being considered for the position, which means I'm going to need a replacement here in District Four. Don't get all excited thinking this is a straight job offer. I'm just letting you know that you're on the list of consideration, if you'd like to be considered."

"Do I get to choose my headquarters?"

"Naturally. My Lieutenants won't be far behind; they're just about used up in their current lives and they've spent a little too much time in this District—about forty years too long. You'll be needing to look for new Lieutenants pretty soon afterwards. Interested?"

District Four meant he could set up camp in Charleston. He could wait for Tommen and possibly be part of the police department that would handle any Missing or Found Child cases. This was a dream come true! "Absolutely."

"Glad to hear it. I'll call you once I know more. At this point, there is no guarantee that I'm even going to get the Manager position. You understand."

"I do. I'll be ready to go, but I'm not exactly holding my breath."

"You got the idea."

So Owain started passively perusing homes for sale and available jobs in the Charleston area. He'd been through the area several times since moving away and it never ceased to amaze him how much the area had grown up. He remembered when a starving man didn't have a prayer of finding civilization for endless miles. Now everything was just a short drive here or there, and even lost hikers had a shot at finding some form of help if they had half a brain to know what they were doing.

As a whole, West Virginia was the poorest state in the U.S., owing most of that to the Appalachians where people did not have electricity or running water. Some of it was true poverty caused by economic misfortune, and some of it was voluntary. The mountain people were a different breed who had no use for your modern technology.

To that end, housing was typically pretty cheap, as long as you stayed outside the city limits. Of course, it also meant Owain had to read the housing descriptions carefully to make sure it had electricity and running water. Could he live without them? Sure, already had for the first forty years of his life. Did he like modern amenities? Yes. Yes, he did.

He tried not to get too invested in the idea, but it was hard. He had a chance to search for Tommen. Not that he couldn't go there anyway once he started to overstay his welcome in Austin, but he liked the idea of a promotion, too. Captain of District Four.

Owain leaned back in his chair and let out a breath he hadn't realized he'd been holding.

I did make something of myself, pa, he thought. *I found Teo, just like you told me to. You and ma. If only you could see me now. I'm doing better. A lot better. I haven't touched a drink in over half a century. I'm a policeman now. It's the first real degree I've ever had, and it's a real job on the right side of the law. You'd be proud of me. I know you would.*

Owain said farewell to 1999 from his cruiser, hauling drunken morons from one party or another back to the holding cells. It was one of the few parts of his job where he felt more like a taxi and less of a police officer. All the same, he did it with little emotion, doling out pieces of advice here and there. He did not get short with them, physical only if he had to. After all, he'd been one of them once.

But the world did not end once the clock struck midnight, and January 1, 2000, was ushered in without the collapse of the computer system, the electrical grid, or world governments, nor did Jesus return on his white stallion, or any other world-ending prophecies of doom and gloom. Or any prophecies at all. It was simply another night and another day.

The year was rather uneventful as far as Owain was concerned. He'd reached a point in his life where he was no longer overly concerned with the affairs of government and world leaders. He fully believed that all the new technology and the Internet changed things, and not for the better, but he'd lived too long to believe anything really changed. Kingdoms came and kingdoms fell. Empires, regimes, they all ended eventually. Borders changed. People did, too. Not that he was rooting for anyone's destruction; he merely accepted it as fact. The most he cared about were local taxes in cities, townships, and counties, and maybe the state government, the governor and all that, depending on what was going on.

He did not hear anything about the Manager or the District Captain positions, so he concluded that either Paul hadn't gotten the position, or else he had, and Owain was not chosen to be his replacement as Captain.

That was the nice thing about technology, he figured. Phone, email, even this texting thing coming around now. Things could get done a lot quicker if they needed to be, and with ten times less effort than jumping around through blind portals.

It was February of 2001 that he got the call for a more formal interview for the Captain position. He went before both Paul and Lonnie. Unlike standard job interviews, with all of them being Time Agents, he was able to give a more complete overview of his history, his accomplishments, his training. He could admit to having seventy years of work experience despite looking only forty or fifty years old. Though it was a relief, he was still anxious about the interview and returned home unsure how to feel about it.

After the interview, he started looking more seriously at homes and jobs in Charleston, even contacted a few real estate agents to put out some feelers, get a sense of what he was walking into.

As far as Austin PD, the only people he told about his prospect of moving were his superiors. They didn't like the idea of losing a good Sergeant, but they could respect his decision to move back to Charleston to "hopefully take care of some family issues." And if he remained a cop with Charleston PD, well, at least it wasn't a total lost cause.

He contacted Charleston PD to inquire about a position. They were more than happy to take a fully-trained officer with a few years of experience. Just let them know when he would be in the area and Captain Steggmann would be happy to interview him and get the paperwork started.

All that remained was the green light from Paul which came in early June. He was relocating to District Two, consisting of basically all of central Canada, from Manitoba to Ontario, and everything north to the Arctic Sea. As soon as possible, Owain had to relocate to wherever he wanted his headquarters to be.

Owain made an offer on a house and was accepted almost immediately (he quickly began to figure that maybe he'd offered a little high). With that settled, he sent in his resignation to the Austin PD and the transfer paperwork to the union, moving from Texas police to West Virginia police.

He arrived in Charleston the same day he was set to close on the house and move in, as well as interview for the position with the police department. He hurried to the real estate office, signed the papers, took the keys, walked into his new home for a shower, found zero hot water, showered anyway, then changed into good clothes for the interview.

Greg Steggmann was a rather imposing fellow in person, Owain thought. Maybe thirty-five years old, six-foot-six or so, two-twenty, with a rather square face, a lopsided mustache, and a mole on one cheek. He had no trouble making himself heard, and he was generally easy to understand as well. He didn't toss in trick questions or play gotcha, though he did ask some difficult ethical questions relating to various cases or scenes. Some of them, Owain had no good answers for, and he admitted as much.

"I appreciate an honest man," Steggmann told him sincerely. "Now, if you were to get the job, are you looking for any department in particular? I know Texas has a lot of border hoppers, but we're a bit lacking in that department."

"Actually, I was more hoping for Missing Persons, especially children," Owain answered.

"Really? What makes you say that? Why children specifically?"

"Ah, I had a nephew go missing some years ago. He's not been found."

Steggmann nodded. "Motivation is a powerful thing. Well, I guarantee nothing, but we'll see."

He left the interview feeling wholly inadequate and certain that he wasn't going to get the job. Well, at least he had his consolation prize, the county mounties.

He went home to more thoroughly inspect his new abode. It wasn't much, a serious step down from how he'd lived in Austin. Maybe he should have shopped around a little more. The interior was very sixties with shag carpet and paisley power furniture. At the very least, it was structurally sound and really not in bad shape, once he got it cleaned up a little. It had one bedroom, one bathroom. An uninsulated storage room might be renovated into an office in the future.

Yes, he'd definitely offered too high. He'd been that idealistic moron the sellers had been counting on, the person who just loved the idea of living in the mountains, having beautiful mountain sunrises and sunsets, everything straight out of a magazine. *Congratulations, you've won the jackass of the year award.*

Nevertheless, it was home.

It was July when he started working for Charleston City Police Department, and, he was told, after he completed a ninety-day probationary period on the road, he would be working in Missing Persons.

Owain still had a few weeks left on probation when 9/11 occurred.

Six of the guys took off the next day to enlist in the Army, and the rest, who were young enough, were fretting that they would receive a draft notice in the mail. Suddenly, Owain was off probation. Suddenly, the book of protocols doubled in size. Suddenly, men in black suits were everywhere. And just as quickly, they were gone, with the stench of increased bureaucracy in their wake. Fear and paranoia were everywhere, almost as prevalent as the religious imagery that began popping up. Most of the symbols were crosses or rosaries, but there were not a few crescent moon and stars with multiple bullet holes as that was now the preferred target at ranges all across the country.

But unlike Pearl Harbor and World War II, the sense of community drifted away before the month was even over, and the desire for war quickly became politicized and as divisive as any sword. Where once the boys in blue were wishing each other well before being shipped off overseas at the behest of Uncle Sam, now they debated whether war was necessary. Who where they fighting, where, why, how? Was it right? Was it moral? God forbid, but could it have been an inside job perpetuated by the government so they could have an excuse to invade yet another Middle Eastern country rich with oil? The conspiracy theories ran rampant.

There was war. Again. No draft notices came in the mail and there was no impending invasion. Because the United States had been in the Middle East for over a decade already, one conflict slid into another and few could even really say what was going on.

The year turned over into 2002.

Owain continued to work Missing Persons, perusing every case since 1970, solved and unsolved. Some of it he declared interesting reading, but he was always on the lookout for Tommen, some indication that he was alive and well and living somewhere in the United States. Even if he was grown and married and had a family, Owain just wanted to know he was okay, find some relief for his conscience.

He found nothing, no indication whatsoever that Tommen was out of the cave. Owain understood that the Band overhanging the cave was strong and made Time go faster, but was it really that strong? Had Tommen really been in there that long? He tried to do the math, figuring how much time he'd spent in the cave compared to his seventy year leap, but couldn't come up with anything concrete. Could be he would be waiting another century before his nephew emerged.

2003 rolled around, about as significant as any other year Owain had seen, and 2004 was no better.

Well, he couldn't say 2004 was a complete waste of time. He ended up going back to school, enrolling in classes so he would have a better shot at promotion. Sergeant could be attained through hard work, discipline, and being a damn fine officer with good ethics and no disciplinary action against him. Anything above that required not only time in service, but time in the classroom, too. It might have made for some late nights, but Owain had a bit of an advantage being able to Band and condense hours of studying into only a few minutes. Hell, it was the only way he could balance working full time and going to school part to almost full time. Sure, he didn't have a wife and kids or other social functions he was desperate to make, but even he enjoyed a bit of relaxing at the end of the day.

Taking psychology classes was harder than he anticipated, and not because the material was difficult. But it was hard to read about certain psychological elements and realize that he was basically reading about himself when he was younger. Alcoholism, violence, sexual activity that was predatory in nature, he identified with almost all of it, though he admitted to nothing. While he knew he had once been that way...he had once been that way. But no more. It was almost as if he were reading about a different man in a different life. A story.

It didn't stop the demons from torturing him at night, however.

He also took a number of medical classes, not forgetting his Plan B of medical school, becoming a doctor and waiting for Tommen that way. At the very least he would be able to get a Medical First Responder license which would allow him to render aid to someone in distress and be of some use to an ambulance.

And somewhere, in the midst of all of this, he was still a Timekeeper Captain. Even as he studied for his final exams in school, he also had to find a couple new Lieutenants. Not just one, but both of his put in their notice of resignation, that they were leaving the District; they had more than overstayed their welcome.

Owain really wasn't sure how to go about it. Up until now, everyone had always called him. Now he had to do the calling. He had to do the research, consider his candidates, interview. He was the boss this time around.

He figured to put it off until after his exams.

He was just finished taking his finals for his MFR license when he was approached by Dr. Lily Guile, one of the proctors who also happened to be a Harvester Time Agent. She worked in the Neonatal Intensive Care Unit at the children's hospital. When she wasn't busy saving lives, she was sucking them clean of their Potential Time—whole lifetimes—to sell in the Time industry. She was fabulously wealthy but with a rotten personality, at least toward other Time Agents. Owain was no exception, Captain Timekeeper or not.

"I hear you're in the market for a couple new Lieutenants," she said, amiably pouring him a cup of coffee.

He took the cup but did not drink; he wasn't a big coffee drinker. "I could be."

"I might have a couple suggestions."

"Can't hurt to listen, I suppose."

"Micah and Micaiah Durvin, identical twins. They're Lieutenant-trained Masters originally from Ireland—about in your neck of the woods I hear. They've been in District One for a while, currently in District Eight but looking for a home to call their own."

Owain raised a brow. "And what's in it for you?" There was no such thing as a free lunch when it came to Harvesters.

She shrugged. "Oh, just keeping my friends close, I suppose."

And she meandered away.

Only out of sheer curiosity did Owain end up calling and adding them to the list of candidates to interview. It didn't take long to figure out the story. Lily and Micah, the younger twin, had been quite heavily involved. Right now they were in an "off" phase, and it was unclear whether they would ever be back "on."

The last thing Owain needed was drama between one of his Lieutenants and a shady Harvester, and he initially passed them over. As he continued to vet each of his options, he started to feel guilty about it and revisited the possibility. Everyone wished everything ran utterly smooth, especially in management. Everyone wished that the chain of command was flawless. That was absolutely preposterous. Everyone would always have a problem with someone, and Timekeepers and Harvesters were notorious for not getting along. And as for Micah and Lily being involved or not being involved, he considered whether it was really different than if, say, the two of them decided to find other Time Agents to pass off as spouses for a time. There would always be drama, always be problems, whenever two people were left alone for a long enough period.

And other than that little kink, he rather liked the twins. They were hard-working, outgoing, and they had no problem with staying in Charleston as Owain had requested. He'd done too many years as a Lieutenant separated from the rest of his superiors, and his inferiors, too (few Time Agents wanted to get mixed up in border-hopping Runner adventures). He liked being able to talk to people in person, bounce ideas off them at a moment's notice without having to go through the hassle of a blind portal. Maybe he was becoming too old-fashioned in a rapidly technologically advancing world.

As it happened, he ended up instating Micah and Micaiah as his Lieutenants. Within four months, they'd opened up Bakery na hÉireann. From what Owain could gather, it was a bit of a dream come true for them, to own their own bakery. Micaiah, despite being the twin who worked out, was primarily the office manager, taking care of business. Meanwhile, Micah, skinnier and clean-shaven, made the magic happen in the kitchen, using Time to crank out ten times what a business their size should have been capable of. And their pastries...Lord above, the pastries were to die for.

"So what made you make Charleston your base of operations?" Micaiah asked one morning as they sat around the bakery having coffee and various baked goods. It was six months since they'd moved to town. The morning rush had passed and they were the only three in the store, watching the snow fall only a couple weeks before Christmas. Owain was not working that day. Micaiah went on, "Most people pick New

York or Boston or someplace."

Owain nodded and swallowed his bite of pastry. He gave them a condensed version of events, about Tommen disappearing and him falling into the same trap trying to find him. Now he was just biding his time until his little nephew came out of the cave.

"That's nice," Micah said, smiling awkwardly. A young woman might have called it adorable. "You think you'll find him?"

Owain sighed and shrugged, shaking his head. "I don't know. I really could be waiting for something that may never happen."

Or maybe not. It was August of the next year, 2005, when he was at home, just about to sit down to dinner, and his phone rang.

"Walt, this is Lisa at the ER." Lisa was one of the head nurses. She was well-known and well-liked by just about everyone in the department, and she and Owain had a good enough relationship that she would often just call him directly on some cases rather than try to go through dispatch or the station.

"Got something for me?" Owain wondered, lamenting his dinner which was going to be cold soon.

"I got...something for you. Not quite sure what it is. Maybe you ought to come see him for yourself."

CHAPTER THIRTY-THREE

THE FATHER

Owain nearly tripped over himself multiple times to get to the hospital. Lisa was not one to just hand out cryptic messages and hang up. She was always very polite and forthcoming, giving out as much information as possible over the phone before it became a matter of privacy. This one was different, though. Very different. And the way she mentioned her patient as a "he" gave Owain hope.

He managed to pull himself together before walking in the emergency room doors. No need to go lumbering in like a bear on a rampage. Technically he was on duty now, about to take an official case. He was in uniform. Despite a few rumples, he had to present himself appropriately. Besides, there was no guarantee that this was Tommen.

And even if it was, he could not display any overly excitable emotion. No one could know or hope to understand their connection or history. Even so, they didn't really have a history. Tommen had no idea who he was or that they could be even remotely related. Considering that this would be a one hundred and fifty year leap into the future, more than double what Owain had done, the kid was probably scared speechless. The less Owain could confuse and frighten him, the better.

Lisa was right there to meet him when he walked in the door.

"Oh, Walt, good of you to come." As if there had been a chance that he wouldn't have.

"You said this would be interesting," Owain told her, following her through the large double doors to the hall of patient rooms. "Anything I should know before I go in?"

"He's eight years old, and either extremely delusional, or...he's got a great fairytale to tell."

Now Owain was really interested. This might just be the one. "What do you mean?"

"Well, he says his name is Tommen Forbes. Like, *the* Tommen Forbes, the one who disappeared into Forbes Cave a hundred and fifty years ago. He says he just went in the cave one day on an exploratory trip, came back out, thought it was night and his pa was going to switch 'im—" She grinned at this. "—and when he was coming back down the mountain, he was attacked by a demon. He was hit by a car, actually. But either way, he is extremely scared of everything and everyone. Half the time, he's not even speaking English."

He raised a brow. "Let me guess, Welsh?"

Lisa nodded, glancing at him. "Yeah. And when he does speak English, it's with a lot of difficulty and a heavy accent. So, good luck getting through to him on that level."

"How is he, physically?"

"Well, wherever he comes from, he comes from poverty nonetheless. Doesn't know what electricity is, or running water. He's not starving, but he's suffering from malnourishment and several vitamin deficiencies. We almost had to sedate him to get lines in him for fluids and supplements. Otherwise, nothing to suggest physical abuse, no wounds in various stages of healing, no burns. Just cuts and scrapes like a normal kid, plus a broken collarbone, ribs, and pelvis from being hit by a car."

"Can't forget that," Owain said dryly.

By that time, they had reached their destination, and Lisa opened the door.

He certainly didn't look eight years old, as scrawny as he was, but he was every bit his father's son with the pronounced cheekbones, high forehead, and thick brown hair flopping over on his head. His eyes were his mother's, the purest chocolate brown you ever did see, always bright for one reason or another. Joy, love, curiosity, determination. Fear.

"Hi, Tommen, how are we feeling?" Lisa asked with all the warmth of a woman who had a ten year old herself.

The little boy looked like he wanted to shrug, but was presently unable. Instead, he just studied his hands and mumbled, "Good, ma'am."

"Tommen, I brought a friend with me. He wants to talk to you and ask you a few questions. Is that all right?"

"Yes, ma'am."

Owain took a chair from its position in the corner of the room and set it at Tommen's bedside. He sat down, trying to appear as unthreatening as possible. "Hi there, Tommen. My name is Walter. I'm a police officer. Do you know what that is?"

"Yes, sir," Tommen said, still not looking at him.

"Tommen, can you look at me?"

He did so, and for just a minute, Owain was sure he'd see the familiarity and the recognition. He was sure the boy would break into a grin; he would even take a cry of fear. But it never came. The boy just stared at him, wide-eyed and terrified. Owain continued on, heart heavy and twisting against the arrow that had just pierced him.

Looking back, Owain figured he shouldn't have been surprised. He and Teo really hadn't looked a lot alike in the first place. He took more after their grandfather and uncles, while Teo had taken after their ma. Add into that many years of fighting, broken bones, scars, and general wear and tear, Owain probably bore little resemblance to the man he had once been, never mind his brother.

All the same, he had hoped.

"Where are you from, Tommen?" Owain asked amiably, hoping his disappointment didn't show through.

"*Ar y mynydd.*" (On the mountain.)

"*Gyda pwy wyt ti'n bwy?* Who do you live with?"

"*Fy ngad, fy ma, fy mrawd a chwiorydd.*" (My dad, my mom, my brother and sisters.)

"Yeah? What are their names?"

"*Teo ydy fy ngad a fy mrawd. Deg blwyddynau hŷn na fi ydy fy mrawd Teo.*" (Teo is my dad and my brother. My brother Teo is ten years older than me.)

"*Pa faint o blwyddyn ydy ti?*" (How old are you?)

"*Wythlwydd.*" (Eight years old.)

"And your ma and sisters? What are their names?"

"Maisy is my ma. Gwendolyn, Mary, and Laurel are my sisters."

Owain nodded. It was all he needed to hear, as if appearance and improbable story weren't enough.

"*Tommen, wyt ti'n gwybod y blwydd?*" (Tommen, do you know the year?)

"*Mil wyth pump deg pump.*" (1855.)

Owain shook his head. "*Nac ydy. Dau mil pump.*" (No. 2005.)

"*Nac ydy!*" Tommen insisted, tears springing to his eyes. "*Mae'n mil wyth pump deg pump! Dw i eisiau fy ngad! Dw i eisiau mynd adref!*" (No! It's 1855. I want my dad! I want to go home!)

"*Dw i'n gwybod,*" Owain said gently, nodded and sighing. "I know. You need to heal first, though, all right? Get some rest."

It killed him to see the boy so confused and helpless. It hurt even more to know that Tommen would never see his dad again. Or his ma or anyone he had ever known. He was completely alone in the world right now except for Owain, and Owain was the only one who knew the truth.

He followed Lisa out of the room.

"He's absolutely petrified," Lisa hummed.

"I don't blame him," Owain said. "I'm going to start a report. I'll need statements from everyone on your crew who's been caring for him and I'll need the names of the EMS crew and the responding officer."

Frank Willis was the responding officer. From what he understood, Tommen had come racing off the mountainside into the road on a bad stretch just on the blind side of a curve. Because of the nature of the curve, the driver had only been doing about thirty-five when he suddenly saw the little boy, but that was still a heavy impact. Tommen had been knocked unconscious and, according to EMS, stayed that way the whole ride into the hospital. The nurses hadn't expected him to survive the night. No one knew what to make of his outrageous claim that he was the same Tommen Forbes for whom Forbes Cave was named.

It was the truth, but it didn't help much when making out a report and trying to follow protocol to locate family or anyone who knew him. There were a few Forbeses in the area, but none of them laid claim to him. Family dynamics were...difficult right now, they said, and no one quite knew who was related to whom. A DNA test was run just in case, but came back as being very distantly related, if at all. Owain found this funnier than he thought it should have been.

As for Tommen, with no family to return to, he couldn't stay in the hospital indefinitely, and was released to the care of a foster family. Owain understood the logistics, but he read the reports saying that he was not adjusting well at all. What really got under his skin was the fact that they actually had a shot at adopting him. It wasn't that he didn't believe the family incapable—in fact, they were very nice people, responsible, and they certainly had financial means—but he couldn't bear the thought of Tommen being taken away and raised as an idiot, as if his whole life in 1855 had never happened, as if he were delusional or maybe mentally retarded.

So Owain put in an application to foster Tommen, arguing that a quieter household, one without eight other children running around, might better suit his immediate needs. The courts agreed, and Tommen was set to be moved after his last doctor's appointment which would clear him of almost all medical needs relating to his injuries.

He arrived at the hospital and sat in the parking lot for a few minutes, trying to gather his nerves. He was terrified; there was no other way to say it. He'd been nervous before when Victoria was born, but back then, he'd hardly cared for more than a few hours or days before he was back to drinking to cope with it, telling himself he was celebrating when really he was running and hiding. This time, he was facing everything completely sober.

He'd picked up a few things for Tommen, some clothes and a backpack to put them in. Everything was rather plain; the boy had no concept of TV, movies, or animation, so all the shirts and backpacks with the animated movie or comic book characters on them would mean nothing. He grabbed the backpack and took it in with him.

"Today's the day," Dina greeted as he walked in. "Are you excited?"

"Nervous as hell," he admitted.

"Well, know that he's nervous, too. Scared out of his mind almost. The doc will write a script for anti-anxiety meds, probably Ritalin."

"He's eight years old."

"And running almost a hundred and fifty beats per minute just sitting down. It's not fair, but he needs to calm down. I don't envy you,

Walter."

Owain said nothing to that, just put on a good face as he entered Tommen's room. He'd healed well from his accident, not the least thanks to Owain who had done a little speeding up of the healing process during their visits. According to all the nurses, Tommen seemed to prefer him, and that had been another factor in why he'd won the case to foster him.

"Are you ready to get out of here and go home?" Owain asked, pulling up a chair.

Tommen nodded.

"All right. Let's get some proper clothes on you, and let's go home."

It was the first Christmas in over a century that Owain had spent with family. It wasn't anything extravagant, just a simple affair with stockings hung on the wall, a nice meal, and a few gifts. Tommen wasn't especially enamored with battery-operated toys—indeed, he was rather afraid of them—and was quite oblivious to all the animated characters from the latest movies and TV shows. Instead, Owain gave him what he might have expected from Christmas gifts: a couple pairs of socks, a new winter jacket, and simple toys made from cloth and wood. Then they sat in the living room and Owain read the Christmas story from the Bible.

It was the first time that Tommen appeared any sort of calm and comfortable, and he fell asleep where he lay on the couch, still healing from his injuries. Owain decided it best just to let him stay there, and the following week, after New Year's, he asked for a DNA test of his own.

The courts didn't believe it, but three independent tests confirmed that Owain was Tommen's biological uncle.

"You know where his parents are, then, right?" the social worker asked in a meeting with the judge.

Owain shook his head. "I wish I did. I was ostracized from the family for a lot of years and only recently came back to the area. I just never got up the courage to go looking, was more kind of hoping to just bump into them first. Teo was never a very social person, though. It doesn't surprise me that he'd hide himself in the hills."

Searches were done for Teo Forbes, Sr. but came up empty. No one came forward claiming to be him, no one knew him or anything about him. Even Teo Jr. was a negative. When Tommen was able to walk and run again, he was asked to show them where he lived, but he couldn't do it. Owain had little doubt that Tommen had been more than knowledgeable about the hills as they had been, but with all the modernization and industry creeping up the mountainside, the poor child got all sorts of confused and broke down crying when he couldn't find home.

"We can't wait forever," the judge said.

"He needs to be with his family," the social worker objected.

"Walter Forbes is his uncle. That is family. I'm sorry his dad is too much of a hermit to come into the city looking for his son, but I don't like seeing kids in limbo forever."

The comment was like a punch to the gut for Owain. His brother loved his boy, loved him a lot. It had killed him not to go running off and searching for him endlessly, no matter the results. It had killed him to have to choose between family and family. There had been no good answer until his wayward brother appeared, looking for redemption.

Well, Teo, looks like everyone gets what they wanted. Pa wanted to be rid of me, and he was. Ma wanted me to be a good man, and I'd like to think I am. You wanted me to find your son, and I have. I wanted redemption, and I think I've found it. Tommen wants a family, and...No. He wants his family. I'm just the best he's going to get.

"What if his dad does come looking for him?" the social worker challenged. "These hills are huge. If he really is a hermit, he may be searching on foot or doing things the old-fashioned way. It's not quick."

"It's been nearly a year, Sam," the judge told him. "We've put out the word and heard nothing back. A decision needs to be made."

"What about the Robertson family? They're a family, children around his age, financially stable—"

"Weren't you the one just saying he needs to be with family?"

"A single uncle in a dangerous profession. He needs love, support, stability—"

"All right, I've heard enough of this," the judge interrupted. "Mr. Forbes, you've been taking care of Tommen for a while. Think you can keep taking care of him?"

"Of course, Your Honor." He did not try to hide the hope that had begun swelling in his chest.

"Good. I'm awarding you full custody of Tommen and I'll have the paperwork drawn up within the week. If your brother does turn up, then he can sue for custody and we can deal with it later. Anyone have any objections? Never mind, I don't care. Next case, please."

Owain left the courthouse in a daze. The next thing he knew, he was signing a bunch of papers fully instating him as Tommen's legal father. Tommen remained outside the judge's chambers until everything was signed and filed away.

"Are you ready to go home?" Owain asked him, feeling light-headed with pride and a certain sense that he just did something he didn't think through completely.

Tommen nodded, not saying a word. He still didn't speak a whole lot, but at least he was finally calmed down enough that he appeared to be adjusting. At the very least, cars didn't scare him as much and he got in the backseat without a fuss.

"Are you my dad now?" Tommen asked, his English heavily-accented so he almost couldn't be understood.

"I suppose so," Owain told him.

When they got home, Owain put Tommen on the couch beside him.

"I know your pa was looking for you, Tommen," Owain said. "I know he loved you very much. Your ma, too. You meant the world to them. But when you went exploring in that cave, you got all mixed up and lost in there, so now you're here. Does that make sense?"

Tommen nodded and wiped his eyes. "Teo said I shouldn't go alone because I might get lost. And now I did and now they're gone."

Owain shook his head. "No. Not gone. Not as long as they're here—" He tapped Tommen's temple. "—and here." His chest. "As long as you remember them, they're never really gone."

The boy sniffed hard. "Okay."

It was tough to judge whether Tommen really understood what Owain was trying to tell him, but it was safe to say he didn't. Yet. In time, he would probably come to terms with it.

"*Ond fy ngad i ydy chi rŵan,*" Tommen stated. (But you are my dad now.)

Owain's heart and mind nearly tore in two as he considered his answer. Tommen was just coming around to accept that his family was gone. He'd planted little seeds in the boy's mind about the Time trap, but how could he explain that he had also gone into the cave, that he'd gone in there because of Tommen? How could he explain why he had gone but his pa hadn't? Probably Teo had never even told his children about his brother sentenced to hang for murder.

Finally he nodded. "Yeah. I'm your dad now."

"Okay."

Regret instantly filled Owain, but before he could say anything more, Tommen hopped off the couch and wandered off to his room to play or do something. The moment was gone. Well, maybe he could tell him another time, once things had settled down and the looming threat of being moved to another home had ebbed.

Thursday, he took Tommen to the bakery. He'd gotten to know Micah and Micaiah pretty well, and they were the ones he went to when he wanted advice on real matters, when he needed true answers.

"So this is Tommen," Micaiah said, leaning on the counter and looking down at the scrawny child who shrank back a few steps. "We've heard a lot about you." He looked at Owain. "You said the adoption officially went through?"

"Tuesday, yes," Owain answered proudly. He put his hand on Tommen's head, but something had caught the child's attention, and he wandered off to investigate. Owain kept his voice down as he added, "He's not leaving the family again."

Micaiah straightened. "I'm less worried about him than I am you." He turned on the faucet beside the coffeemaker on the counter. As he dumped the old coffee and rummaged in the cupboards for a fresh package, he went on, "Question is, are you going to tell him?"

Owain faltered. "I haven't decided. He's just starting to adjust; I don't want to surprise him or confuse him more."

"The longer you wait, the harder it's going to be. I mean, once he gets to be a teenager, well, things could end badly. That's the only way things really could end, once he gets it in his head that he's a man he doesn't have to listen to you. You don't need to suddenly dump an armload of fuel on that fire."

"I know what you're saying. I just don't know a good way to tell him. I've already Suppressed him, and I don't plan on taking him before the Hands anytime soon. Telling him without showing him could end badly, too."

Micaiah flipped the switch on the coffeemaker, and it sputtered to life. He turned and watched the boy for a minute as he stood and just stared at the television, completely mesmerized by the moving images. He looked back at Owain. "You said he's just starting to adjust. Everything is new to him, and he's terrified. No, he might not understand the hows and whys, but he needs something solid and familiar to hang onto."

"But the explanations and everything else —"

"Walt, he's eight years old. He doesn't have to know all the details and all the Time involved; he just needs to know that you're there, and you're family. Do you even speak Welsh with him?"

"Not really, here and there. He does need to learn English, though, before I can put him in school, and he doesn't exactly have a bunch of friends who can help him. I'm all he's got."

"Exactly," Micaiah said. "You're all he's got. Don't be a stranger to him, Walt."

He stopped speaking as the boy walked along the large display case, marveling at all the baked goodies contained within.

Gingerly, he walked up to Owain and tugged on his shirt. *"Fe merdr'i 'r rhôl 'na, os gwelwch yn dda?"* (Can I have that roll, please?)

Micaiah raised a brow. "What's he want?"

Owain showed him the roll in question, a kid-sized sticky bun which Tommen took gently, as if afraid it would disappear. As he bit into it, he mumbled, *"Diolch, Tad."*

Micaiah looked from the child to Owain. He didn't need to speak Welsh to know what Tommen had just called him. He sighed.

"Have a nice day, guys." He leaned on the counter again and addressed Tommen. "Enjoy the sticky bun, okay? *Go dté tú slán.*" (Bye.)

They left the bakery and returned to the car. Owain helped Tommen into the seat so he wouldn't get sticky fingers all over everything, and soon enough, they were heading home.

"Your birthday is coming up soon," Owain said conversationally. "Do you want any presents? Do you want to have a party?"

"Why?" Tommen wondered.

"For your birthday. Do you want a birthday party?"

The child just gave him a confused look as he continued to chew his sticky bun thoughtfully. Then he swallowed and again asked, "Why? Why is there a birthday party?"

"It's...it's just something some people like to do for their birthday. It doesn't have to be a big party or anything." Owain might have suggested inviting a few friends over for a sleepover or something, except Tommen really didn't have any friends.

Tommen shook his head. "No party. Thank you."

"Do you want to do anything special? See a movie, go to the park, anything like that? It's your call."

"Who's calling?"

"No, I mean, it's your decision. *Dy fenderfyniad.*" (Your decision.)

"Oh."

"Do you?" Owain goaded.

He was silent for a minute or two before answering, "No. We do that stuff anyway."

"Do you want to do anything for your birthday? What about presents?"

"No."

"Not even some new clothes, a new toy, nothing?"

"No. My clothes are fine."

Of course they were. Tommen was still mentally living in an era where a person wore the same clothes all week, except for Sundays when you got out your Sunday best. And those same clothes were worn just as long as possible, until they were so thin they may as well have been strung up as screen doors. When that happened, well, just patch up any holes and keep wearing them. Tommen had a hard time being persuaded to change his clothes, but he had no trouble staying clean. He was more than happy to shower or bathe or wash his clothes with water he didn't have to haul up from the creek.

Tommen adjusted better over the summer, when he could play outside on his own, once the babysitters learned to just stand back and let him do his own thing. When permitted to be alone for a time, he gradually came around to being social on his own. He improved his English with the babysitters. After Owain got home from work, Tommen would tell him about his day, the trees he had climbed, the hills he had conquered, and insects he had discovered.

Owain still did not tell him about their blood relationship. As much as he wanted to, he still feared for Tommen's mental well-being. How would that look to suddenly tell him they were related? What's more, Owain was Tommen's uncle, his pa's older brother, the one Teo had probably never told him about. More than that, what if it caused him to clam up again? Or worse, what if he started to act out, blame Owain for his family's disappearance and his misfortunes?

Thousands of ideas and scenarios ran through Owain's mind until he could no longer distinguish the rational from the irrational fears. Micaiah chided him for his procrastination, but he couldn't help it. He'd hit a wall of fear and uncertainty, different from any fear he'd ever really known. It took him a while to identify what made this fear so different.

One, it was because there were other people involved.

Two, it was because he cared.

Three, it was because he loved Tommen like his own son.

He didn't want to see Tommen hurt as much as Owain did not want to be hurt himself. Even if Tommen knew that they were related, there was nothing either of them could do about it. They couldn't go back in time, couldn't make the cave work in reverse. Tommen was finally coming around to some semblance of normal, and they were living together as father and son. Tommen fully understood that he was adopted, but to him, Owain was his new dad. That was their dynamic, and it was the one they would share...at least for a little while. Owain knew that the DNA results would come up when Tommen turned eighteen and received his adoption box from the courts, but by then, they would have a long-standing relationship and Tommen would be better equipped to process the information.

That didn't mean there weren't days when Owain still thought about telling him. Tommen's birthday, for example. It seemed an appropriate time. No one knew his actual birthday, so they just went with the date he came stumbling out of Forbes Cave—August 12. One year after his tumble into the modern world seemed like a poetic time to tell him the truth. But Owain kept silent. And on the first day of school, third grade, Tommen said goodbye to his dad before he got on the bus, and Owain found he didn't want to tell.

But even as he felt pride at being called dad, there was still a little lingering shame, as if he were trying to replace his brother, as if he were doing something dishonest or dishonorable.

Then Thanksgiving rolled around. It was one holiday Tommen really got into. He loved to eat and he seemed to enjoy cooking as much as Owain, and he tried to help in any way he could, even when it was unneeded or unwanted. Owain managed to make several dishes familiar to Tommen and make up a small harvest festival for his son. It was the first time Owain saw Tommen as Teo had likely seen him, joyful and full of life, brimming with curiosity and hope. Owain didn't realize the stress he felt over Tommen's more withdrawn nature until the burden was lifted. There was hope that this little boy would grow up to be normal, happy, and productive.

Micah and Micaiah came over to partake as well. The dinner might have been better suited for the twins' house which was considerably larger, but they decided on the Forbes household as a celebration of family. Owain offered to lead the prayer.

"Wait, wait!" Tommen said. "I want to pray!"

Owain nodded. "All right. Why don't you start, and then if anyone else wants to take a turn, they can, and I'll finish. How does that sound?"

Tommen did not wait for an agreement or answer of any form as he folded his hands, closed his eyes, and began praying just as if he were holding a regular conversation.

"God, thank you for today. It's a beautiful day." Actually, it was rainy and dreary. "Thank you for the food was cooked." Grammar wasn't his strong suit. "Bless the hands that made the food and the animals came from and the farms and the farmers, too." Takes one to know one. "God, thank you for Uncle Micah and Uncle Micaiah." Owain wasn't sure when that had started, but he wasn't going to discourage it; the twins weren't bad role models. "Bless their bakery and all the good food in it and keep them safe and away from fire." Always important. "And thank you for Dad and how much he loves me. He has a nice house and running water and gave me a room all to myself." The simple things. "God, please help Dad to sleep better and not have more bad dreams." Owain's eyes came open at that; he hadn't realized Tommen was aware of his nightmares. He closed his eyes again as Tommen continued. "And God, wherever my family is—my ma and pa and Teo and all my sisters—please keep them safe and happy and healthy and help the crops grow on the farm so they can have a nice harvest festival, too. And thank you for Dad for taking me in. Amen."

Owain exchanged glances with the twins, all of them stunned and not a little emotional in their own way. Owain let out a breath as he started his own prayer.

Epilogue

To
Father Arthur Forthill
County Beaumaris Chapel

Father Forthill,

We have received and transcribed all correspondence you have sent to us regarding the man Owain Fforidd who was imprisoned in Beaumaris Gaol, bound to hang for the murder of his ex-father-in-law and five associates. It is a stunning tale to tell and would surely depict the love and mercy the Lord bestows upon any who merely ask for forgiveness and so receive salvation.

There is, however, the matter of Fforidd's escape from prison and subsequent disappearance. While we acknowledge that every man has free will, it is the opinion of the Welsh chapel community and the Catholic Church that to continue to propagate Fforidd's story could be indirectly misconstrued as an endorsement of his actions and similar actions, that is, escaping lawful justice. It is unknown the state of Fforidd's mind or soul when he escaped and he is solely under the eye of the Lord now. While we understand that you believe he is a changed man and may seek to do some good, we will await further developments.

To that end, copies of his story will no longer be made or circulated, except, perhaps, as gentle reminders to the rest of the flock of the sinful nature of human beings. Many in Wales already know his name and his crimes, so the story will not be new, but perhaps some perspective will shed light on an otherwise dark situation.

Therefore, in respect to your hard work and firm belief that he is or was, in fact, a changed man, several unaltered copies will remain in storage for a time. It is the hope of the Lord and His servants everywhere that great good for the Heavenly Kingdom will come of this adventure, in due time. After all, the Lord works all things together for good for those who love him. He can bring life to dry bones and greenery from the sand.

We also received word of your resignation from your post at Beaumaris Gaol and the installation of James McArtur as your replacement. It is our understanding that you will be assisting Father Peitr Worthington in his duties until such time as he is unable to perform them or else passes to be with Our Lord. It is our recommendation that you also seek an assistant for yourself posthaste.

It should go without saying that prayer ought to be of the utmost importance concerning Fforidd — or any endeavor, but especially in light of recent events. It is not only imperative that we pray for the Lord's will to be done concerning his actions and his future, but for you as well, knowing that he was in your charge at the time of his escape and you had been counseling him for some time. We pray for wisdom and a peaceful spirit for you.

The Lord's peace and mercy be upon you in whatever you do.

"Bydd pobl gyffredin yn gweld hyn ac yn dathlu. Felly codwch eich calonnau, chi sy'n ceisio dilyn Duw! - Salm 69:32"

Sincerely,
Father John Woods
Caerdydd Chapel

WHEN THE HUMBLE SEE IT, THEY WILL BE GLAD;
YOU WHO SEEK THE LORD, LET YOUR HEARTS
REVIVE

PSALMS 69:32

Author's Note

If you have already read *The Chivalrous Welshman*, then you may already be loosely familiar with the characters, and certainly more familiar with Time and how it works, but you have almost certainly noticed the dramatic shift in tone and mood. If this is your first *Timekeeper Chronicles* story, you may be slightly confused and wondering where all the Timekeeping, science fiction-y stuff was.

The answer to both of those concerns is that *Of Saints and Sinners* is far darker and more introspective than other *Timekeeper Chronicles* stories. Rather than focus on action or dialogue, the main idea here is to get inside Owain's head and live his life with him, to see how he got from the noose to adopting his nephew as his son, to see what kind of man he has become, how he got to where he began in *Time to Kill*. *Of Saints and Sinners* has less than half the dialogue of *Time to Kill*; even the first few parts are split between narration and reflection. There is also far more religious imagery and thoughtfulness, which I believe is an integral part of *The Timekeeper Chronicles*, but is essential to Owain's development as he struggles to find his way in the universe.

Earth has never been a major player in the Time industry, and such themes are only just starting to be explored in *The Chivalrous Welshman*, which means it's not as big of an issue beforehand, in *Of Saints and Sinners*. Timekeeping is minimal, and Owain had no involvement in the Dispersal. His biggest concerns in life have more to do with life itself, Earth-side, how he is going to deal with these stunning revelations about life and the nature of the universe itself, whether he wants to continue on in his search for his nephew or give up and ask Mark for a mercy killing.

Of Saints and Sinners also plays a role as a narrative and chronological anchor, providing some perspective and a measure of realism to events only mentioned in *The Chivalrous Welshman* as we see Cassius in his role as a gaoler, meet Owain's mentor Mark, and touch on how the twins got to be the District Four Lieutenants, courtesy of Lily Guile. So it sort of acts as a cross-reference to other points of the story already established. As more books and series come forth (such as *The Hands of Time*, which will focus on Rifun and Cassius and their role in the Dispersal), characters and events will intersect more and more, providing greater context and fulfillment in the series as a whole.

So, no, *Of Saints and Sinners* was not a massive, stunning, action-packed thrill-ride with suspense on every page that isn't blatant action. It serves a different purpose, one that is a little less in your face and a little more in your head, I hope, provoking thought and providing context. All the same, I also hope you enjoyed walking beside Owain and seeing his path of redemption. Maybe you can relate.